THE FIGHTERS OF FREEDOM

Duncan MacLaren

AuthorHouse™ UK Ltd.
500 Avebury Boulevard
Central Milton Keynes, MK9 2BE
www.authorhouse.co.uk
Phone: 08001974150

First published by AuthorHouse   03/16/2011

ISBN: 978-1-4567-7632-9 (sc)
ISBN: 978-1-4567-7633-6 (e)

Any people depicted in stock imagery provided by Thinkstock are models, and such images are being used for illustrative purposes only.
Certain stock imagery © Thinkstock.

This book is printed on acid-free paper.

Because of the dynamic nature of the Internet, any web addresses or links contained in this book may have changed since publication and may no longer be valid. The views expressed in this work are solely those of the author and do not necessarily reflect the views of the publisher, and the publisher hereby disclaims any responsibility for them.

Introduction

"Look after yourself!" Hayley kissed Fletcher softly on the cheek.

Fletcher passed with his hands over the red curls of his wife's hair then he stopped over the baby she held in her arms. "Pay attention to the small one! I'll be back in a few days."

"Do you promise?"

"I promise," Fletcher kissed his wife again then he jumped on his horse, picked up the reins, gave the sign to depart to his group – the Horsemen - and let his horse run.

Hayley sighed during she looked behind her husband and the Horsemen, as they left the village to go and help others. The Group of the Horsemen had been designed to do exactly that; they were a lot of lawless men and a few women and they had to make good what they all had done wrong once in another life. And they all followed what they had been ordered to do; they hadn't any other choice.

It wasn't the first time that Hayley had to stay back in the village, as she had been pregnant and looked after her son now but it was every time the same. It felt terrible to watch the Horsemen riding away; all she wanted was to be with them. She had been the leader of the Horsemen, as only woman who rode with them, together with her husband Fletcher.

Hayley kissed her baby on the cheek and said finally: "Let's see what the others are doing." And she turned around and went over to the market place where the other women were sitting, sewing, talking, playing with the children.

Hayley sat down beside Mandy and Amanda, her best friends in the village, and started a normal conversation...

1

It was in the evening, the second one after Fletcher and his Horsemen had left the village. It was a nice evening, warm but not hot; the sky was clear and the night came almost unexpected over the horizon.

Hayley had left her baby with Amanda to have a bit of time for herself – and especially for the house she lived in with Fletcher and her son. The whole afternoon she had spent cleaning it and it looked like new. Now she wanted to stretch out for a moment on the bench in front of the house and enjoy the quietness around her.

A couple of birds flew over the village around, and they whistled a song in different tones.

Hayley observed the birds from under her eyelashes.

Suddenly – the birds flew away with a screech.

Bang! Bang!

Two loud shots could be heard.

Hayley reacted at once. She still felt the training till deep down in her bones so she jumped up, grabbed after her rifle, which was leaning beside the door and ran the street along to the wall around the village.

Two of the older men who lived here followed her at heels.

Hayley reached the gate, which burst open in the same moment and Hayley got thrown hard against the wall. For a second she was unable to do anything and first, as she felt foreign hands on her body, she awoke completely out of her dizziness and kicked out as hard as she could.

The three men who had thrown themselves on her were completely unknown to Hayley. She turned, got her arm free and hit one of the men so hard over the head that he fell against the wall. But in the next moment the other two men were over her again and finally Hayley had to notice that she had no chance against these men. They pulled her on to the belly and tied her hands firmly together. Hayley had lost her rifle as the gate broke and now as she was tied, she felt helpless like never before.

The two men who had followed her were lying not far away from her dead on the ground. As she understood what had happened to them, she felt worse; worse because she felt happy that she was still alive. But this feeling she should lose quite fast.

The foreign men who had stormed the village threw a third dead body to the others before they went further on through the village.

Hayley swallowed three times before she could breathe normal again. She turned her head away from Russ' dead eyes, which stared at her accusingly. Hayley didn't know what was going on here but she felt sick about everything what already had happened.

The foreign men searched every house and forced everybody out on the market place. As almost all the men had left two days ago with Fletcher, it was mostly women and children who were forced out of the houses on to the market place.

Only Patrick with his broken arm and Richard, a nurse who looked after the village's patients, were pushed outside as well.

Two men stepped nearer to Hayley and grabbed after her arms. They pulled her up and brought her over to the market place as well. They threw her back to the ground and Hayley had trouble to stay conscious, as she hit hard the ground.

For a while nothing happened.

Hayley recovered from the fall and pointed her ears.

Some of the women were crying quietly; only sobs could be heard now and then.

"Who of you is leader of this terrible bunch?" A loud, hard voice asked into the half silence of the village.

Hayley turned her head to see who had spoken. She saw a big burly man on a big white horse looking curiously around. He was dressed like a Sheikh but he was a west man with blond hair and only light brown skin.

"That would be me!" Hayley said clearly.

The man on the horse looked down at her – and suddenly grinned mockingly: "Well, at least one good thing beside all the other rubbish here." He made a hand movement, which included the whole village. Then he gave a sharp order: "Bring the women and children into this big house there. (He pointed to the Hall.) She comes into the house there." Now the man pointed at Hayley and then at the white house to his left, which was Hayley's home. Then he gave his last order. "Kill the two men!"

"No!" Hayley interrupted the man. "Leave them alone! They have nothing done to you!" She pleaded for the lives of the men.

The man looked down at her. He jumped of the horse and went over to the place where Hayley was still laying on the ground. He gave the silent order to pick her up and half a minute later Hayley got pulled up to her feet.

The man stared at her mockingly: "And what do you want to give me when I spare the men's lives?" He asked curiously.

"What do you want?" Hayley asked firmly back.

The man grinned. "Good try! But it doesn't work, as I will get it so or so! Kill them!" He turned to one of his fellow comrades.

"No!" Hayley cried out and kicked out at the men surrounding her.

But the men were already prepared and got her into the knees before she could hurt somebody earnestly. They turned her around that she had to face Patrick and Richard.

Both men had been forced to the ground; they looked scared over at Hayley.

Hayley only looked back with tears in her eyes. There was nothing she could do to stop this insanity. She looked away, as two men pointed their rifles at Patrick and the other man – and shot.

Luckily the men were merciful.

The shots hit the two men direct into their heads, and they were dead in an instant.

Hayley could follow how the eyes of the men broke, and fear ran ice cold down her back. Yet Patrick had been a good friend to her from the beginning and Hayley took the loss very hard.

Then Hayley got pulled up and was led over to her house. The men brought her up to the first floor and into the room, which she normally shared with Fletcher. She got thrown onto the bed and the two men disappeared after locking the door again.

Hayley was alone.

A long time went by before Hayley really understood what had happened and why Patrick and Richard as well had to die. She was lying on the bed and looked around. She felt sick, and she got up and went over to the window. She looked out to the street, which was normally full of the women and children but now it was quiet out there now; only sometimes one of the foreign men was riding through the street. Otherwise nothing could be heard or to be seen, and the Hall where the women and children had been brought to lay completely in darkness, which had come over the village in the last minutes.

Steps could be heard on the stairs coming up but Hayley didn't turn around. First she moved her head, as the door got unlocked and somebody came inside. Once more she stared into the face of the big burly man.

"What do you want from us?" Hayley asked, trying to stay calm.

The big burly man sat down on the bed. He pointed at his side. "Sit down!"

Hayley stayed where she was and looked only at the man.

The man grinned. "Okay, stay where you are. What we want from you? That's quite easy. We got informed that here are a lot of women and we need a lot of them. The market is big." He shrugged his shoulders.

In this second Hayley discovered the whole truth about what happened here. Somebody had betrayed them – it was impossible to find them here on this spot if you didn't know it. And whoever it was; he wanted that they got destroyed and everybody got sold as slaves on the market.

Hayley grew pale.

The man laughed. "Ah, you understand. Then we can come to the next business."

"And that would be?" Hayley tried to give her voice a firm sound.

The man got up and came over to her. "You are a really great looking girl! Not like the others who start to cry at once. I like women like you!" He stretched his arm out and touched her curls, which fell into her forehead.

Hayley tried to avoid the touch but she had the wall in her back and there was no way out to the sides. And as her hands were still tied together, there was really nothing she could do.

The man laughed again. "No way out for you!" And he grabbed her arm and forced her down on the bed.

Hayley kicked out but the man caught her legs without any problems and pressed her into a lying position. Then he lay down on top of her so that Hayley couldn't do anything anymore. She turned her head to the side that she hadn't to see him and swallowed in order not to get sick here and now.

The man only grinned, as he started to tear Hayley's clothes off. He tore at her blouse till it ripped apart and with one more grab the bra Hayley wore fell to the side as well.

Hayley pressed her lips hard together, as she felt the man's hands on her breasts, stroking them softly and pressing his lips on them. He kissed Hayley's breasts, sucked at her nipples till they grew hard.

Hayley shook lightly for anger and disgust but she couldn't prevent the fact that her nipples grew hard under the man's caressing hands. Tears came up into her eyes but she suppressed them as best as possible.

The man didn't seem to notice how bad Hayley felt. He pressed his lips now on her mouth and kissed her wildly during his hands massaged still her breasts. Finally he let go of her breasts and went with his hand over her stomach down to her trousers. He slipped a bit to the side that he could open the belt and then the trousers without problems. With a foot he pressed her legs down, as she started again to defend herself and the man solved his lips from hers and slipped down in order to pull the trousers off.

Hayley tried to kick out but now her own trousers hindered her.

The man sat down on top of her legs and pulled her boots off, then the socks and at last the trousers. So there was nothing left what Hayley would protect and could.

The man lay down on her, pressing firmly his body against the naked body and grinned at Hayley. "Now we will have some more fun, won't we?" He laughed.

Hayley turned her head to the side.

The man pressed his mouth on hers, searching with his tongue through her mouth.

Hayley let it happen; she had problems to fight her nausea down, as she felt his hands all over her body again.

At last the man pressed Hayley's legs apart with his own one and slipped with his hand down and started to stroke Hayley on her softest spot.

"You like that, don't you?" He asked after he had let go of Hayley's mouth. He pressed with his hand firmly against her spot and Hayley made a face out of pain.

The man laughed again. Then the man opened his own trousers then he rolled again on Hayley, pressing at the same moment with full power deep into her.

Hayley groaned up for pain but the man grew more and more excited through that. He pushed himself forward and forward, deep into her, again and again...

As the man finally left up from her, Hayley was only lying on the bed and didn't move at all anymore.

The man dressed again, satisfied, but not finished with Hayley at all. He still had a surprise for her left. "Don't you want to know who told us that you all are here – unguarded?"

"The devil told you?" Hayley pressed out of her mouth, not paying attention to the man only trying to have her still under control.

The man laughed loudly. "Yes, you could say so. But he will tell you the rest of the story personally. I'll let him in. Have fun!" The man got up and left the room.

For five minutes it was quiet in the room.

Hayley breathed deeply in and out, getting a bit angry; angry because she was helpless and angry because of everything what had happened and which she hadn't been able to prevent.

The door opened again and a man stepped inside. He closed the door and examined Hayley on the bed.

Hayley looked over at the man at the door. "I knew it was you." She said quietly.

Brian stepped over to the bed. "Certainly you know. Finally I was the only one who didn't show up outside, as it happened, right? But you can go out from the fact that nobody else will notice that. And you won't have a chance to tell anybody." He laid his hand down on her cheek.

Hayley turned her head away. "What do you want to do with me? Kill me – how you allowed it with Russ, Patrick and the others?"

"No nothing like that." Brian sat down beside Hayley and started to caress her softly. "We will sell you as well on the market but we will make sure that you never will come back again, doesn't matter what happens."

Hayley felt her chest got tied up that she couldn't breathe anymore. She felt so sick that she didn't notice at all what Brian was doing to her. The only thing she could think of was – she never would see her husband again; she never would see Fletcher again. And if she could keep her baby, that was more than unlikely.

Hayley fell into a big black hole.

Brian left her, as the morning came up again.

Hayley got forced to dress then she was taken outside and tied up to the wooden cross of the well on the market place. Hayley didn't care anymore; she was so deep lost in the big black hole that she couldn't find a way out. She didn't notice what happened to her and she didn't notice what happened around her.

Some of the women were let out of the Hall to serve the men water whenever they wished it.

Mandy, who was one of them, asked for permission to give Hayley water as well, as she noticed that she didn't have anything for hours through she was kneeling the whole time direct in the intensive bright light of the sun.

Mandy bent down to Hayley. "Hayley?" she asked carefully.

Hayley didn't react.

Mandy wiped with a towel over Hayley's face. "Please, Hayley!" She murmured quietly, worried. "Don't give up! If you give up we haven't any chance anymore! Help us!"

Hayley looked up. "I'm sorry, Mandy! I can't see a way out. All I can offer you is a piece of advice: Don't trust anybody! Especially not, when you think, he is trustworthy!"

"What do you mean?" Mandy held a cup to Hayley's mouth, and Hayley drank carefully a little bit of water. Then she swallowed. "You will find out!" She said, sinking her head.

"Don't give up!" Mandy pleaded her again.

"I don't! Or I try not to." Hayley added quietly.

"Go on!" A man came up to Mandy and Hayley and pushed Mandy away.

Mandy went on but as she threw a look over her shoulder she discovered that the man who had pushed her away touched Hayley in a very unfriendly way.

And Hayley didn't react at all at him.

Next morning the women and the children got loaded into some wagons the foreign men had organized for the transport.

Some of the men steered the wagons during the others rode on horses beside them. They all had weapons; and nobody had a chance to run away.

That Hayley had to notice as well. She had a terrible night behind her – similar to the first one – and now she was tied to one of the wagons in the back, firm and strong, and she had to go behind it without being given any other chance. Somehow she hoped this whole horrible affair would stop and she would wake up from this nightmare.

But it didn't happen.

Around noon Hayley broke together and she didn't remember for a long time what happened next…

2 – Two years later

Fletcher shrugged his shoulders. "Do we have any trouble with the Fighters of Freedom?" He asked more or less curiously, as he already knew the answer.

The Fighters of Freedom had already a name; a good and a bad one, which ran through the mouths of every living man and woman - even here in the village. The Fighters of Freedom were known to be fighting for revenge - but also as support for every poor or helpless man or woman.

And now one of the Fighters of Freedom was standing in front of their gate.

Like Fletcher had thought he only got in denial shakings of the heads from his comrades. So he sighed. "Then let him come in! We can offer him the safety of our village, some food and water and hope that he decides to go on fast again."

Tim nodded. "I'll keep an eye on him." He said, got up and left the Hall.

In front of the gate and the wall, which went completely around the village, was a young man on a camel, waiting. He was dressed from top to bottom in black and the only thing, which could be seen from his face were the eyes.

So it was only a guess from Tim that it was a man and that he was young. He stared down at him from top of the wall but finally he gave the sign to open the gate. Then he stepped the stairs down to greet the newcomer.

The Fighter of Freedom jumped down from his camel and came over to the gate. He examined Tim who stood in the middle of the open gate and the two other men who had opened the gate. "Thanks for letting me have a break here." He said, laying his hand on his heart and then stretching his arm out in a half circle, palm of his hand up.

Tim knew the sign, which was a sign of freedom, and gave it back to the foreigner. "It is an honour for us to have you here." He answered quietly. "Come inside!" He stepped to the side and let the Fighter come inside.

The Fighter didn't hesitate to come inside; he led his camel through the gate and looked interested around.

"This way," Tim led the Fighter down the street to the market place where he stopped. "Unluckily we haven't any empty room where you could stay. But if you like you can stay here at this place. For your camel we will find a space on the grass behind the village."

"Thanks." The Fighter spoke with a quite dark voice, deeper cause of the scarf he was wearing in front of his face. He turned to the camel and started to take the saddle down. Then he placed it upright against the well so that it could catch the last warm rays of the evening sun.

Tim took the camel at the reins and gave it over to Luke who brought it away.

"What else can I do for you?" Tim asked curiously.

The Fighter opened a belt around his hips and laid a big sword, which had been hidden under the cloak, he wore, down beside the saddle. "Is the well working?" He asked.

"Certainly, it is." Tim nodded. "I'll get you some wood for a fire." And he waved to another man to get it for him.

The Fighter noticed that Tim didn't move away and he grinned under his scarf but he didn't say anything. He went over to the well and got himself a bucket of water out of it. Then he sat down beside his saddle and said inviting: "Why don't you sit down with me? As you seem to watch me that I don't do anything wrong, you can sit down with me as well." He added mockingly.

"I'm sorry but we are a bit suspicious when foreigners come. Here happened too much." Tim sat down beside the Fighter.

The Fighter nodded. He began a normal conversation and it needed not a long time till he and Tim were setting up a fire together and Mandy, Tim's wife, came to join them with a selection of meat and vegetables. After that it wasn't long anymore till more and more men and women joined them at the fire.

Even Fletcher came and sat down beside Tim and Mandy. But he bent backwards, tipped Tim on the shoulder and asked quietly: "Why is he here?"

Tim shrugged his shoulder. "I couldn't find it out. He doesn't talk much but he seems to have good intentions and is quite nice."

"I hope you're right." Fletcher was still a bit suspicious.

The evening went on and the more the men drank wine and beer the louder they became.

The Fighter observed the men thoughtfully. He saw how Mandy laughed and joked with the other men and one especially and he frowned slightly. Luckily nobody could notice that.

Brian had a good time. He was drinking quite a lot, and his jokes grew stupid. He looked at the Fighter and mocked: "The dark clothes must be completely warm in the heat of the sun. You must be melting."

"Not more than you in the light beige clothes." The Fighter answered in the same mocking voice.

Brian examined him with astonishing clear eyes. "You probably think you are something better only because you have a sword."

"At least it's better than to hide behind a rifle like you do." The Fighter had no problems with answering back, and he did it with a calm voice and a touch of an aggressive undertone.

Brian grew angry about the Fighter's attitude. "So you think it's cowardly to handle a rifle? Perhaps you want to see me handling a sword? I'm good at it as well." He mocked.

That was it.

The Fighter got up, "Why not? I would like to see you trying." He pulled a sword out of his clothes and held it over to Brian.

Fletcher got up. "You both stop right now! We have here a friendly sit together and nobody is blowing up a fight here! Sit down, both of you!" His voice was firm and didn't let any contradiction through.

Still the Fighter ignored him completely, holding the sword in his hands and looking over at Brian. "Are you the coward I think you are?" He said quietly.

Brian threw a look over at Fletcher then he took the sword. "I'll show you who the coward is here." He answered calmly.

Tim got up and stopped Fletcher who wanted to step between the two angry men. "Let them fight if they want to. At least it will clear the air."

"Nice man, yes?" Fletcher glared at Tim but Tim shrugged his shoulders.

The Fighter pulled a second sword out of his clothes, took the cloak off and turned over to Brian.

The men and women stepped to the side and left in the middle a space for the two fighters.

Brian swung the sword a little bit to get a feeling for it.

The Fighter on the other side let his sword sing with a swing through the air; at least it sounded like that. Then he put his whole attention over at Brian.

The fight went on for a long time. Both men glared at each other, trying the swords out at the other one.

The Fighter noted every weak point of the man opposite him, and he played a little bit with him.

Then Brian hit quite violently out at the Fighter but the Fighter ducked down and the sword glided over his head through the air. At once he let his sword talk and Brian jumped backwards, holding his left arm where the sword of the Fighter had scratched him.

Brian grew much angrier now. He hit with the sword out at the Fighter that he had to go back step-by-step.

The women and men spread to the side and the Fighter hit the wall from one of the houses around the market place.

Brian hit out again and pressed the Fighter against the wall. "Are you taking back that I'm a coward?"

The Fighter grinned behind the scarf, "For sure not. You were always a coward and you will die being a coward." He answered sharp.

"What do you mean now?" Brian pressed a bit more.

The Fighter lifted one leg. "Think about it! It's now two years ago!" Then the Fighter kicked out at Brian so that the man flew backwards on to his back. For a moment he stopped and stared at the Fighter who came slowly over to him. He got up again and faced the Fighter. "Ha...?" He started to ask and he was so quiet that only the Fighter could hear him.

The Fighter nodded calmly. "And now you know why you have to die!" He said and hit out with the sword.

Brian did his best to answer on the hits but he hadn't much experience to stand for long against someone like the Fighter in a rage.

The Fighter of Freedom had learnt to fight with a sword quite well and he had no problems to bring Brian into a difficult position. Finally he hit so hard at his own sword; hold by Brian, that Brian lost the hold of it.

The Fighter didn't hesitate for long; he lifted the sword and hit out at Brian.

Brian tried to stop the sword but he could not manage it. He got the sword full into his side. He groaned up, double bent forward then he broke down, slowly.

As the Fighter stepped nearer, he noticed the dying eyes of Brian staring at him. Slowly, very slowly the glance disappeared out of Brian's eyes, and his head rolled to the side. Slowly the Fighter put his sword away again then he picked up the sword he had lent to Brian.

"May I ask why you are letting our friendship down by killing one of us?" Fletcher came up to the Fighter who still stood beside the dead body.

"You don't seem to be so sad about the dead guy." The Fighter noted.

"I have my reasons. But that doesn't matter for you." Fletcher frowned. "I would like to hear your reasons for killing him. It can't be only the small discussion at the fire."

The Fighter sighed. "What do you know about the Fighters of Freedom?"

"Nothing much," Fletcher looked still at the Fighter in front of him without recognizing him at all.

The Fighter pointed over to the fire. "Why don't we sit down again and I'll tell you something about my friends and myself?" He suggested.

Fletcher nodded, "After you."

During Fletcher followed the Fighter over to the fire two other men came and removed the dead body.

Mandy at the fire sighed. "I liked Brian a bit." She said quietly but used to sudden deaths she only shrugged her shoulders.

The Fighter looked over at her but he didn't say anything. He sat down again and picked up a bottle of wine. He led the bottle under the scarf to his mouth and took a long sip before he looked around.

All the women and men had gathered around again and waited interested for whatever would follow now.

Fletcher made an inviting hand movement and the Fighter swallowed. He cleared his throat and began his story to tell: "It all started around two years ago. If I'm correct informed, it happened here." He stopped for a moment.

Mandy frowned. "Are you talking about the time, the foreigners wanted to sell us as slaves?"

The Fighter nodded. "Exact."

"What did you have to do with that?" Mandy asked.

The Fighter wasn't prepared to tell the whole truth now. "I have a friend who lived here. She told me the whole story of what happened here."

"As it can't be one of us here – the only two women who never came back were Amanda and – Hayley." Mandy noticed with a side look at Fletcher. "Who of these two told you the story?"

The Fighter knew he had to tell them about Amanda's death so he decided fast not to go too far away from the truth. "I heard it from Hayley." He said calmly, avoiding looking at Fletcher.

Fletcher looked up. "How and especially where is she?" He asked quietly.

The Fighter shook his head. "One thing after the other." he answered and started to tell his own story to the listening group of men and women, as if he had never been there and as if he really only had heard it…

3

As Hayley woke up again, she was lying in one of the wagons, still tied up but in the shadows. She felt terribly sick and her skin was hurting all over her body. Somehow she wished she could cry but as much as she tried she felt empty and no tears wanted to come.

For a long time nothing happened.

Hayley didn't know how long she was already lying in the wagon and she didn't know how many seconds, minutes or hours had gone by since she had woken up again.

The journey went on for a very long time, and Hayley lost completely her feeling for time.

In the nights the caravan made a short break where they all got something to eat and drink and where the foreign men caught some sleep, one after the other. Almost a week went by before they reached the next town.

In all this time Hayley had seen the other women and the children only from far away; the men kept her alone and tied up the whole time.

Hayley had lost the interest completely of what would happen with her. The only thing, which kept her going at that moment was the sight of her son she saw daily lying in Mandy's arms, far away from her but alive. Otherwise she really didn't know what would happen to them all and she couldn't keep up anymore.

The day they reached the town was the day a new life would start for Hayley; even she didn't know it yet.

All the women and the children were led away, and Hayley was sure she wouldn't see them again. Her baby went together with Mandy, and on one side Hayley was relieved because she knew he was in good hands but on the other side it broke her heart, as she knew she would never see him again. From that she was convinced about since a long time now.

The men let Hayley lying in one of the wagons; she didn't get the chance for a walk, for a cleaning up or something else. Again a lot of time went by but the only sounds she heard were sometimes shouting. She didn't care what it was; she only asked herself, not conscious about that, what now would happen to her.

It was already dark, as the big burly man came back to the wagons and entered the one, in which Hayley was lying. He sat down beside her and smiled: "Your friends made a really good price for me on the market. Everybody has now a new home – and for you I have something special."

Hayley examined him. "You really sold them as slaves?" She asked, not believing for a second what she just had heard.

The man grinned. "What did you think? That we drive you around out of pleasure?" He mocked laughing. "And aren't you curious where you will go to?"

"Not in the least, as I won't stay there." Hayley answered firm.

The man laughed again. "Your friends made me rich but you will make me richer. And you won't have a chance to leave that place. You will enjoy it!"

Hayley made a face but she didn't answer anything.

In this moment a man came up to the wagon and called softly: "Sheikh Farrar? The Prince is here."

The big burly man – now Hayley knew his name: Sheikh Farrar – got up and smiled at her: "Soon you will be in a new home as well. The prince is here to have a look at you." He looked at her from top to bottom. "You don't look so well at the moment but it will be enough to impress him." Athletic he jumped from the wagon and waved to two other men. "Get her out and see to it that she doesn't look so bad anymore."

The two men nodded and came over to the wagon. They opened up the covers and grabbed after Hayley's legs. They pulled her out of the wagon and looked at her.

In the meantime Sheikh Farrar went over to the place and greeted the prince, Prince Alban of Tarragon, like the old friend he was. They talked for a time but finally the prince grew impatient. "What do you have this time for me?"

Sheikh Farrar smiled. "A jewel, but she is a wild cat – you have to be careful."

"Where is she?" Prince Alban was curious.

15

Sheikh Farrar gave a sign.

The two men who had pulled Hayley out of the wagon brought her over to the two waiting men. They had straightened her clothes, cleaned her face and combed her hair. Then they had cut the ropes and prepared new ones. As they brought Hayley over now, she was tied to ropes at both wrists that the men could lead her freely. As well her ankles were tied so that she only could do small steps.

Sheikh Farrar and Prince Alban looked at her with interest, one calculating how much he would get, one with sudden lust and fire.

Prince Alban stepped nearer to Hayley. He put his finger under Hayley's chin and lifted her head.

Hayley looked at the Prince. She saw a tall man in fine clothes, somewhere in the middle of his forties. His dark skin fitted together with the dark eyes and the black hair. He was a handsome man but Hayley didn't feel anything, as she looked at him.

Prince Alban stared at her. He examined her from top to bottom, opened her mouth to look at her teeth, opened the shirt a bit to look at her breasts then he went around her and looked at her back. At last he went over to Sheikh Farrar again and nodded. "You're right. She's a jewel. What do you want for her?"

For a while both men were discussing the price of Hayley before they finally agreed and shook hands on it. Then the Prince turned and said, looking at Hayley again: "Give her my sign and dress her into the clothes I brought with me that I can take her back."

Sheikh Farrar nodded. He gave some hand signs but Prince Alban was faster. Once more he went over to Hayley and started to open her trousers.

Hayley swallowed in order to get over the shame, which came upon her and she only hoped that she could take revenge for everything what happened to her – again.

Prince Alban pulled her trousers down that she finally stood half naked on the place. The Prince examined the sign she had on her left leg then again he went around her. He pressed his body against her from the back, laid one hand on her mouth and one hand on her left leg and turned it a bit. "Burn at first the sign away before you give her mine." He ordered shortly.

Sheikh Farrar nodded. He took one hot gleaming stick off one of the men who had brought it and another one and came over to Hayley.

Hayley saw the stick and knew what would come now. She stiffened and prepared herself for the coming pain.

Sheikh Farrar had no problems with what he had to do. He pressed the hot gleaming stick against Hayley's leg, to be exact against the sign of the Horsemen she had there.

Hayley breathed deeply in and groaned, as she felt the pain crawling through her body. She would have liked to cry but the hand on her mouth prevented that she could do more than groan.

And Sheikh Farrar hadn't finished with her. He gave the first stick back where he had it from and took the second one. Again he turned to Hayley and for a second time he pressed the stick against her leg, this time under the first mark.

Tears came up into Hayley's eyes. She couldn't help herself but that was too much for her. It happened so much to her in the last days that she couldn't cope anymore. For a moment she broke completely.

Finally Sheikh Farrar threw the second stick away and looked at his work. Satisfied he nodded.

Prince Alban let his hold of Hayley go, went around her and looked at the burned mark on Hayley's leg. He as well nodded satisfied. "Bring her over to my tent." He said shortly, pointing over to a tent at the side and the two men led Hayley how she was over to the tent.

Prince Alban followed them slowly.

Inside the tent Hayley had to sit down on some soft pillows and the men tied the ropes to some wooden barriers on the sides. It prevented that Hayley could lie down what she really would have liked in that moment, as the pain still ran through her whole body. But so she was sitting on the pillows with wide-open arms and had to wait for what would come now.

Prince Alban came into the tent and examined her thoroughly again. "Let me see your leg. I don't want that you get an infection." He said firmly and sat down in front of Hayley. He grabbed after her left leg and pulled at it till he could see the marks.

Hayley had no power left to reject against Prince Alban. She didn't look at him, as he started to care for her leg.

Prince Alban smeared cooling crème on the marks then he looked up again. He dried his hands on a towel, which was lying beside the pillows. At last he sat down beside Hayley and started to stroke over her hair.

Hayley wished from the bottom of her heart that he would leave her alone for a moment but Prince Alban was fascinated from her. He passed with the hand over her cheek and took then her face between his hands.

Then he forced her to look up. "Listen carefully!" He started firmly and tried to catch her look. "You belong to me now and you have to do what I want. Every time you aren't obedient you will be punished." He was silent for a moment then he continued: "But I really like you. If you decide to be nice to me, I'll make you to my first wife. You will have a good life then." He bent forward and pressed his lips on Hayley's mouth. As he didn't feel any response, he solved his lips again. "Think about it. And now we want to see that you will be presentable when I'll bring you over to my palace. Are you able to dress alone or do you need guards around you?" He asked mockingly.

For the first time Hayley looked up and stared at him. She didn't say anything but her look said everything.

Prince Alban got up. "Let me tell you that there are a lot of guards around the tent. Sheikh Farrar, he and his men, they are still here as well as you know. No way out." he cut the ropes from the barriers and pointed over at a big wooden box. "You find everything you need inside there. Dress – or I drag you naked through the streets!" Prince Alban turned around and left the tent.

Hayley looked after him. She knew he was right with his bits of information about the guards; she had enough seen of them outside, staring at her. The last thing she wanted now was to see them again; to try to run away was impossible. So what else was there for her?

Hayley pulled at the rope around her ankles till they fell off then she got up. During she pulled her trousers up she went over to the box and opened it. For a moment she stared at the fine dresses in the box then she turned around. Searching she looked around.

"Do you need something?" Prince Alban stepped back into the tent.

Hayley stepped back every time Prince Alban came a step nearer to her. She almost fell over the box with the dresses during she tried to get her power back for an answer.

Prince Alban noticed that and stopped at once.

"If you... Would have... Some water, please. I'd like to... wash myself... a bit." Hayley still felt the shame and the embarrassment from before that she started to stutter. As well she hadn't recovered her full power yet so she felt terrible afraid.

Prince Alban smiled. He clapped into his hands and a man appeared in the opening of the tent. He made a bow and looked asking at the prince.

"Bring some water, soap, shampoo and a hairbrush - at once!" Prince Alban ordered cold.

The man bowed again and disappeared.

"You'll get everything you need. And if you need more, ask Ahmed." He pointed to the opening and Hayley understood that he meant the man he had given the order to.

"I'll wait for you outside till you are ready. But don't let me wait too long." Prince Alban warned her then he left the tent again.

Hayley cowered together on the box with the dresses. She didn't know anymore what to do. She felt so bad.

Ahmed came inside. He had everything with him what the prince had ordered to bring her. He placed the things on a table on the side before he turned to Hayley. "Do you need something else?" He asked quietly.

Hayley looked up. She saw the things on the table and shook her head.

Ahmed bent forward, still looking at Hayley. "I know it's difficult but it would be better for you if you do what Prince Alban says. And he's not as bad as it looks like now, you can believe me." Ahmed suddenly told her.

Hayley brought somehow a smile up on her lips. "Thanks, Ahmed." She whispered. Then she let her head sink down again.

Ahmed disappeared.

A while later Hayley got up and went over to the table. Automatically she started to wash herself, using soap and shampoo a lot. Then she dressed in a simple green dress she had found in the box and which looked very good on her with the red curls as contrast.

Somebody cleared his throat outside the tent. "Are you ready?" The impatient voice of the prince came into the tent.

Hayley nodded. Then she noticed that he couldn't see it and answered quietly: "Yes, I just finished."

Prince Alban came into the tent again. He examined Hayley and nodded more than satisfied. "You look great." He said with a smile. "You will impress everybody, I'm sure."

Hayley looked down on the ground, not responding at all to the words.

Prince Alban sat down on the pillows. He pointed at the pillows next to him and ordered: "Sit down with me! We have to talk about some more rules."

Hayley looked around where else she could sit down but there wasn't much choice without the pillows. So she sat back down on the box with the dresses.

Prince Alban grew angry. "Damn girl! If you don't come over here now, I'll hit you over. Believe me, I'm able to." He sat and grabbed after the whip he carried at the side of his clothes.

Hayley shook together, as she noticed the hand movement. Afraid she got up and came over to him, slowly, very slowly.

Prince Alban pointed on the pillow direct beside him, and Hayley sat hesitatingly down. The prince smiled at her. "First rule: Obey – or get punished! You'll learn it or you'll end up in my cells. Second rule: Be always nice to me or you have to endure the same I said before." He laid his hand on Hayley's leg.

Somehow Hayley endured it. So many foreign men had touched her in the last days that she wasn't able to feel anything anymore. Still it made her angry that she now was only a subject of lust and nothing more. But she also knew if she would defend herself here and now it would make everything worse.

Prince Alban came nearer to her. "We still have a bit of time. My men are not ready yet with loading the stuff we bought. There's another girl as well but you are thousand times better." He whispered. His hand wandered up her leg, passed her hip and came to a rest over her breasts.

Hayley swallowed. She was terrified; she didn't know what to do and she didn't know if she could keep herself under control till the right time had come.

"Prince Alban? We are ready to go." A man came inside with a bow.

Prince Alban took his hand away from Hayley and turned to the man. "Bring her to the other girl into the wagon. We start as soon as possible." He didn't let show if he was angry about the interruption.

Hayley only felt relieved that she had come around it again and that she was safe for the moment.

The man bowed and came over to Hayley. He grabbed after her arm and pulled her up.

"Tie her up or she will escape you!" Prince Alban informed his guard mockingly.

The guard picked up the rest of the rope from the rack and followed the order of his commander. He tied Hayley the hands firmly on the back, and Hayley stood still between the two men and let it happen. She knew she had no chance at the moment.

Prince Alban examined her longingly for a last time that evening then the guard pulled Hayley outside and pushed her over to a row of wagon, which had been prepared for the journey of Prince Alban, back to Tarragon. In the middle of the wagons the guard opened up a wagon, grabbed after Hayley, lifted her up and threw her inside.

Hayley fell hard into the wagon and she groaned slightly.

The wagon was closed up again and it was dark inside.

Hayley recovered fast; she felt somebody near herself and she turned a bit around.

It was a woman beside her she noticed, as some long hairs touched her body as she turned. The woman cried quietly and even Hayley had problems to keep her eyes dry. She heard the silent cries and she thought she recognized the voice.

"Amanda?" Hayley asked quietly into the darkness.

The cries stopped for a moment, "Hayley?" Amanda's voice came carefully back.

Hayley slipped over to the other woman and pressed her face shortly against the face of Amanda. "What happened to you all?" She asked quietly, as she rested her head back on the ground.

Amanda swallowed. "It was terrible. We had to undress, wash and then they brought us up on a platform in front of a crowd of people and sold us to them one by one." Amanda's voice almost broke. "I got then pushed into a tent, got a dress and was brought into this wagon. I'm here since a long time; two or three times some men came to look at me but that's all."

Hayley pressed her body at Amanda's. "Ssssh!" she made quietly to calm Amanda down. The other woman had started to cry again.

Hayley didn't know what else to do, as she had herself to fight against her feelings.

For a long time both women lay only there and tried to find out if they could cope and what would happen next. Then the wagon was opened up again and a lantern shone inside.

"Are you both comfortable?" A mocking voice asked.

Hayley recognized the voice of Prince Alban and she blinked into the light. "Some pillows would be nice. It's quite hard here." She answered quietly, suddenly feeling that she had the power at least to make it more bearable for them in the wagon.

She was right.

Prince Alban nodded, turned and gave some sharp commands.

Five minutes later the women were lying on some very soft pillows and were covered with some blankets. Then the wagon was closed up again and darkness surrounded them once more.

"Why is he doing it?" Amanda was astonished. "He seems to make what you want."

Hayley sighed. "But that has a reason. He hopes I'll be willing to become his wife when he helps me now to feel comfortable."

"But you are already married!" Amanda said horrified then she stopped short and said much calmer: "I'm sorry, Hayley. I didn't mean to…"

"It's okay." Hayley pressed out through her teeth. "Do you know what happened to my son?" She asked finally quietly.

"Mandy didn't let him for one minute out of her arms. She claimed that he is her son and has to look after him. They seemed to believe her and brought her everything she needed for him. I don't know who… who… who bought them but they went together." Amanda started to stutter, as she had to talk about the fact that they had been sold on the market.

Hayley swallowed. "It may be good for her that they think she's a mother. Perhaps she has it a bit easier then." She murmured.

Amanda heard her murmur, lying direct beside her. "Why didn't you tell them that he is your son? Perhaps they would treat you better then."

Hayley actually brought a smile on her lips at this suggestion. She shook her head. "Wrong." She said. "They know it."

"How can they know?" Amanda asked astonished.

Hayley sighed again. Then she told Amanda in short, almost quiet words about Brian and his betrayal. After that she lay still on her pillows.

Amanda breathed deeply in. "I would never have thought that about him." She said, shocked.

"What does it matter now?" Hayley felt terrible, as talking about Brian had brought back the memory of these horrible first nights in captivity.

Amanda slipped carefully over to Hayley, lying her face down so near to her that her nose touched Hayley's. "Listen, Hayley. Is there nothing we can do?"

Hayley noticed in time that Amanda seemed to get crazy soon. She kissed softly Amanda's nose tip and whispered: "Stay calm, Amanda. I don't know yet what we can do – but I promise you that we won't stay wherever they bring us to. We will be free again – and we will go home again. I promise!"

"Really," Amanda whispered asking back, sounding more comforted than before.

"I promise." Hayley confirmed firmly.

Both women fell silent after this promise. Again they had to wait a long time till they finally noticed that the wagon started and their journey began. They were lying side by side and felt only relieved about the fact that they had each other.

The caravan of Prince Alban went on the complete night and the whole day through, only stopping two, three times for meals.

Hayley and Amanda slept most of the time; when the wagons stopped they got the allowance to leave the wagon and to have their meal out in the sun.

As they were out in the desert again, Prince Alban and his guards saw everything a lot easier. They didn't tie Hayley and Amanda up anymore, as the possibility of running away was very small. The sun in the desert would kill everybody who didn't know how to handle it, and without water and food it was impossible to survive.

Hayley knew this as well, and she didn't make a move through Amanda pressed her to do something. But she explained to her that it would need nothing if they would die here in the desert, and at last Amanda accepted her decision to wait for a better possibility...

4

After almost eight days on the way, the caravan reached a town at the edge of the desert, in the near of some hills.

It was the hometown of Prince Alban - Tarragon.

Hayley and Amanda heard the welcome shouts for the Prince, as they went through the gate and along the streets. It was a big noise and went on for quite a time. But in the end it grew quieter, and the wagons stopped.

Hayley wished to have enough power and courage to peep through the opening of the wagon to see where they were but she still hadn't recovered her usual self and didn't dare to do anything. She said to herself that she would see it soon enough when they would get them out.

It needed around half an hour till the wagon was opened up and Prince Alban looked inside. "Come out now!" He ordered.

Hayley followed the command, as they hadn't any other chance and she climbed out of the wagon. Amanda was just behind her and she clutched to Hayley's hand anxiously.

"Bring them to the ladies harem. Organize enough food, wine and clothes for them that they are comfortable." Prince Alban gave his next orders out to Ahmed who stood waiting some steps behind him.

Ahmed bowed and waved to the women to follow him.

Hayley got a push into the back and made some steps forward. She pulled Amanda with her and through the guards beside them and behind them they had no other chance than to follow Ahmed.

These all left them no time at all to look around. They only caught a glimpse on the building they got led into: it was a big building, white marble and cold.

Ahmed led them through a big hall to a door on the left side. He opened the door and said quietly: "Ladies Quarter. I'm not allowed to go on but I will organize everything you need from here. Please go inside!"

"Thanks, Ahmed." Hayley murmured and stepped through the door.

Amanda followed her at once.

Ahmed closed the door behind them, and Hayley heard that he – or somebody else – locked the door at once.

Both women looked around. They were standing in a corridor, lighted through lamps under the ceiling.

Hayley noticed a door at the end of the corridor and she pointed at it. "It needs nothing when we stay here. Let's see if somebody else is already here." She grabbed very firm after Amanda's hand and pulled her with her through the corridor to the door. Then she opened the door and looked inside.

The room behind the door was very big. On the left were benches, tables and chairs; in the middle was a big swimming pool and to the right a lot of doors. Behind the pool were big glass doors, which were open and led to the outside into a garden.

At one table in the middle three women were sitting and talked together. Two others were sitting at the edge of the swimming pool.

All the women wore nothing than short bikinis and a light robe over it.

Hayley cleared her throat. "Hi!" She murmured, as she stepped inside and pulled Amanda with her.

Amanda let the door go and it slipped close with a soft noise.

The women in the room turned around. Astonished they examined the newcomer, and Hayley and Amanda stared confused about the visible wealth in the room back.

One of the women at the table got up and came over to Hayley and Amanda. "Hello! I'm Shannon, Prince Alban's first wife – till now." She added, as she examined Hayley from top to bottom. "But I think he will prefer you instead of me." She continued without regret in her voice.

Hayley shook her head. "You can have him I would say if I would have a say." She answered calmly. "I'm Hayley – and that's Amanda." She then introduced herself and her friend.

"Welcome." Shannon smiled. She liked Hayley's outspoken type and shook her hand vigorously. "I'm afraid you won't have a say in this matter.

But before we go deeper into this area, come and let me introduce you to the others." She turned and went back to the table.

Hayley and Amanda followed her slowly. So they had time enough to recover from their surprise of the surroundings and the foreign women here. As they reached the table, the two women from the pool had come over to them as well and Shannon led the introduction, which made quite clear that the other women had accepted her as first wife of the Prince.

"Ladies, that's Hayley and Amanda." She pointed first at Hayley then at Amanda, Then she turned to the two women and continued: "That's Bethany and Elaine; Nicole and Orinda are the wives of the Prince's brother. Let's sit down!" She offered.

Hayley nodded in greeting at the women during she sat down. She examined the women who still looked interested at her and Amanda as well.

Bethany was at least as tall as Hayley; she had beautiful blonde hair and blue eyes. Elaine was just the opposite, small, very thin with black hair and dark blue eyes. Nicole had brown hair and brown eyes; Orinda had black hair and black eyes, she was an Asian woman.

Shannon herself had long blonde hair and sparkling blue eyes. She was tall and had a very female figure.

With these five very female women around, Hayley started to feel unwell. She knew that she looked good with her fire red long curls and the green eyes but she had an athletic figure and couldn't be said very female. Even after the birth of her son she had got her figure back at once without any problems; a fact other women were jealous about it.

Amanda on the other side fitted better in. She was as young as Hayley was, unmarried, just not so tall as Hayley but with a very female figure, long black hair and dark eyes.

Bethany smiled. "Good. Now we can go out from the fact that we get a first class meal and something to drink. – Not, that we don't get anything on other days but it is really better when new women arrived." She added hastily, as she saw that Hayley lifted an eyebrow.

Hayley smiled at her. "Is this all or are there more rooms?" She asked curiously.

Shannon pointed over to the doors. "Some bedrooms are on the other side but that's then all. More than enough for us, don't you think so?" She asked.

Hayley hadn't the same opinion but she only asked further on: "Is there no gym or something like that? Is the pool everything?"

It was Elaine who suddenly understood. She laughed loudly: "Hayley, wasn't it?" She asked, still smiling.

Hayley nodded.

Elaine bent forward and looked at her. "You don't seem to understand where you are now. This here is the harem of the Princes of Tarragon and all we are allowed to do is looking after ourselves and care for ourselves. You won't get a chance for training or something like that." She threw a look over at Bethany before she continued: "And if you try it – you will suffer."

Bethany sighed. "I tried it and I suffered." She said quietly and turned her back to Hayley. She let go of the thin robe she wore and showed her bare back to Hayley and Amanda. It was covered with scarves, bright and red.

Hayley sighed as well. "I'm afraid that will be the same with me. I don't intend to stay here – I have responsibilities somewhere else."

Amanda laid her hand on Hayley's shoulder and pressed it shortly.

Bethany looked over at Hayley. "What do you mean?" She asked astonished.

Hayley breathed out. "I'm already married and I have a son. Also I have a good job." She pressed her lips together.

Shannon on her other side suddenly understood her feelings. She pressed shortly Hayley's hand. "You have to forget them. You must." She said urgently. "There is no way out of here."

Hayley shook her hand off and got up. "Just the opposite - I'll never forget and I never forgive." She said calmly and went over to the open doors to have a look into the garden.

Shannon bent over to Amanda and asked quietly: "Is she always so stubborn? Can't she see that's hopeless and that she only hurts herself when she goes on like that?"

Amanda nodded. "She is like that, always. And I can understand her – I feel the same. But I don't know if I will have the courage she possess."

Hayley in the meantime stared into the garden. Her feelings were in chaos, and she felt afraid that she might not be able to survive what happened with her here. Also her leg started to hurt again like in the last days so often and she wished she would be able to cry. But the only thing she did was, pressing against the left side of her left leg in order not to feel the pain anymore.

"Are you all right, Hayley?" Shannon asked carefully. She observed Hayley's hand on her leg.

Hayley nodded. "Yes, I'm all right." She answered and took her hand away.

But she got stopped from Shannon who knew more as she wanted to tell. "Is it the burned mark?" She asked calmly and grabbed after Hayley's leg. Before Hayley could react, she got hold of it and turned it that she could look at the mark. In the same moment she shrugged together. "Hayley, listen! That doesn't look good. If you don't let me treat it, you will be dead without any other help. – Come back and let me have a good look at it, please!" She looked so intensive at Hayley that Hayley started to like the woman. She looked at her. "What will happen to you if I refuse and die?" She asked curiously.

Shannon shook her head. "You really don't want to know. Come now." She reached Hayley her hand, and Hayley took it.

Together they went over to the benches where Shannon asked Hayley to lie down and to show her the marks.

Hayley did what Shannon asked her to do, and Shannon touched the area around the marks carefully. She noticed that Hayley twitched together in pain and stopped. "Elaine!" She called the small woman. "Get me fresh water and the herbs from the shelf in my room, please."

Elaine disappeared through one of the other doors and came back five minutes later with a bowl of water and a glass of herbs. She went over to Hayley and Shannon and placed everything on a table nearby.

Shannon washed the marks on Hayley's leg carefully then she made something like a crème out of some of the herbs and put it on the marks.

Hayley bit on her lips in order not to cry out for pain.

Shannon shook her head. "It would be better if you would cry. It makes it easier for you. And now don't move! If the infection spreads out, you'll die."

Hayley nodded only.

Shannon washed her hands and dried them carefully. Then she disappeared into her room.

Elaine sat down beside Hayley. "Shannon will report that you are sick and that the Prince should leave you alone till you are all right again. That will give you a bit of time to be able to accept all these here." She said comfortingly.

Hayley pressed a smile on her lips. "Thanks." She only murmured then she closed her eyes. A second later she was asleep.

"Amanda!" Shannon turned to Hayley's friend. "Hayley has now a bit of time but - can't you convince her to see that there is no way out of here and that she should get used to this fact?" She asked worried, as she came back from her room.

Amanda looked at her. "If you would know Hayley, you would know that she can't be convinced from anything when she has another opinion. But what's wrong?"

Shannon sat down back at the table. "I spoke with the Prince. He told me that he really likes Hayley, and when she doesn't obey him, he will break her. And you know what that means."

Amanda nodded slowly. "But will he wait till she is all right again?"

"He will wait but not longer than necessary. In the meantime..." Shannon looked at Amanda.

Amanda leaned back and closed her eyes. "How shall I convince her when she sees what he's done to me?"

Shannon shook her head. "Listen, Amanda. Prince Alban is a gentleman, especially in bed. You have nothing to fear, believe me. If you do what he asks you to do, you will have a great time. And then you won't have any problems to convince Hayley of the same."

"We'll see." Amanda felt unwell at the thought of it but she knew that she wouldn't have the power to fight against Prince Alban. She never had been a fighter like Hayley...

Five eunuchs served a delicious meal to the women in the harem. Beside meat and potatoes there were a lot of fresh fruits, exotic ones and they looked gorgeous.

The women woke up Hayley who seemed to lie in a half unconscious sleep and brought her something to eat.

Hayley didn't eat a lot; she was exhausted and the infection did the rest: she fell asleep again after only some bites of the delicious meat and a potato.

Shannon observed her worried; the infection seemed to be more dangerous than she had thought before. She took a chair to the bench where Hayley was lying on and sat down beside her, examining her leg from time to time and watching the woman carefully.

Amanda on the other hand had no time at all to look after Hayley.

Bethany and Elaine saw to it that Amanda washed totally and shampooed her hair then dried herself and ate enough.

In the meantime Nicole and Orinda had searched for a suitable dress for Amanda, and after Amanda had finished her meal they helped her dressing and brushing the hair till she looked really beautiful.

But then came the last bit, and Amanda knew that these all was not quite true.

Bethany brought a belt over to Amanda, which was made out of leather and silver chains. She laid it around Amanda's hips and closed it, during Amanda watched her asking. "A security measure Prince Alban wants to have. Don't be afraid of it!" She explained shortly, as she noticed Amanda's look. Then she connected to the belt a chain, which she led over Amanda's back and also wound it around Amanda's wrists.

Amanda couldn't move her hands anymore.

"You'll get used to it. The Prince will take them off you." Elaine whispered to Amanda, seeing her bewildered look. "But he wants to make sure that we don't do anything on the way to him."

Amanda sighed. "But it's humiliating!" She answered quietly.

Elaine shook her head. "You will soon notice that every other woman in the palace will envy you about that. It makes you feel good and gives you the position you belong into. Finally – you are one of Prince Alban's wives!"

Amanda didn't answer. She didn't know what to say and she still felt unwell.

Elaine touched her shoulder in comfort, and then Bethany came up and took Amanda at the arm. "Come on now." She said quietly and led her away from the other women. She brought her over into a small side room, which was only equipped with a chair.

Bethany pressed Amanda down on the chair and said calmly: "Listen, stay here and be calm. The guards will come to get you and they will bring you over to Prince Alban. Do what you get told and you will be okay. See you tomorrow!" Bethany left the room and locked the door behind her.

Amanda looked helplessly behind her, waiting for whatever would follow...

Hayley woke up the following afternoon. She felt better than before and her leg didn't hurt so much anymore. She looked astonished around the big room, in which she laid till she started to remember. Carefully she got up and listened to find out where the other women were.

Different voices came through the open doors out of the garden over to her.

Hayley followed the laughter and the voices till she saw Shannon, Amanda and the rest of the women sitting and lying on the grass in the middle of the garden.

Amanda discovered Hayley at first. She waved over to her and called friendly: "Hayley! Come over and join us!"

The other women turned around and smiled at her.

Hayley brought a smile on her lips and stepped over to the women. "Hi!" She said quietly and carefully.

Shannon smiled at Hayley. "Sit down, Hayley. How is your leg?" She pointed at the blanket beside hers.

Hayley sat carefully down. "Better, thanks. It doesn't hurt so much anymore."

Shannon leaned over to her and looked at her leg. "It looks better but it will still need time till it's really okay." She murmured. "You had another mark. What was it?"

Hayley made a face. "It was the sign of the Horsemen." She answered shortly.

Shannon shook her head. "I have never heard of them. What are they?"

"They are a bunch of criminals who try to make good what they once did wrong. Is it right?" Orinda looked at Hayley.

Hayley lifted an eyebrow. "Where do you know that from?" She asked astonished.

Orinda hesitated. Then she confessed: "My sister married one of them and moved into their village." She stopped short before she continued: "When you both belong to the Horsemen then…" Her voice broke.

Hayley frowned. "What's the name of your sister?"

"Olivia. Her husband's called Serge." Orinda whispered.

Hayley and Amanda exchanged a look. "I know Olivia. She is a fine girl. – But she is now a slave like the rest of us." Hayley added carefully.

Orinda stared on the ground. Nicole slipped over to her and laid her arm around Orinda's shoulders and pressed them.

"Olivia is a strong girl. She will survive, whatever may happen to her now." Hayley said comfortingly.

Orinda sighed. "I think you're right. She always had her own head." She shrugged her shoulders and was silent.

Shannon left the garden and came back five minutes later with a tray of glasses and a pot of crème. She placed the tray in the middle of the women, offering the glasses with cold juices around. The pot of crème she gave over to Hayley and said only shortly: "Put more of the crème on your leg. It will help you."

"Thanks." Hayley did what Shannon told her to do and she felt shortly after how her infected leg cooled down. Then she accepted one of the cold drinks.

For a long time the women sat together and talked and laughed.

In the evening they got again served a delicious meal, and this time Hayley was able to enjoy the food. She ate with appetite, as she hadn't had so much good food for a long time. At last she leaned back and enjoyed an orange, slowly, bit by bit.

Again Amanda hadn't joined into the meal. She had her bath once more and then a bit of food.

After the other women had finished their meal, they helped Amanda into her dress.

Hayley observed interested how Amanda got dressed and how Bethany finally put her into the chains. She frowned.

Shannon smiled, as she noticed Hayley's look. "It will be Amanda's turn to chain you when you go to the Prince." She said laughing. "It looks more terrible than it is. And you can ask her yourself tomorrow morning, if it is so terrible to sleep with the Prince."

Hayley smiled, as she heard the suggestion. "You don't understand." She noticed. "It is not that I don't like the Prince or don't want to sleep with him. I can't – even if I wanted to. The problem is that I'm already married, and I have a son. I don't want to betray them because I love them and I want to go back to them." She stopped short and looked at Shannon. "How long are you already here?"

Shannon shrugged her shoulders. "I came over here, as I was nineteen and still a virgin. That's now just over ten years ago." She thought about it. "I was brought up to live in a harem so I don't know how it is – outside."

Hayley understood. "And you are happy here?"

"I am." Shannon smiled. "I was unable till now to give him the son he wants to have. So I have no problems to accept the other women he pulls into his bed. That's normal for a harem." She looked around. "It is only a small harem here but…"

"You see!" Hayley bent over to her. "I could give my husband a son, and I won't like it to see other women next to my husband. I… God, I miss them!" Hayley laid her hands over her eyes and bit on her lips to stop herself crying.

Shannon laid a hand on Hayley's shoulder. "It will be good; everything will be fine!" She murmured in comfort.

Hayley breathed deeply in and out. She needed two minutes till she had herself under control again. She looked up and saw how Bethany locked the door behind Amanda. "Thanks, Shannon. We will see how it will go on." She said quietly.

Bethany and the other women came back to the table where Hayley and Shannon still sat.

The evening went on and as it grew late, Shannon showed Hayley the room she could share with Amanda.

Then it grew quiet, and the women went to bed…

Next morning was a very beautiful morning.

Hayley was up early. She didn't feel any pain anymore in her legs so she decided to go swimming. In one of the cupboards she found a bikini in her size; she slipped into it and went then over to the pool.

The water was warm, and Hayley divided it with her strong arms without problems. She swam through the whole length of the pool and back, again and again.

As finally the other women came for breakfast, Hayley was sitting on the edge of the pool and relaxed.

"Morning, Hayley. You are early up!" Shannon greeted her smiling.

Hayley smiled back. "Morning, Shannon! I'm most of the time early up, now I need only a cup of coffee and I'm like newborn."

Shannon laughed. "Then we want to see what we have here." She went over to the dining table and looked at it.

Hayley got up and looked searching around.

Bethany noticed her look and pointed over to a cupboard at the side. "You'll find a robe inside there." She said smiling with an air of jealousy, as she looked at Hayley and her athletic figure.

Hayley smiled at her and got a robe out of the cupboard. She pulled it over and went over to the others to the dining table. As she noticed Bethany's look, she shook her head. "Don't look at me like that! You have a figure; I always wanted to have when I was together with my husband. I might be athletic but I haven't a soft skin and I haven't so nice breasts – like you for example."

Bethany breathed deeply in. "And so we are all jealous of each other!" She laughed. "But I don't believe you that your breasts are so terrible. Let's see!"

"What?" Hayley was confused.

Bethany came around the table and stepped behind the chair on which Hayley sat. "We are under us – so don't be shy!" She said quietly. She laid her hands on the robe on Hayley's shoulders and pulled it down. Then she opened the bikini and looked over Hayley's shoulder.

The bikini fell down and Hayley sat half naked on the chair.

Interested the women looked at her. Bethany knelt down beside the chair and laid a hand on Hayley's breast. "Your breasts are great. I really don't know what you have against them." She said and started to massage them softly.

Hayley looked at her. She needed a second to get over her surprise before she could answer: "You may think so. You know the difference – I don't."

Bethany stopped. "What do you mean?"

Shannon laughed loudly. "Come on, Bethany! You know it exactly! She wants to see your breasts as well."

Bethany grinned. "Well, when it is so." She resumed and pulled off her own robe. Then she opened her bra and pulled it down. At last she laid her things on an arm of the chair beside Hayley's and sat down on it. Calmly she showed her breasts to Hayley.

Hayley examined her carefully. She leaned over to Bethany and touched her breasts gently. "I still think yours are better than mine." She smiled.

The other women grinned. "You both are crazy!" Shannon shook her head. "Come on now, let's have breakfast!"

Both Hayley and Bethany pulled their bikinis over again then everything turned back to the breakfast. Only Hayley still felt Bethany's hand on her breast; it wasn't a bad feeling but it made her unsure about herself.

The women had almost finished breakfast, as the door of the small room opened up and Amanda came inside.

Bethany jumped up and went over to her. She undid the chains and came back to the table with Amanda following her.

"Morning, Amanda! Are you all right?" Shannon greeted her softly, and Hayley and the other women turned around to have a look at her.

Hayley stared at her friend. "Amanda?" She asked quietly.

Amanda pulled herself together. "Good Morning! I'm all right." She answered, suppressing her real feelings. Her eyes were dry but her look was sad.

Hayley didn't say anything anymore; she knew how it is when you had to deal with something, which is great ballast to your soul. She foresaw that Amanda didn't want to talk about it at that moment, and she accepted it.

Amanda sat down at the table and took a cup of coffee. She said nothing, heard and saw nothing; she nipped only up and on at her coffee.

The women needed a long time more to finish with breakfast.

Hayley brought Amanda into the room they would share together and put her into the empty bed. She pulled a blanket over her and left her then alone. There was nothing she could do for her now than to give her a bit of peace.

As she went outside, everybody without Bethany had gone into the garden again. Bethany was still sitting on her chair at the table and stared into her cup.

Hayley went over to her and sat down again beside her.

Bethany looked up. "You know that I like women as well?" She asked quietly.

"I noticed it, as you touched me!" Hayley nodded.

Bethany sighed. "The others can't understand it. I hoped you perhaps…"

Hayley felt even more ballast on her shoulders. "I had once something with a cellmate, as I was in prison. But…"

"I know you're married and you have a child. But they are not with you now. Can't we keep each other company?" Bethany pressed the lips together as a try to suppress the question she just had asked.

"What will the others say about that?" Hayley asked curiously, not in the last embarrassed.

Bethany shrugged her shoulders. "I don't think they will say much more than they already did. And perhaps they would think then that you finally get used to being here." She was silent for a moment then she asked very quietly: "Would you take me with you when you leave here?"

Hayley bent over to her. "If this is your wish, I'll take you with me." She confirmed in the same quiet voice. "Do you have here a room on your own?" She asked, thinking hard for a moment.

Bethany nodded. She pointed over to one of the doors. "That's my room. Nobody wanted to share with me because – I meant trouble, always."

Hayley got up. "I don't think so." She said firmly, grabbed after Bethany's hand and pulled her up. "Show me your room." She pleaded.

Bethany led her over to her room and opened the door.

Hayley stepped inside and looked around. She noticed the big bed in one corner and went over to it. Slowly she sat down on it and lay finally down.

Bethany stared for a second at her then she made sure that the others were still outside before she also entered the room and closed the door. She came over to the bed, sat down on the edge and stretched out her hand.

Hayley caught her hand and pressed it down on her heart. She got up a bit again and sat eye to eye beside Bethany.

And suddenly Bethany bent over her and started to kiss her wildly.

Also Hayley opened her mouth and pressed her tongue over into Bethany's mouth. As they touched each other's tongues, the kisses grew more wildly and Bethany pressed with one hand Hayley's head firm at hers.

Only after some minutes they finally solved their lips from each other and Hayley stroked Bethany softly over the cheek. "I haven't been kissed like that since a long time." She confessed.

Bethany smiled. "So wild?" she asked curiously.

But Hayley shook her head. "No. The men who… had me in the last days were always… wild but none of them was at the same time… soft and… loving."

Bethany, who still had her hand at the back of Hayley's head, stroked her gently. "I know what you mean. And you won't get it with the prince either – so, please, let's be together and give each other what we need." She pleaded.

Hayley bent carefully over to Bethany and kissed her softly on the mouth. She laid her arms around her, hugging her gently and murmured, her head pressing against Bethany's throat: "I could do with a bit of love." Tears dropped out of her eyes and down Bethany's throat.

Bethany pulled her up a bit and looked at her. "Ssssh!" she made and kissed the tears, one after the other, away.

Hayley enjoyed Bethany's lips on her face and her tears soon stopped running. She laid her head on the side, and Bethany went with her mouth and tongue over to Hayley's ear and throat. Her hands went down and pushed the robe to the side. Then they passed over to the back and opened up the bikini top.

Hayley pulled the robe from her arms and threw as well the bikini top away. Finally, under Bethany's hands, she lay down on the bed again.

Bethany looked smiling down at her during she let her own robe falling to the ground. And the bikini followed shortly after. Then she pushed her left leg over Hayley and sat carefully down on her. Softly she started to massage Hayley's breasts.

Hayley grew excited under Bethany's touch and she groaned lightly.

Bethany grinned. She bent forward and pressed her lips on Hayley's breast, passing with her tongue softly over her nipples. Again and again till the nipples grew hard and Hayley began to move for excitement.

Hayley stretched her hands out and touched Bethany's back, going up and down.

Bethany lifted her head and she slipped a bit up till she reached Hayley's head. With one hand massaging the breast, she pressed her lips on Hayley's mouth again.

Softly but full of excitement both women kissed each other for a long time.

Hayley went with her hands up to Bethany's breasts and started to massage them. She pressed so much her nipples that Bethany finally solved her lips from Hayley's and breathed groaning out.

Hayley smiled. With one hand she went down till she reached the second half of the bikini. She pushed her hand under it and touched Bethany's soft spot.

"What..." Bethany couldn't finish her sentence; she groaned once more.

Hayley pulled her hand away. "Get out of this thing." She murmured.

Bethany needed a second to understand. Then she got carefully up and pulled the rest of the bikini down.

Hayley did the same then she lay back down again, her legs a bit apart and the arms stretched out to Bethany.

Bethany came back again and again she sat down carefully on Hayley.

Hayley pulled her down, and both women kissed each other first softly, then wildly. Hayley laid her hand back on Bethany's breast during her second hand wandered a bit around over her body. Bethany had her hands on Hayley's breasts as well.

At last Hayley reached again, this time without problems, Bethany's soft spot and started to stroke her gently.

Bethany solved her mouth once more and groaned slightly.

Hayley went with her finger inside and found the right spot. She caressed the spot and stroked over it again and again.

Bethany over her groaned now loudly, lying down with her upper body down on Hayley, and in between the groans she tickled Hayley's ear with her tongue.

Hayley enjoyed the feeling as well; she pressed her finger deeper into Bethany and listened to the woman gasping after air. She pressed one more time and then again and finally Bethany groaned loudly up. She let herself fall completely down on Hayley and tried to catch her breath.

Hayley laid her free arm around Bethany and stroked her softly.

"Where did you learn that?" Bethany turned astonished to Hayley.

Hayley smiled. "I told you before that I once had something with a cellmate. She was kind of… crazy."

Bethany giggled. "I believe you." She rolled to the side, breathed deeply in and got a bit up again. "And now I show you how crazy I am." She said grinning and bent over Hayley again. Softly she kissed her but stopping her hands at the same moment. She laid her hands beside her own hand before she went down over Hayley's chin, her throat till she reached her breasts. She pressed her lips on them, passing with the tongue over her nipples till they grew hard under her touch.

Hayley opened her mouth and groaned quietly. She gave herself completely into Bethany's hands and enjoyed the feeling she received through her touch.

Slowly Bethany kissed for a last time Hayley's breasts and massaged them gently, Then she went down, licked around the navel and came finally down to Hayley's soft spot.

Hayley spread out her legs willingly and her hands went down in order to touch Bethany's hair. She breathed deeply in.

Bethany pressed her mouth on the spot and drove with her tongue inside. She touched the right spot and passed over it again and again.

Hayley's hands got cramped into Bethany's hairs and her legs moved up and down. She groaned deeply.

Bethany grew wilder; she embraced Hayley's legs and pressed her face firmly against Hayley's softest spot.

Hayley groaned again.

Bethany licked her more and more then she went with one hand down and pressed her finger into Hayley, still kissing one more time the spot. Again and again she pressed her finger deeper into Hayley and Hayley groaned every time deeply.

Bethany got up a bit without removing her finger, just the opposite, once more she pressed it deeply into Hayley, bending forward and kissing her nipples at the same time.

Hayley groaned. She passed with the hands over Bethany's shoulders and she shook at her whole body. As Bethany pressed her finger one more time into her, Hayley groaned up loudly. She got up a bit, driven by the excitement and pressed Bethany's shoulder a bit. Then she let go of Bethany and fell backwards again. With a deep groan she breathed out.

"And how did you like that?" Bethany lay down again beside Hayley and stroked her softly over the breasts.

Hayley sighed. "That was at least so good like what I did with you." She grinned and replied the caress she received from Bethany.

Bethany smiled. "And now the best comes." She said and bent over Hayley again…

Hayley and Bethany joined the other women in the garden after more than two hours. They sat down with them as nothing had happened and started to talk with them like the day before.

Shannon examined the two women intensive but she said nothing. What the women did in the time they had to spare was not from interest for her, the other women or somebody else.

The day went fast and was followed from a lot more.

Hayley got the chance to cure her completely, and as the Prince had left for a short trip into the country, she was not in danger to have to do something she didn't want to do.

But that changed after a while.

One evening the eunuchs brought a good evening meal. But before everybody sat down, Shannon stopped Hayley. "Wait a moment!" She said quietly.

Hayley examined her curiously. "What is it?" She asked back.

Shannon was embarrassed. "The Prince is back and he knows that you are all right again. He wishes to see you tonight. You have to get ready for him."

Hayley hadn't changed a bit. She looked mockingly at Shannon. "The Prince can wait." She said and went over to the table where the others all had sat down already.

Shannon hurried behind her and grabbed after Hayley's arm. "You can't do that. What shall I say to him?"

Hayley turned to Shannon. "Show me how and I will tell him personally that he can spend the night alone, that I won't come." She said firmly.

Shannon shook her head. "You are so stupid! You will regret it!"

Hayley shrugged only with her shoulders. She sat down at the table and started to eat like everybody else as well.

Shannon hesitated but then she followed the examples of the others and sat down for dinner. But she was worried what would happen now to Hayley. She had started to like her immensely.

Nothing happened that evening - nothing at all.

Shannon grew more and more worried the more time went by. She knew Prince Alban quite well and she knew he would do something to get what he wanted. And she knew that Hayley would regret that she didn't go to the Prince tonight.

Later the evening the women grew tired and they all went to bed.

Hayley went to bed as well, not caring in the least that she had upset the Prince that night. Fast she was asleep, turning in her bed due to curious dreams.

5

Hayley woke up, as she thought she had heard a noise in her dreams. That she had heard correct, she noticed a second later, as a hand was pressed down on her mouth. She lifted her arm in defence at once but somebody else grabbed her arms and tied her wrists hard together before she could do anything. As well her ankles got tied up; she couldn't do anything, as her legs were completely covered from a blanket, which helped the men who attacked her.

Before she completely knew what happened, she got gagged then lifted up and carried out of her room.

Everything happened so fast and so quiet that Amanda in the bed opposite Hayley's didn't notice anything at all.

Hayley was carried through a door, along some corridors, a staircase up till she didn't know the way anymore and was finally dropped on the ground in a big room. The men who had attacked her left her lying on the ground and went out of the room.

Hayley turned till she came into a sitting position. She looked around where she was during she tried to get rid of the bound around her wrists.

"Finally you're here!" A mocking voice interrupted her tries.

Hayley turned her head a bit and looked into the way the voice had come from. She winked and then she discovered the person who came over to her. It was Prince Alban.

Angry she stared at him.

"Well, you should have known that I react allergic to disobedience. For that you will see what you get out of it. But at first I want to have some fun with you." Prince Alban cut the rope around Hayley's ankles and pulled her up.

Hayley couldn't do anything as she was still tied at her hands and gagged.

Prince Alban pushed her over to his bed and pressed her down on it.

Hayley looked helplessly around for a way out, but Prince Alban laughed only. With short movements he pressed her into a lying position then he picked up another rope and tied her hands to the bed frame. At last he pulled the gag out of her mouth.

"And what are you doing now?" Prince Alban asked interested, stroking her softly over the cheek.

Hayley almost couldn't bear his touch. She bit on her lips and tried to stay calm. "I think I have to bear what you do with me. But you will regret it as well, I tell you." She pressed through her teeth.

Prince Alban laughed loudly. "Tied up to a bed but making threats – that's good. Then it's clear what we have to expect from one another. Let's go down to business." He bent forward and pressed his lips on Hayley's mouth during his hands pulled the last bit of her clothes from her body…

Two hours later Prince Alban was finally satisfied. He lay down beside Hayley and closed his eyes for a while.

Hayley tried to suppress the tears, which stood in her eyes. She felt so bad, used and she knew for certain she couldn't bear that one more time. Before she had to, she would kill herself. Perhaps she would find then the rest and the freedom she was looking for.

Prince Alban got up and rang a bell. He pulled a robe over, and during Prince Alban knotted the belt around his hips, he looked down at Hayley.

Two guards with guns came inside and bowed to the Prince.

Prince Alban pointed at Hayley. "Get her up and dress her in normal clothes. Then bring her down to the cells and lock her up."

The guards nodded, and Prince Alban left the room.

The rope around Hayley's wrists got cut but one of the guards held her at gunpoint so that she couldn't do anything. She got a pair of trousers and a shirt in which she had to dress.

One of the guards looked at her wrists, which were covered in dry blood. He put a bandage around them before he tied Hayley up again.

Finally the two guards let Hayley out of the room, some staircases down till they reached the cellars. They knocked at an iron door and somebody let them in.

Hayley stepped into the prisoner track, led by the two guards. They forced her to go on till the end of the corridor where a big cell was. A dark man opened the door of the cell and Hayley got so hard pushed in that she fell to the ground. Behind her the door was locked again.

Hayley pulled herself up into a sitting position and looked around.

The cell was quite big but there were already some prisoners in it. And they all were men.

Hayley felt cold, as she examined the men around her who came slowly up to her. She was afraid, more than she wanted to confess to anybody right now.

Suddenly – the men had closed her already in – they got pushed to the side.

A man, still in guard's uniform knelt down beside Hayley and started to open the ties around her wrists. "Aren't you the girl Prince Alban bought from Sheikh Farrar?" He asked quietly.

Hayley examined him carefully. He seemed familiar in one-way to her but she couldn't remember where from. "I am. But who are you?" She asked quietly.

"I was one of the guards who looked after you." He reminded her. "It's good to see that nothing very bad happened to you. I felt sorry for you."

Carefully Hayley got up. "Is that the reason why you are here now?" She asked curiously.

The man shook his head. "I tried to help some poor people who were in the way of the Prince. He didn't like it at all – so I ended up here."

Hayley nodded. She looked around, as she felt a hand on her shoulder. She turned. "Take your dirty fingers off me or you will regret it!" She warned the man behind her who went with his fingers now up to her hair.

The man grinned. "I hadn't for a long time a woman in my hands. It feels good." He touched her hair.

"Not long anymore!" Hayley pressed out. She made a fast movement, lifted her leg and kicked violently out.

The man got thrown against the wall and sank slowly to the ground, unable to do anything.

The guard grabbed after Hayley's arm and pushed her over into another corner before one of the other men could react on her. "Stay here! Perhaps I can hold them off you then!"

Hayley nodded. "Thanks for the help!" She answered quietly.

For a long time it was quiet in the cell. The men went into other corners after they noticed that neither with Hayley nor with the guard it was good game to play.

The guard looked after Hayley and brought her water and food when they got something thrown into the cell. He also had a look at Hayley's wrists, which didn't look so good.

Hayley asked herself the whole time how it should go on now. She knew that the guard couldn't watch over her the complete night. And what would happen then to her?

Was it that what Prince Alban hoped for her? That she got raped again and again and that it broke her? That she would be willing then to become his wife?

Everything seemed so hopeless.

Hayley turned to the guard who had sat down beside her and looked at him. "What's your name?" She asked curiously.

The guard looked up. "My name is Arthur. Arthur Macmillan. My parents are English and I'm born there but I grew up here." He informed her quietly and added: "And you?"

Hayley smiled lightly. "Hayley Houseman. I'm married and I have a son. Normally I would ride now with the Horsemen." She answered calmly, even she felt like panicking.

Arthur nodded. "I thought so. The way you were brought in didn't seem to me like that you were a slave. But – what are the Horsemen?" He asked back.

Silently Hayley told him about her life and explained what the Horsemen were. Then she told him what had happened to them all and how she had come into this position.

Arthur listened quietly. He didn't say anything but he understood now why Hayley was like she was. He examined her carefully.

Hayley finished her story. In silence she stared in front of her.

Arthur got up and organized a pillow and a blanket. He reached it over to Hayley and said quietly: "Lie down and try to sleep. I'll watch over you."

Hayley smiled at him thankfully. "Wake me up when you get tired. I'll look after you then."

Arthur nodded and Hayley lay down. A second later she was asleep.

The morning was already almost over, as Hayley woke up. She looked around, not knowing if it was day or night, as the cells had no windows at all.

Arthur looked up. "Awake again?" He asked quietly in order not to disturb anybody else.

Hayley nodded. "How long did I sleep?" She asked in the same voice.

"Around seven hours." Arthur answered after a look at his watch.

"Why didn't you wake me up?" Hayley asked astonished.

Arthur shrugged his shoulders. "I thought it would be good when you get enough sleep that you are fit again. I can get some sleep now – if you look after me."

Hayley got up. "Certainly I do. Lie down." She offered him her pillow and blanket and Arthur accepted it thankfully. He lay down and was a second later asleep.

Hayley had a look around in the cell. She organized some water for herself and after she knocked out a second man who tried to touch her, the men left her alone. She sat down again beside Arthur and nipped at the water. As she leaned back against the wall, she noticed that parts of the wall fell down behind her. She paid a lot more attention to the wall and after some minutes it was clear for her that she could get out of the cells through this wall. She worked secretly but like possessed to get a big hole into the wall.

"You know certainly that not the walls keep us in here – that it is the desert outside the town?" Arthur looked at Hayley who astonished noticed that he was awake again. She shrugged her shoulders. "But there are hills as well, am I right?"

Arthur sat up. "What do you want to do?"

"I want to get out of here – doesn't matter what it costs me. If I'm out of here – well, I know how to survive in a desert and I know how to survive in hills. And I will find a way to get my revenge!" She spoke the last words with all the hatred she felt in her and turned back to the hole she had scratched into the wall.

Arthur observed her for a moment. Then he got up and sat down beside Hayley. He started to scratch at the wall as well, and again Hayley looked astonished up.

Arthur smiled. "I can't let you go alone, can I?" He asked carefully.

Hayley stopped. "If you really want to come with me – I have to warn you. One betrayal from you and I'll kill you instantly. If you follow me and do what I say, you will survive. It won't be an easy life, as I want to have my revenge but it will be better than this life. Do you really want to come with me?"

Arthur nodded. "I'll come with you. And I'll help you to get what you want." He promised.

"We have a deal?"

"We have."

Arthur and Hayley shook hands then they turned back to the wall.

6

Seven days Hayley and Arthur scratched at the wall; one after the other in order not to let anybody know what they were doing there. Early evening of the seventh day the hole was big enough to let them out.

Hayley stretched her head out and noted that she still was a floor above the ground. But she looked to the back of the palace and the hills behind it. She pulled her head back and smiled. "It's good. Better than I thought." She looked around in the cell. "Get the carafe with water and the bread. Then let's see that we get away from here. It's dark enough outside."

Arthur did what she had said and came back to Hayley a minute later.

As Hayley threw a look outside again, the other men in the cell noticed that something was going on and stepped nearer.

"What are you doing there?" one of the men asked curiously.

"Doesn't matter for you," Arthur answered.

Suddenly Hayley grabbed after his arm and stopped him. She turned to the men and explained calmly: "We're breaking out. If you want to take the chance, you can go as well – after us. Good luck." She looked again through the hole.

"Why did you do that?" Arthur whispered to her. He bent forward and grabbed after Hayley's arms, as she started with her legs first to climb out of the hole.

"If they leave as well, they will stay around and give us the chance to escape without anybody noticing it in time." She whispered shortly back. Then she slipped through the hole till she only hung on Arthur's hands. She looked at the ground, hardened her muscles and jumped down. She rolled over her shoulder, as she touched the ground and was on her feet and leaning against the wall at once again.

Arthur threw the bread down to her then he let carefully the carafe down on his belt. Finally he crawled through the hole and jumped as well to the ground.

"Take care of the water!" Hayley pressed him the carafe into his hands, as Arthur stood on his feet again then she looked around, "This way!" She said and started to run the way down between wall and hill.

Arthur followed her, looking after cover and a hand pressed on top of the carafe to save the water in it.

Hayley chose the next path into the hills and Arthur followed her without contradictions. They climbed up the hill, slipped down on the other side and climbed the next one.

It wasn't easy, as Hayley hadn't any shoes on and as well the bread in her arms, and Arthur still carried the carafe with water.

At last Hayley saw a cave in one of the rocky hills and pushed Arthur over to it. "We can rest in there for a moment." She said, reaching the entrance and sitting down on the ground.

Arthur followed her example relieved and put the carafe beside him on the ground. "I don't think they will follow us. I saw other guys leaving the cell as well." He said quietly.

Hayley looked up. She just wanted to confirm it, as she noticed a shadow on the hill they had come down some minutes ago. She made a sign to Arthur to be quiet and watched the shadow carefully.

Arthur bent forward and threw a look outside as well. "He's alone. Easy game," he murmured.

"Stay here!" Hayley ordered shortly and pressed the bread into his arms. Then she slipped out of the cave and slid quietly over the grass to the shadow. She picked up a branch and jumped up behind the shadow, picking the branch into the shadows back. "Freeze!" she ordered. "What are you doing here?" She asked firmly.

The shadow stopped. "I was looking for you." The shadow answered. It was definitive a male voice.

"Why?" Hayley asked further on.

The man in front of her lifted his arms. "I have no weapons. I only saw how you defended yourself in the cell and I was impressed. I want to come with you – I think it's the only chance to survive." He answered.

"Why were you in the cell?"

The man didn't answer.

Hayley pressed the branch into the man's back very hard.

"Okay, okay." The man gave in, probably thinking that it was a gun in his back, which was the thought Hayley wanted to make him believe. "I'm a thief. They caught me, as I tried to break into a rich man's house. That's the reason why I was in the cell. And if they catch me again, I'll probably lose more than my hands, which they had promised me for now. I don't want that. – Please, let me go with you. I will do everything you want me to." He promised.

Hayley hesitated. Then she pushed the man again. "To the right, move!" she ordered shortly.

The man started to walk to the right, and with short orders Hayley led him over to the cave where Arthur was waiting for her.

Arthur moved to the side, as the man stepped into the cave.

Hayley threw the branch away and sat down on the ground. "What's your name?" She asked the man who turned now around to her.

"I'm Rick Moleskin." The man sat down beside Arthur and leaned back. He looked intensive at Hayley and examined her.

Hayley on her side stared at Rick with a frown. Finally she turned to Arthur who watched both of them and said quietly: "Divide the bread through three and hand over the carafe."

Arthur reached her the carafe, and Hayley took a long sip out of it. Then he divided the bread, gave the biggest one to Hayley, one part to Rick and kept the last one.

Hayley gave the carafe back to Arthur before she pulled a bit up from the bread and munched it in silence.

Rick ate his piece of bread in a hurry; he seemed to be very hungry. Then he took the carafe from Arthur and drank a bit.

"If you want to come with us – you have to accept two rules." Hayley started and watched the sun coming over the hill. But out of the corner of her eyes she saw over at Rick. "First of all, don't betray us. I'll take every betrayal very serious and revenge it with death. And it doesn't matter if you betray Arthur or me. Is that clear?" She turned and faced Rick directly again.

Rick looked from one to another. "I promise not to betray one of you." He said firmly.

Hayley nodded. "Secondly, we are on the way not only to survive but to get revenge as well. Are you ready to play the game?"

Rick sighed. "I never had a chance before. I'll do what you want me to if I get the chance to survive – undamaged."

"I can't give you the guarantee that you will stay alive and… undamaged. It is a risk to come with me but I will promise you that I will care for you as best as I can." Hayley was silent for a moment. Then she continued: "And as you both know how I treat anybody who dares to touch me – I wouldn't try it if I were you."

Both Arthur and Rick nodded.

"Does one of you know the area here?"

Arthur shook his head. "I was only in the desert around the town but never in the hills."

Hayley looked over at Rick.

Rick hesitated for a second but then he answered truthfully: "I came as well through the desert into this area. But perhaps this may help." He pulled some sheets out of his pocket and handed them over to Hayley.

Astonished Hayley took the sheets and spread them out. It was a map of the area. "Where did you get them from?" She asked amazed.

Rick smiled. "I told you, I'm a thief. I didn't know what it was but I thought it might be useful. It looks like I was right."

"Do you have more such surprises for us?" Arthur grinned.

"Let's see." Rick emptied his pockets. Two knifes came out of it, a thin bunch of rope, a packet of herbs against headache, a pen, some small papers and a cross.

Hayley shook her head about this arsenal. "Perhaps you would be useful." She murmured and picked up one of the knives. "No weapons, yes?" She asked mockingly, as she tried out the knife.

Rick shrugged his shoulders. "I didn't think about the knives at that moment." He confessed.

Hayley put the knife into her pocket. Then she turned back to the map.

"I have something more in my pockets. It may not what you hope for but it will help you." Rick said quietly.

Hayley looked up again. "What do you mean?"

Rick pointed at Hayley's bare bloody feet. He took some bandages out of his shirt and slipped over to Hayley. "Let me take care of your feet. You won't come forward anymore if I don't." He added, as he saw that Hayley wanted to protest.

Hayley bit on her lips. Her feet were hurting her a lot but she didn't want anybody to see it. Now she knew that Rick knew as well and she didn't contradict, as he took her feet into his hands, cleaned them as best as possible and put the bandages around them.

After that Hayley felt a little bit better and she pressed out: "Thanks."

"That's okay." Rick slipped back on his place beside Arthur.

Once more Hayley looked down on the map. Her fingers found the town they had escaped from then the way up to the cave they were now in. At last she looked over the whole map to find out if there was a place nearby where they could go to. She stopped over a curious sign at one side of the map. Some letters were written there as well but Hayley couldn't make them out. "Who of you can read that?" She asked quietly.

"What?" Arthur bent forward and looked down at the map.

Hayley pointed the words out for him.

Rick as well bent forward. Slowly he spelled out: "Temple of Freedom."

Hayley examined him suspiciously.

Again Rick shrugged his shoulders. "I learnt old Arabic from my parents. That's long ago."

"A temple is it, yes?" Hayley asked only.

Rick nodded.

"Perhaps we are lucky and we can get there what we need." She threw another look at the map. "We should be able to reach the temple in two days."

Arthur nodded. "But we have to save the water then." He said calmly.

Hayley folded the card together. "We should see that we get some sleep. We can't go on in the day, it's too dangerous."

"We should keep watch as well." Rick suggested.

Hayley stretched herself out. "Fine, you have the first watch." And she closed her eyes.

Arthur grinned at Rick before he stretched himself out beside Hayley. "Wake me in two hours." He murmured and was the next second asleep.

Rick examined the two sleeping people and sighed. He got up, went carefully around the two and sat down beside the entrance to be able to watch the hills.

It was already afternoon, as Arthur woke up Hayley. "It's your turn, Hayley." He murmured and sank down to the ground.

Hayley wiped over her still half open eyes till she could open them totally. She looked at the two sleeping men and then to the outside. For a second the sun burnt in her eyes and she closed them again. Then she sat down at the entrance and stared outside.

For almost two hours she watched over the two sleeping men.

Suddenly the sun disappeared behind the hills and Hayley noticed that it must have been later than she thought. She gave the men some more minutes but at last she got up and woke her companions. "Arthur! Rick! Get up! We have to get on!"

Arthur sighed with closed eyes. He got up, opened his eyes and brushed shortly his clothes down. "I'm ready." He said shortly, picking up the water carafe.

Rick rolled around and got finally up as well. "Me too." he murmured, rubbing the sleep out of his eyes.

Hayley in the meantime had thrown a look on the map again to find out the way to go. Now she nodded at the men to follow her and led the way out of the cave and around the next hill.

They were never to know that they left just in time.

Prince Alban's army had found traces of bloody footsteps on one hill and had followed them till they reached the cave where Hayley, Arthur and Rick had rested. They noticed that the three people couldn't have left a long time ago but now there were no bloody traces anymore.

The small army left searching just to the opposite way Hayley had led Arthur and Rick into...

Two days long they went through the hills, searching for the Temple they had found on the map.

Arthur kept an eye on the water that nobody drank too much and that they had enough for the days of walking, which wasn't quite easy, as they were all thirsty though climbing through the hills.

Hayley had saved mostly of her piece of bread and she gave from time to time a bite to the men to keep them going. She herself hadn't much of the bread; it was most important to her to have something for the men. She was used to have less than everybody else.

At last they reached the top of a hill and the men threw themselves down into the grass.

"I don't go one more step!" Arthur groaned.

Rick nodded at him. "It's really enough."

Hayley observed the men worried; the last thing she would need now was to lose her companions cause of exhaustion. But she had to confess to herself that her feet were killing her, she felt sick and still she was hungry too. She didn't understand what was happening to her and she pushed everything on the long days on the run.

Hayley sat down beside the men who were lying by now in the grass and stared down the hill. There was something at the bottom of the hill but she was too exhausted for a moment to really see what it was. Then she looked harder down the hill and she discovered the buildings, built into the side of the hill.

Hayley sat up straight and stared down.

"What do you have?" Arthur murmured, looking over at Hayley.

Hayley didn't look away from the buildings at the bottom of the hill. "Come over here and tell me if you see the same like I do." She said quietly.

Arthur groaned but finally he got up, went over to Hayley and sat down beside her. "What?" He asked. In the same moment he got a push from Hayley into the side.

Hayley only pointed down the hill.

Arthur followed her finger, looked down the hill – and drew the air deeply in. "Fucking hell!" He called out in surprise. "Rick! Come over here!"

Rick looked up. "What is it?" He asked astonished.

Hayley turned around to Rick. "I think we found what we were looking for." She only said but it was enough to get Rick up and running over to them.

Rick stopped beside them and stared down the hill. "Dear Lord!" He sighed, "At last!"

Hayley smiled. "Can I get you to go some more steps?" She asked.

"Certainly!" it came back two-voiced.

7

Hayley, Arthur and Rick started to climb down the hill towards the buildings. They needed two hours to climb over the rocks and slipping down the grass and the earth. But finally they reached the wall around the buildings.

"You led us very well!" Arthur laid his hand on Hayley's shoulder.

For once, without noticing it, Hayley accepted Arthur's hand on her shoulder. She sighed only and said calmly: "Let's find a way in!"

They all went together around the wall and half way around they found a gate.

Hayley knocked on the gate.

Nothing happened.

The three looked at each other.

Hayley lifted her arm to knock again – but in this moment the gate opened a crack.

A monk looked through the gate and examined the three people in front of the gate. "Can I help you?" He asked astonished.

Hayley nodded. "We would need some water and food and a place where we can recover. Can you help us?"

The monk looked at her from top to bottom. But only as he saw Hayley's feet he grew softer and opened the gate a bit more. "Come inside!" He pleaded them. "We will see what we can do for you."

Watchfully and still a bit suspicious Hayley stepped inside and Arthur and Rick followed her at once.

The monk closed the gate behind them and asked them to follow him. He went over to one of the buildings and let them enter. Then he asked them to take a seat and he would see after the rest.

Hayley sat down carefully into a chair and looked around.

Arthur and Rick sat down on two other chairs.

Arthur sighed. "Perhaps we are right here now." He said hopefully.

Rick only nodded.

The monk came back and placed some bowls he had carried on the table in the middle of the room. "We don't have much but you are welcome to share with us." He bowed and pointed at the bowls.

"Thanks." Hayley offered him a tired smile. Then she nodded at Arthur and Rick and the two men got up and went over to the table. They checked the food and were soon eating hungrily.

Hayley in the meantime crunched together on her chair. She felt bad and it didn't go away.

An elderly woman came into the room and smiled at the two men. Then her look went over to Hayley and she frowned. Fast she stepped over to her and grabbed after her hand, "My dear child! Are you feeling sick? Let me help you!" She said in a warm motherly voice.

Hayley looked up at her. She didn't say anything but she didn't contradict, as the woman helped her to get up and led her out of the room. They went over to a nearby room where a big bed was inside.

"Please lie down and let me have a look at your feet!" The woman asked Hayley.

Hayley nodded. She lay down on the bed and stretched herself out. But as much as she tried to stay awake, she couldn't manage it. Almost at once, after her head had touched the pillow, she was asleep.

Hayley woke up; as the sun flooded into the room and onto the bed she was lying on. She blinked some time before she remembered where she was. For a second she stretched herself out again then she got carefully up and went over to the window. Interested she looked outside.

In front of her window a big patch of grass stretched out. After that some acres lay in the sun and a lot of people were working on them. Around them Hayley could see other buildings and far away the wall around all.

Hayley went back to the bed and looked down at herself. Only now she noticed that she was completely naked, her wounds cared for and her wrists and her feet bandaged. She looked around for her clothes but she couldn't see them. But in a corner was a cupboard and she went over to it and opened it.

Inside the cupboard hang some clothes in black, trousers, shirts, waistcoats and even boots.

Hayley didn't hesitate for long. She found the size which fitted her and she slipped into the clothes and the right boots. After she finished dressing she turned to the door and left the house, curious to find out where she actually was.

"I knew you would choose black." A voice said behind her, as she stepped out of the door.

Hayley turned around, a frown on her forehead. "What do you mean?"

Arthur got up. "Don't tell me, you don't know." He said astonished. "It was the first thing Rick and I got told here."

"I really have no idea what you are talking about." Hayley shook her head.

Arthur stroked over his dirty old clothes. But before he could explain something, another voice joined into the conversation: "Well, I see, you are all right again."

Hayley turned and looked at the monk who had stepped nearer to them. She nodded. "Yes, thank you, my feet are still hurting but it is okay."

The monk nodded. "May I ask you why you chose the black clothes?"

Hayley frowned again. "I don't know what it matters but there was nothing else in the room."

Again the monk nodded. "I thought so. Your feelings are so strong that they don't leave you a choice." The monk turned around to Arthur. "And what is the way you will go, my dear boy? And where is your friend?"

"I'm here." Rick came from the other side to the group in front of the house. As well as Arthur he still wore his own dirty clothes. He smiled at Hayley. "You look better."

"Thanks." Hayley stared at him. "I would like to say the same about you but that's not possible."

Rick grinned. "I know. We," he looked over at Arthur, "we decided to make our decision after you did yours. And I see you made it."

Hayley turned around to the monk and looked asking at him.

But the monk only smiled and took her hand. "Come with me, Fighter. You can't do the decision for your companions; they have to make their own decisions. You influenced them already enough." He led her away from Arthur and Rick over to another building.

Hayley threw a last look over her shoulder at her companions then she followed without contradictions the monk over to the building he led her to.

Arthur and Rick exchanged a look then they retired back into the house they had been standing at.

The monk led Hayley into the entrance hall of the building. "I have to leave you here. Wait – and they will come to see you." He said with a bow.

Hayley frowned once more. "Who will come?" She asked curiously.

"Wait and see for yourself." The monk smiled then he turned and left the building again, closing and locking carefully the door behind him.

Hayley looked around.

The hall was empty, almost empty. At the side was a wooden bench, some doors led into other rooms but they were closed and at one end a small staircase led up to the upper floors. But otherwise the hall was empty.

Carefully Hayley went along the walls, looking at the doors but not touching them. After a long time of waiting she finally sat down on the ground, leaning against one of the empty walls.

"Kneel down and show your respect for the higher ones." A voice sounded through the hall.

Hayley got up in a trace. "I don't kneel down for somebody I can't see and I don't know; don't speak even of respect." She answered firmly.

For a while it was quiet again.

Then a door opened to the left of Hayley and a man came into the hall. He was dressed in a long white robe with golden embroidery but his head was free and showed short black hair. Urgently he examined the woman in front of him.

Hayley stared not at the least frightened back at him.

"You are an impressive woman – to look at and in your manners. You are not frightened when you should be. At least you don't show it. And you make a point. But tell me why do you want to fight? Why don't you look for a husband and have a good life?" The priest that was what he was, looked intensive at Hayley, asking his questions.

Hayley swallowed but she didn't hesitate. "I am married and I have a son. But that life was taken away from me and I was forced to do things I never would have done on my own free will. I seek revenge for it – maybe able to go home one day as well."

The priest nodded. "If we help you to get your revenge – what are you willing to give us for it?"

"I'll give you my life, if I only would be able to get revenge – and to see one more time my husband and my son." Hayley said without hesitation.

"Follow me!" The priest turned back to the door through which he had come inside. "Don't be afraid now, your companions will follow you soon."

Hayley frowned slightly but she followed the priest without contradiction. She seemed suddenly to know that here she could get what she wanted and she was eager to get it. So she followed the priest, hoping that soon she would be on her way again.

The priest led Hayley through a long corridor, then a staircase down till they stood in front of a big wooden door.

"We come now into the temple of our god. Don't enter if you are not willing to swear what you just told me." The priest warned Hayley then he opened the door and entered the temple.

Hayley still stood at the entrance and looked into the temple.

The temple was a big room underneath the earth. Massive pillars at the sides gave it a very gloomy look and the stone figures in black between them didn't make it better. Torches were hanging at the pillars and with the flickering light over the walls the temple was only in half darkness. At the other end of the room was a big stone altar and behind it was something that looked like a tomb.

The priest who had led Hayley to the underground temple room walked straight through the empty room and knelt down in front of the altar.

Four other priests, also dressed in white robes but different embroideries, entered the temple through a side entrance and knelt down to the left and the right of the first priest.

Hayley stepped into the temple and closed the doors behind her. Then she went over to the altar.

"Why do you come into the secret temple of Harder, God of Freedom?" One of the priests looked up and at Hayley.

Hayley cleared her throat. "I'm looking for help; help to get revenge for something, which was done wrong and to make it right again."

A second priest got up and went around Hayley to stand behind her. "Revenge is not always the best way to make something good, do you know that?" He asked quietly.

Hayley turned a bit of her head. But otherwise she didn't move. "I know that revenge may not be always the right way. But I think that in my case revenge is the only way to get a bit of my freedom back."

"Freedom?" a third priest got up and stepped to her right.

"Freedom of heart and soul," Hayley answered shortly.

The priest who had spoken at first and the fourth priest got up as well so that now only the priest who had brought Hayley into the temple knelt in front of the altar. The fourth priest stepped to the left side of Hayley and took her arm. He opened the button of the arm sleeve and pulled the sleeve up.

Hayley let it happen without saying or doing something.

The other priest stepped to the head end of the altar. "If you trust Harder, God of Freedom, you will get what you seek for. But he needs something as repayment for his help. What are you willing to pay for getting your revenge?" He asked firmly.

Hayley looked over at him. "I will give you my life after I got my revenge and I have seen my husband and my son for a last time." She answered as firmly as the priest had asked his question.

"If you trust Harder, God of Freedom – lie down on the altar that we can prepare you for your task." The priest spoke again.

Hayley hesitated for a second then she stepped over to the altar, sat down on it and slipped around till she could lie down properly on the stone altar.

The four priests stepped to the four sides of the altar. The priest to Hayley's left side picked up her arm again and stretched it out.

Now only Hayley noticed another metal stick beside the altar with a handcuff on top of it.

The priest let her arm over to the stick and closed the handcuff around Hayley's wrist.

Hayley couldn't move her arm anymore.

Now the other priests laid their hands down on Hayley's head, her right arm and her both legs. They started to sing a melody, which was unknown to Hayley but sounded warm and welcoming.

Hayley closed her eyes.

The priest who had brought Hayley down to the temple got up and came around to Hayley's arm, which was still stretched out. He laid his hands on her arm and murmured something in old Arabic. Then he checked carefully her arm before he turned to Hayley. Ignoring the song he said quietly to Hayley: "It will hurt you a lot now but I'm sure you'll be okay with that. It belongs to the tradition." He added, as he saw that Hayley wanted to say something.

"All right," Hayley whispered only her agreement.

The priest got himself a chair, sat down and picked up an instrument, which wasn't more than a stick with a hot needle.

Hayley frowned. It was astonishing that the priest here should have an instrument like that, as that belonged more into the western world. Also the priests didn't look like, as if they would go on journeys.

The priest smiled softly, as he started the machine.

Hayley shook together, as she felt pain running through her body. She wanted to move but the six hands kept her in place.

Hayley knew suddenly that the instrument was a tattoo machine of a special kind. Normally you wouldn't get such pains, as she got them now. Again she closed her eyes, concentrating on the melody the priests were still singing.

8

Hayley didn't know how much time had gone by, as she finally woke up again. She was laying on a simple bed, no pillow, and no blanket. Covered she was with a black cloak, which she threw to the side now.

Slowly she got up and stepped over to the window. Her arm hurt her and she held it firmly. She didn't notice at all that she was bandaged.

Outside it was quiet and nobody was around.

Hayley frowned. She looked down at herself to check if she was dressed completely then she went over to the door and opened it. She stepped into the corridor, which was empty and slipped through the last door outside.

It was a light sunny day. The sunrays were warm and put everything on earth into different but nice colours.

Hayley enjoyed the feeling of the sun on her skin, and she breathed deeply in. After a moment she looked around, searching for somebody who could explain to her where she was. But nobody was around.

As Hayley stepped from one building to the next, she noticed that she seemed to be in a small round of houses, inside the walls of the Temple of Freedom where they had knocked at the gate.

"That's right." A dark voice confirmed her thoughts.

Hayley turned around. She was astonished, as she was sure that she hadn't spoken aloud.

"And right again." The man who looked at her grinned and bowed. "Please, forgive me, Fighter, for reading your thoughts. But they were lying so openly around..." He shrugged his shoulders.

Hayley had no other choice than to smile. Somehow the man seemed to be funny to her. But still she frowned and examined him. "And who are you?" She asked curiously.

Again the man bowed. "I'm sorry, Fighter, for not having introduced myself. But it is long, long ago since we had the last visitor here. I'm Salazar Magentas; I'm responsible for your health, body and mind." He tipped at his forehead.

Hayley smiled. "I think we will understand each other quite good. I'm Hayley Houseman. – But where am I here?"

Salazar Magentas smiled. "This only your teachers can answer you. I don't know why you are here or what you shall do here; I only know", he looked examining at Hayley. "That you really need something to eat. Come with me; I'll show you."

Hayley followed the man into a house and after some minutes she sat in a friendly and comfortable room at a table and was eating a very good dinner.

Salazar looked satisfied at her and so did the priest who had come inside.

"May I sit down with you?" The priest asked calmly.

Hayley nodded. With a hand movement she offered him a chair at her side.

The priest smiled and sat down beside her. "If you are ready, we have a lot to talk through." He started.

Again Hayley made an inviting hand movement.

"You noticed that everybody calls you 'Fighter'?" The priest asked.

Hayley nodded.

"You are the first one here who gave everything to get her revenge. Only a fighter can do so, so we will turn you into one. And as we are here at the Temple of Freedom, you will be the first Fighter of Freedom we will have."

"So?" Hayley frowned, "But why? I mean, why are you helping me?"

The priest smiled. "We have our reasons why we help you. I can't explain it now – one day you will understand." He was silent for a moment then he continued: "Which training do you have already?"

Hayley shrugged her shoulders. "I can Judo, Karate but only self-defence and shooting. That's all."

But the priest nodded satisfied. "There we can build on." He got up. "Let me show you around then you can show your companions everything tomorrow."

"They decided to follow me?" Hayley asked, really astonished.

The priest nodded. "They told me that you three have a... a deal together. They don't want to let you down, not even now when there is more to ask than a handshake cause of a deal."

Hayley looked down to the ground in order to hide her smile. She swallowed and asked curiously: "When are they coming?"

"At the moment they are down in the Temple like you were. We will bring them up in the evening. – Shall we put them into another house or do you want to have them near you?"

Hayley frowned. She calculated shortly through and said then hesitatingly: "I would like to have them in my house – if I still find it myself." She added, frowning.

The priest pointed to a house to the right, which was held in a light yellow colour.

Hayley nodded. "Will they be all right tomorrow morning?"

"Like you." The priest confirmed it.

Together the priest and Hayley wandered over the small yard. The priest pointed all the interesting places out to Hayley like the gym, the swimming pool, the arena and many more. At the arsenal he stopped. For a moment he looked examining at Hayley again then he cleared his throat. "Let's look for the right weapons for you." He said and knocked at the door to the arsenal.

A man in his early thirties, similar dressed like Hayley opened up the door. He greeted the priest with a light bow but then he looked astonished at Hayley, examining her from top to bottom.

The priest introduced her shortly: "That's Hayley Houseman, first Fighter of Freedom. Hayley, that's Harold Bluestone, specialist for weapons. Can we come inside?"

"Certainly," Harold Bluestone opened the door, and Hayley and the priest entered a dark room, which was only lit by some candles. And still it was possible to see the swords hanging at the walls and lying on the table in the middle.

Hayley looked astonished around.

The priest turned to the Weapon Specialist. "She needs her weapons."

"I thought so." Harold Bluestone nodded. He opened the door again and said calmly: "If you would wait then outside, please. You know – the choosing of the weapons is a delicate procedure."

The priest nodded and left the house.

Hayley had followed the short conversation with astonishment, now she turned to the Weapon Specialist.

Harold Bluestone locked the door and looked smiling at Hayley, "Like to drink something? We need a personal atmosphere here that you will be able to choose the right weapons for you."

"Thanks." Hayley nodded at him and took place on a chair the Weapon Specialist had pointed out to her.

Harold Bluestone came back with two glasses. He sat down on a chair opposite Hayley and reached her one glass. Thoughtfully he looked at her during he held his glass up. "Hayley it was, right?"

"Harold, is it right? Or do you like Harry more?" Hayley shot back.

"Harry, yes, why not?" The Weapon Specialist grinned. "I haven't anything heard from you. Do you like to tell me something?"

Hayley shook her head. "I prefer not to tell anything." She said quietly.

Harry nodded. "Okay." He looked to the ground then up at Hayley again. "Then it's only revenge you seek?"

Hayley put her glass on the table. "I know that they told you. So you know exactly what I want. Why do you ask all these questions?"

Harry sighed. "Listen. All I try is to find a good atmosphere that you won't get problems during you choose your weapons. I would be able to help you a bit – if you would open up for a moment and would tell me something. Or, at least, try to answer my questions truthfully."

Hayley frowned. "Listen, Harry. I will be truthfully to you: I don't want to talk about what happened to me. The only thing, which is now important to me, is to get my revenge. It may sound hard but you can believe me – the people deserve to get killed." Hayley grew silent, as Harry got up and went through the room. Straight he grabbed after one sword and came back with it to Hayley. "Try this one!" He said only.

Hayley got up and took the sword out of Harry's hands. She pulled it out of the cover and looked at the blade. Carefully she weighed the sword in her right hand – but suddenly she had the feeling that it wasn't right. She tried it with her left hand but it was definitely not right. She pushed it back into the cover and shook her head. "Not good." She said calmly.

Harry smiled. "It was only the first try." He said and brought the sword back to its place. "Is your wish for revenge the only wish you have?" He asked, standing beside another sword.

Hayley shook her head. "No, it's not." She sighed inwardly. "I have two wishes. Revenge is only the first and the strongest one." She added.

Harry picked up another sword and brought it over to Hayley. "Try this one!"

Hayley took the sword and went through the same procedures like before. But only this time the sword lay in her hand like a piece of longer arm. She smiled. "That really feels good." She said impressed.

Harry grinned. "Fine." he answered only, looking at Hayley thoughtfully. "Two wishes, two swords. What is your second wish?"

Hayley pressed the lips together and looked down to the ground, still holding the sword in her hands.

"Is he friend, lover or husband?" Harry smiled softly.

Hayley sighed. "Husband." she confessed.

Harry went through the room, holding his hand above the swords till he suddenly stopped. He stepped back and picked up a sword with a big stone in the middle. With the sword in his hands he came back to Hayley. "I don't know." He said quietly, looking from Hayley to the sword and other way round. "But this sword might be quite right for you. Try it!"

Hayley looked down at the sword. It seemed quite big to her but she got up and stretched out her hands.

Harry laid the sword down into her hand.

Hayley weighed the sword in her hands – as suddenly the stone in the middle started to glow in a deep green colour. Hayley observed the glow with admiration, and then she laid her hands on the handle, hiding the glow. She pulled the sword out of its cover and lifted the sword.

"I knew it! You are the one!" Harry stepped back in admiration.

Hayley put the sword back into its cover and turned to Harry. "What do you mean?" She asked, laying the belt of the sword around her hip and closed it.

Harry smiled. "This sword is a special one. Under no circumstances you should ever give this sword out of your hands. It will protect you and everybody you care for. More I can't say; you will find out. – And I think you know already; otherwise you wouldn't have put the sword already around your hips." Again he smiled.

Hayley looked down at herself. As she looked up again, she as well smiled. "You are right." She confessed. She picked up the other sword and laid it as well around her hips so that the swords crossed on her back. "Still, there is one more thing. May I look around?"

Harry nodded. "Look around as much as you like, Fighter." He bowed and retired to the door.

Hayley went through the room, looking at the swords. "Harry, can you do me a favour?"

"Certainly," Harry came nearer again.

Hayley turned to him. "Please, my name is Hayley. Nothing else, all right? And don't bow to me. Do you promise?"

Harry looked down to the ground. He shook his head. "I can't. You are a Fighter – no, you are *the* Fighter, we were looking for. You have the right to get treated like the one you are. I'm sorry!"

"Come over here!" Hayley was standing in a dark corner, looking at a two-hands-sword.

Harry stepped over to her side. "That's a fine sword as well. You have a good eye!"

"Let's try it!" Hayley said and grabbed after the sword. She pulled it with both hands out of its cover and turned it against Harry. She laid it down at his chest. "What do you think now?" She asked curiously.

Harry swallowed. "You won't kill me. You still need me to show you how to handle the swords."

"Are you really sure?"

Harry nodded.

"Maybe you are right." Hayley looked intensive at Harry. "But if you don't start to treat me a little bit as a human being, you will regret it soon. Is that clear?" She put a bit of pressure on the blade of the sword at Harry's throat.

Harry swallowed. "Please..." He stuttered.

"Please, what?" Hayley asked hard.

"Please... Hayley," Harry stuttered his sentence to the end.

Hayley let the sword sink down. "Was that so hard?" She asked calmly. She turned the sword to look at it more closely. Then she pushed it back into its cover and held it up. "Third wish – third sword!" She said smiling.

Harry smiled. He said nothing; he only threw a look at his watch. "It's time for dinner." He said and made a hand movement over to the door.

"Do you like to join me? – I have some more questions." Hayley added, as she stepped over to the door.

"It would be an honour." Harry smiled. He opened the door and let Hayley step outside. Then he closed and locked the door behind him and followed Hayley over to the house where the dining room was.

Salazar smiled, as he noted that Hayley was punctual for her meal. He served Hayley and Harry then he waited till the next ones showed up.

Hayley understood that he would get his meal first when everybody else had had theirs.

Hayley talked quietly to Harry but she didn't let the other tables out of her eyes. Whispering she asked Harry out about the other people who came inside the dining room and whom she didn't know.

Harry looked carefully around and said in the same quiet voice: "You know the priest who brought you to me. That's Priest Hassan. He looks after the houses and their equipments. Also he greets everybody who is new. – The guy beside him in the grey robe is Doctor Balthazar. You will see him this afternoon – he has to check that you are all right to do the job. – The guys in black are the trainers; you will get them to know, one after the other. Salazar you know already. Then there is only the High Priest who joins us only from time to time. – You won't see any other priests here; don't ask me where they are. – That's all I can tell you."

Hayley nodded. "And from the looks they send over to us, I would say they are jealous." She grinned.

"Maybe," Harry grinned as well. "I will get to hear something later on. But – when I think now about it – it's for sure not bad – for both of us!"

Hayley and Harry finished their meal and Harry said good-bye. He left the dining room and went back to his house.

Hayley leaned back and closed her eyes.

On the table at the other side the man in the grey robe got up and came over to Hayley. "May I?" He asked friendly.

Hayley opened her eyes again. "Certainly." she offered him the chair opposite.

Doctor Balthazar sat down and examined Hayley curiously. "I would like to see you soon in my practice. You don't look so good to me."

"I'll come for sure. But I think I'm only tired because of what happened in the last days." Hayley smiled at the Doctor.

"This decision you can leave to me. – Come to the small white house at the end, in one hour, all right?" Doctor Balthazar pointed to the left end of the room.

"All right, Doc." Hayley nodded.

Doctor Balthazar winked at her, got up and left the room.

Thoughtfully Hayley stared behind him.

9

An hour later Hayley knocked at the door of the small white house where Doctor Balthazar lived and had his practice.

"Come in!" A voice called from inside.

Hayley opened the door, stepped inside and closed the door. Curiously she looked around.

The room she stood in was like a waiting room in a hospital. It was plain white and some chairs stood around. A door opposite the entrance door was half open.

"Come in, Fighter!" Doctor Balthazar called and put his head around the door. He waved to Hayley, and Hayley stepped into the next room.

This room was clearly a Doctor's practice. A desk, some chairs, a liege, cupboards, instruments, medicaments and so on.

"Take a seat." Doctor Balthazar offered Hayley a chair in front of the desk then he sat down behind the desk.

Hayley sat down, only half prepared for the following examination.

Doctor Balthazar asked a lot of questions about the illnesses Hayley once had had; any operations and similar things. He stopped short, as he heard that Hayley had given birth to a son only just over three months ago. Finally he finished off his questions and started with the real examination.

Hayley had to undress completely and Doctor Balthazar checked her carefully through. He stopped short again on some points but he didn't say anything.

Doctor Balthazar was very careful. He checked and he double-checked.

Hayley was astonished about the attention the doctor paid to her.

Finally Doctor Balthazar asked her to dress again and sat down behind his desk again. He wrote a lot down and put everything together into a big file. But he left it open, turning to Hayley and staring at her.

Hayley finished dressing and sat down in front of the desk. Calmly she looked at the doctor: "What is it?"

"What do you mean?" Doctor Balthazar watched her carefully.

Hayley sighed. "How sick am I? I mean, for nothing you don't write so much."

Doctor Balthazar laughed. "No, no. You're strong and healthier than most of the others, I checked. Okay, your feet are not in the best state at the moment – I'll give you a crème for that. Otherwise you are completely all right and… your baby as well."

Hayley looked up. "What did you say?"

Doctor Balthazar got up and stepped around the desk. He sat down on the edge of the desk and faced Hayley. Intensively he stared at her during he said, "Listen to me, Hayley. I can't say a lot at the moment, as it is still quite early but it is for one hundred per cent sure that you are pregnant. I know it doesn't fit into your plans but it is important that this baby will be born. Don't ask me why. You are off the job for the moment – the baby is more important."

"No!" Hayley threw her hands in front of her eyes and supported her head with the arms.

Doctor Balthazar laid his hands on Hayley's shoulders, "Hayley, child! Listen to me! It's not so terrible you may think now. All you have to do in the coming months is – to pay attention to yourself – and nothing else. Go, have a rest and think it out. Then you will understand why it is important. – And let me tell you one thing: You won't be able to harm yourself. There will be from now on every time somebody around you who is looking after you. He – or she – will see to it that you will fulfil your purpose." He added.

"Stop it!" Hayley looked up. "Stop it! I do understand." She got up and turned to the door. There she turned around for a moment, stared at Doctor Balthazar but then she left the practice in a hurry.

Hayley went straight back to the house where she had woken up in the morning. She sat down on the bed, which was more a wooden bench and rolled up on it. For a long time she lay there, trying to keep her eyes dry.

"Hayley?" a male voice asked carefully.

"What is it, Harry?" Hayley spoke very quietly.

"I only wanted to know if you are all right. Doc told me that you have a... a problem." Harry added softly.

"Are you one of my guards?" Hayley mocked half-hearted.

"In first place I'm here as your friend. Secondly I'm here because I have a problem. And third, I'm one of your guards, too, yes." Harry confessed.

Hayley turned around to Harry and examined him. "What for a problem do you have?"

"I don't know..."

"You can tell me; you know I won't say something. And perhaps it will bring me on other thoughts." Hayley interrupted him at once.

Harry smiled, "Probably. Your two friends arrived. The problem I have is – do you want them near you or shall I bring them into another house?"

"I thought Priest Hassan is responsible for that." Hayley frowned.

Harry shook his head. "He wouldn't be able to bring them up. I do that every time." He grinned at Hayley. "I also brought you up here." He stopped short then he continued: "Priest Hassan greets the newcomers in the morning and he looks after the houses and their equipment."

Hayley nodded.

"And where do you want me to bring your friends to?"

"Please bring them here into the house. I like to have my friends around me." Hayley answered slowly.

"Okay." Harry nodded. He got up and stepped over to the door. There he hesitated, "Like to come with me?"

Hayley stared for a moment at him then she got up and went up to the door. In silence she followed Harry over to the temple and down to the hidden temple room in which she had given her oath. She didn't remember the way out and she looked curiously around.

In the hidden temple Arthur was lying on the altar, unconscious like Rick who was lying on the stone floor just in front of the altar.

Priest Hassan, now Hayley recognized him – he was the fourth priest in the celebration of her oath, looked over at Hayley and smiled.

In the back of the room another priest waited patiently.

Hayley stepped over to the altar. She stared for a moment down at Arthur then she grabbed after his arm and looked at the sign on it. Finally she pulled the sleeve down again and buttoned it. She looked up at Harry.

Harry nodded over to the priest before he stepped over to Priest Hassan and pulled up one of Rick's arms. Together the two men carried Rick out of the temple.

Hayley and the other priest followed with Arthur.

As they reached Hayley's house, Priest Hassan and Harry waited for Hayley. They looked asking at her, and Hayley made a short decision. She nodded over to a door to the left during she directed the priest who helped her over to the right. She opened a door and together they laid Arthur down on a wooden bed, similar to hers. At last she grabbed after a cloak, which was hanging beside the bed and laid it down over Arthur.

The priest had already left, and Hayley stepped now quietly outside and closed the door behind her.

Out of the room opposite Harry and Priest Hassan came and nodded at her. She nodded back before she turned to her own room and lay down again.

"Come on, Hayley. It's time for dinner!" Doctor Balthazar's voice came through to Hayley's ear.

Hayley turned around. "Already?" she asked astonished.

Doctor Balthazar smiled at her. "I was here once before, and you were sleeping so nicely that I didn't want to wake you up. But now you should really come with me that you still get something to eat. And you will need it." He added, his hand lying on her belly.

Hayley sighed. "Yes, Doc." she hummed and got up. She went over to the side to a cupboard, took a carafe, which was standing there and filled a bowl with water. Then she splashed the cold water into her face till she was really awake again. She turned around.

Doctor Balthazar reached her a towel.

"Thanks." Hayley took the towel and dried herself. "What is with Arthur and Rick?"

"Are they your two friends? They will sleep through till tomorrow like you did. – I had a look at them; they are fine." He added smiling.

Hayley didn't say anything; she picked up the cloak and laid it around her shoulders. As she turned to leave her room and the house, with Doctor Balthazar at her heels, she asked suddenly interested: "Are here other women as well?"

Doctor Balthazar shook his head, "No, normally not. This is not an area for… for normal women – if you know what I mean." He seemed to be embarrassed.

Hayley smiled. "Yes, I know what you mean. But there are exceptions for every rule?"

Doctor Balthazar nodded. "We will make an exception for you – we already made an exception for you – in taking you in." He was silence for a second then he continued: "We will give you the possibility to look outside our walls for somebody you like and trust in order to help you in the next months. Let's say – tomorrow? Then Priest Hassan has time enough to inform your friends what's going on."

They reached the house where the meals were served and together they entered the room.

"Yes why not?" Hayley answered Doc's last question and looked at him. "Are you coming with me?"

"I will. Finally I know the people outside. And Harry will come as well. He has the responsibility for you." Doctor Balthazar confirmed.

Hayley didn't answer anymore. She understood completely that everything had been taken out of her hands for the moment and her only job at the moment was to look after herself. She sighed.

After a moment Hayley sighed again. She noted that all of the teachers, trainers and priests had gathered around one big table and had their meals.

Doc took his place among them and started to eat as well.

For Hayley a table in a corner opposite the big table was prepared.

Hayley didn't hesitate. She picked up her plate and the pot, which was standing there, and went over to the big table. She pushed one of the men in black into the side and completely surprised he slipped to the side. Hayley sat down beside him, as it would be the natural thing in the world.

Stunned Priest Hassan, who seemed to be something like the father of the group and kind of leader, looked over at Hayley. He cleared his throat: "You know for sure what you are doing?" He asked mockingly.

Hayley looked up from her plate. "I know it. And you?"

"I must say, at the moment I'm completely surprised and have no idea why you do that." Priest Hassan confessed.

Hayley smiled. "Then I'll try to explain. First of all, I hate eating alone. Secondly, I noticed when I ask somebody to keep me company that the rest of you are completely jealous. Third, I'm quite aware of the fact that I'm the only woman here at the moment but also I tried to find help here to get my revenge, I'm at the moment in need of much more help. As I'm not allowed to do anything anymore, I'm no risk to any of you but much more in need to get to know you all. There is no reason at all to handle myself as something different – if better or bad doesn't matter. I'm not."

Harry looked over at her. "You forgot something." He said calmly.

"And that would be?" Hayley asked curiously back.

But the answer came from Doctor Balthazar: "We all know your story, through not from you. But we know that you are pregnant from Prince Alban, the most powerful man here in this area. A child from him makes the mother to the most powerful woman in the area. You have the right to get treated better than we would do it with anybody else."

"That was really the last thing I wanted to hear." Hayley murmured. She laid her fork to the side and leaned back. "Why don't you accept then my wish to have dinner with you?" She asked curiously.

Priest Hassan shook his head. "That's not so easy. We..."

But Hayley didn't give him time to finish off what he wanted to say. She got up, said calmly: "I understand." and left the table.

10

Hayley went straight back to her house where she hesitated for a moment. Then she opened the door to her left and threw a look at Rick.

Rick was still sleeping deeply.

Hayley closed the door again and went over to the right door. She opened it and stepped inside. Quietly she went over to the bed in which Arthur was laying and sat down on the edge. She wiped him some strands of hair out of his face and stared thoughtfully at him. She didn't notice at all that tears were running over her face and dropping down on Arthur's hand.

"What's wrong, Hayley?" Arthur murmured, without opening his eyes.

"I'm sorry! I didn't want to disturb you in your sleep. I…" Hayley's voice broke.

Arthur supported himself on his arms that he could get up. He looked at Hayley. "Come on, Hayley! After all you went through, nothing could be so worse here that you have to cry." He laid his arms around Hayley and pressed her softly at his chest.

Hayley allowed the soft touch without contradiction; she snuggled up at him and tried to get herself under control again. After a time she looked up at Arthur: "You have to know that I'm pregnant from Prince Alban." She said quietly.

Astonished Arthur looked at her. But he was fast in thinking it through and said then comforting: "Listen, Hayley. That brings you in a very good position and eventually it will bring you what you want to have. Give the baby a chance; it's not his fault."

"His?" Hayley smiled lightly over Arthur's words.

Arthur nodded. "I don't know why but it will be a boy, believe me." He stopped for a moment before he continued: "There's a legend, saying that the day will come, a woman will destroy the kingdom but her son, who's a secret son of the last prince, will built up a new kingdom and lead it in a wise and good way. – Perhaps it's time now that the legend comes true."

Hayley moved uneasy around, "But why me? And is that the real reason for you to come with me?"

Arthur took Hayley's hands and pressed them softly. "One of the reasons why I came with you was that the legend is quite clear over some points. It says that the woman never comes alone, a simple guard, a thief, a sword master and a priest are her main companions. I have the ambition", he smiled lightly, "to be that guard. And I'm convinced that I'm right since Rick joined us. You know he is a thief."

Hayley looked down at the ground. "And what does the legend says about what happens with the woman?" She asked, suddenly feeling interested.

"Mainly it's said that she found her freedom again. Is that not what you are looking for?" Arthur asked.

"As well, yes," Hayley laid her head back on Arthur's shoulder. "Listen, Arthur. I don't know this legend and I don't think that it will be me who is fulfilling this legend. All I need is a bit of understanding and help in the next days. Will you help me?"

Arthur stroked softly over Hayley's back. He made a great effort not to show Hayley what he just felt in this moment, as he held her in his arms. Sometimes it was really difficult to handle the situation. "I'll help you – you know that." He said, his voice sounding a bit hoarse.

Hayley heard it and she hesitated for a moment. Then she looked up at Arthur. "Please, help me now." She whispered, coming with her head nearer to Arthur's.

Arthur swallowed. "How?" he asked, leaning back in the same speed Hayley came nearer to his face.

Hayley stopped him with laying her arm around his shoulders. "Arthur, what do you think? Would our friendship become deeper if we become an item for a time or would it destroy everything?"

Arthur swallowed once more. "I think," he started nervous, "never something will come between us, which will destroy our friendship. But… are you sure you want that – after all what happened to you?"

Hayley smiled lightly. "I know you won't rape me – you will love me. And that's it what I need now." Again she came nearer to Arthur but this time he didn't give way. As Hayley hesitated, he came the next millimetres and touched with his lips softly Hayley's mouth.

It was a shy kiss, and perhaps cause of that Hayley enjoyed it so much.

They exchanged a look to make sure it was in both sides favour then Arthur laid his arms around Hayley's body and pulled her more up at him. Then he laid his lips again on hers and as he felt that she responded, he carefully opened up her lips and went with his tongue into her mouth.

Hayley grew a bit excited, as she felt his tongue in her mouth and she touched it softly. As she felt his hand at the back of her head, pressing her more against him, she kissed him more wildly. Finally they solved their lips from each other and looked excited at the other one.

Arthur caressed softly Hayley's cheek then he went down over her throat and started to open the cloak she wore. He let it fall to the ground and went over her side to the beginning of the black waistcoat. He started to untie the leather strings and Hayley helped on the other side. Finally she pulled the waistcoat over her head and let it fall on top of her cloak.

Arthur opened his own leather strings of the waistcoat and pulled it over his head. He fired it to the ground and looked again at Hayley. Then he bent forward and pressed again his mouth on her lips. In the same moment he went with his hand under her shirt and closed softly his hand around her bra, feeling her breast through it.

Hayley grew excited and she pressed herself more against Arthur.

Arthur took it as invitation and started to unbutton her shirt. He pulled her shirt down, threw it to the ground and started to open her bra. After he had finally managed it, he let it fall to the other things on the ground and solved his lips from hers. He looked down at Hayley's breasts and passed softly with his hand over them. "You are beautiful!" He murmured quietly.

Hayley felt his look and his touch on her body and she moved lightly.

Arthur noticed her movement and pulled her down on the bed. With a fast movement he pulled his shirt off then he lay down beside Hayley and started again to stroke her softly.

Hayley enjoyed his touch and she started to tremble lightly.

Arthur pressed his mouth on Hayley's breasts and kissed them, first softly then more and more intensive. He pressed his lips on her nipples and passed with his tongue over them again and again.

Hayley groaned lightly.

A noise stopped them and let them look up.

"Sorry, I really didn't want to disturb you both. I was only looking for the toilet." Rick grinned mockingly at Arthur and Hayley.

Hayley sighed. She looked at Arthur and Arthur stared back at her.

"Are you up for a game?" Arthur asked quietly. "He wasn't searching for anything – he heard us."

"I know." Hayley murmured. She sighed again then she had decided herself. "Try it!" She supported him.

Arthur grinned. He got up and turned around to Rick. "You have to know that we don't believe you. You heard us, didn't you?" He stepped towards Rick.

Astonished Rick examined him. "Well, at first I was really searching for the toilet. But as I came nearer to this room – well, yes, I could hear you. And I grew curious."

Hayley supported herself on her arms and looked over at Rick. The fire red curls of her hair fell wildly around her shoulders, and her naked breasts were good visible; she stretched out one hand and said calmly: "As you are here now, come over. I think it's time that we all get to know each other."

Completely stunned Rick looked over at Hayley then he stared at Arthur.

Arthur stepped beside him and pushed him into the back that Rick hesitatingly stepped forward. "Don't you think we will be able to satisfy her? Especially you – with your fast fingers," Arthur made a hand movement and Rick blushed.

Hayley laughed quietly. "Come on now. I don't bite."

Rick threw another look at Arthur and at last at Hayley. His eyes landed on her breasts and he couldn't keep his eyes off her anymore. As Arthur pushed him again, he stepped willingly over to the bed.

Arthur started to open the leather strings at Rick's waistcoat and Rick pulled it finally up and over his head. It landed on top of Hayley's clothes.

Hayley slipped into the middle of the bed and Arthur swung himself over to her left side.

Rick sat down on the bed and pulled his shirt off.

Hayley stretched out her hand again and laid it down on Rick's shoulder. And Rick couldn't stop himself anymore; he lay down and pressed his mouth on Hayley's.

His kiss was much more intensive than Arthur's but Hayley noticed that she still enjoyed him touching her lips and discovering her mouth with his tongue. She caressed with one hand Rick's naked body during her other hand lay on Arthur's shoulder.

Arthur began softly again to caress Hayley's breasts, first massaging them softly then pressing his mouth on her nipples and passing with the tongue over them, again and again.

Hayley moved and solved her mouth from Rick's. She groaned lightly.

Rick bit her softly into her earlobe before passing with his mouth and tongue all over Hayley's face. Then he went with his tongue over her chin and down her throat, which made Hayley groan again. She grew from second to second more and more excited.

Arthur gave one breast free and massaged the other one.

Rick softly touched Hayley's breast, pressed the nipple and massaged it intensive.

Arthur bent forward and kissed Hayley again.

For a while both men played with Hayley; one kissed her on the mouth and massaged one breast, the other one kissing and licking her nipple. Then they changed.

Hayley was out of breath after a while and she groaned again, as Rick gave her mouth free again.

Rick smiled and instead of kissing her breast again, he went down over her belly and the navel till he reached the trousers. He started to open the trousers and Arthur went with his arm under Hayley and lifted her up so that Rick wouldn't have any problems to pull her trousers and underwear down. Then he laid her softly down again.

Rick threw her clothes down on the ground and stared at Hayley's legs.

Hayley started to tremble again and Arthur kissed her softly.

Rick stroked over Hayley's legs and spread them out softly. Then he sat down between them and laid his hand lightly on the hairs between her legs.

Hayley turned her head to the side and gasped for excitement.

Arthur kissed her on her breasts and Rick bent forward to kiss her on the spot. First he kissed her softly on top then he drove with his tongue inside her. He drove up and down and discovered finally a spot where he felt Hayley twitching and groaning when he touched it. He licked this spot more and more intensive.

Hayley groaned. Her hands cramped around Arthur's head and Arthur kissed and licked her breasts wildly now, driven on from her touch. Hayley groaned loudly.

Rick stopped. He got a bit up and pulled his trousers down. He threw them away and turned back to Hayley. Then he led his hand under Hayley's bottom and carefully he drove his penis deep into Hayley. Finally he lay down completely on her and during he went up and down, he kissed Hayley all over again.

Hayley groaned once more; she laid her legs around Rick and pressed him, in his rhythm, more and more deep into her. Her hands passed wildly over his back.

Arthur lay beside them and stroked them both again and again.

Finally Hayley couldn't stand it anymore; she groaned up loudly and in her excitement she felt and heard Rick getting to orgasm as well.

They both needed quite a while till they caught their breaths again then Rick rolled to the side and stroked once more over Hayley's breasts. "You are really good and you are really beautiful." He murmured.

Hayley smiled. "You are not bad either and your body – well, training you don't need." She changed her smile to a grin.

Rick leaned back. His hand went over her breast down to her belly. "Do you really think it's good what we are doing here?" He asked carefully.

Hayley swallowed for a moment. "I'm sure it's good." She said quietly, turning her head toward Arthur and looking sadly at him. "At least it is what I need now."

Arthur bent over Hayley and kissed her softly. "Ssssh!" he made quietly and caressed Hayley's cheek. "You're lying with two guys in bed and still you can't stop thinking about what happened? What else do we have to do that you start to relax?"

Hayley laid her hand on Arthur's chest. Softly she started to caress him and her hand went down and down till she reached the trousers Arthur still wore. She started to unbutton it. "At the moment I have only one thought: Are you better than Rick? And then I think about what I have to do to find that out." Hayley found her smile again.

Arthur threw a look over at Rick. "I really don't want to know who of us is better but you can make your decision – if you want to." He bent over Hayley again and kissed her softly. His tongue pressed Hayley's lips apart and Hayley opened her mouth. Their tongues touched each other and the kiss grew wilder.

Rick observed the two smiling; his hand was still lying on Hayley's belly and he stroked her softly.

Hayley moved and solved her mouth from Arthur's. With half open mouth she lay there and enjoyed once more the caresses of the two men. From time to time she groaned slightly.

Arthur passed with his lips and his tongue over to Hayley's ear, softly biting her lobe. Still feeling Hayley's hand on his body he went down over Hayley's throat till he reached her breasts. There he stopped and looked up at Hayley; his hand enclosing her breast.

Hayley had closed her eyes and sighed silently. Her hand passed over Arthur's back and her other hand lay down on Rick's shoulder.

"I fear I'm too excited to give you now, what you want to have. Let's change the order, shall we?" Arthur asked quietly.

Hayley opened her eyes and looked smiling at Arthur. "That's fine with me." She answered calmly.

Arthur grinned. He pulled his trousers down and threw them to the ground. Then he laid his leg down on Hayley's and pressed them apart. Carefully he sat down between her legs and pushed his hands under Hayley's body. Softly he lifted Hayley up and pulled her towards him.

Hayley supported herself on her arms and helped from her side as best as possible.

Arthur pushed his penis direct into Hayley and held her around her hips. "Lie down and enjoy!" He murmured and pressed her body against his.

Hayley lay down and gave Arthur the space with her body he needed. She groaned, as Arthur pressed himself against her again.

Arthur bent forward during he pressed against Hayley's body and laid his hands on her breasts.

Rick, who still lay beside Hayley and Arthur, kissed Hayley fast on the mouth then he turned and sat down beside Arthur. He passed with his hands over Arthur's back that the powerful man looked astonished at his companion. Rick didn't care what Arthur might think about him; he pushed his hand under Arthur's bottom.

Arthur gasped. He felt Rick's hand between his legs and it aroused him more as he already was.

Even Hayley felt it. She groaned up, as she felt Arthur moving in her and as his hands pressed her breasts hard, her body started to tremble and her hands cramped down into the sheet of the bed.

Arthur groaned loudly up, as Rick moved his hand for- and backwards and suddenly he pressed himself firm against Hayley. Then he sank forward and down on Hayley.

Also Hayley had to catch her breath again and after she had calmed down, she asked astonished: "What was that?"

Arthur got up and lay down beside Hayley. "Ask him!" He pointed at Rick who just lay down again beside the other two. "He has really fast fingers."

Rick only grinned.

Hayley sighed. "At least – we all got what we wanted to have."

"Not quite." Arthur laid his hand on Hayley's body, as he discovered a bruise on her breast. "Did I hurt you?" He asked apologizing, stroking over her breast.

Hayley threw a fast look down her body before she shook her head. "I didn't notice. Forget it." She laid her hand on Arthur's.

Softly bent Arthur over her and kissed her on the mouth. Then he kissed carefully the bruise on her breast then he enclosed with his lips her nipple and licked it again and again.

Hayley closed her eyes once more. "I'm still so excited, I could groan again." She said lightly, enjoying the feeling Arthur built up in her.

"I love to hear your groan." Rick murmured and started to kiss her cheek and ear including the lobe. As he finally reached her mouth, Hayley opened it expectantly. Rick went around Hayley's lips with his tongue before he carefully pushed it into her mouth.

Hayley felt his tongue inside her and touched it longingly. The kiss grew wilder and wilder.

Arthur went slowly down Hayley's body till he reached the certain point between her legs. He started to stroke her softly.

Hayley turned her head away from Rick and groaned slightly.

Arthur played with the time; softly and slowly, very slowly he caressed Hayley on the spot before he pressed finally his mouth on the spot.

Hayley groaned up loudly and Rick pressed his lips on her nipples and massaged her breasts again. Hayley's hands went over Rick's head and his back in excitement.

Arthur embraced Hayley's legs and felt her trembling during he touched with his tongue her spot and licked her again and again.

Hayley groaned up loudly and her body stiffened. Then she slowly relaxed.

Arthur stopped licking her and turned around. "Satisfied?"

Rick looked up as well.

Hayley grinned down at the two men and nodded. "Completely – for the moment." she stopped for a moment then she continued: "But if you both would come up now, we have to discuss something."

"Now," Rick asked and sounded flabbergasted.

"Yes, now." Hayley grinned. "It's the best time – now we can't hide anything before each other anymore or can we?"

"No, we can't." Arthur grinned, as he lay down beside her again. "We haven't even a blanket to cover ourselves up."

Rick turned on his belly and supported himself on his arms. "What do you want to discuss?" He asked curiously.

Hayley examined her two companions carefully. "Listen – I don't know what made you come over here and why. I also don't know what you swore down in the temple. Fact is – I had no idea what's on but I was relieved to hear that you followed me. I needed you here and I still will need you, probably more than ever in the next months. I…"

"You mean to say that you had no idea if we are friends or not? Cause of the short time we know each other and all the circumstances?" Arthur asked calmly.

And Rick added: "And you want to know all the facts that you can be sure about us?"

"Kind of," Hayley confessed. "I really don't have any idea anymore what's happening, what's happening with us. So I want to be sure about us."

Arthur and Rick exchanged a look. Then Arthur cleared his throat: "Well," he said. "Perhaps you want to tell us everything about yourself…"

Hayley nodded weakly, "Yes, why not? Somebody has to start." She was silent for a moment then she continued: "Do you know that I'm married and that I have a son?"

Arthur laid his hand on her belly and looked calmly at her. "You told me before, I believe. But go on; tell us everything from the beginning."

And Hayley told the two listening men her whole life story from the day on she had seen the Horsemen till the point she had ended up in Prince Alban's prison cell. Then she cleared her throat once more and confessed to the two men what for an oath she had given to Harder, God of Freedom.

After that she felt relieved; she had no secrets anymore. But she still didn't know anything more about her… friends?

11

Arthur was the next one to tell his life story; he made it short and told Hayley and Rick only the main facts of his life. He told them as well about the rests of the food he had given out to the poor of the town and how the Prince had heard about it – the reason why he finally had ended up in the prison cell where he in the end had met Hayley. Then he hesitated. "I told you already one of my reasons why I followed you. The legend kept me going but it wasn't that alone." Again he was silent.

Hayley looked at him. "What was it then?" She asked curiously.

Arthur still hesitated and threw a look over at Rick.

Rick nodded at him. "Tell her – she has to know! Tell her what you swore in the temple." He reassured him.

Arthur wetted his lips. He stared to the opposite wall and said then quietly: "Perhaps you remember? The evening Prince Alban bought you from the Sheikh? For the transport they brought you into a wagon, together with another girl. You asked for pillows and blankets and a guard came to bring you everything?"

Hayley frowned. "I remember the situation but I don't remember the people around me. I was too wrapped up in myself. – Err. – You were the guard?"

"I was." Arthur confessed quietly. "And then happened something, I would never have dreamed of."

Hayley looked intensive at him but she said nothing.

Arthur sighed. "I fell in love. I fell in love with a girl with beautiful fire red curls and a body to die for. I knew at that time that I wouldn't have a chance to get you and that it was stupid to lose my heart to somebody I didn't know at all – but I couldn't help myself. If you would have asked me to help you to escape – I would have done it and I would have come with you already at that point. As you didn't say anything, I stayed to be in your vicinity and waited for my chance to come – what happened."

Hayley laid her hand down on her mouth. "Then it was a mistake what we just did." She whispered, for a second terrible afraid.

Arthur felt Hayley trembling and laid again a hand on her belly. "Listen, Hayley. You wanted to know the truth to be sure of our friendship. Since you were brought into the cell and you told me that you are married – I knew once more that I wouldn't have a chance to give you my love. Down in the temple I swore," he hesitated again and wetted his lips, "I swore to love you forever and to be there for you every time you need it. But as this love can't be fulfilled, I have to marry somebody who loves me and to make her happy under every circumstance. – You can imagine that the second part of my oath was a real problem for me." Arthur was silent again.

"Yes, and I don't make it easier for you." Hayley nodded understanding.

Surprisingly Arthur shook his head. "No, you did help me. You gave me more I ever hoped for. I think I will be now more ready to fulfil my oath than I was at the time, as I gave the oath."

Hayley examined him thoughtfully. "You followed me out of love, only to get the life sentence, always to be with me but not to get me. – Well, that's a hard sentence."

"Only for a short time till you fulfilled your oath." Rick joined back into the conversation.

Hayley and Arthur turned their heads over at Rick.

"What do you mean?" Hayley asked astonished.

Now Rick hesitated. "If I understood you correct – you will die after you got what you wanted. After that Arthur won't have so many problems – as you won't be here anymore. Correct?"

Hayley closed her eyes. "Yes, that's correct." She turned back to Arthur, opened her eyes slowly again and winked, mainly to suppress the tears, which had come into her eyes. "You have to take in the next months what you can get from me – after that I will see that I can fulfil my oath. And I won't hesitate to come back here after I got what I want."

Arthur nodded. "I know." And he bent over Hayley and kissed her softly.

Hayley replied the kiss but then she turned to Rick. "You are now the only one who is still a secret to us. We told everything, what about you?"

Rick sighed. "Well, what has to be done has to be done." He answered philosophical and continued then more slowly: "Best is, I start with the oath I gave. I swore never, never to betray you both, which will not be easy for me, as I never did anything else, as to betray other people. I also swore never to steal out of fun anymore, only when our group would be in need of it. The part, which makes my oath really difficult for me, is that I had to swear to train somebody up and to show all my tricks to him in order to help him to fulfil his destiny. They told me that it will be your son I have to train but…"

Hayley shook her head. "You have to see it other way round. If it's for the good of my son to know your tricks – it will be good to show him."

Rick shook his head. "I was taught that in the moment you give your tricks further on, your own powers grow less and you remain back, old and unable to do anything. That's not really the future I expect for me."

Hayley laughed. "The time will show what will happen. My son is not even born, no reason to worry now about it. Perhaps you will be already an old man before you have to give any secrets out. So it won't be too bad."

Rick smiled at her, as he laid down his hand on Hayley's belly beside Arthur's. "I didn't say, which son of yours." He said quietly.

Hayley frowned slightly.

Rick laid his finger of his other hand on the mouth and smiled at Hayley. "The oath was almost reason for me to leave again." He confessed. "But then I thought about the days we were on the run together, and I couldn't. I can't say that I love you both", he grinned mischievously, "but there was something, which didn't let me go. I don't know what it was – and is – but it has me, you have me completely in your hands. – I was born a thief, I lived as a thief but you saved me for being treated as thief. Perhaps there is something more in this body than – a thief."

In silence Hayley and Arthur listened to Rick's confession then Hayley leaned back and smiled lightly. "Don't you both think now as well that it was good that we told each other everything? It helps to understand – at least I know now what I have to expect from you and what I never should ask you."

"Well," Rick smiled, "we know now that we are really friends, aren't we?"

"We are." Hayley confirmed and laid her arms around Rick and Arthur's shoulders.

But Arthur tipped thoughtfully with a finger on top of his nose. "Yet – something is still missing." He murmured.

"And that would be?" Hayley asked astonished.

Arthur smiled. He supported himself on his arms and looked at Hayley and Rick, saying quietly: "A sword master and a priest!"

12

"Are you ready?" Harry looked into the dining room where Hayley still sat over her breakfast.

Hayley was tired after the long night she had spent with Arthur and Rick but she had been awake again early in the morning. It had been impossible for her to sleep longer.

Arthur and Rick on the other hand still slept over the narcotics they had got in the temple and which hadn't disappeared out of their bodies completely.

Hayley now looked up. "Ready for what?" she asked astonished.

Harry came completely inside and examined Hayley thoughtfully. "Don't you remember? We wanted to go outside to look for a companion for you? A woman who will help you in the next months? Or don't you want anymore?" Then he added carefully: "Or are you too tired?"

Hayley smiled lightly. "I'm not too tired – and I really want to go. But please, let me finish my… whatever it is." She finished, staring into her cup.

Harry grinned. "I think they call it here herbal tea." He said and sat down opposite Hayley. "Let me guess – you would prefer a coffee!"

Hayley winked at him. "It's true, I would prefer a coffee. This tea doesn't help me to wake up and especially good it isn't either." She confessed.

"Then, come on! We'll get something better – outside." Harry pulled Hayley up and led her out of the room.

Together they went outside and Harry led the way over to the house where the temple of Harder was underground.

Hayley remembered the way they had gone the day before, as they picked up Arthur and Rick. "Do we have to go through the temple to come to the outside?" She asked curiously.

"Luckily not," Harry laughed. "If we would go every time through the temple we would be always quite a long time on the way. There is a shortcut – I'll show you." And he stepped as first one into the hall of the house.

Hayley followed him slowly, looking carefully around to be able to remember the way. But she noted that it wasn't necessary, as Harry pulled a key out of his pocket and opened a door at his right side. He closed it carefully again after they had both entered the room. Then he led Hayley through a flood of rooms and corridors till they reached the other end of the house where Harry opened and closed once more a door.

Hayley was confused and she showed it. "The house doesn't seem so big." She murmured and continued: "Why do you have to lock the doors?"

Harry smiled. "Not everybody should be able to come inside the temple without problems. You will soon notice why."

Hayley frowned. "You said temple. But the temple is underground and for everybody available." She said, now completely confused.

"Well," Harry searched for words to explain the situation, "everybody outside thinks the whole area where we live is the temple. And somehow they are right. You will notice that as well."

Hayley nodded only. She was happy after all the empty rooms and corridors to come into the open air again and she waited impatiently till Harry had opened the outside door.

Outside both of them stood at first still, trying to get used to the sun and breathing the fresh air.

Then Harry turned to Hayley and pointed a path down. "I have here a very good friend. Let's see him – where we start to search for a friend of yours doesn't matter. As you don't know anybody, every place will be so good like another." He added.

Hayley accepted it. "Let's see your friend." She said quietly.

Harry followed the path down and led Hayley over to a nice small house at the edge of the small village around the temple, direct at the wall. He knocked at the door and waited patiently for an answer.

"Come in!" A voice called loudly.

Harry opened the door and let Hayley step inside.

Hayley looked interested around.

The inside of the house told Hayley intensive who lived there: Just opposite the entrance door at the other end of the wall was an altar with some flowers on it. Otherwise the room was almost empty, only some pillows were lying on the ground in the left corner around a small table.

It was the typical house of a priest.

"Al?" Harry called.

"Is it you, Harry? Sit down; I'll be with you in a moment." A voice came back from the right side where obviously bath and bedroom had to be.

Harry grinned. He pointed over at the pillows, and Hayley sat hesitatingly down. Harry sat down on a pillow and stretched himself out. "Al is all right, you can believe me." He said, as he noticed Hayley's concerned look.

Out of one of the rooms came a man and looked over to the corner.

"Hi Al," Harry greeted friendly.

Hayley looked over to the man – and bit on her lips to pretend not to laugh loudly.

The man was completely naked and had only a small towel in his hands, wiping his hands in it. For a moment he seemed to be speechless then he lowered the towel and said reproachfully: "You could have told me that you have a female guest with you!" He turned and disappeared into the next room.

"I'm sorry, Al! I thought it would nice if she sees you like you are!" Harry called grinning back. Then he threw a look over at Hayley and shrugged his shoulders.

Hayley shook her head but she couldn't hide a smile.

Five minutes later the man came back, now dressed in a white robe. He came over to the sitting area and bowed in front of Harry.

Harry got up and embraced his friend. Quietly they exchanged some words before Harry sat down again and the man in the white robe turned to Hayley.

"Welcome to my house!" The man said and bowed.

Hayley got up. "It's a pleasure to meet you." She answered and bowed slightly back.

The man laid his hands on Hayley's shoulders and smiled: "I'm Priest Alfonso – but you can call me Al. Every friend of Harry is my friend too. Sit down."

Hayley sat down again.

Priest Alfonso crossed his legs and sat down on a pillow between Harry and Hayley. Again he turned to Hayley: "You have to excuse my dress from earlier but I didn't know Harry would bring such a jewel into my house. What are you doing here, my daughter?"

Hayley felt more and more impressed from the man in front of her. He seemed to be only a touch older than she was and he had a really good body, which she had seen before. It was a real pity that he was a priest and untouchable. So she smiled and answered quietly: "To be truthfully: At the moment I'm not allowed to do anything – without looking for a female friend and companion. As I don't know anybody here, perhaps you can help me?" and explained shortly her situation.

Priest Alfonso nodded. "It won't be easy but I think I know somebody who would be right for you. Only a suggestion, as I don't know you yet. But why don't we go and you have a look for yourself?"

"Yes why not?" Harry got up and reached Hayley his hand to be able to get up more easily during Priest Alfonso got up lightly.

The priest went to another room and came back with some sandals at his feet. He opened the door and bowed over to his friends. "I'll show you where the women are now. Then you can choose."

Hayley followed the priest quite curiously and Harry stepped behind both with a careful look at Hayley. But nothing happened and they came undisturbed to the area where the women sat together and washed clothes in big basins.

"Good morning, my ladies!" Priest Alfonso greeted friendly.

An echo of the greeting came back to him, and the women smiled at the Priest. It was quite clear that the women liked the Priest. But for that they eyed Hayley and Harry suspiciously.

Priest Alfonso smiled at Hayley, as he noticed the looks of the women around him. He saw the same like them; a woman dressed in black with swords around her hips. She was similar to Harry who only wore the swords with much more pride. But the women didn't stare so much at Harry, as they already knew him, as they did with Hayley who was completely new to them.

Hayley on her side had no problem to stare back. Under her look the women started their work again and looked away. Hayley replied the priest's smile.

Slowly the two men and the woman went through the washing area to the other side where the fields started. Some women worked on the fields as well.

Hayley stopped, as she noticed a young woman of her own age standing alone at a basin, washing her clothes. The woman was thin with long black hair and a sweet but very sad face. The other women didn't talk to her and didn't help her at all; they ignored her completely.

Hayley felt pity for the woman and she turned her steps away from the fields and over to the woman. "Hi!" She greeted the woman friendly. "Can I help you?"

The woman looked up. "Hi!" She answered very quietly. "It's okay; I can manage."

Hayley smiled. "Don't be ridiculous! It's a lot to do, don't you think so? All your own or do you wash clothes for somebody else as well?" She asked calmly, grabbing after a skirt and starting to wash it carefully.

The woman looked up once more. "You know what you do here?" She asked astonished.

"I do." Hayley confirmed. She threw a look over at the other women and asked quietly: "Why aren't the others helping you?"

The woman stared back into the basin. "I'm a bastard; they don't like me cause of my mother having a child and not being married. My mother is dead but I have still to fight against it. – It would be better for you not to talk to me anymore if you want to make friends here." She added very quietly.

"Oh, God," Hayley grinned. "I never made a difference between legitimate and illegitimate born people. And I hate people who make such a difference. – And my friends, well, I like people who are truthfully. And at the moment I like you. What's your name?"

"They call me Arachnarella – that means so much like: Woman who tries to live." The woman answered quietly, looking shyly but intensive at Hayley. "And yours?"

"My name is Hayley. Don't know if it means anything," Hayley laughed.

"But what are you doing here? I don't think that I have seen you here before." Arachnarella asked curiously.

Hayley smiled. With short words she informed Arachnarella why she had come to this place but she didn't mention what she was looking for at that peculiar moment. She finished off with the skirt and threw it over into the basket with the clean clothes. But before she could take another piece of the clothes, a voice called loudly: "Hayley!"

Hayley turned and discovered Harry and Priest Alfonso standing at the edge of the fields and waving over to her. She turned back to

Arachnarella and asked calmly: "Will you be okay alone? My friends are waiting for me."

"Certainly I am. And – thanks for your help." Arachnarella smiled shyly again.

"It was my pleasure." Hayley winked at her then she stepped over to the two waiting men.

Priest Alfonso smiled at her. "Then I was right." He nodded.

"You were right? With what were you right?" Hayley asked astonished.

"Well," Priest Alfonso smiled wide, "the only two women in this area who are different to all other women here. You were bound to find each other and to like each other." He explained.

Hayley threw a look over at Arachnarella. She smiled. "Perhaps – we'll see." She answered shortly and stepped further on.

Hayley spent an interesting morning with Harry and Priest Alfonso in the village around the temple. She got to know some of the other women as well and closed some independent friendships with the men and the women of the village.

And the more Hayley showed her interest into the people the more the village people grew friendlier towards her. They noticed that she wasn't a fraud, that she was in fact only one of them.

Finally they came back to the house, which was the entrance to the Temple of Freedom where they had started their journey.

Harry turned back to Priest Alfonso and asked calmly: "Do you want to come with us? You weren't in the temple for a long time."

"Perhaps you're right. I should come with you – and refresh my memories." Priest Alfonso nodded. He looked over at Hayley. "And you? Did you get what you wanted?"

Hayley hesitated. "I don't know. But it was for sure interesting." She smiled.

Harry opened the door and they all stepped inside. Again after a walk through endless corridors and empty rooms they finally reached the other side of the house and with that the inside of the temple.

"It is dinner time!" Harry grinned and pushed Hayley over to the house where the dining room was.

Hayley didn't contradict. Even though she had noticed that she was on the way to become good friends with Harry, she still remembered that he was her guard with the order to keep an eye on her and to see that she looked after herself. To keep to the dinner times was only one of the small jobs he did.

In the dining room was everybody already there.

Hayley noticed that Arthur and Rick were sitting in a corner of the room, opposite the big table where the priests and trainers had their place. One more plate was on the table, and she went over to her two friends and greeted them friendly: "Hi Arthur! Rick! How are you?"

The two men looked up at her and smiled.

"Sit down, Hayley. We were waiting for you. Where were you?" Arthur asked curiously.

"I had a look around the village outside." Hayley replied the smile. "And what did you do?"

Rick shrugged his shoulders. "We had a short induction around and got our time tables."

"Then we were at the Doctor's and also organized some blankets and pillows – for you as well." Arthur added.

"Thanks." Hayley looked over to the other table where Harry and Priest Alfonso had taken seat and enjoyed their meal. "And how is your time table?" She asked curiously.

Arthur shook his head. "We got told not to let you know, as for the next months your time table is completely different to what we will do. Only to avoid that you get jealous and that you will do something – well, stupid." He said carefully.

Hayley grinned. "Yes, they are very worried about me. But I'm not stupid, in neither way. I can imagine how your timetable looks like but, at the moment, I have to confess that I'm not interested in fights or something like that. I still feel not so good and..." She stopped, as suddenly a sharp pain went through her body. She snapped after air.

Arthur and Rick let their forks fell down on the table and they caught Hayley in their arms. Arthur steadied her and murmured quietly: "We'll bring you back – you should lie down." His voice was worried.

Doctor Balthazar at the other table got up as well and came over to the table. He laid his hand on Hayley's throat to catch the pulse and frowned. He turned to Arthur and asked quietly: "Can you carry her over to her house? She belongs into bed."

"On my way," Arthur only hummed. He pulled Hayley into his arms and Hayley laid her arm powerless around his neck. With the face at his shoulder, she accepted to get carried out of the room. She only felt the pain in her body; she really didn't register at all what happened around her.

The doctor and Rick as well as Harry and Priest Alfonso followed Arthur hastily, as he carried Hayley over to their house only some steps further down the street. He entered the house and brought Hayley straight back into her room. There he laid her down on the bed, her head on a pillow and pulling a blanket over her body. Kneeling beside the bed he stared anxiously down at her pale face.

"Please, leave! I'll look after her." Doctor Balthazar laid his hand on Arthur's shoulder. "She will be all right again, believe me."

Arthur nodded. He got up and left the room but not without throwing a last look over at her from the door. Then he closed the door and stepped over to Rick who waited in the middle of the lobby.

The two friends looked in silence at each other.

At the entrance to the house Harry and Priest Alfonso stood and stared over to the closed door.

Priest Alfonso shook his head. "That's not good." He murmured and turned to Harry. "Please go back to the village and bring Arachnarella over here. She will be the best to look after Hayley." He pleaded him.

"Arachnarella," Harry examined him astonished. "Are you sure?"

Priest Alfonso nodded. "Please go – now!" He said urgently.

Harry frowned slightly but he turned and left the house.

Priest Alfonso turned to the two men in the middle of the lobby. "Excuse me, my dear friends." He said to them and stared into the astonished faces of Arthur and Rick. "There is no need at all for you, waiting here. Why don't you go back and finish your meal?" He asked calmly.

Arthur frowned. "I don't like to be unfriendly to a priest – but when you think I leave Hayley completely alone here and in pain during I finish off my meal, you must be completely mad!" He answered strongly.

To his surprise Priest Alfonso smiled. "Yes, perhaps I'm completely mad." He confessed. "Because I don't think that you can help her by being starving. This is your first meal after more than twenty-four hours so you must be very hungry and it won't be good for anybody if you don't finish it off. Doctor Balthazar is more than competent to look after Hayley for the moment and I will look after her as well. And Harry is gone to get one of the women of the village to come and help Hayley. Don't you think that will be enough?"

Still the two men hesitated.

Arthur cleared his throat. "But she doesn't know you like she knows us. She will like it to see somebody familiar as soon as she is able to again." He contradicted.

Priest Alfonso examined him thoughtfully. "You really love her, don't you?" He asked out of his thoughts. Then he shook his head and smiled again. "Believe me – when she wants to see you both, we will send for you."

Arthur and Rick exchanged a look.

"You do know the legend, don't you?" Priest Alfonso turned direct to Arthur. "Trust me, you won't regret it." He added carefully.

Arthur looked at the priest for a second then he grabbed after Rick's arm and pulled him with him. "We're in the dining room." He informed Priest Alfonso over his shoulder.

The two men left the house.

13

Hayley opened her eyes carefully, as somebody laid a wet cold cloth on her forehead. She winked till she saw clearly again and examined astonished the woman sitting on the edge of her bed.

The woman noticed that Hayley had moved and looked at her with a smile.

"Arachnarella," Hayley asked surprised.

The woman nodded. "Harry asked me to come and care for you in the next months. They all seem to think that you need female accompany. Somehow I doubt that but it's all right with me to be here."

Hayley frowned. "I asked for a female friend, not for somebody to care for me – and who really doesn't care." She said and turned her head away.

Arachnarella shrank back. "I'm sorry, Hayley. I didn't want to hurt you and it's not what I got told. Well, and you don't look like somebody who is able to look after herself at the moment."

Hayley sighed. She turned her head back to Arachnarella and examined her carefully. "Perhaps you are right. Don't listen to me; sometimes I'm not fully aware of the situation – like now. Ignore me then." She sighed. "Still I'm happy that you are here." She looked around.

"Do you miss something?" Arachnarella asked astonished, as she noted Hayley's look.

"Well, not something." Hayley answered slowly, "Somebody. Where are Arthur and Rick?" She inquired.

"Wait – I'll fetch them." Arachnarella jumped up and left the room.

Five minutes later Arthur and Rick entered the room.

Arthur went straight over to the bed and bent over Hayley to kiss her on the cheek. "How are you now?" He asked worried.

"Better since you both are here." Hayley smiled. She stretched her hand out to Rick and Rick greeted her softly as well.

"What happened?" Hayley asked calmly.

Arthur shrugged his shoulders. "You didn't eat anything. It seemed that you had a lot of pain and you lost consciousness. Doctor Balthazar checked you through but he couldn't find anything. Are you still in pain?"

Hayley searched fast through her body for any pain but then she shook her head. "No, it vanished." She answered quietly. Carefully she sat up and sighed. "What is now expected from me?" She asked further on.

Arthur smiled. "For today we all expect you to stay in bed. Tomorrow – well, we will see."

Hayley smiled lightly. Then she noted something and asked concerned: "Do I keep you from something important?"

Rick shook his head. "Nothing could be more important than your health and well being. We were together with Harry and Al. They seem to be okay."

"They are. At least Harry is. About Al I don't know so much either." Hayley sighed.

Arthur and Rick exchanged a look.

"I'm quite sure that they are all right." Arthur smiled reassuring at Hayley. "If you remember what I told you."

Hayley looked frowning at him. "You want to drag them into it as well?" She asked suspiciously.

Arthur shook his head. "No, I won't. But I can't stop destiny, can I? – And Al knows about the legend as well; he has the intention to be the priest out of it."

Hayley shook smiling her head. "You all gone crazy, haven't you?" She leaned back again and closed her eyes. "I think I sleep a little bit longer. I'm tired." She murmured.

Arthur got up and kissed her softly on the cheek. "Sleep well. We'll look later again after you."

Rick did the same then the two men left quietly the room.

Arachnarella noticed the two men leaving and went on silent feet back into the room. But Hayley had gone back to sleep and didn't notice anything anymore.

14

Next morning Hayley felt so well again that she was out of bed, washed and dressed before Arachnarella who slept on a bed in a corner of the room even could open her eyes.

"What are you doing?" Arachnarella asked astonished, after she finally had opened her eyes and sat up.

Hayley shrugged her shoulders. "I like to catch some fresh air. Do you want to come with me?"

"Give me five minutes!" Arachnarella swung herself out of bed and went to get washed and dressed.

Exactly five minutes later she was ready and the two women left the house. Together they stepped over the green of the street and breathed the fresh air.

"Good morning, my daughters! How are you this nice morning?" A voice spoke to them from the back.

Hayley turned. She bowed lightly and answered with a smile: "Good morning, Al! We are fine – and you?"

"I'm fine as well." Priest Alfonso stepped nearer. "It's good to see you on your feet again. But you should be careful; you only came yesterday just around it."

"I came around what?" Hayley frowned.

Astonished the priest examined her. "Did nobody tell you?"

"Tell me, what?" Hayley asked again.

"You had contractions. So you need to be careful in the next days. Finally you don't want to risk anything, do you? Did you see the Doctor?" Priest Alfonso explained.

Hayley shook her head. "I haven't seen him yet. And Arthur and Rick didn't say anything."

"They probably don't know either." Priest Alfonso waved it away. But then he changed the subject. "What would you think about a nice good breakfast?"

Hayley grinned. "Well, I would have nothing against some fresh fruits and bread. Now where you mentioned it – I'm really hungry."

"Come on then!" Priest Alfonso led the two women over to the house with the dining room.

They stepped inside – and Hayley noticed astonished that they were the first ones.

Priest Alfonso shrugged his shoulders. "It's very early." He explained shortly before he pressed Hayley on a seat at a table and turned to the kitchen to search for Salazar to get something to eat.

Hayley turned to Arachnarella who sat down opposite her at the table. Thoughtfully she stared at her, without really seeing her.

Arachnarella blushed under her look. "What is it?" She asked quietly.

"Why did they bring you over here?" Hayley asked curiously, "Why you?"

Arachnarella frowned. "Don't you like me?" She asked astonished.

"No, it's not that." Hayley sighed. "But you are completely different to me – and you remind me of somebody."

"I remind you of whom?" Arachnarella grew curious.

"I had a good friend in the village where I came from. Mandy was the wife of my husband's assistant. I don't know what happened to her; I only hope she's all right." Hayley stopped short before she continued: "In some ways you are like her and that makes me feel uncomfortable. – Why you?" she asked again.

"Harry and Al only meant that we both hit it off right away." Arachnarella started, and Priest Alfonso who came back to the two women at the table added: "And I wasn't completely wrong, was I?"

Hayley shook her head. "No, you weren't completely wrong." She turned back to Arachnarella and examined her softly. "I really do like you – but I don't know if you will be able to change me how they want to have me here. I'm…"

"But I already did." Arachnarella smiled lightly.

"How did you change me?" Hayley frowned.

"Well," Arachnarella looked at her with a smile; "yesterday you still carried your swords with you around. Today you left them back in your room."

Priest Alfonso laughed loudly. "You both are good! I really like you both!"

Hayley had thrown a look down her clothes and had noted that Arachnarella was right. She had forgotten to take her swords with her. Sighing she looked at the two smiling people in front of her: "I take everything back I said. You are good and perhaps exactly what I need." She confessed, knowing exactly that if she would have had more time to finish dressing she would have taken her swords with her. "What's for breakfast?" She asked instead.

Priest Alfonso smiled. "Everything you want to have." He answered and pointed over to the door where Salazar came inside with a big tray of tea, fruits, bread and porridge.

Hayley smiled with hungry eyes at him and hungry she started to eat.

After Hayley, Arachnarella and Priest Alfonso had finished their breakfast; they left the dining room and wandered a bit over the green.

Hayley sighed again. "And what shall I do now?" She inquired.

"Well, you can choose." Priest Alfonso answered her smiling. "You can get used to some of the stuff every woman is doing and which Arachnarella can show you. Or you can observe your two friends when they make their first tries in their training. Then you would know what lies ahead of you. Both have its good and its bad sides. It's your choice – but if you like a piece of advice..." He looked at Hayley.

Hayley nodded at him.

"Well, your two friends are quite nervous, even though they would never confess to it. If you show up to watch them, they will make a lot of mistakes. Don't make it worse for them – stay with Arachnarella and enjoy your life for the next months. You will see early enough what the trainers are expecting from you." Priest Alfonso looked straight at her.

Hayley looked down at the ground. She kicked against some small stones and watched them rolling away. Then she sighed. "Well, I think at first I go and see the doctor. Then we'll see further on." She said calmly and turned her steps over to the house where the doctor had his practice.

Arachnarella looked astonished at Priest Alfonso. "What does that mean now?"

Priest Alfonso smiled. "She's searching for good reasons why she hasn't to watch her friends. Only in case they ask her." He nodded satisfied. "It makes her calmer as well, and that's good."

Arachnarella agreed without saying anything.

Hayley let herself check through from the doctor and was somehow relieved to hear that everything was all right. She knew when something would happen to her child; she would have a very bad time. So she decided for herself not to let anything happen to her or her child.

After the check up, she went back to her house, where she ran straight into Arthur and Rick.

The two men greeted her friendly. "Morning, Hayley! How are you today?" They asked in chorus.

Hayley smiled. "I'm okay. I just had a check up and everything is all right. But Doctor Balthazar meant it would be better if I rest a lot. – And that I should do." she nodded lightly.

Arthur laid his hand on her shoulder. "You should do that. We'll look later after you, okay?"

Hayley nodded. "Have fun!" She wished them before she went into her room and lay down on the bed.

15

Some months later Arthur and Rick were much more confident about their training and they grew really good.

Hayley in the meantime had much more problems with her pregnancy. But finally her time came and with the help of Doctor Balthazar, Priest Alfonso and Arachnarella she gave birth to a beautiful baby boy who cried out of full lungs to announce his arrival.

Hayley leaned exhausted back, as Arachnarella laid the baby into towels and cared for him. Hayley observed her during Doctor Balthazar finished his job and finally she sighed: "Arachnarella?" She asked quietly.

The dark woman turned around.

"Arachnarella - can I see him? Finally I'm his mother!" Hayley sighed.

Arachnarella smiled. "Certainly." she said quietly and picked the baby carefully up. Then she went over to the bed and laid the baby down into Hayley's arms.

Hayley examined the baby in her arms. Softly she stroked over his cheek and said very quietly: "So, that's you, young man! And one day you will be a very good king over this kingdom, as you are the only son of the last Prince. Well, you should always remember that you are a Prince; even though your mum is only a Fighter." She whispered.

The baby in her arms moved and for a second it looked like, as if he would smile at his mother.

"Come on, Hayley. You should rest a bit. Your son will be fine; we'll look after him." Priest Alfonso said quietly and stretched out his arms.

But Hayley laid her arms strongly around her son and caressed him softly. "I'm quite capable to look after him." She said urgently.

Priest Alfonso wanted to say something but Arachnarella stopped him. "You asked me to teach her some things, which I did. I taught her to love her son – perhaps he wasn't conceived on free will but he is still her son, too. What you see now, is the result of it. Her mother instincts are coming through. She wants to look after her son, how every other mother would do it. Let her do it, it will be for her best - and his." She explained quietly.

Priest Alfonso hesitated for a second then he nodded. "You did a great job." He murmured.

"Hungry?" Hayley smiled, as her son suddenly started to cry. She sat a bit up, opened a bit the shirt she wore and laid her son at her breast.

The baby started eagerly to suck at her nipple.

Doctor Balthazar nodded satisfied. "Everything's all right now. Arachnarella - are you staying here?" As he got a nod from the dark woman, he continued: "Then Al and I go and announce the arrival of the new Prince. Come on, let's go!" He grabbed after Priest Alfonso's arm and pulled him outside.

"I hope they are not doing anything stupid." Hayley murmured during she observed her son drinking at her breast.

Arachnarella smiled. "They will celebrate – finally is today a great day! But you should see that you get a bit of rest, for you it was very exhausting." She added.

Hayley laid her son onto her shoulder after he had stopped drinking and clapped him softly on the back. She held him for a moment then she nodded. "Yes, you are right. I'm tired out. Where can I lie him down?" She asked.

Arachnarella pushed a cot over to the bed and took the baby out of Hayley's arms. She bedded him carefully in the cot and smiled at Hayley. "You will be able to see your son any time. But now try to sleep a bit that you will be fit soon again."

"Yes Ma'am." Hayley threw another look at her son who slept peacefully and closed then her eyes.

Arachnarella left the room on tiptoes, as she heard the regular breaths of Hayley.

"He has your eyes." Arthur noticed astonished, as he looked at the baby in Hayley's arms. "But he is so small."

Hayley laughed lightly. "Once you were so small as well. He will soon grow; you will see. What do you think?" She turned to Rick.

Rick grinned. "He definitely has your eyes. If he got only half of your intelligence and feelings – he won't be only a handsome man but a very clever and good young man." He answered quietly.

Hayley smiled at him. "Thanks for that."

"It was a pleasure." Rick smiled at her.

Arthur shook his head. "If you go on like that, you will be as good with compliments as with your fingers." He made the hand movement of stealing and grinned at Rick.

Rick only frowned at him.

"What's his name?" Arthur continued.

Hayley was uncertain. "I thought about it. Perhaps it would be good to name him after his father that there will be at least one connection. What do you think?" She asked again.

"Well," Arthur hesitated, "If it won't be too... too painful for you."

Hayley looked down at her son. "I don't know. But I think it will be good." She patted softly her son's cheek during Arthur and Rick held their fingers up and the baby grabbed after them.

"Alban Junior," Rick mocked a bit, "To bring your two cultures completely together. Well, why not?"

Hayley leaned back. On her face was a light smile but she still felt exhausted, though it was already one day after she had given birth.

Arthur noted it and said quietly: "We should leave. You still need rest and should sleep a bit. We'll come back later."

"Thanks." Hayley smiled tired at her two companions.

Arthur and Rick threw a last look at her and her son then they left the room.

Hayley got up. She put her son back into the cot, pulled carefully the blanket over his body then she sat down on the bed. Before she even had lain down correctly, she was asleep.

Three days later Doctor Balthazar allowed Hayley to go outside again.

Hayley didn't let herself ask twice; she dressed in her black clothes again, which fitted her miraculous again, picked up her son and left the house. Outside she breathed deeply the fresh air in and enjoyed the slightly warm mountain sun on her skin.

"First walk?" A voice asked calmly behind her.

Hayley turned smiling around. "Harry! Yes, we are on our first walk. How are you?"

"I'm fine. And you both?" He looked smiling down at the baby in Hayley's arms.

"We're doing great." Hayley laughed.

During Hayley and Harry talked quietly, more and more men came out on the green of the street and gathered around them. In silence they stared at Hayley and especially at the baby.

Hayley suddenly noticed the men around her and looked up smiling. "Hello! Come to see my son?" She asked laughing.

"Well," Salazar answered calmly. "To see and to show him the respect he earns." And he knelt down on the ground.

Hayley examined him astonished. But before she could do anything, the other men knelt as well down in front of her.

Only two men at the side stayed upright.

Arthur and Rick only bowed lightly over at her.

Harry stood still on the same spot like before. He hesitated. "Am I a sworn man to you like Arthur and Rick or do I have to kneel down as well?" He asked quietly.

Hayley looked at him. "When you kneel down – you will lose my respect and friendship. I think I will have enough to do to accept everybody else – after that." She nodded around at the men.

Harry smiled. "Tell them."

"You mean?" Hayley frowned.

"Yes." Harry nodded.

"Well," Hayley cleared her throat and turned to the kneeling men. "Get up! You will have enough time later on showing your respect to my son." She said loud and clearly.

The men around her stood up again.

"You have to excuse that but you are the mother of the new prince. To see you both for the first time out here, is a great moment for us. We're grateful and thankful towards Harder that he had let your steps come to us." A man, dressed in simple black informed Hayley shortly.

"And I'm thankful that he had let me come to this place. My son and I are in the best hands of the world." Hayley answered with a small bowing towards him.

The men looked at each other then one of the men stepped forward and bowed: "If you would allow me a favour?"

"And you are?" Hayley asked against.

"Will, Ma'am."

"And the favour you want, Will?"

Will hesitated. "May I hold your son for a moment? It would be a great honour!"

Hayley grinned. She stepped over to him and laid carefully her son into the arms of the young man. "Hold him like this and you won't have any problems." She said quietly.

Will stared at the bundle in his arms and he smiled.

Hayley counted with the fact that everybody now wanted to hold her son but she was surprised, as Will after a while turned back to her and gave her the baby back. "It was an honour." Will confirmed, bowed and vanished from the street.

Hayley sighed quietly, as the baby in her arms suddenly started to cry. "One thing is quite clear: He has very good lungs!" She murmured and held the baby up. She sniffed, "Well, such a protest only because you have your pants full. Let's go and get them changed." She grinned at the remaining men then she turned and went back to her house where Arachnarella just put fresh clothes into a cupboard. In silence Hayley changed the nappy then she went outside again and finished her walk. But still to which place she ever came, the men bowed to her and showed her and her son all the respect.

Hayley disappeared quite soon into her house again.

Arachnarella smiled only, as Hayley poured out her worries to her. "Don't take it too personal. They are only happy to be here at these great moments. Finally you are about to write history here – to let a legend come true!"

Hayley sighed. "I only wish in between you all would see what we really are: a mother and her baby - and nothing else."

"As soon as they calmed down, they will." Arachnarella promised her. Then she hesitated: "But my job is done here. Do I... do I have to go back now?" She asked hesitatingly.

Hayley came over to her and laid her arm around her shoulders. "If you leave me now alone, I will never forgive you. I need you here – I need you to look after my son when I haven't the time to do so. And I won't have much time in future, as I have to think now about my training. – Will you help me?" She asked carefully.

"I will." Arachnarella smiled relieved.

They both knew exactly what waited for Arachnarella when she would return to the village outside. So Hayley used the opportunity and gave her some more work to keep her in safety before she would decide what the best was for Arachnarella...

16

The training was hard and intensive, and there were days where Hayley couldn't move anymore at all in the evening. She had a warm bath to relax her muscles again but after that she was only able to crawl into bed.

One thing was quite true: She hadn't any time at all for her son anymore. She still breast fed him but she also tried that he got used to milk out of the bottle, as she hadn't much more milk in her breasts left.

And she wouldn't need to interrupt her training lessons quite so often anymore...

Hayley learned to handle her swords; first with one hand then the two-hand-sword and finally she learned to fight with a sword in each hand. After a while she was able to let her swords 'sing' and to dance the sword dance wasn't difficult for her.

Harry was a good teacher and he showed her all the tricks she needed to know to become a good fighter.

Finally one morning Harry organized that Arthur joined them in training; he wanted to know if Hayley was near the point to become a good fighter.

Arthur had grown under his watchful eyes to an excellent fighter.

So Harry set up a training fight between them. Shortly he laid the rules down: "Listen! I don't want to have any injuries here, so – please – when you notice that the other one doesn't react on your hit, stop it. Otherwise fight till we have a clear winner."

Hayley and Arthur looked at each other.

Then Hayley shrugged her shoulders and stepped a bit away.

Arthur got in position as well. He drew his sword.

"Okay. And go!" Harry looked from one to the other.

Arthur stepped carefully nearer to Hayley who looked waiting at him. With one fast step Arthur came nearer to her and lifted his sword for the first attack. With power he let his sword 'sing', totally aware in an emergency to stop it.

But it wasn't necessary.

Arthur noted a fast movement and concentrated completely on what he was doing. His sword hit with full power on another that it sparkled.

Hayley had drawn her sword and had lifted it in defence. As now the swords sparkled, she ducked away with a side step.

Arthur followed her at once and again their swords 'sang' and sparkled again.

Twice, during the fight, Hayley lost her balance but Arthur hadn't any chance to use that for his purpose. She was too quick on her feet again and stepped to the side before he could think about a new attack.

Otherwise the fight was quite even. Harry noted every weakness on every side and studied their attack technique.

Finally Arthur became a problem; he scrambled over some green patches, as he lifted his sword to defend himself against an attack of Hayley and he fell to the ground.

Again this time Hayley was faster than Arthur and with another hit against his sword, the sword flew away.

Hayley caught the sword and turned back to Arthur who was still lying on the ground and breathing hard.

"I have enough!" Arthur lifted his hands in defence and Hayley smiled. She reached him a hand to help him getting up.

Arthur scratched some grass from his trousers then he looked up. "You got very good in this short time." He said approvingly.

"Thanks." Hayley smiled.

"Well," Harry joined into the conversation. "Without two or three small mistakes on both sides – it wasn't bad. You two are good sword dancers. Let's see what went wrong." And he started to put everybody back into the position of the first mistake. He explained what went wrong and how to make it better. They played it through till Hayley and Arthur knew the steps and the hits even when they would sleep then they went on to the next step.

The morning went fast under this training and then Hayley had training in self-defence, Judo, Jiu-jitsu, Karate and many more things.

The more Hayley learned the more she became confident and her old hatred for Prince Alban and the other men and the strong feeling of revenge came full back to her. She knew with every day now she came nearer to the point where she would get what she wanted and she confessed only to herself that she was impatient till the day would come. In the meantime she trained like possessed, and her body came back into the old good shape of a trained woman.

And just over a month later – after Hayley had got ahead of Arthur, Rick and... Harry – she and her friends got called down into the Temple of Freedom...

Hayley saw astonished that the temple area was full of people, dressed in simple black. But she hadn't any time to wonder about it, as the High Priest called out: "Kneel down in front of the altar!"

Hayley stepped into the temple and in front of the altar. There she knelt down and put her head down in awe.

Arthur and Rick exchanged a look then they followed and knelt down beside Hayley, Arthur to her right, Rick at her left side.

"We are here to celebrate the first Fighters of Freedom! But..." The priest stopped and looked confused at the empty pillow on the ground in front of the altar, beside Rick.

Hayley looked to the right and at Arthur; he nodded at her. Then she looked to the left and got the agreement from Rick. At last she opened her mouth and said quietly into the silence: "Harry! You're needed here!"

"Am I?" An astonished voice came back.

Hayley turned her head a bit and pointed over to the last pillow.

Out of the back a shadow moved forwards and Harry came towards the altar. He looked surprised but Hayley smiled at him and he knelt down on the pillow in front of the altar.

The priest started from the beginning: "We are here to celebrate the first Fighters of Freedom. We are here to give them our support and want to encourage them to stay always at the side of Harder, God of Freedom. Their way may go over a difficult path but with our support they will never leave the path. Let's pray!" And during the loud outspoken prayer the priest went over to Hayley, lifted her chin and drew a sign on her face. Then he asked her to get up and slowly Hayley got up.

Two priests stepped into her back and laid a wide long black cloak around her shoulders. Then one of them took her hair into his hands and rolled the red curls till he had the control over it. He wound a black band around it and knotted it carefully.

Finally a forth priest stepped forward with a long but small scarf in his hand. He laid one end on Hayley's shoulder then he wound the scarf around Hayley's head till only her eyes were visible. Nothing else was to be seen anymore, even not her fire red curls.

Satisfied the priest stepped back again.

The High Priest came up to Hayley again and laid his hands on her head. He murmured some words; Hayley couldn't understand then he pressed her down on the pillow again.

The High Priest turned to Arthur and the procedure repeated itself. Then it went on with Rick and finally with Harry.

The High Priest started to sing a melody, which the men in the temple picked up, and the priests dropped some water from behind on the heads of the Fighters.

Half an hour longer the Fighters had to kneel in front of the altar during the High Priest followed up with the celebration before he came to the main point. "The legends tell us that a woman with red hair will destroy the kingdom. In her company are four men, her best friends and also some riders. But at the moment there are not enough. Is there perhaps anybody who wants to ride with and as a Fighter of Freedom?"

For a moment it was quiet in the temple.

Suddenly a voice could be heard: "Not as Fighter but as friend I would like to join the group and ride with them." Priest Alfonso stepped forward and knelt down in front of the altar beside Harry on the blank stone.

The High Priest nodded calmly. "I knew it would be you who will look after them. Our best wishes are going with you, Priest Alfonso." And he bowed slightly.

Completely in silence some of the men dressed in black got up and knelt down behind Hayley and her friends.

Again the High Priest nodded. "It's time for us to leave now, my friends. You Fighters will stay here for the rest of the day and the night in order to get to know each other. Tomorrow we will give you your camels, food and drink for your way. After that you can go on your way to get what you want with Harder's help. We here did what we could to prepare you for your task; there's nothing more we could do. Good luck!" The High Priest bowed to the Fighters of Freedom, turned and left the temple.

The priests followed him in silence.

Hayley felt in her back that the other men had got up as well and disappeared now back to the outside. She turned her head to the side and threw a look backwards. After she noticed that they were alone in the temple, she made a sign, turned and, using the pillow as seat, sat down in front of the other Fighters who still knelt on the stone floor.

Arthur, Rick, Harry and Priest Alfonso followed her example.

"Why don't you sit down?" Hayley asked quietly. "As we will spend a long time down here, we should make it comfortable for ourselves."

One of the men who knelt in front of her lifted his head. "Well," he started but Hayley shook her head. "Will, don't start again! Sit down!"

Will hesitated then he sat down to the side and pulled his legs into the front. Calmly he looked over at her.

And all the other men followed his example.

"One question", Hayley counted the men fast through and noted that fifteen men had accepted to come with her. "Why do you want to come with me?" She looked from one to the next.

Will frowned. "Well, it's a holy journey – even if you may not see it like that. We want to be part of it, a good reason."

"Are you the speaker of everybody?" Hayley asked amused.

Will blushed. He let his head sink down and didn't say anything anymore.

Hayley sighed inwardly. Carefully she took the scarf off her head; the priest had put around, and pulled the band out of her hair. She shook her long fire red curls and laid the scarf to the side. Then she examined the men in front of her again but without Will she recognized nobody. "Listen!" She said calmly. "When we want to work as a team together then it's the best you forget at first the legend and everything connected with that. All I want to do is having my revenge, that's what keeps me going – and I'm the one who would be honoured if you would help me. Everything altogether – we should see that we get to know each other and you should know that you can talk freely to me – if you want to stay with me." She added carefully.

The men in front of her exchanged some looks.

Then a big burly man lifted his look and said in a very calm and quiet voice: "The reasons why we want to follow you are different to yours and probably different to the reasons of your friends. We want to follow you but you should never try to change our reasons for that. It would destroy the team."

Hayley nodded. "And your name is?"

"Clarence."

"All right Clarence. Perhaps our reasons are all different but the problem is that we are a team from now on and when you treat me like you did till now – I'll be the one who is leaving the team. Is that clear to you?" Hayley asked urgently.

Clarence stared at her. He swallowed one time then he suddenly jumped up. "If you think we would let you go like that – you are wrong! We are one team like you said and we stay together whatever happens. Fuck you – if you don't start to accept what you are and whatever you do that you will never get rid of us!"

Hayley leaned over to Arthur and murmured: "Did you hear that? He can swear!"

Arthur who laid the scarf from his head over his shoulder grinned back. "Was this what you wanted?" He inquired.

"Something similar to that," Hayley confessed. She turned back to Clarence and looked at him. She stared so intensive at him that Clarence started to feel uncomfortable. He blushed slightly and looked around, as if he would search for help.

The other men stared to the ground and didn't dare to say something.

"Hayley – stop!" Arthur laid his hand on Hayley's shoulder.

Astonished Hayley turned around to him. "What shall I stop? I didn't do anything."

Rick on the other side grinned. "Don't you know that a look out of your green eyes is a terrible thing to bear? If you go on like this you will be able – one day – to kill somebody with this look. And see what you did with Clarence! At first you manage that he acts like a normal man and then you put him back into his old position through staring at him. He's completely confused now."

Hayley stared speechlessly at Rick. She frowned till she noticed what Rick had said. Then she tipped with her finger against her forehead and said mockingly: "You're crazy!" She turned back to Clarence who still stood nervously in front of her. "Ignore him! From time to time he has such a crazy flash. – At least I'm happy that you showed me that you still could react like a normal man. I like it more to have men around me who are swearing than chatting sweet. Do you think you can keep that up?"

Clarence examined her astonished. "Aren't you angry with me?"

"Why should I?"

"Well," Clarence stopped and finally shrugged his shoulders. He grinned. "I start to understand what you mean. It's all right with me."

"Fine," Hayley smiled at him. "Who of you will be your leader?" She asked into the round.

"I don't understand." Another man looked up at her. "You are the leader."

"That's not what I mean." Hayley answered. "I don't know most of you and I need somebody I can turn to if there is a problem. At least till we get to know each other better."

The man agreed. "Okay. As far as I know – you know Will and you got to know Clarence. You can choose yourself."

Hayley smiled at him. "Well," she started, imitating Clarence, "I could choose but I don't want to, as this person has to represent you. And it doesn't matter if I know the person already or not. Why don't you discuss it for a moment? We'll leave you alone for a moment." She gave a sign to Arthur and got up. Then she looked down at Rick and said loudly: "Move your ass up from here! We have to go to the back!"

Rick smiled again. He turned to Harry; during he got up and said mockingly: "Did you hear the sweet voice? I love it – again and again!"

Harry laughed only loudly.

17

Hayley went over to a dark corner at the other side of the temple and sat down. With her back she leaned against the wall and closed her eyes.

"One question to you now," Harry sat down beside her and observed her steadily.

Hayley opened her eyes again and turned her head into his way. "What is it?" She asked curiously.

Harry looked for the right words. "Why? I mean – why did you ask me to come forward and join your team? Why did you ask me?"

Hayley threw a helpless look over at Arthur before she answered slowly: "There are two reasons: for one, I think Arthur infected me with the legend. It says that four men – a guard, a thief, a sword master and a priest – are always at... my side. Well, a guard and a thief are already around me and I knew that Al wanted to join us. And you are a sword master, aren't you?"

Harry nodded, and Hayley continued: "Secondly, you asked me to one time yourself. Don't you remember? It was on my first walk outside with my son. As everybody..." She stopped.

Harry nodded. "I remember. But I didn't know that you took that seriously. I mean..."

"Don't you want to come with me?" Hayley asked surprised.

Harry sighed. "No, I really like to come with you. It's only..." Again he stopped himself.

Hayley turned to him. "Tell me – what is it? We shouldn't have any secrets for one another, that wouldn't be good, as we have to work strongly together." She inquired.

Harry still hesitated.

Priest Alfonso looked over at him. "Tell her. She needs to know what you feel."

Hayley frowned.

Harry sighed. "It's only – err – I was in your house, the night, the first night of Arthur and Rick in the temple." He confessed finally quietly.

"Wait." Arthur frowned. "You mean the night Hayley, Rick and I slept together?"

Harry nodded.

Hayley understood. With a smile on her lips she said quietly: "And you would have liked to join us, wouldn't you? But you didn't dare to come completely inside, did you?"

Harry stared embarrassed onto the ground.

Hayley sighed. "I can't sleep with every man who is attracted to me."

For a moment they were quiet; everybody stared in front of each other, never noticing something from the others.

It was Rick who finally broke the silence. "Al, did you swear to stay abstinence?" He asked out of his thoughts.

Priest Alfonso shook his head, "God, no. Why should I? But what has that to do with everything?"

"Well," Rick leaned back, turning to Hayley. "I think, Hayley, you have to see everything from another point of view. If you take Arthur away; it's only a connection between us. I mean, err, I don't know what I mean." He suddenly stopped.

Hayley frowned deeply.

But Arthur understood. "What Rick means, is, that it is you who is talking the whole time about being a team. But Rick, you and I shared something together what made a firm connection between us. And the rest is jealous of it. That means – if you want to have a firm team – I mean, if you wish to have a firm team around you who you can trust, you have to share with everybody what you shared till now only with Rick and me."

Hayley sighed. "With other words: Only if I sleep with all of you, I will have the guarantee that we are – friends. And that I can trust you, right?"

Rick grinned. "Jealousy can go unexpected ways. Will you risk anything?"

"I would risk everything already if I would do it. Don't you think so?" Hayley mocked back.

Arthur examined her astonished. "Why are you so – so mockingly? Is it so absurd what we just said?"

Hayley hesitated. "It's only so that I can hear clearly that you both want to sleep with me as well. I... I don't know what to say."

"Say yes." Arthur smiled softly at her. He threw a look over at the group of men at the other side of the temple and continued: "I think the guys will still need some time to discuss everything. Prove to us that you mean what you say."

"Here and now?" Hayley was for a second terrified.

Priest Alfonso shook his head. "Not here. At the side here is a small room; there is nothing in it but for that case." He shrugged his shoulders.

Hayley sighed. She looked from one to another and finally got up. "Well, let's see. But I don't think I can manage all of you at once."

Arthur grinned. "Go and wait! I think we can organize the rest."

With a shrug of her shoulders Hayley left the group and went into the room Priest Alfonso had pointed out to her. Inside the room she looked around.

It was true that the room was empty but it was clean.

Hayley pulled the cloak away from her shoulders and laid it down on the ground. Then she sat down on it, laid her swords down beside her, lay finally down and waited in patience of what would happen next.

"We know exactly that you are not really in the mood for that. But perhaps we can change that." Arthur sat down beside Hayley and wiped a hair out of her face.

Hayley smiled. "I know that you all are in the mood. And I accept your reasons, so I'm sure I will come into the right mood." She turned her head and looked at Priest Alfonso. "But I must say – I'm surprised about your choice." She turned back to Arthur.

Arthur grinned embarrassed. "Well, I thought it would be good to have him near me, as I think he can understand what I feel – and can stop me when I go too far."

Hayley laughed. "That makes me feel much more comfortable now." She grinned.

Arthur smiled, as he bent over her and kissed her softly.

Hayley laid one arm around him and replied the kiss carefully. Her other arm still lay stretched out beside her.

Priest Alfonso sat down and took her hand. Softly he began to kiss Hayley's finger.

Arthur stretched himself and pulled Hayley up. Hayley came up just in front of Priest Alfonso and looked at him. Al used the opportunity and kissed Hayley softly on the mouth. He stretched his tongue out into her mouth and started to discover everything.

Hayley grew a bit excited, as she felt his tongue and she responded at once on him. She didn't notice that Arthur had opened the leather strings of her waistcoat and his own and finally pulled his off. Then he took off his shirt before he pressed himself against Hayley's back and started to stroke her softly.

Hayley removed her lips from Al's and sighed lightly. She pulled at her waistcoat and Al and Arthur responded on it. Together they pulled the waistcoat off her and threw it to the side. Then Al started to unbutton her shirt during Arthur pushed it up from the back.

Hayley leaned against him and closed her eyes. Her hands slipped over Al's shoulders and stroked him over throat and cheeks.

"You already saw me naked." Al grinned, as he took her hands and led them down to the beginning of his dress.

Hayley grabbed after his dress and pulled it over Al's head. Then she threw it to the ground.

Al opened the last button of Hayley's shirt and Arthur pulled it away. Then Arthur opened the bra and as it fell down, Al stared at her. "You are beautiful." He said quietly and started to stroke her softly over the breasts.

Hayley lay down again and she pulled both men with her.

Arthur bent over her and kissed her, first softly then wild.

Al laid his hands down on Hayley's breasts and massaged them hard. Then he pressed his lips on her nipples and licked them vigorously.

Hayley turned her lips away from Arthur's and groaned deeply. She laid her hand on Al's head and cramped it into his hair.

Arthur kissed softly her cheeks then he went down over her throat and the shoulder till he reached her breast. He released Al and started to kiss Hayley around the breasts, then sucking and licking at her nipples till they grew hard under his touch.

Al pressed in the meantime his lips on her mouth and they kissed each other wildly.

Arthur went with his hands down her body and opened her trousers. He got up, pulled her complete clothes down and then his own. Finally he lay down again, pressed his mouth again on her breasts during his hand went down and stroked her softly between her legs, which were slightly apart.

Again Hayley turned her head away, this time from Al, and groaned loudly. Al bit into her earlobe and kissed her on her cheek. Hayley laid her arms around him and stroked him softly, trembling herself a lot.

Arthur went down her body and pressed his face down between her legs. He searched with his tongue for the right spot and licked her intensive there.

Hayley groaned again.

Al pressed his hands on Hayley's breasts and massaged them again. He licked her nipples and bit them carefully.

Hayley trembled; she tried to close her legs, which didn't work, as Arthur was still sitting between them and kissing her on the spot. Finally she groaned loudly.

Arthur slipped a bit up and pressed his way deep down into her.

Hayley groaned up again and Al lay down beside her. Arthur lay down completely on her and pressed more till he groaned up as well. Satisfied he rolled to the side.

Before Hayley could relax, Al was over her again. He kissed her wildly, one hand pressing her breast hard and one leg between hers. He was completely naked; he never wore something under his robe.

Hayley was soon out of breath again and she groaned once more after Al gave her mouth free and pressed his on her breasts. She didn't notice that Arthur had dressed and had slipped out of the room and that somebody else had come inside. She only noted that it had happened, as another mouth was pressed down on her lips.

Harry was at least as wild as Al, perhaps even more. He discovered Hayley's mouth completely with his tongue and licked her tongue intensive, which made Hayley crazy. She embraced him hard, noticing astonished that he had already undressed.

Al bent down between her legs and discovered Hayley's spot with the finger. He rubbed her over the spot and opened her softly up before he bent completely down and kissed her there gently.

At the same moment Harry gave Hayley free, and Hayley groaned loudly. She still embraced Harry firmly, and Harry kissed her all over her face. Hayley breathed kisses on his face as well, every time she hadn't to groan.

Al pushed his hands under Hayley's bottom and lifted her softly. He slipped nearer to her and pressed his way into her, still sitting on the ground. Holding Hayley firmly at her hips, he pressed her again and again hard against himself.

Harry finally pulled Hayley up till she sat on Al's lab and, as he hadn't moved, direct in front of him. They kissed each other again and Hayley pressed herself down on Al till he started to groan as well.

Harry pressed himself against the back of Hayley and his hands wandered forward and lay down on her breasts and massaged them.

Then Al lay down on his back and pulled Hayley with him till she finally lay completely on him. Astonished she looked at him but she grew more astonished, as she felt Harry at her bottom, forcing his way from behind into her. She groaned up, not knowing what happened to her.

Al stretched his tongue into her mouth, touching hers but without pressing his lips on hers. So both of them were free to groan every time they felt they had to. And they had to quite often.

Harry pressed Hayley's breasts hard, pushing against her once more and at least groaning up in excitement. Then he lay down on Hayley and sighed.

"How often did you do that already to a woman?" Hayley asked curiously, as she had caught breath again.

"Well, quite often." Al grinned at her.

Harry nodded, softly stroking her over the back. "And they always liked it very much." He added.

"You can put me into this category as well." Hayley sighed, "Crazy – but very good."

"I would like to take you from the front as well." Harry whispered into her ear.

"Then you have to get up that I can get up." Hayley grinned.

Harry solved himself from Hayley, and Hayley got up. She winked at Al who turned then away to get dressed again during Hayley lay down on her back. For a moment she breathed deeply in and pressed her legs together. Then she relaxed and looked up at Harry.

Harry pressed Hayley's legs apart again and sat down between them. He stretched his finger out and laid it on Hayley's spot where he started to rub her softly.

Hayley supported herself on her arms and looked at Harry. "Wanting to get me straight up again?" She grinned and couldn't stop her legs to react on what Harry was doing.

"Yes certainly. As long as you can keep it up," Harry grinned.

"Not long. I'm too excited for that." Hayley lay back down and bit on her lips during she tried to hold her legs straight. But Harry bent forward and started to lick her intensive at her spot.

At this moment somebody pressed his mouth on Hayley's breast and massaged the other one wildly.

Hayley groaned loudly again and what she experienced now, she never expected.

Harry forced his way into her, pushing it five times deep into her before he let her go. In the next moment Rick was over her, pushing his way into her, five times pressing hard then he sat down beside her again.

Once more Harry was over her and during he found his way firmly into her, he pushed his tongue into Hayley's mouth and kissed her hard.

Again they exchanged and Rick pressed Hayley's breasts during he pushed against her.

Hayley groaned and she couldn't stop anymore. She didn't know who of the men was in her and who beside her and she didn't care. Kissing the men, trembling and groaning was all she could do and all she wanted at that moment.

Harry groaned up, as he was just pushing against her and holding her breast hard. He let her go and rolled to the side.

Before Hayley could react, Rick was over her again and once more he found his way into her. He pushed and pushed, pressing his mouth onto hers and massaging her breast. Hayley felt helpless under him, unable to do something and groaning up so that her mouth got firmly sought against Rick's.

Rick solved his lips and groaned up as well. He fell down on Hayley and sighed.

"Was it now so bad?" Rick turned to Hayley after he had given her free.

Hayley shook her head. "No. Now I know at last how crazy you all are." She answered with a grin.

"Good. So it should be." Harry smiled at her during he dressed. "Are you coming as well?"

"Give me five minutes to recover!" Hayley sighed.

Harry and Rick nodded and left the room after they had dressed.

Hayley lay quietly on the ground and had closed her eyes.

"Do I disturb you?" Arthur asked quietly, as he sat down beside her.

Hayley opened her eyes again and smiled at Arthur. "No, you don't disturb me. As a matter of fact – I was waiting for you."

"How did you know that I would come again?" Arthur asked astonished.

Hayley sat up and looked straight into Arthur's eyes. "You were so fast, so different from the last time. I couldn't believe that that should have been all." She answered quietly.

"You are right." Arthur smiled lightly. "I hoped you would have a little bit more time for me now – without the others in our back."

Hayley laid her arms around him and sighed quietly: "But you know why I do it?" She asked.

Arthur nodded. "I know." He confirmed and embraced Hayley softly before he laid his lips softly on hers. He pressed her lips apart and discovered lightly her mouth.

Hayley enjoyed the kiss, which was full of love and desire – and all she wanted now.

Arthur's hand slipped over her back, the side – which excited Hayley at once – and came finally to the front, touching and massaging her breasts.

Arthur was completely dressed, and Hayley hadn't any chance to come under his shirt. So she left it with stroking him over his hair and his throat.

Finally Arthur stopped. "Would you do me a favour?" He asked quietly.

"What is it?" Hayley leaned against him.

"Well, can you… I mean… would you…" Arthur stuttered.

Hayley smiled. "Sure I do. No need to stutter." She confirmed calmly and pressed Arthur down till he lay on his back. Then she opened up his trousers and bent down. She led his penis into her mouth and licked him wildly during her hand closed around it and went up and down. She felt his penis growing hard in her mouth and heard Arthur groaning. Then she stopped, swinging her leg over him and pushing his penis down into her. Softly she pressed herself against him, feeling his hands moving up her body and stroking gently over her breasts. She stretched herself, enjoying thoroughly the feeling of his hands on her body and his penis in her. Then she bent forward and kissed Arthur softly.

At last Arthur groaned up and he pulled Hayley down on him.

Hayley lay down with her head on his shoulder.

"Did you enjoy it at least a bit?" Arthur asked quietly, stroking over her face.

Hayley sighed. "I did. I don't need to have an orgasm the whole time, only to prove to everybody that I enjoyed it. Sometimes the quiet way is the best way."

Arthur laid his arm around her and pressed her softly. "The only thing I don't like is to know that you do something you don't like. But perhaps you will tell me when this will happen."

"Ah, Arthur," Hayley smiled. "You can do whatever you want with me – it never will be wrong!"

Arthur pressed Hayley against him and turned till Hayley lay on her back and he was on top of her. "Do you know what you are saying there?" He asked quietly, searching through her face.

Hayley looked at him. "I know what I say. It's an offer I made till today only to one person, as you know. But I think to make this offer to you – it will give us the opportunity to get what we need – and it will give me the safety of knowing that you will always stay at my side."

Arthur stroked gently over her face. "Don't you really know that you don't need to make this offer to me? That, I will always be at your side?" He hesitated before he continued: "The others will be satisfied with the bond we just made. Through that they always will be at your side as well. I don't need that bond. You should know that by now. I can't change – I'll be satisfied already to be near you."

Hayley looked clearly at him. "But it's not enough for me." She answered quietly, embracing him firmly. Then she sighed again. "The others will be waiting for us already. We should see that we dress and join them again." She stroked him softly but then she moved a bit to the side.

Arthur gave her free and closed his trousers again. Interested he observed how Hayley got dressed again then he got up and opened the door to the outside.

Both left the room and joined the others in the corner.

18

Rick, Harry and Priest Alfonso stared at Hayley and Arthur.

"Everything okay," Priest Alfonso asked gently, as Hayley sat down beside him.

Hayley examined him and turned then her eyes over to Harry and Rick. She asked quietly: "Do we have a strong bond now?" And she stretched her right hand out into the circle.

Arthur laid his hand on hers; his fingers enclosed hers.

Rick followed his example after a moment; closing his hand around the other two.

Harry sighed. He laid his hand on top of the others and pressed them.

Priest Alfonso stretched out his hands and enclosed the other hands from the top and the bottom. "I think we have here a very strong bond." He answered and pressed the hands firmly.

Hayley smiled.

As they just solved their hands, a quiet voice asked: "May I disturb you for a moment?"

Hayley looked up. "Who are you?"

"I'm Nick Bolder. " The young man introduced himself. "The others decided to make me to their leader."

"Okay Nick. Sit down." Hayley offered him a seat in her circle. Then she continued: "I'm Hayley, that's Arthur, Rick, Harry and Priest Alfonso."

Nick nodded at the others during he sat down and the others stared curiously at him.

"So you know the others all quite well?" Hayley inquired.

Nick nodded. "Yes, since a long time already."

"Okay. Then I will tell you why I wanted to have a leader…" Hayley started but got interrupted from Nick at once: "Because you don't know them?" He asked solemnly.

Arthur grinned. "At least he's not stupid."

Hayley pushed him her elbow into the side. "Shut up!" She said and turned back to Nick. "That's only one of the reasons. But the main factor is that sometimes the situation asks for some special requests and I need you in these situations to find at once the right person for doing the job. Do you understand what I mean?"

"Well," Nick started but got this time interrupted from Hayley. "If I ask you now that I would need two men who can walk without making any sound – who would you send to me?"

"Will and Jean," It came back like a pistol shot.

Hayley nodded, "All right. I see you understand. But be also aware that your position is absolute important. If you make a wrong decision, our lives can hang on that. All of our lives!" She added urgently.

Nick only nodded.

Rick bent over to Hayley and whispered something into her ear.

For a moment Hayley looked thoughtfully at him then she nodded. Again she turned to Nick and ordered clearly: "I would need now two men who are good in hiding in shadows. Also they should be quite powerful." She looked asking at him.

Nick needed only a second to decide. He turned his head and called loudly: "Clarence! Martin! Come over here!"

Two men got up and came fast over to the small group in the corner.

Hayley nodded at Rick, and Rick got up. "I think we need to organize some food and drinks. Come with me!" He said to the two men and went over to the next door. He opened it – only Harder knew how – and slipped through it.

Clarence and Martin followed him at once.

In the meantime Hayley got up and said calmly: "We should join the others. Perhaps you can introduce everybody to us, Nick?"

Nick got up as well and nodded.

Arthur, Harry and Priest Alfonso followed their example and together the four men and the woman went over to the rest of the Fighters who were still sitting in front of the altar.

Hayley sat down at the edge of the group without the Fighters noticing her, as they turned their eyes over at Nick and the others who sat down in front of the group by the altar.

At a nod of Hayley, Nick started the introduction: "Well, Will you know already. He is specialist in knife throwing – if you ever need that, he can do it for you. At his right side is Damon, well, he is a dreamer. You will find out soon what that means. Gerry and Richard, Jean and Ian, Guy and Sean, Brad and Austin, Mick, Ken and Hank are Sword Dancers like you are. Everybody of them has his special talent but that's a bit difficult to explain now."

"Why did you explain then Damon?" Arthur hummed.

Nick threw a look at him. "I think it's important that you get to know him. He is, well – find it out for yourself."

Hayley examined the dark man interested from the side.

Damon gave the impression of being the black man. Dressed completely in black like all the others but with his dark skin, black hair and, how Hayley noticed later on, black eyes he was a dark figure. He held his eyes closed during his introduction and had only a light-mocking smile on his lips.

Hayley asked herself what he was thinking at the moment. His introduction had been mysterious, and she really wanted to know why. But she foresaw that it wasn't the right moment now.

"There we are!" A funny voice sounded through the Temple.

Rick stepped up to the altar and threw a big black sack on it. Clarence followed with a second sack and Martin carried a basket with – wine bottles. They started to unpack and put everything nicely out on the altar.

Brad made a slushy sound, and Arthur turned grinning around to him. "It's for you, so get it. Enjoy!" He slipped to the side, giving the way to the altar free.

Brad got up and went over to the altar. He wasn't the kind of man who you had to tell everything twice. Normally – and especially when it went around food and drinks – he obeyed the first order.

The other men followed him slowly. They chose their food carefully and shared together some of the bottles of wine.

After they had settled down again, Arthur, Rick, Harry and Priest Alfonso got something for themselves, only Hayley waited a little bit longer. She was sitting in her corner and frowned during she observed the men.

Arthur noticed that Hayley didn't move, as he just wanted to sit down again. He stopped, placed his plate on the ground and stepped back to the altar. He filled a second plate, picked up another glass and bottle and got finally his own stuff. Then he went over to Hayley in her corner and sat down beside her. "You have to eat something as well." He said quietly and reached her the plate.

Hayley examined him thoughtfully. "Perhaps I should." She confirmed quietly, accepting the plate after a long time.

Arthur filled a glass of wine for her.

Quietly they ate and drank till they finished everything on their plates and in the bottle. Then Hayley leaned back and closed her eyes. "I'm tired." She murmured.

Arthur laid his arm around her shoulder and whispered: "Do you want to lie down in the small room where we were before or do you want to rest here?"

Hayley sighed. "Don't make it so complicated. I lie down here where I am." And she turned, laid her head on Arthur's lab and closed her eyes. A minute later she was deeply asleep.

The Fighters still talked together but time after time the men lie down as well and fell asleep.

Rick and Harry crouched together behind the altar for a nap, only Priest Alfonso stayed awake for a little bit longer. He observed with a smile on his lips Arthur who drifted away for some seconds till his head fell onto his chest so that he woke up again. But Arthur didn't dare to move, afraid that Hayley might wake up again.

But at last even Arthur and Priest Alfonso fell deeply asleep.

19

Next morning, as the High Priest entered the Temple, the Fighters of Freedom were all awake and looked more or less fit.

"Come with me!" The High Priest ordered shortly and stepped through the Temple to the other side where he opened a door. He stepped up the staircase, along the corridor, through the entrance hall and finally through the door to the outside.

The Fighters of Freedom followed him in silence. Already now, the levels of authority in the team were clear: Hayley, as the leader, was the first one behind the High Priest then followed Arthur, Rick and Harry.

Nick, as leader of the Fighters, was the next one to follow, the team closely behind him.

As last one, Priest Alfonso stepped into the fresh morning air, observing everything and everybody, having all in his eyes.

The High Priest went straight over to the gate in the wall, which enclosed the complete area of the village, the fields and the Temple of Freedom. The gate was open and outside it was possible to see the village people beyond a row of camels.

The High Priest stopped and turned around to Hayley: "We promised you to give our best camels to you – what we do now. The first one, the big dark brown one, is yours. It's the most powerful and fastest camel we have. Now," the High Priest examined Hayley carefully, "I wish you that you will find what you are searching for. I think you are good prepared and you will make us proud of you. Harder, God of Freedom will be on your side; never hesitate but if you need help – come back to us. We're also prepared."

Hayley had laid the black scarf around her head so that only her eyes were visible.

The High Priest made the sign of Freedom in front of Hayley's face and finally over her head. "Remember always the oath you gave to Harder! If you stand with your oath, nothing will happen to you." He murmured again then he released Hayley and turned to Arthur. The same procedure went on...

Hayley turned around and took the reins of the big brown camel, which had been led over to her. Still she didn't climb up the camel; she looked searching around.

A woman stepped out of the darkness of a corner, as if she had waited for Hayley to appear - which was the complete truth. She had a baby in her arms, which she carefully turned that Hayley could see its face.

Hayley smiled under her scarf, and she nodded at Arachnarella who nodded back at her. Then Hayley turned away, climbed up her camel and looked at the Fighters.

Arthur, Rick and Harry were already on their camels, also Nick and a few of the others. The rest of the Fighters followed one by one till only Priest Alfonso was left.

Priest Alfonso kissed the big ring on the High Priest's left hand and bowed at the same moment.

The High Priest made a hand movement over his head and, as he pressed his hands as goodbye, he said calmly: "We organized for you a wagon, pulled by horses. We thought it would be better and much more suitable for you as to ride on a camel. Also you need to take food and water with you, which we loaded into the wagon. – Keep a good eye on the Fighters! - Freedom for you, my son!" he finished up.

Priest Alfonso bowed a last time and turned then to the wagon and the horses, which had been led over to him. He climbed up the wagon and sat down during he picked up the reins.

Hayley, who had waited for this moment, gave the sign to depart. She gave the camel the head free that it could run like it wanted and held only softly the reins.

The camel started to walk over the grass and the others followed. At last the horses pulled the wagon forwards and half an hour later the Fighters of Freedom were out of sight of the Temple of Freedom.

"Where are we going to?" Arthur pulled his camel up next to Hayley's.

Hayley sighed. "Now where the time is here, I don't know any more if it's right what I want to do." She murmured. Then she noticed that Arthur examined her astonished and continued, more confident: "I had a look onto the map. We are on the way back to Prince Alban and his town and his palace. I have something to do there – also I promised two women there to take them with me when I leave. I couldn't do it before, as you know, so I have to do it now. Finally I have to keep my promise, haven't I?"

"You have." Arthur smiled.

Another camel came nearer from backwards.

"Sorry to disturb." Nick grinned innocently. "The guys only want to know when we break up for a rest. We are not used to riding for hours without any breaks and we really would need one now, before we all get sore." He looked at Hayley.

Hayley sighed. "We break up for a rest at the next possible place. Here it wouldn't be good, as we could get killed here in this trap. We should see that we get out of here as soon as possible." She pushed her camel forwards, and Arthur followed her at once.

Nick informed the Fighters, and they rode on.

Two hours later the Fighter of Freedom came to a wide grass area, lying between some hills.

Hayley stopped her camel and gave the sign to stop for a break. As she climbed down from her camel, she felt as well stiff and sore from the ride.

The rest of the Fighters were groaning and they stretched out on the grass.

Only Priest Alfonso seemed to be fit; he gave a bit of food and some water out to the Fighters before he thought about getting some rest as well.

Hayley stretched out between Arthur and Rick and crossed her arms under her head.

Both Arthur and Rick turned to her and looked asking at her but Hayley didn't say anything.

Finally it grew too much for Rick and he murmured: "What will we do now?"

Hayley threw a side look at him. "I just thought about it. With the camels we have to go more around the hills, so it will take some time to come to Prince Alban's town. Till then we should be at home on the camel's backs and..." She hesitated. She got a little bit up and called: "Nick! Come over here!"

At the other end a man got up and came over to where Hayley and the other leaders were laying on the grass.

"What can I do for you?" Nick asked calmly.

"Sit down and rest as long as there is time." Hayley answered shortly and observed the man who sat down and stretched himself out on the grass in front of Hayley's feet. Then she turned back to Arthur: "Do you have any experience in killing people?"

Arthur nodded. "You know that I was a guard. It belonged to my job, sometimes, to kill people." He confessed quietly.

Hayley turned to Rick and looked asking at him.

Rick sighed. "Well, I normally would never have done it but…"

"Come out with it!" Hayley nodded at him reassuring.

Rick closed his eyes. "I broke once into a house I thought would be empty. It wasn't and the owner was quite… well, I had no other chance than to kill him."

"And you can do it again – when the situation asks for it?" Hayley inquired.

Rick looked at her. "For that I trained." He confirmed.

"Harry?" Hayley turned to the next man beside Rick.

Harry hummed only.

"Yes or no," Hayley asked grinning.

Harry looked over at her. "I'm a Sword-Master. Yes, I did kill people before for good reasons and I would do it again – for a good reason."

"You get your good reason." Hayley turned away and sat up. She examined Nick and asked quietly: "What is with you, Nick?"

Nick nodded. "I had to – and I can do it again."

Hayley didn't let him go. "And the others?" she asked curiously.

Nick shrugged his shoulders. "There are some who never have done it. They got trained at the temple, waiting for this chance. Like all of us; not one will refuse to follow an order you give, even when it means to kill somebody." He answered seriously.

Hayley leaned back again. She stared for a moment into the sky before she said quietly: "I don't know if you will be in danger to have to kill somebody, probably only in self-defence. I'll show you the town from the outside – then I need a good plan to come into the town without killing too many people."

Nick felt positive about that and said it: "That won't be a problem."

Arthur looked frowning at him before he looked at Hayley: "And then?"

Hayley sighed. "I will kill Prince Alban; I have to."

Nick sat up and examined the woman in front of him. "So you're sure to make the legend really come true?" He asked astonished.

Hayley looked at him. "Why are you so surprised?" She asked calmly. "As far as I know, most of you only come with me because of that they think the legend is now to come true."

"Well, yes." Nick answered slowly. "But…"

Hayley shook her head. "Listen, Nick. I heard first of the legend in the temple, as Arthur told me about it. At this time I had already made up my mind – I want to have revenge for everything what happened to my friends and me. And that's now exactly what I intend to do – legend or not." She was silent for a moment before she continued calmer: "You and your friends – you should decide now if you still want to go with me or not. If you decide not to, you are still near enough the Temple to find your way back. If you decide to come with me, you have to get used to the fact that I do what I have to do. – Go now and tell the others! Make your decision – and make it soon!" She pushed him away.

Nick followed the order and went over to his friends. Shortly after, he was talking to them urgently.

Arthur whispered quietly into Hayley's ear: "Why did you do that? Will you get them out of your way?"

"No." Hayley whispered back. "But I think that they didn't know till now what I meant to do. It's better when they hear it now before it is too late – because I won't change my mind anymore."

Arthur nodded. "And what will you do after you killed Prince Alban?"

Hayley hesitated. "I have to look after the women in the harem. You know I promised two of them to bring them away."

Arthur confirmed it. "But what's then?"

"Then", Hayley sighed again, "then we go to the next one on my list."

Before Arthur or one of the others could say something, a voice joined in again: "Did you ever think about that you may not be able to kill the prince? What shall we do then?"

Hayley looked up at Nick who had spoken. "I never think that I can't do it. I've got a good training and I'm able to kill somebody. And – don't I have the legend in my back?" She mocked.

Nick shook his head, as he sat down again. "Why don't we forget the legend from now on? First of all you should prove to us that you mean what you say."

"You can have that." Hayley agreed. She got up. "We go on!" She said and caught her camel.

The Fighters got up and climbed on their camels.

Five minutes later, the Fighters were on their way again.

20

Seven days after the Fighters had started out for their journey, they reached the border of the town where Prince Alban lived. They could clearly see the wall around the town, the houses and a little bit higher up, the palace.

Hayley brought her camel to a sudden stop. She stared over to the gate in the wall and frowned for a moment. Then she slowly grew angry, her eyes sparkled and her hands cramped around the saddle till the blood was pushed out of her fists and the bones were clearly to see.

Arthur examined her astonished. "What is it, Hayley?"

Hayley didn't react; she still stared down at the gate.

Arthur followed her look and frowned. Then he got up and stared down at the gate as well.

On the top of the wall, direct over the gate, a wooden rack had been installed. At this rack a woman was tied to, good visible for everybody who came nearer to the town. She must have been hanging there already for a long time; her face was fallen in and she seemed to be a skeleton without flesh now. Only one thing was still good visible – the long black hair.

"Do you know her?" Arthur asked quietly.

Hayley nodded. "Yes, I do. That's... that's Amanda, my friend I had to leave back." She hummed angrily and continued then: "The bastard will pay for that as well!" She turned around and called at Nick: "Nick, I need somebody here with a high intelligence and fix ideas! Hurry up!"

Nick nodded and turned his camel. He searched under the Fighters till he found for whom he was searching for and sent him straight over to Hayley.

Stunned Hayley looked at Damon, as he stopped his camel beside hers. "You were looking for me? How can I help?"

"Well," Hayley doubted Nick's intelligence but decided to give it a go. "We need to come into this town unseen and unheard. Finally we want to surprise everybody – and Prince Alban especially."

Damon nodded and looked down at the town, "Unseen and unheard? That's wrong." He murmured and frowned deeply.

Hayley picked it up. "What do you mean?"

Damon turned to her. "It's impossible to come inside there – unseen and unheard. There is only one possibility for us, which will work well, as nobody knows us till now."

"Which possibility is it?" Hayley grew impatient.

Damon smiled. "Did you ever come on the idea that they don't know you how you are now? Why don't we ride down to the gate and knock on and ask for quarters for the night? Perhaps we even come into the Palace on that way without any great problems. Nobody will know it's you, seeking revenge and nobody will recognize us, as nobody knows us till now as well." He was silent.

Stunned Hayley exchanged a look with Arthur. "Well, yes." Hayley nodded. "You have the right idea. Thanks."

"It was my pleasure." Damon turned his camel but before he rode back he grinned at Hayley: "But you should see that you don't give yourself away. Your eyes and your hands speak a clear language." He pointed at Hayley's hands.

Hayley looked down and at once solved her grab around the saddle. She nodded at Damon who then rode back. Hayley decided fast: "We do it. Let's go!" She gave the sign and pulled at the reins till her camel turned and slowly took the slope down the hill they had been stopped on before.

The Fighters followed her in a row and an hour later they reached the gate of the town.

Hayley looked up at the female skeleton and for a second she flashed her eyes in anger. But then she had herself under control again and gave Harry the sign to knock on the gate.

Harry did it and they waited patiently for a result.

"Who's there and what do you want?" A voice could be heard behind the gate.

Harry answered formal: "We are riders on a long journey. We don't want to do any harm – we're only looking for a meal and bed overnight."

Hayley almost laughed loudly. The lie seemed to be funny to her but she bit on her lips and suppressed the feeling.

The gate was opened carefully and a soldier came to the outside. He examined the group of riders and finally shook his head. "Who are you?" He asked once more.

Harry pulled the scarf down from his face and smiled at the soldier. "We are from the Temple of Freedom. We do look for a good meal and a bed."

"Be patient. We'll ask the Prince if he wants to see you." The soldier stepped inside again and the gate closed behind him.

Harry threw a look over at Hayley but Hayley stared at the gate.

Almost half an hour later the gate opened once more and the same soldier like before stepped outside. "Prince Alban sends his regards. You can stay in the Palace for the night; he said he always offers his help to the Temple of Freedom. Come inside and be welcomed."

Hayley pushed her camel and it stepped through the gate, following the soldier the street up to the Palace. All the others followed her; they grew curious.

In the yard of the Palace they all left the camels in the hands of a stables man and looked interested around.

Hayley noticed that this was the ground where she had been one time before: On the day she had arrived here. She remembered to have seen at that time only the Palace in front of her nose, now she noted as well the beautiful view over the town. Once more she searched in herself for an anchor, and as she thought about her revenge she found the anchor she needed now.

A Palace Guard greeted them friendly and showed them over to a side part of the Palace. "Here you can rest from your ride. Prince Alban awaits you later for dinner in his rooms. I will show you in time." The guard bowed and left the Fighters alone in the big room.

Hayley looked around. "Still, it's comfortable. Who's taking the first watch?"

"Do you really think that's necessary?" Rick asked interested.

Hayley nodded. "I don't trust anybody here. It'll be better if we are on guard that nothing happens to us – before its time."

"I'll be on guard then." Rick nodded and asked two other men with a hand movement to keep on guard as well.

Hayley lay down on a soft bench with pillows. She closed her eyes.

The others, without their guards certainly, followed her example and it grew quiet in the room.

As it got dark outside, the Palace Guard entered the room again and bowed. He then led the Fighters over to a big room where a table with food and drinks and pillows to sit on were prepared. "Have a seat! The Prince will join you soon." The Palace Guard bowed and disappeared.

Hayley stopped at the end of the table, opposite the seats, which were definitely signed out for the Prince and his family. "I better don't sit near the Prince or his family or I won't be able to stop myself." She hummed.

Arthur grinned under his scarf. "What does it matter? If you kill him here or somewhere else, is there a difference?"

"Yes, there is." Hayley suppressed a grin. "Somewhere else I won't have so much witnesses, especially not in the own group."

"I understand." Rick sat down beside Arthur. "You will bring us around the fun to see you fighting."

Hayley rolled her eyes. "You got it!" She mocked and pulled a bit at her scarf that she would be able to eat and drink without taking the scarf down. Carefully she watched that nothing, no hair, really nothing, could be seen.

"Prince Alban, Prince Lateran and their wives." A voice announced, and everybody jumped up again.

Hayley observed her surroundings and looked over to the curtains through which at this moment Prince Alban came. At his side, the arm on his, stepped Shannon along.

Behind them followed the Prince's brother, Prince Lateran, with one of his wives in the arms, Nicole.

Hayley was happy to see the two women and to notice that they looked fine. She was relieved about it but she stepped a bit back, suddenly afraid that they might be able to recognize her. But over the distance of the whole table, it was stupid.

"Welcome to my Palace! You are from the Temple of Freedom?" Prince Alban greeted and turned with his question over at Priest Alfonso who had sat down wisely direct on the first place beside the family.

Priest Alfonso nodded. He mimed the leader at that moment. "Yes, that's right. We are already a long time on the way and very grateful that you allow us to stay here. Freedom to you all!" he finished up.

Prince Alban put his head down for a second. "Freedom to you too." he answered. "It's a pleasure to have you here. Please, take the food; I can get more if it's not enough." He smiled.

The Fighters accepted it and started to eat and drink a lot. They all knew what would happen in the night and they were carefully to eat as double as they drank, only to stay sober.

The only one, who didn't drink and ate, was Hayley. Her throat was sore since she had seen Prince Alban again and she couldn't manage to get something down into her stomach.

"Drink that! It will help you to be able to eat something." Arthur whispered to her and pressed a glass of wine into her hand. "If you don't – he will notice."

Hayley nodded and took the glass. She tried the wine carefully, suppressing the feeling to get sick at once and drank a little bit more. The knot in her stomach vanished and her throat felt better and she looked surprised at Arthur.

Arthur only grinned.

Hayley ate a little bit of bread and fresh fruits during she concentrated on her target. She observed Prince Alban who led an intensive conversation with Priest Alfonso. Also she had the two women in her eyes; the women, who seemed to be happy but didn't eat much, drank almost nothing and didn't say a word. Hayley was convinced that she had to rescue them, somehow.

It was almost midnight, as the Fighters said good night and went back to their quarters. On the way they mysteriously lost some of them; Hayley hid behind a pillar and Arthur behind a curtain. Nick and Damon hid in the next corridor behind some furniture.

Rick and Harry went back with the rest of the group, as Hayley had said that she might need them to keep their backs free.

Hayley followed with her eyes two guards who had in their middle a woman she didn't know. The woman was dressed in a very fine blue dress and the chains she wore over it, still looked familiar to Hayley. She had seen them, as Amanda wore them. This woman was brought from the guards to one of the Prince's.

Hayley decided fast that she would follow them. Perhaps she was lucky to find so Prince Alban…

Hayley followed the guards in a safe distance.

The guards went along some corridors till they stopped in front of a posh door, there wasn't any other explanation. They knocked on and entered the room behind the door, pulling the woman with them. Then the door closed.

Hayley hid behind a curtain.

After a while the door opened again and the two guards left the room. They had the chains in their hands and disappeared some doors further on into another room.

Arthur placed himself beside that door, his sword in his hands and he nodded at Hayley.

Hayley ran up to the door and listened. She heard some whispering and she opened the door very quietly. Then she peeped through the crack.

Shannon was lying on the big bed and stared to the ceiling. She was completely naked.

Prince Alban, dressed only in some pants, went around the other woman and examined her from top to bottom.

The woman trembled at her whole body and she clinched her hands.

As Prince Alban laid his hand on her shoulder and started to open her dress, Hayley pulled her sword out and stepped into the room. "I wouldn't do it if I were you." She said calmly, pointing her sword at Prince Alban.

Prince Alban didn't seem to be surprised. He left his hands sink down and stared at Hayley without recognizing her.

The two women pressed in horror their hands in front of their mouths; Shannon crouching under a blanket and the other woman stepped away from the door and the black figure, which stood there.

"What do you want here? Do you think I entertain you here as well?" Prince Alban was angry over the interruption.

Hayley examined him mockingly. "Well, I'm searching for entertainment but not how you mean it. I'm looking for a partner for a sword fight." She stepped completely inside and closed the door with a kick against it.

"You want a swordfight - now and here? You are crazy." Prince Alban said firmly. "Go – before I call the guards!"

"Call them if you need to. That won't stop me and – yes, I want to fight you now. It's the best time – to kill you!" Hayley smiled under her scarf.

"You want to kill me? Why?" Prince Alban frowned, stepping back to the wall where his sword hung.

Hayley stepped a bit to the left. "Revenge!" she only said.

The woman ran over to the bed to be out of the way.

Prince Alban stopped in the middle of the movement, as he wanted to grab after his sword. "Revenge?" he said astonished. "Revenge for what?"

"For everything you did to me." Hayley answered quietly. "I promised you that you will regret it, don't you remember?" She asked mockingly.

Prince Alban took the sword down and examined the dark figure again. "Who the devil are you?" He asked angrily.

Hayley smiled under her scarf. She took the sword with her left hand and pulled the scarf from her head. Then she threw it on to the bed and shook her long red curls.

"Hayley," Shannon sat up in bed and looked half astonished, half terrified at Hayley.

Prince Alban grinned. "I remember. But I must have made a deep impression on you that you come running along to me."

Hayley looked mockingly at him. "Running to you I wouldn't say. Finally I have a weapon and won't make it easy for you even to come near to me. – Otherwise I got already enough from you. Your son is sweet, much sweeter than you ever can be – and now I only want one more thing – to see you die!" She took the sword back into her right hand.

"Well, I don't like to see you die, as you are still a nice wild cat. When I win, you take your place in my harem again, all right?" Prince Alban saw himself definitely as winner.

Hayley grinned mockingly. "That won't happen!" She promised and lifted her sword.

Prince Alban hit out shortly but Hayley caught the hit without any problems with her sword and she hit out at once again.

For a while the two only exchanged some hits to find out what the other one knew then suddenly Prince Alban let go some hard hits and pressed Hayley so against a corner and brought her into a difficult situation. "Do you give up?"

Hayley grabbed after the top of her sword and pressed against it. "Never!" she said and lifted her leg. Fast she kicked out and hit Prince Alban against his stomach that he flew some steps back and fell against a table. Hayley ran the steps behind him and hit out with her sword. Prince Alban tried to hold the hit but his sword got caught between the legs of the table and he couldn't get it out in time. Hayley's sword hit him full power into the side – he groaned up.

"Get up!" Hayley pressed out. "I don't kill somebody who's helpless."

"Then perhaps I should lie here and not get up." Prince Alban pressed his hand against his side and got very slowly up. His hand cramped around the sword and he turned to Hayley. "That was only luck." He hummed. "And that will change now." He hit out with his sword but Hayley was prepared. She caught the hit and turned it around. She hit out, saw the coverless side and scratched the Prince over his chest.

Prince Alban groaned up. His cover went totally, as he tried to press his hand against his chest and his sword fell to the ground.

"You should finish it now. We haven't so much time anymore before the guards will notice something." Nick said calmly. He leaned against the frame of the door.

Hayley laid her sword on Prince Alban's shoulder and said calmly: "I hope you made your last will." But before the Prince could answer, Hayley took the sword firm into her hand and pulled it over his throat.

Prince Alban broke down; he tried to breath, couldn't and finally it stopped. His eyes broke and then he lay dead on the ground.

Hayley put her sword away again and turned over to the bed. She picked up her scarf and looked over at the two women. "Are you two all right?" She asked carefully.

Shannon looked at her. "So – you really did it. You know that Amanda had to die cause of you?"

"That wasn't to oversee." Hayley nodded.

"And what happens now?" Shannon asked quietly.

"First of all..." Hayley stepped around the bed. "It's good to see you again." She smiled.

Shannon got up, naked how she was and embraced Hayley. "It's good that you're back." She answered quietly. "But what happens now?" She asked again.

Hayley grinned. "First of all – you should dress again. Then Nick will show you where you can stay – without being in danger."

"Then – it's not over?" Shannon sank back onto the bed.

"It just started." Hayley said calmly and patted her friend on the shoulder. "Dress now."

Hayley stepped back from the bed and went over to the door.

Nick still stared to the outside.

"Nick! Can you bring them down to our quarters? They will be safer than here." Hayley asked him quietly.

Nick nodded. "Certainly." he let Hayley slip out of the room and closed the door.

Hayley went down the corridor and stopped at the door where the guard had disappeared through. Arthur still leaned against the frame. Hayley made a sign towards Arthur but Arthur shook his head. He went with his finger over his throat and shrugged then with his shoulders.

"You're crazy." Hayley shook her head and went further on the corridor along.

Arthur and Damon followed her slowly.

Hayley stopped in front of another posh door and opened it a crack. Only soft snoring could be heard. Hayley shook her head and switched the light on.

The snoring stopped; a man wiped the sleep out of his eyes and finally looked up from his bed. As he noticed Hayley at the door, he grinned amused: "Well, well, well! Did you come to have some fun with me?"

Hayley frowned. "I can't understand how you all come on the idea I want to sleep with you when I stand in front of you with a sword in my hands."

Prince Lateran climbed out of his bed and pulled his trousers up. "What do you intend to do then? Kill me?" He mocked.

"Why shouldn't I? I already killed your brother." Hayley answered calmly.

Prince Lateran frowned. "You killed Alban? You're crazy!"

"Perhaps," Hayley weighed her sword in her hands.

Prince Lateran picked up a sword and examined Hayley thoroughly. "My brother was always a bit weak. With me you will have a problem." He mocked and attacked Hayley in the same moment.

Hayley was prepared and defended herself very well. At first she only defended herself but as Prince Lateran pushed her into a corner, she woke up and answered with a series of hard blows so that the prince flew back. Hayley hit once more and she caught Prince Lateran at his chest. Prince Lateran panted up but he caught himself again. He lifted his sword but he hadn't any chance anymore to hit out. Hayley hit again and she caught him this time neatly over the throat. Prince Lateran looked astonished at her; slowly he went down into his knees, his eyes broke and then he fell forward onto the floor.

Hayley shook her head. "You're both weak." She murmured then she took her scarf and put it around her head. At last she went over to the door and slipped out.

Arthur and Damon looked at her and Hayley nodded.

"What are you doing here?" A voice asked from the other end of the corridor.

Hayley, Arthur and Damon turned around. Interested they examined the guards who came nearer to them.

Hayley turned over to Arthur and said quietly: "whose turn is it ?"

Arthur pointed over to Damon.

Hayley grinned under her scarf. "We leave them then to you. Finally we want to know how good you are." She said quietly to Damon.

Damon shrugged his shoulders. "My pleasure." he said calmly and drew his sword. With fast steps he went over to the three guards and before Hayley was able to lean against the wall – the three guards lay dead on the ground.

"You should remember this for the next time." Arthur whispered over to Hayley. "That's the right way to do it."

"I'll try to." Hayley hummed back. She went the corridor along, stepped over the dead men and examined Damon. "Do you have another hidden secret I should know about?" She asked calmly.

Damon shrugged his shoulders. "I don't know. I'm sure you find out." He answered steadily.

Hayley grinned. "We'll see. Let's go!" She said and stepped on.

As the three Fighters came back to the ground floor, the other Fighters had blocked the outside doors and locked some of the other guards into their rooms, how Rick shortly explained to Hayley. Then he pointed over to another door. "Ladies Quarters!" he said grinning. "We left it for you to open it up. I don't know if they already noticed something."

Hayley nodded. "Okay. I'll have a look." She went over to the door, which was still familiar to her and she remembered the first time she had entered through that door. Then she gave herself a push and tried the handle.

It was locked.

Without thinking Hayley lifted her leg and kicked hard against the door. The door cracked and flew finally open.

"Well, now they know it." Arthur said mockingly, shaking his head about the noises Hayley had made.

Hayley shrugged her shoulders and entered the corridor. She went it along till she reached the end of it and stepped at last through the door.

Arthur entered behind her the harem and looked interested around.

Hayley remembered the days she had spend here and sighed quietly. Her eyes wandered through the room till she noticed the women crouching together at the other end of the room, near the door to the outside.

But just as Hayley wanted to step forward, five eunuchs stormed out of a side room, the swords lifted and attacking the intruders – Hayley and Arthur.

Hayley drew her sword and fell onto her knees to come out of the reach of the first hit of one of the eunuch's swords. Then she attacked herself and the first eunuch almost fell into her sword and died. Shortly after, the second and the third eunuch fell dead to the ground.

Hayley turned around to Arthur and noticed that he had done his part as well. To his feet lay the last two eunuchs, definitely dead.

Hayley nodded at Arthur and he stayed where he was, covering the area with his sword. Hayley put her sword away and stepped slowly around the swimming pool towards the women who had grown very, very quiet in their corner. Stunned and scared to death they stared over to the dark figure, which came towards them.

Six women altogether but Hayley only recognized four of them: Bethany, Nicole, Elaine and Orinda. The other two must be new women like the one she had seen in Prince Alban's room together with Shannon.

Bethany was the only one who had still a little bit of courage in her body. She looked at Hayley without recognizing her in her dark clothes and the black scarf around her head. "What do you want from us? And what did you do to Shannon and Ezra?" She asked, trying to give her voice a serious and firm sound.

Hayley smiled under her scarf. "That's the wrong question. There is nothing I want to do to you or Shannon or the others. But there is something I had to do and that you know exactly."

Bethany frowned. Astonished she examined the dark figure again, searching for something familiar.

Hayley helped from her side; she took the scarf and pulled it slowly off. Then she shook once more her long red curls and looked asking at Bethany.

"Oh, my god," Bethany murmured, her face pale like the white marble of the wall, "Hayley!" Then she ran the last steps over to Hayley and fell into an embrace, which Hayley replied firmly.

For a moment Bethany only pressed Hayley at herself then she looked at her again. "I really missed you. We only heard that you were thrown into the cells but not what happened with you there. Then – two months ago – Prince Alban fetched Amanda and let her being strangled to death over the gate as a warning for us. We had to watch how she died – cause of you. Do you know that?" Suddenly angry Bethany punched Hayley on the shoulder.

Hayley caught her hand and pressed it. "Yes, I know. That wasn't my plan – and you can believe me that Prince Alban regretted it. But I'm here now at least to fulfil my other promise: To take you with me – if you still want to." She added quietly.

Bethany sighed. "I thought you've forgotten me – down in the cells. How did you manage to come out of there?"

"I'll tell you later; we haven't much more time." Hayley turned to the other women. "Are you all alright? Nicole? Elaine? Orinda?" she asked quietly.

The three women came over to her and hugged her shortly. "Yes, we're all right." Elaine confirmed. "But…"

"Attention, Hayley! Look behind you!" Arthur's voice echoed through the room.

Hayley turned and pulled in the same moment her sword out of its cover. She caught the hit a guard had tried to make from behind and – by sheer mistake – pulled her sword over the only place he didn't cover, his throat. The guard broke down, dead before he hit the ground.

Hayley examined the grounds outside. "Go over to Arthur! Run!" She said quietly.

Bethany, who had stepped backwards, as Hayley killed the guard, grabbed after Nicole and Orinda's arms and pulled them with her. Elaine followed her at once, pushing the other two women in front of her to the entrance as well.

Hayley covered their backs but nothing happened.

Arthur opened the door again and waved the women to follow him. He led them out of the harem and then to the side into the room, which had been their quarters for the night.

Nick was at the window, staring outside, whilst Shannon and the other woman sat on a sofa in a corner and looked afraid around. They shook together, as Arthur entered the room but were happy then to see Bethany and the other women.

During the women gathered together, Hayley pushed Arthur over to Nick and said quietly: "Nick! I need you outside. – Arthur, please, can you stay with the women here; I'll make you responsible when something happens to them. Understood?"

Arthur nodded.

"Okay. Let's go Nick." Hayley pulled her scarf around her head again and left the room, Nick at her heels.

Arthur looked calmly behind them; he knew exactly why it was him who had to stay back and to keep an eye on the women. Hayley did trust him, he knew, and the women here were her friends – and could be a good reason for a deal if they got problems. That Hayley didn't want to leave them in anybody's hands; it was clear why she had chosen Arthur.

Thoughtfully Arthur pulled the scarf from his head and laid it together on a chair. Then he turned and looked over at the women.

It was Shannon who noticed him first. She jumped up. "Are you not one of the guards of the Prince?" She asked, suddenly going pale.

Arthur shook his head. "I was – a long time ago." He answered quietly.

"The question is: On which side are you now?" Shannon inquired seriously.

"Well, I don't know if it will comfort you – but I'm sworn to Hayley and I never would betray her. I also don't know what you think about Hayley but that doesn't matter. She asked me to keep an eye on you and that's exactly what I intend to do."

Shannon examined him. "I don't believe you. You plan something."

Arthur shrugged his shoulders. "Believe what you want to believe. But I give you a piece of advice: Stay here and wait till Hayley comes back. Then you can ask her yourself."

"I don't intend to go outside when there are fights going on – if it's that what you mean." Shannon mocked.

Arthur didn't give any answer anymore. His eyes caught a figure outside and he stared interested behind the figure.

Hayley in the meantime had gathered together the rest of her team and gave short instructions, with Damon's help, how to catch the other guards without needing to kill so many. As they left the main part of the palace, Hayley felt a look in her back and she turned to see whom it was. She discovered Arthur at one window and nodded reassuring at him before she turned and went over to the next building.

Through the night Hayley and the rest of the Fighters managed to shut most of the guards and servants into their rooms without having to kill them. Two, three people crossed the way of Hayley or one of the other Fighters and had to let go off their lives – with the exception of one man. That man almost ran directly into Hayley's arms and he stepped afraid back at once.

"Ahmed!" Hayley said astonished and withdrew her sword.

The man stared at Hayley without recognizing her at all and asked, still afraid: "Please, don't kill me! I haven't done anything wrong."

Hayley knew they were almost finished with their work and pulled her scarf down. "Ahmed, don't you recognize me anymore?" She asked calmly, "The woman, who was brought over here under force some months ago?"

Ahmed examined her from top to bottom. "I remember." He said slowly. "I told you what to do in the tent of Sheikh Farrar." He stopped short before he continued: "You changed but you still look very well. But what do you want to do now?"

Hayley smiled. "I won't kill you, if it's that what concerns you. I still have you in a very good memory. Come with me." She stretched out her hand towards Ahmed.

Ahmed hesitated then he took her hand and followed her to the outside.

In the yard Hayley looked around till she discovered Priest Alfonso who had gone with them every step but kept in the background. She went over to him and said quietly: "Al, that's Ahmed. Can you bring him over to Arthur? – And see that he stays alive, I still need him." She added whispering.

Priest Alfonso nodded. "Come with me, my son." He said, even though he was younger than Ahmed.

Hayley nodded at Ahmed and the man followed the priest up to the main part of the palace.

Hayley herself needed some hours longer till she had everything under control and could turn back to the room where she had left Arthur and the women back. She entered the room and looked astonished at the picture in front of her.

The women had stretched out on the beds and sofas in the room and so had Arthur. But on his lap was laying Bethany's head, which made the picture a bit confusing.

Ahmed was sitting in a corner in a small daydream; only Priest Alfonso was wide-awake. He turned to Hayley, having the rising sun in his back, and smiled. "Lie down for a moment – you need a rest. I look after you." He said quietly. "Arthur is unluckily already occupied." He changed his smile to a grin.

"Perhaps that's all right like that." Hayley answered quietly. She went over to the next sofa and stretched herself out. Almost instantly she fell asleep.

21

Hayley woke up because it was so quiet in the room. She looked confused around and noticed that she was alone in the room. Still tired she got up and left the room in order to search for her friends.

Harry, Brad and Jean were in the hall in front of the room in which Hayley had rested. Harry smiled at her, as she left the room and informed her shortly: "We have some guards down at the gate and Brad and Jean make at the moment the in-between-runners. Arthur, Al and Ahmed are with the women in their quarter, if you look for them. They felt safer there. Otherwise is everything calm. In the town they don't seem to have noticed something."

"You think so." Hayley smiled tired. She turned over to the harem and entered through the broken door. Already in the corridor she heard laughter. As she stepped through the door, she discovered the women in the pool, playing and laughing around. Arthur, Al and Ahmed were sitting at a table near the pool and enjoyed some fruits.

Hayley didn't hesitate; she knew she had to wake up for the next step she had to do – and what was better than having a bath? She went over to a cupboard, took a bikini out of the drawer and disappeared into a room beside the cupboard. Fast she exchanged her clothes and went then over to the pool. She slipped into the water and dived down.

The cold water woke her up immediately. Hayley wiped her eyes and looked over at the women at the other side of the pool. They hadn't noticed her at all till now.

Hayley swam a length of the pool and back before she came nearer over to the women.

Shannon leaned against the wall of the pool and stretched herself out on the water. "Well," she said. "Still I want to know how it's going on now."

Nicole, who had stretched herself out on the belly, shrugged her shoulders. "We'll find out." She said quietly.

Bethany dipped into the water and combed her wet hair with the fingers, as she came out of the water. She listened to the conversation and opened her mouth to say something, as...

Hayley laid her hands on Bethany's back and stroked her gently. "You are still so soft like I have you in my memory." She whispered her into her ear.

Bethany grabbed with her hands into her back and caught Hayley's arms. "But you are much stronger than I remember you." She murmured then she let her go and turned around. "Otherwise you are still the same old stubborn girl I know." She stroked softly over Hayley's cheek.

Hayley smiled. She pressed Bethany at her body and sighed quietly. But before she could say something, another voice joined into the whispered conversation: "Hayley! It's good to see you again – especially without your swords. But perhaps you can tell us how it will go on now?"

Hayley wiped a tear out of Bethany's eyes then she turned over to the other women who stared at her. She shrugged the shoulders and said carefully: "You know, Shannon, why I had to come back and you knew what would happen then. How it will go on? I know what I have to do. What you will do? Tell me – and I'll organize it for you." She looked calmly over at Shannon who stood now upright in the water.

Shannon grew angry. "Does it mean that you haven't a plan in store what will happen to us? Did you everything without thinking about the future?" She shouted so that Arthur, Priest Alfonso and Ahmed looked astonished over to the swimming pool.

"You don't know me a bit, do you?" Hayley mocked back. She turned to Bethany. "What do you think?"

Bethany smiled. "As far as I know you – you have at least two plans in store. It only belongs how we and the town people react on what you did to which plan you follow. Am I right?"

Hayley grinned at her. "You definitely know me better than Shannon does." She murmured. She turned, swam back to the other side and pulled herself out of the water. Then she went over to the room where she had changed before, dried herself and dressed again in her black clothes.

A man stormed into the harem, looked around and finally stepped over to Arthur, Priest Alfonso and Ahmed. He started to talk quietly but excited to Arthur.

Arthur got up just as Hayley came opposite out of the room where she had changed. She noticed at once the excited faces of Arthur and Nick who had come inside with the news. Hayley stepped around the pool.

Arthur and Nick came towards her and with a nod of Hayley's head, Nick started to tell what he had already told Arthur: "The town people noticed that something is wrong here. They are curious; they want to know what's going on. It's time that you inform them."

Hayley nodded. For a second she stared at Arthur then she turned her head, looked over Arthur's shoulder and called to Priest Alfonso: "Al! Can you see to it that the ladies come out of the pool and dress? In a serious way please? Perhaps we need them later on."

Priest Alfonso lifted his hand and nodded. And during Hayley, Arthur and Nick left the harem; Priest Alfonso got up and stepped over to the pool. He smiled at the women and said calmly: "You heard what Hayley said. Please, leave the pool and dress. Probably you will be needed soon."

Bethany, Orinda, Nicole and the others nodded and started to move to the other side of the pool but Shannon was stubborn. "What is when we don't do what Hayley wants? She can't command us around how she wants to have it." She said coldly.

Priest Alfonso smiled down at her. "It seems to me that you still don't understand what's going on here. Let me try to explain to you – to you all. Through Hayley's act of killing the prince, she got the power over the palace and the town with everybody who is in there, including all of you. Hayley is in control – and if you don't obey, you have to take on the consequences. I think you still know what that means." He looked straight at Shannon who looked uncomfortable back. "Hayley only wants the best for you all, this I can assure you. But even I won't accept that you are disobedient. I maybe a priest but I'm not in Hayley's group cause of that. So, if you don't want to have any trouble now – go and dress!" Priest Alfonso's voice changed from a comfortable to a very hard tone.

Bethany climbed out of the pool. "Come on, Shannon! It's no use – or do you want to be dragged in front of everybody like you are now?"

Shannon looked over at her; she hesitated for a second longer then she gave herself a push, swam over to the other side and climbed out of the pool. Together with the others she went into the rooms to dress.

Hayley, Arthur and Nick in the meantime had gone down to the hall where it had been normal to welcome the town people when they had problems. Now the hall was bursting full of people…

Hayley understood why Nick had been so excited, as here in the hall was a lot of shouting and trouble going on. Hayley and Arthur went along the side of the hall to the front during they listened to what the people were saying.

"What happened here?"

"Where is the Prince?"

"What are you doing here?"

These were the most asked questions Hayley and Arthur got to hear, as they listened.

Rick and Harry who sat on chairs in front of the people looked helplessly at each other. They weren't used to the attention they received and didn't know what to answer the people.

Hayley asked politely her way through the crowd till she reached the front.

Rick and Harry breathed relieved out, as they saw Hayley and Arthur coming towards them. Rick got up at once. "It's time that you come. They're asking a lot of questions, we can't answer. You're the best for that." He murmured.

"Okay, okay." Hayley smiled lightly then she turned to the crowd. She examined the excited men and women before she whistled loud and hard: "Calm down, everybody!" She called over the heads.

The cries died down and the people turned to her and examined her astonished.

"Listen! The Princes are dead and we took over here! Any questions?" she asked but added in the next moment: "One after the other!"

An elderly man stepped forward. He bowed shortly then he said quietly: "I'm Alderman Archery, Maitre of the town. Prince Alban is dead?"

Hayley replied the greeting and answered calmly: "That's right."

"And what is with Prince Lateran?"

"He is as well dead."

Alderman Archery examined Hayley from top to bottom. "We should have counted with that." He confessed, now calm as well. "Are you taking over here?"

Hayley hesitated, "Only for the time being. I intend to leave the town in good hands, as I have to go on. But I want to make sure that here everything will be all right when I leave. Therefore it would be good if you would like to help us." She looked straight at the Maitre.

Alderman Archery was astonished. "You want us to help you – after all you did to us?"

"Do you want to tell me that you had nothing against the Princes? That you liked what they did?" Hayley mocked.

"Well," the Maitre started to stutter. "I don't... I want... I mean..."

Another man stepped forward and bowed, interrupting the Maitre: "I'm Rocco Macchino, Assistant to the Maitre. I didn't understand your name..."

Hayley bowed. "I'm Hayley Houseman, Fighter of Freedom." She answered quietly.

Rocco Macchino nodded. "Then it's true?" He asked.

Hayley frowned. "What do you mean?"

"I mean," the assistant hesitated for a second before he continued: "Is it true that you let the legend come true? You already destroyed the kingdom – has Prince Alban a son?"

Arthur stepped to Hayley's side. "Be careful!" He whispered. "The people here take the legend very serious. So don't mock about it – and destroy with that everything you did." He warned her urgently.

Hayley nodded. She looked at the Maitre and his assistant and confessed for the first time: "Yes, the legend comes true – and Prince Alban has a son."

The murmur under the town people grew loud.

The Maitre and his assistant exchanged a look. Then the Maitre cleared his throat: "Where is he? Shouldn't the son of the prince grow up here where he belongs to?"

Hayley examined him carefully. "No, he shouldn't. He should grow up in an environment, which is completely different from this one here that he will be able to understand the value of everything here when he comes back. He is in the best hands; a good friend of mine is looking after him like after his own. Prince Alban's son will come back when the time is ready for that."

"As you wish – you are his mother?" The Maitre had seen through the connection.

Hayley hesitated. She exchanged a look with Arthur, who nodded reassuring at her, before she answered calmly: "Yes, that's right."

The murmur in the hall grew much louder. And then something surprising happened: One man after the other, one woman after the other knelt down and bowed their heads. As well the Maitre and his assistant knelt down but they looked with respect at Hayley.

Arthur smiled lightly, "Very good! Now you have them full in your hands." He whispered to her.

Hayley sighed. "I only hope that they accept then my choice." Again she turned to the Maitre and said clearly: "I intend to leave the town and the palace in the hands of the first wife of Prince Alban. She has my full support and she will act under my orders. It is my wish that you accept her as regent in my orders – if I get to hear that you don't follow her, you all will regret it. Is that clear?" Her voice was hard.

The Maitre bowed his head. "Yes, my Lady." He answered shortly. "When will we meet her?" He added carefully.

Hayley looked thoughtfully at him. "I will introduce her to you all in half an hour – be my guests in the meantime and have a drink." She gave a sign to Nick and seconds later servants enter the hall, loaded with bottles of wine and glasses.

Hayley nodded at Arthur and together they left the hall again. As they went back to the upper part of the palace where the harem was, Arthur turned to Hayley and asked astonished: "Are you sure that you want to hand the palace and everything over to Shannon?"

"Well," Hayley smiled, "Shannon is not happy at the moment – with me, because she is afraid. But that will change soon, and she is absolutely trustworthy."

"You know I trust your opinion." Arthur opened the hall door for Hayley but as she stepped through it, he stopped her, taking her at her hand. "What did you mean with that your son is in the hand of a good friend of yours? He's still in the temple."

Hayley leaned for a second against Arthur. "I don't intend to leave my son in their hands. It wouldn't be good if he would grow up as a priest, he must live with normal people and learn how it is. I think I will leave him with Ahmed; he will have it good with him – and Ahmed owes it to me."

"Do you really think that's a good choice?" Arthur was sceptical.

Hayley shrugged her shoulders. "May I remind you that Alban will grow up, doesn't matter what we decide now? I'm ready to trust Ahmed; he was more than one time a good friend to me." She said steadily.

Arthur bowed his head. He opened the door to the harem and side at side they stepped back into the harem.

Shannon, Bethany and the others had dressed in the meantime and had taken seat at the tables near Priest Alfonso and Ahmed. Now they looked up with interest, as Hayley and Arthur came over to them.

Hayley examined the women from top to bottom. She was satisfied with what she saw. "Did you make your decision?" She asked calmly.

"What for a decision?" Shannon asked back.

Hayley looked over at her. "The decision who of you will stay here and who of you wants to go away." she explained shortly.

"Didn't you make the decision already?" Bethany asked astonished.

Hayley turned to her. "I made the decision for one of you – to be exact; I made the decision for Shannon. But I need to know who of you wants to stay here with Shannon and who wants to go away."

Shannon frowned. "And I have nothing to say in this matter?"

Hayley stepped over to Shannon and knelt down beside her chair. "Listen, Shannon." She said quietly, urgently. "You know that I have to leave again but the people here need somebody who leads them. You are the only one who can do that; you were Prince Alban's first wife; you have the authority and probably the knowledge. The town people will accept you, if you will accept me and my reasons to go on. Trust me; you will have a good life here."

Shannon looked down at Hayley and felt the old friendship coming up again. Suddenly she smiled. "You are a bitch!" She said, smiling wide. "You had this plan in your mind the whole time, hadn't you? And you know that I like to stay here, don't you? It was an easy game for you!"

Hayley smiled. "You are right. Shannon, will you do it? Will I have a home here when I come back?"

"You will have a home here, forever. Promise," Shannon bent forward and embraced Hayley lightly.

Hayley gave the hug back then she got up again. She looked at the others. "Your decision?" she turned to Elaine who sat next to Shannon.

Elaine sighed. "I'll stay with Shannon." She answered quietly.

"Nicole?"

"I'll stay."

"Orinda – What is your decision?"

Orinda hesitated. "If I come with you – would it be possible for me, one day, to see my sister again?" She asked quietly.

Hayley avoided her look for a moment then she looked straight into her eyes. "I can't promise anything but my guess is – yes, you will see your sister again."

Orinda nodded. "I'll come with you."

"Bethany?" Hayley's voice was quiet.

Bethany looked at her then she threw a fast side look over at Arthur. "You promised me to take me with you – I don't want to stay here." She confessed.

Hayley had noted her side look at Arthur and smiled. "Is there, perhaps, another reason for you to follow me as well?"

Bethany blushed and looked down at the table.

Hayley turned to the last women but none of them wanted to come with her. Finally she stepped away from the table over to the priest and the servant. "Al?" She asked thoughtfully.

Priest Alfonso got up and looked asking at her.

"Take Bethany and Orinda under your wings, will you? They should pack some things together and see that they are ready when we want to leave again. Understood?"

Priest Alfonso nodded in silence.

Hayley turned to Ahmed. "I want to see you outside – now!" She pointed over to the green outside the harem.

Ahmed bowed.

22

"Ladies and Gentlemen - Her Royal Highness Shannon and her ladies!" a butler announced in the hall and opened the portals in the back of the hall, in front of the people.

Shannon entered the hall. For a second she stopped, as she noticed the crowd of people in the hall but then she went on till she reached the top chairs at the top table, which had been brought in the meantime.

The men at the table got up and bowed.

Shannon nodded at them and sat down.

Nicole, Elaine and the others followed her example then finally the men sat down again as well.

Maitre Alderman Archery and his assistant Rocco Macchino started a light conversation with Shannon and after Shannon got over her first embarrassment she came up with new ideas, she told the Maitre and his assistant. And they seemed to be happy about that...

During Shannon mastered her first banquet; Hayley and Ahmed went together through the garden in front of the harem.

"You have to do me a favour, Ahmed." Hayley started slowly.

Ahmed stared at her.

Hayley sighed. "You want to go home, don't you?"

Ahmed nodded. "If you let me go – I would love to."

"I let you go – if you do me this one favour." Hayley said quietly.

"What for a favour?"

Hayley hesitated. "I need somebody who can look after my son for me. I have still a lot to do and can't do it myself. Would you do this favour for me?"

Ahmed sighed. "Well, I... I haven't any experience with children. Perhaps my wife..."

"You are married?"

"Yes, since half a year before I got forced into this job."

"And you haven't seen your wife since?"

Ahmed shook his head.

Hayley examined him thoughtfully. "Forget it! Go home and look after your wife! – When you go outside, ask Brad to organize you a horse that you come faster home. Is that all right?"

Ahmed hesitated. "Thank you, Hayley, but... I'm sure my wife will be delighted to look after your son for you, as thank you for letting me go home. Where can I find him – he's not here, is he?"

Hayley shook her head. "No, he is not here. He is in the Temple of Freedom; a girl named Arachnarella is looking after him at the moment. Listen, are you sure that you will look after my son?"

Ahmed took carefully Hayley's hand. "You'll do me the favour of my life – you let me go home. Somehow I have to say thank you for that. And when the only chance of thanking you is to look after your son then I want to do it. – What do I have to do that they will hand him over to me?"

"I will give you a letter, which will explain everything to them. You won't have any problems, promise." Hayley pressed hard Ahmed's hand. "And I have to say thank you for that." She added.

Ahmed smiled. He looked down at his hand and pulled a small silver ring with a diamond down from one finger, his only valuable possession. For a moment he looked at it then he pressed the ring into Hayley's hand. "If you ever will send somebody for getting your son back, give him the ring. Then I will know that he comes from you."

Hayley looked at the ring, "Okay, but if I can't come to pick him up – it will be Fletcher, my husband. Remember the name, Fletcher Houseman. Otherwise my son will stay with you – and you have to tell him where he comes from and what his purpose is. – Is everything okay?"

Ahmed nodded smiling.

For a while they talked still further on, a letter exchanged the owner but at last they hugged each other for a moment before they said goodbye and Ahmed left the harem. Hayley stayed back and stared up into the blue sky. She felt a little bit better than before and now after everything was organized she felt relieved.

Slowly Hayley knelt down and bowed her head...

Priest Alfonso stepped quietly up behind her and laid his hands on her head. "Harder, God of Freedom is with you – wherever you are. Get up, my daughter! You haven't to kneel before him in his environment." He said quietly.

Hayley got up. She turned to the priest, looked at him – and gave him a sudden hug. Then she left the garden and went back down to the hall where Shannon, her friends, the Maitre and the town people were sitting together for a meal. Unobserved she sat down at one table where the Fighters had gathered together and enjoyed her meal...

23

Two days later, the Fighters of Freedom were on their way again.

Bethany and Orinda were sitting on the wagon beside Priest Alfonso and enjoyed the journey.

Rick had organized some more maps from the area and one big one for the whole country.

Hayley had had a look at it and had noticed that she wasn't at all anymore in the country she had been in before. She had been brought into another land…

They were already for over a week on the way, as they finally came to a village.

Hayley stopped her camel at the entrance of the village and looked frowning around. "Something is wrong here. It's so quiet." She murmured.

"Perhaps everybody left?" Arthur suggested.

Hayley threw a mocking look over at Arthur. Then she gave her camel free and entered the village.

One after the other the riders followed her till they reached the middle of the village with the market place and the well.

The Village was for sure left; not one single living human was around.

"Ghost Town," Harry murmured. He felt uncomfortable.

As they came to the market place, Hayley stopped her camel again.

The sight they all saw here wasn't nice and some of the Fighters bit on their lips in order to get over it.

Hayley seemed to be the strongest one. She jumped down from her camel without hesitation and knelt down beside a body, which was lying on the ground. She turned the body around and stared into the dead eyes. Then she got up again and stepped on to the next body.

She did the same with the second body like with the first one, followed by a third, fourth and fifth one. At the sixth body she suddenly stopped. She stared at the clothes of the man, as if she would dream and finally sighed. As she knelt down and searched for the pulse, she suddenly shrugged together.

The man had opened his mouth and groaned lightly.

Carefully Hayley felt over the man's body then she turned him around. As she looked at his face, she sighed. "Jeff, can you hear me?" She asked in a normal voice.

Once more the man opened his lips and groaned lightly.

Hayley turned and waved over to Priest Alfonso who just stepped over to the second body and made Harder's sign over it. Now he looked up, saw Hayley waving and came over to her.

"How good are you in curing sick people?" Hayley pointed down at the Horseman. "Jeff is still alive but not long anymore if you can't help him."

Priest Alfonso knelt down and checked the man carefully through. "I think I can help him. Who is he?"

"Jeff Walters is a Horseman – you know, the group I was riding with before… all this s… all these happened. I know him quite well." Hayley explained.

Priest Alfonso nodded. Carefully he picked the man up and brought him over to his wagon. The two women, Bethany and Orinda, helped him to make space in the wagon and to lie down the injured man. Then all three of them cared for the man.

Two days later, after they had burned all the dead people, the Fighters went further on their way. There had been nothing more they could have done.

Jeff Walters, the Horseman, was still lying in the back of Priest Alfonso's wagon, unable to move or to speak. But he was already on the way of getting better.

Hayley asked herself for at least the hundreds time since she had found Jeff what the Horsemen had done in this far away corner of the country. Also it wasn't quite normal that they would have attacked the village people – normally they would have defended them. But Jeff's being there made it quite clear that they had attacked the village people. Why? She couldn't find any answer.

For that she found Sheikh Farrar and his caravan, only a way in front of them on the third day after they had left the village.

Sheikh Farrar was on his way again, probably searching for new women he then could sell as slaves on the market.

Hayley felt anger coming up her body, as she stood beside her camel on a small hill and observed the caravan of the Sheikh, which just went out into the desert beneath her.

"Keep cool! We need a plan if we want to get him. He has a lot of guards around him." Arthur spoke quietly, as he stepped up beside Hayley.

Hayley sighed. "I'm cool – and I think I have a plan. But it will only work till we are next to him."

"And why not further on?" Arthur asked astonished.

"Well," Hayley threw a fast look at Arthur before she stared down at the caravan again. "The problem is that I will kill Sheikh Farrar as soon as I come near enough to him. He doesn't deserve to live one minute longer."

"We'll see." Arthur stayed on the firm ground. "What's your plan?"

Hayley turned around to him and faced him. "I can't imagine that Sheikh Farrar will recognize us – especially not when we wear our scarves. So let's go and visit him like we are now. Perhaps we offer our service to him?" She smiled lightly, a scornful smile, full of anger but as well with a touch of mockery.

Arthur examined her thoughtfully. "Well, it could work." He said slowly. "And if not then we have to kill everybody." He shrugged his shoulders, as if it wouldn't matter but his voice was full of sarcasm.

For a moment they stared at each other then Hayley turned around again and stared down into the desert.

"When do we start?" Arthur asked quietly.

Hayley stopped short and closed her eyes. Finally she opened them again, breathed through and answered more or less calmly: "Get them ready! We start as soon as possible."

Arthur nodded. He went away, back to the rest of the Fighters at the other side of the hill. Telling them what Hayley and he had seen at the top of the hill was one, getting the Fighters ready to go was the second thing Arthur did.

And five minutes later he gave the sign for departure.

Hayley in the meantime had left the top of the hill and had taken a short cut down the side of the hill. Not leaving the caravan for one second out of her eyes, she prepared herself for her second fight. She checked that the mask was fitting perfectly then she checked her swords and knifes of easy ability to reach them and their sharpness. Then she looked that she had nothing what would give her away.

At that point the other Fighters joined her and together they were riding along and out into the desert, following the caravan.

As the caravan came only slowly forward, the Fighters reached them quite early.

Hayley led her camel around the last wagons and rode along the caravan to the front.

The front of the caravan was made out of one wagon and five riders on horses. They had stopped, as they noticed the Fighters coming along; eying them suspiciously, the hands ready at their guns.

But Hayley had herself under control; even though she discovered Sheikh Farrar in the middle of the riders who looked at them. Hayley made the sign of Freedom and asked curiously: "Where are you going to?"

Sheikh Farrar examined her, not recognizing her dark voice under the scarf. "Where the wind is blowing to." he answered carefully.

Hayley let her eyes sparkle a bit. "What a coincidence! We're going the same way! Do you have something against when we ride with you?"

Sheikh Farrar looked at her camel. "With your camels you are much faster than we are. Why do you want to keep up with us?"

"It's dangerous here in the desert. I thought you might want some additional help." Hayley answered calmly.

"Help that you can rob us during we sleep?" Sheikh Farrar was sarcastic.

"We are Fighters, not thieves. I only offered our service to you, as you don't seem to be strong enough to fight against attackers." Hayley answered mockingly.

Sheikh Farrar looked at her, not minder mockingly. "Against people like you?" he asked laughing. "We would take you in without any problems."

"Do you like to prove it?" Hayley was still mockingly, seeing her aim in front of her eyes.

Arthur beside her only sighed quietly.

"Yes, I like to prove it." Sheikh Farrar turned to his companions and gave some short orders.

The riders rode over to the wagons and after some minutes of ranging the wagons were standing in a wide circle.

Sheikh Farrar made an inviting hand movement into the circle. "After you!" he mocked.

Hayley turned to Rick. "Place everybody around the wagons for an emergency. Arthur, you come with me." She said shortly and jumped from her camel. With certain steps she entered the circle and stepped over to the other side. There she laid down her cloak and laid her big two-hand-sword on top of it. Then she turned around and faced Sheikh Farrar.

The Sheikh had gone over to one of the wagons where he laid down his cloak and took over a sword, one of the guards reached over to him. As he turned around, he asked calmly: "How long do we fight?"

"We fight till one of us is dead. The survivor gets the command over the rest of the group." Hayley answered slowly.

Sheikh Farrar nodded. "It's all right with me. But will your group accept it?"

"They will. And yours?"

"They will as well." Sheikh Farrar grinned. "But that won't be necessary, as you won't have a chance against me." He stepped more into the middle of the circle. "Take the scarf down! I want to see against who I fight."

"If you don't get embarrassed then," Hayley smiled. She took the end of the scarf, pulled it down and threw it over to her cloak. Mockingly she looked at Sheikh Farrar.

The Sheikh was stunned, as he stared at Hayley. Her face, the red curls were still good in his memory and he smiled, as he remembered the time he had had her. "Wild Cat!" he said surprised with a mocking undertone in his voice. "I don't know how you escaped from the Prince's harem but it is a pleasure to see you again. When I finished with you – no, I think, I let you live. You will be able to give us all some more pleasure." He laughed; a terrifying sound.

Hayley's eyes started to sparkle for anger. "We will see." She only answered. She pulled her sword and made some movements with that through the air. Her sword cut the air and made a singing noise. Hayley was ready.

Sheikh Farrar tested his sword only shortly. He turned to Hayley – and attacked her straight away.

Hayley caught his sword with only lifting her own. She held the hit without any problems and looked angrily at the Sheikh. "Do you really think you will come forward with that?" She mocked.

Sheikh Farrar prepared his next attack and hit out at Hayley again.

Hayley started to dance and it was clear after some minutes for the Fighters that the Sheikh hadn't any chance at all against Hayley. She danced her sword dance without effort; scratched the Sheikh at arm and leg and played a game, without letting the Sheikh have a chance to come near to her.

Sheikh Farrar began to sweat. He had to notice that the woman he fought wasn't anymore the helpless woman he had had once for his enjoyment before he had sold her to Prince Alban. This woman now was a strong fighter and not easy to handle anymore. He started another attack.

Arthur sat down beside Hayley's cloak and leaned against a wagon. Almost bored he watched the fight.

Hayley had enough. She caught the hits against her and answered at once with hits so powerful that Sheikh Farrar almost lost his sword, as he stopped the hits. But Hayley hit out again and again and the Sheikh stepped backwards in order to get away from Hayley. Suddenly he lost his balance and fell down to the ground. Hayley hit out at once again but Sheikh Farrar still had his sword and could manage to catch the hit. With enormous effort he got up again, hit out at Hayley to keep her at distance and pulled himself together. But in the next moment he stepped out of cover – and Hayley saw and used her chance. Her sword sang, as she let it through the air and with enormous power she caught the side of Sheikh Farrar's body.

Sheikh Farrar groaned up. He stamped some steps to the side, his sword fell out of his hand then he stood still for a moment. Slowly he went into his knees; finally he fell forward. At last he was lying motionlessly in the dust of the desert.

Hayley breathed deeply in. She stepped forward and pushed with her sword against the body. But the Sheikh didn't move.

Hayley picked up the sword of the Sheikh and turned back to Arthur.

Arthur got up and went over to her. "Good fight!" He praised her quietly. "But did you think about the consequences now?"

"You mean – the rest of the Sheikh's group?" Hayley sighed.

Arthur nodded only.

Hayley turned around and examined the men of Sheikh Farrar who stepped over to the dead body on the ground. They checked that the Sheikh was really dead then they looked up at Hayley. The oldest, and probably the highest in rank after the Sheikh, came over to Hayley and Arthur. "Well," he said slowly. "Then we can go out of the fact that you will take over the Sheikh's business?"

"Was he just on a business trip?" Hayley asked against.

The man nodded.

"Has he already stuff?"

Again the man nodded.

"I want to see it." Hayley ordered shortly.

The man bowed, turned and gave some orders to the other men. The men stepped over to three of the wagons, opened the linen curtains and shouted something inside. Then they pulled out of each wagon four women and pushed them over into the middle of the circle near where Hayley and Arthur were waiting.

Arthur whistled shortly through his teeth.

The women were tied up and they were all terrible afraid. All of them had stains of tears on their faces.

Hayley stepped over to the first of the women and examined her from top to bottom. The woman wore only a shirt loose over her body, just covering the important parts. Hayley looked sharply at her skin, searching for any marks, which would tell her if that woman was a slave or a free woman. She stepped around her and looked at her arms but nowhere could she find a mark. "Where are you from?" She asked quietly.

The woman lifted her head a bit and looked carefully at Hayley. "I'm from a village in the hills; they kidnapped me, as I was searching for wood for my fireplace." She answered quietly.

"Free born?"

The woman nodded.

Hayley took her knife and cut the ties around the wrists of the woman. Then she stepped on to the next one.

Hayley checked every woman carefully through and asked every time the same questions. And she cut the ties from every woman. At last she turned and asked Arthur: "Can you please ask Bethany and Orinda if they can look after these women? They need clothes, food and drink."

Arthur bowed and went away to the wagon outside the wagon circle. He exchanged some words with somebody in the wagon then two women left the wagon and followed Arthur into the circle over to the women.

Bethany and Orinda examined the women carefully. Bethany noticed that one of the women was still more self-confident than the others and looked shyly around. She came over to the woman and stretched out her hand: "Hallo! I'm Bethany and you are?" She asked friendly.

The woman looked at her. "Azara, Ma'am." She answered quietly.

"Bethany, not Ma'am," Bethany corrected her smiling. "Come on – all of you! It's time that you get something to eat and drink! You need it!" She added, as she looked more closely at Azara.

Orinda helped Bethany to bring the women over to the side of one wagon where Rick in the meantime had discovered the food and water supply of the Sheikh. They sat down beside the wagon and Bethany and Orinda helped giving out the food and water. As they finally sat down beside the women, they noticed the cloak and the sword from Hayley lying beside them on the ground…

Hayley in the meantime had gone over to the rest of the Sheikh's group and examined the men. Some of them were still familiar to her, some she didn't know at all. Altogether there were twenty men, most of them the drivers of the wagons. Guards there were only seven.

Hayley looked at the man she had talked to before and asked calmly: "What's your name?"

"Takim, Ma'am." The man answered calmly.

Hayley looked at him thoughtfully. Then she shrugged her shoulders. "First of all: Bring the body out of the circle and lie him down into a grave. Well, after that you can do what you want."

"Which means?" Takim asked astonished.

Hayley smiled mockingly. "You can take some of the wagons and can go wherever you want to go to. But one thing I have to tell you: If I ever find one of you in such a business again – or something similar – I'll kill you all. Did I make myself clear?"

"Yes, Ma'am," Takim stuttered. He turned to the other men and gave some sharp orders.

The men went into the circle, picked up the dead body and carried it outside where they started to dig a hollow grave.

Hayley looked around till she noticed Nick not far away from her and waved at him to come over to her.

Nick came nearer and bowed.

"Nick, get some of the guys and check the wagons. Take everything we could need and put it into the Priest's wagon and two more. Get the best horses to pull these two wagons. The rest leave to these guys." She nodded with her head over to the men who had started to dig the grave for the Sheikh.

"Consider it done!" Nick bowed and vanished between the wagons.

Hayley turned and went over to the women who sat beside the things she had left on the ground some time ago. She sat down on her cloak and leaned back against one wagon, the eyes closed.

Bethany turned to Azara after she had noticed that the woman had finished eating and drinking. "Tell me, where exactly do you come from?"

Azara looked carefully around, as if she still feared to get into trouble when she said something. Her look stopped at Hayley who sat half behind her and seemed to sleep. She turned back to Bethany and looked asking at her.

Bethany smiled. "Hayley is a power woman but in the beginning she wasn't more as you are. You are under friends – you can say whatever you want."

Azara wetted her lips. "What do you mean with that she wasn't more like we are? You for example look quite well – from a good house, I mean." She said quietly.

Bethany nodded. "I lived at last in the harem of Prince Alban, that's the reason why I have so good clothes. Before that – I grew up in a good house but I wasn't more than the daughter of a guard of the house. Hayley on the other hand is free born like you. As far as I know she had been always a fighter but she was also married and had a son before she got kidnapped from the Sheikh and his group. She had a lot of problems and all she's doing now is – seeking revenge for what had happened to her."

"Is it not a bit harsh?" Azara asked astonished, knowing by now that nothing would happen to her when she spoke.

"You have to see it from another point." Hayley answered before Bethany had a chance to do so. She opened her eyes, as she felt the eyes from all the women on her. "I don't only seek revenge for myself – also for the women who got kidnapped together with me. And you should think about what would happen to you if I hadn't come and done what I did. Would you like that – or would you like it more to go home again?" She asked quietly.

Azara avoided Hayley's look. She looked to the side and murmured: "Don't think I'm not grateful for what you did. I am. But does it really mean we can go home? And if it does mean yes – how?"

Hayley smiled at the younger woman. "All you have to do is – tell us exactly, where you come from. Everything else you can leave to us."

Azara swallowed. "As I said, I come from a village in the hills – behind these ones. I don't know the way – but I know that we are already a long time on the way. It must be a long way; I've never been so far in my whole life."

Hayley nodded. "Are you the only one from that village?"

Another woman joined in the conversation. "I'm from the same village – so is Lilly." And she pulled her head in, afraid to get a hit for speaking.

Hayley examined her carefully. Softly she asked: "And your name is?"

"Susie, Ma'am." The woman answered hesitatingly.

Hayley shook her head. "My name is Hayley, nothing else. Who of you is Lilly?"

A third woman looked shyly up. "I'm Lilly." She answered quietly.

"And where are you others from?" Hayley inquired again, waiting this time for a detailed description.

Only slowly the women got used to the fact that nothing happened to them when they spoke. They warmed up one after the other, and they told Hayley, Bethany and Orinda everything they wanted to know.

Hayley saved the information in her brain; she knew it would be a long way to bring the women back to where they were at home.

"Hayley, may I disturb you?"

Hayley looked up at the Fighter who had spoken to her. It was Harry. She made a hand movement, which allowed the Fighter to speak up.

Harry cleared his throat. "Priest Alfonso wants to see you. The Horseman woke up."

"I'm coming." Hayley got up and together with Harry she stepped over to the wagon, which was still outside the circle. She looked asking at the Priest who just poured some water into a cup.

Priest Alfonso stretched himself and smiled at Hayley. "He woke up again – and he can talk. He's asking a lot of questions I can't answer. It would be good if you would have a talk with him." And he pressed Hayley the cup with the water into her hand.

Hayley saved an answer; she took the cup and turned to the wagon. Carefully, not to split any water, she climbed into the wagon and sat down beside the man who was still lying on the ground of the wagon.

Jeff Walters opened his eyes. He winked till he saw clear again then he stared stunned into Hayley's eyes.

"How are you this nice afternoon?" Hayley smiled at him.

"I must be dead. You are, aren't you?" Jeff stuttered.

Hayley laughed quietly. "No, I'm not dead, Jeff. And you aren't either even though it was pretty close this time. What for a business did you have in this village?"

But Jeff wasn't so far to answer any questions. He had too many question, "By God – Hayley! What happened to you? What are you doing here? And where am I here in all words meaning?"

"Well, that's a lot of questions at once." Hayley smiled again. "I will try to explain it to you." She was silent for a moment then she continued: "You are here in safety of my new team – the Fighters of Freedom. To make it short: I put a team together to be able to get revenge for everything what had happened to us. And this I do now. But we came through a village where we found you – and I would like to know what you did there."

Jeff had problems to get all the information in Hayley was telling him. She could see it clearly on his face. Finally he came to an end with his thoughts and said quietly: "You always have been a fighter – why should it be different now?" He noted. "But I still don't understand why you picked me up on your tour. I must be ballast for you."

Hayley shook her head. "We are Fighters, not murderers or something else. You were still alive, as we found you, so we took you with us. The Priest and the two ladies who are looking after you belong to my team as well as this wagon. You haven't been ballast; just the opposite, as you can tell me everything I want to know – and I'm happy that you survived."

Jeff looked at her asking, and then his look fell on the cup, which Hayley still held in her hands.

Hayley noted his look and nodded. "I'm sorry! I'm a bad woman. Let me help you." She pushed her arm under his head and helped him to get up a bit. Then she held the cup on to Jeff's mouth, and Jeff drank thirstily. As the cup was finally empty, Jeff sank back and sighed. "What do you want to do with me now?" He asked curiously.

Hayley smiled. "You have the choice: You can ride with us or you look for your way back home again – alone."

"You won't go back home, home to Fletcher?" Jeff asked astonished.

Hayley leaned back. For a second her sight blurred then she winked the tears away. Calm to the outside but excited inside she asked: "What is with Fletcher? How did he react on what had happened?"

Jeff sighed once more. "Fletcher was, no, he still is very angry and very, very sad. He changed since you disappeared. He doesn't laugh anymore but he never lost hope to find you again. Fletcher grew a bit better, after we found Mandy – and with her your son. It made him feel better at least to have something from you." Jeff was silent. The exhaustion he felt through his injuries broke through again.

Now it was Hayley who sighed. "I swore to give my life for the opportunity to see Fletcher again but it is not the right time now." She looked down at Jeff and continued: "You look tired. Go back to sleep! Everything else we can discuss when you are all right again, okay?"

Jeff nodded barely noticeable. "I feel better already to know that you are here." He murmured then he closed his eyes and fell instantly asleep.

Hayley climbed quietly out of the wagon and stepped around it. She leaned against the wagon with the sight open to the desert and let her tears run.

"Hayley - what's wrong?" A soft voice whispered into Hayley's ear and a finger caught a tear from Hayley's cheek.

Hayley took the hand belonging to the finger and pressed it away from her face, "It is okay, Arthur. Give me only some minutes alone."

But Arthur shook his head. "If you are sad, it reflects on to us all. – Did he raise any bad memories?" He pointed to the wagon.

Hayley pulled herself together, as she noticed that Arthur wouldn't let her be alone. "Not bad – lost memories." She answered quietly and couldn't help that the next tears ran over her face.

In silence Arthur pressed Hayley firm at his body, as he understood what she meant. For a moment they stood in silence together; Hayley's head leaned on Arthur's shoulder and she still cried silently. Arthur stroked her softly over the back and the back of her head till he noted that Hayley grew quieter. "Is it better now?" He whispered.

Hayley laid her head onto his shoulder. "I think it will never be better. But you helped me to come over it – for the moment. How can I say thank you?" She asked, looking at him with big red, now dry eyes.

"I ever will be there for you when you need me." Arthur murmured. "You know that. There is no need to thank me."

Hayley sighed. She embraced Arthur a bit firmer, breathed a kiss on his cheek before she let him go again. She leaned back and wiped over her eyes. "Well, I think I have to use some make-up to cover the strains." She murmured.

Arthur shook his head. "It is too late for that. Everybody here knows that you cried though they don't know why."

The sigh Hayley let go was big and Arthur grinned, as he heard it. Then Hayley shrugged her shoulders. "What does it matter? I have no secrets." She murmured. "Come on, Arthur. We have to make some plans." Slowly she stepped around the wagon then she stopped suddenly. She turned, Arthur still at her side, and watched the rest of the Sheikh's group leaving with the wagons Hayley had given back to them. They left in a hurry and didn't look around.

Hayley frowned for a moment then she turned her head and called: "Nick!"

Nick came around a wagon and ran over to Hayley. He frowned as he noted that Hayley had still big red eyes from crying but he said nothing, he bowed only.

"Nick, send somebody out to shadow these guys. He has to be very careful; I want to see him back alive but I think it's necessary. They plan something." Hayley added calmly.

"All right," Nick nodded, bowed again and ran over to a place where two-three of the Fighters were standing together. He exchanged some words with one of them, Gerry, and after a moment Gerry left the others and followed the Sheikh's group back into the hills where they had gone.

Hayley looked at Arthur. "We have to get ready!" She only said and went on.

24

"Are you sure that they will come?" Rick lay down beside Hayley and stared into the darkness.

Hayley smiled grimly. "They will come. I took everything from them what meant something to them. They'll come back and try to get it back."

"Hope you are right." Harry murmured, only a space away.

"I think the same." Arthur, lying to Hayley's right, came to her support.

Hayley smiled into the darkness. She heard a sound and stopped the others talking.

For a while they only lay on the ground and listened.

Then the noise came again.

Hayley shook her head. It was not clear to her how somebody who wanted to try to surprise and kill somebody could make such loud noises. The only clear thing was that really somebody tried to come near the camp.

Damon, the dreamer had proved again, that he was very good in organization. He had set up a camp with the three wagons, which were still left, in a half circle and had pulled a rope over the empty space where he had tied up the camels and the horses. This was the only real space where somebody could enter the camp and it was the space where Hayley and her friends were lying and waiting for an attack.

The women had been packed onto the floors of the wagons and hopefully were sleeping peacefully with guards, watching over them, between the wagons.

A thin figure pressed itself down between Hayley and Arthur and murmured quietly into Hayley's ear: "If you really think that I stay in a wagon, packed with women, during you fight here – you are wrong. I may not have your training but I'm still good."

"Be quiet!" Hayley hissed.

At the same moment the noises came again, much nearer than before.

Hayley pulled her sword out of its cover, hesitated for a moment then she pressed it Jeff into his hands. Then she took the second sword and got quietly up onto her knees. Carefully she looked through the horses and tried to make something out in the complete darkness of the desert night.

Arthur, Jeff, Rick and the others knelt down beside her; everybody with his sword in his hands, Jeff's hand cramping around Hayley's sword.

In front of Hayley a shadow could be seen, outlined from the darkness. Then a second shadow came and a third. Finally a group from around fifteen men could be seen from the kneeling position Hayley and her team was in.

"First the guards – then we will see what we do with the rest. Be as quiet as possible. They don't expect us." The first man whispered to his comrades and stepped forward.

In the same moment Hayley got up and lifted her sword.

The man stepped direct into Hayley's sword and on his face came up an astonished and painful expression.

"It's a pity that you didn't take my warning for real, Takim." Hayley said calmly and pushed her sword much more into the man's body.

Takim opened his mouth but nothing came out of it. Blood ran down his mouth ankle and his chest and without another sound he broke together.

His comrades needed some seconds to understand what had happened. Then they looked for a way out of the trap they had walked into.

But Arthur and the rest of Hayley's team didn't stay back. They forced the attackers into a fight and, slowly but steady, one attacker after the other fell dead to the ground.

Hayley had picked out another strong man to fight against, only to be able to dance her sword dance again. She did it, fully enjoying it and didn't feel at the least sorry, as the man fell to the ground and died.

Almost an hour later the fight was over.

The Fighters of Freedom removed the dead bodies and burnt them outside the camp, looking that the smoke didn't hit the camp at all.

Hayley made sure that nobody from her team was hurt and that the women were still all right and alive. Then she turned over to Jeff who had sat down beside a wagon and leaned against a wheel.

"Are you okay, Jeff?" Hayley asked quietly.

Jeff looked up. "I'm okay, thanks. It had been only a bit exhausting; I think I'm not as fit as I thought I would be."

"But you were pretty good." Hayley smiled. "And for you it's not over yet."

"What do you mean?" Jeff frowned.

"Well," Hayley sat down beside him. "You fought with us and proved to be one of us. You need to be initiated to us now – or do you really believe we would let you go after tonight?"

"Guess not." Jeff sighed. "But I'm prepared – I'm prepared since I took the sword from you. And I don't think it's bad to belong to your team – again."

Hayley smiled. She took her sword back, which Jeff reached over to her and put it back into its cover. Then she got up and waved over at two Fighters to come over.

Adrian and Ian followed the command, came over to Hayley and Jeff and bowed.

Hayley nodded at them. "Take Jeff with you and prepare him for the initiation. He also gets the tattoo and we have to burn a mark away." She explained shortly.

Adrian and Ian exchanged a look. "Okay." They both hummed like out of one mouth and turned then to Jeff who still looked astonished up at Hayley and tried to understand what she just had said.

"Come on, Jeff! Let's go!" Ian asked Jeff calmly.

But Jeff hesitated. Only as Hayley looked at him reassuring, he got up and followed the two Fighters to a wagon on the left side.

Hayley went over to the wagon of the Priest and looked around till she saw Priest Alfonso sitting between the wheels.

"What on earth are you doing down there?" She asked astonished.

Priest Alfonso shrugged his shoulders. "The wagons are too full with all these women, as that there would be any space for me. I prefer to sit here."

"Do you really?" Hayley teased him, remembering the night in the temple.

Priest Alfonso grinned. "Well, at least I prefer a more... a more personal atmosphere."

Hayley sat down beside him. "You have to help me. I need an initial ritual for Jeff with everything what comes with that."

Priest Alfonso nodded. "I thought about it since the day we picked Jeff up in the village. I guessed at least one day we would need such a ritual. If you send me the others over than I can prepare everything. – Where is Jeff?" He added.

"Adrian and Ian are looking after him." Hayley sighed.

"What is it?" Priest Alfonso looked sharply at Hayley, seeing her through the light of some torches only shadow like.

"Well," Hayley searched for words. "I don't know if it's right that I want to do that."

"I know what you mean." Priest Alfonso laid his hand on Hayley's shoulder and pressed it shortly. "But don't you think it will be right **to ask Jeff** if he wants to join. If he wants to – then it can't be wrong."

Hayley took the hand from her shoulder and breathed a kiss on it. "You're right. I get the others to help you. But – if possible – don't disturb the women. Let them sleep."

But once more Priest Alfonso shook his head. "I know that I will hurt you now a lot but it must be." He was silent for a moment then he continued: "We have to wake up Bethany. It's time that she fulfils her purpose."

Hayley stared at the Priest. "And which purpose would that be?"

Priest Alfonso took once more Hayley's hand and held it firmly. "She loves Arthur – you may have noticed it. And Arthur – you know what he gave for an oath. It's time that they come together."

Hayley went stiff. "You want to marry them?"

"Well, it's not that I want to steal your best friends from you but they both are meant for each other. Think about it and you will find out that I'm right. And we shouldn't wait any longer with that."

Hayley closed her eyes. "I know you are right. But it still hurts."

"You won't lose them completely." Priest Alfonso comforted her. "They both will still be there for you; they couldn't do anything else."

"Well, I think from now on you have to count with the fact that I come more often to you." Hayley got up, turned to the Priest and asked calmly: "In which wagon is Bethany?"

Priest Alfonso pointed half up and half behind him.

Hayley nodded. "I'll send the others to you before I wake up Bethany. Will you be okay to prepare everything?"

"Certainly," Priest Alfonso shooed her away like a hen, and Hayley ran over to the place where she saw Arthur, Rick and Harry coming back into the camp.

Five minutes later the three men and the priest were busy to build up a small altar behind the horses and camels, far away from the wagons in order not to disturb the sleeping women.

Hayley in the meantime went back to the wagon where she had sat in front of before and opened the curtain from it a bit. She flashed with a torch inside to find out who of the bodies Bethany could be. As she noticed finally Bethany lying on the left side of the wagon, she pulled softly at her leg.

Bethany murmured something quietly and tried to free her leg.

Hayley held on and pulled once more.

Bethany opened her eyes and winked.

"Bethany! It's me, Hayley! Can you come out for a moment? I have to talk to you!" Hayley called softly into the wagon.

Bethany blinked again, looked astonished at Hayley and at last she started to move. Carefully she crawled out of the wagon and a minute later she was standing beside Hayley. Still astonished she examined her: "Is somebody hurt? Or what else do you want now?"

Hayley pointed to the ground. "Come on, let's sit down. I have to talk to you." And she sat down and waited till Bethany sat down beside her.

"What's the matter?" Bethany asked again.

Hayley hesitated. "You are in love, aren't you?" She asked finally, very quietly.

"You got me out of my dreams to ask me that?" Bethany frowned.

"Not really." Hayley answered slowly. "But I need at first an answer from you."

Bethany swallowed. "You know exactly that I'm in love. But there is no way that he ever will notice me." She answered quietly.

"Would you accept that he only likes you but will look after you – after you got married?" Hayley's voice was only a breath in the air.

"How will you get Arthur to marry me when he doesn't love me?" Bethany shook her head, not aware that she had spoken out the name of the man she loved. Hayley hadn't mentioned it at all till then.

Hayley threw an apologizing look over at Bethany. "Well, you have to know that Arthur swore to marry somebody who really loves him with all the consequences – but not his big love. Would you be willing to marry him, knowing that he doesn't love you at the moment?"

Bethany looked at her intensive. "As much as you are willing to give him up, as much I am willing to marry him - if I only could get him." She sighed.

"One last question," Hayley wetted her lips. "How would you like it to marry him – tonight?"

"I… I… I mean… I would…" Bethany couldn't stop stuttering.

"Calm down!" Hayley pressed her shortly on to her body. "I can't give you a big wedding and party you probably dreamed of – it will be only a small ceremony in front of Priest Alfonso. Is it all right with you?"

Bethany embraced Hayley intensive. "I'm happy with everything if only I can get him. You will be at my side, won't you?"

Hayley sighed. "I wish you both that you will be really happy. And I will be there for both of you if you need me. But don't ask me to attend the ceremony. It would make me sadder than I already am."

"You are not happy about us getting married, am I right?" Bethany noted.

Hayley shrugged her shoulders. "I know that you both are meant for each other. But it wasn't a really good day for me today."

"Err…" Bethany wasn't sure what to say.

But Hayley made it easy for her. "Don't say anything anymore. See if you have something nice to dress but – please – don't wake the others! They all will need the sleep they can get. I'll come and get you when it's time for it." She got up and left without saying anything more. Slowly she went over to the camels, stroked them softly during she passed through them and stepped over to the place where the Fighters had build up an altar and had lit some torches around it. She nodded satisfied.

"We can start." Arthur smiled at Hayley, as she came over to him and the other Fighters.

"All right," Hayley turned to Rick. "Go and tell Adrian and Ian to bring Jeff over here."

Rick bowed and vanished into the darkness outside the altar.

In the next ten minutes Priest Alfonso instructed Hayley and the others what they should do. But mainly it was only to hold Jeff firm down on the altar when it was time for that; otherwise they had only to stand still.

Hayley stood behind the altar, looking after an iron stick, which stuck out of a bucket with a small fire burning in it.

Arthur stood at her right, at the top of the altar. Rick, who had come back only a moment ago, was standing opposite him at the end of the altar. Harry knelt in front of the altar, near the top. And Priest Alfonso stood at the end but in the front of the altar, waiting for Jeff to arrive.

The other Fighters sat in silence in a half circle in front of the altar.

Adrian and Ian led Jeff into the half circle and stopped at a sign of the Priest.

Jeff was embarrassed; he was naked without a string of underpants, just hiding all the necessary things. The wounds he had got in his last fight with the Horsemen were still visible but healing well. Jeff shivered in the cold night air.

"Come over and kneel down in front of the altar!" Priest Alfonso ordered shortly, and Jeff followed the order. He went over to the altar and knelt down, not far away from Harry.

"Are you here on your own free will?" Priest Alfonso asked quietly.

Jeff nodded. "I am." He answered firmly.

"Are you willing to join the Fighters of Freedom in their journey to Freedom?"

"I am." Jeff answered firmly again.

"What are you willing to give us when we accept you in our group?"

Jeff frowned. "What do you want to have?"

Priest Alfonso shook his head. "It's you who has to tell us the price you are willing to pay for the honour to ride with the Fighters of Freedom."

Jeff looked helplessly over the altar at Hayley but Hayley avoided his look. He frowned deeply again, thinking about what he could offer. At last he shrugged his shoulders. "You took the last things from me, I possessed. There is nothing anymore I could offer you, without my knowledge and… and my word that if I will ever possess anything that it will belong as well to the group as it will to me."

"Do you want to accept this offer?" Priest Alfonso turned over to Hayley.

Hayley nodded. "I accept the offer." She answered clearly.

"Get up!" Priest Alfonso ordered, and Jeff got up. "Before we can present you to Harder, God of Freedom, we have to burn the mark away you carry on your leg. Harry, Arthur!" Priest Alfonso nodded at the two men and they went over to Jeff. Harry stepped behind Jeff and laid his strong arms around Jeff's body and arms. Arthur grabbed after Jeff's left leg and pulled it apart from the other one, turning it till the mark could be seen.

Hayley picked up the gleaming iron stick and went around the altar to Jeff. "This will hurt you a lot." She murmured, as she came nearer and she lifted the stick.

Jeff pressed the teeth together.

Hayley pressed the stick firmly against the mark on Jeff's leg and made sure that all what stayed back was burnt skin without a visible sign of the mark. Then she took the stick away again and reached it over to Rick who threw it in a bucket with water.

Jeff hung more in Harry's arm than that he stood on his own feet. Not one sound had come over his lips but a bit of blood dropped down his mouth ankle.

Harry pushed Jeff carefully over to the altar and helped him to lie down on it. He laid his right arm down beside his body and pressed it with his hands down.

Arthur stepped back to the topside and laid his hands carefully but firm on Jeff's head.

And during Rick laid his hands firmly around Jeff's ankles, Hayley took Jeff's left arm and stretched it out. She laid his hand on a small wooden table, pulled a rope over to his wrist and knotted then the rope around the table. Finally she went one step backwards and laid her hand on Jeff's shoulder.

In silence Priest Alfonso sat down in front of the outstretched arm, picked up the small tattoo machine he had taken with him for this purpose and set to work. After a time he finished up his work and got up again.

The Fighters let go their hold of Jeff and Hayley cut the rope. "Be careful!" She warned Jeff, as he got slowly up. "Don't touch the tattoo – if you want that everything goes well."

Jeff nodded only.

"With that you belong now official to our group. Rick will look for some clothes for you and Harry will give you your sword. But you have to wait for your own camel – which I can't shake out of my sleeve." Hayley smiled. "You can drive one of the wagons for now – if this is all right with you."

Jeff nodded. "Thank you." He smiled thinly at Hayley, still feeling the pain in his leg and his arm.

The Fighters grinned satisfied at each other and they all got up.

"One moment please!" Hayley called softly over the altar. "We're not finished here."

The Fighters turned astonished to her and even Arthur, Rick and Harry stared surprised at her.

"We have someone under us who gave a certain oath to Harder. It is time now that he fulfils his oath." Hayley explained.

Damon frowned. "As far as I know it's only you, Arthur and Rick who gave the oath to Harder. Isn't it right?"

"It's right." Hayley confirmed it.

"Well – who of you is it now?" Damon inquired curiously.

Arthur closed his eyes. He knew the oaths of the other two and he foresaw that Hayley was talking about him.

Hayley looked over at Arthur. "You know the oath you gave to Harder. There is somebody who loves you, ready to marry you with all consequences. Are you ready to fulfil your oath?"

Arthur sighed. "Do I have a choice?"

"I'm afraid not." Hayley smiled. She went over to him and whispered: "You will be satisfied, believe me. And I wish you all the best." She embraced him shortly before she continued: "I'll get her now."

"Are you staying for the ceremony?" Arthur asked quietly.

Hayley shook her head. "You will better manage without me being here." She smiled once more then she took Rick's hand and pulled him with her into the darkness.

"Bethany?" Hayley asked into the darkness near the wagon where she had left her.

Bethany hesitated for a second then she stepped forward. "Is it okay so?" She asked shyly and turned one time around.

Rick whistled through his teeth.

Hayley grinned. "For these circumstances – you look sweet! Arthur will be very happy!"

"Do you really think so?" Bethany looked down at her clothes.

"I think so too. I could get jealous." Rick laughed. "Come on, Bethany. I'll bring you over to the altar." He stretched out his hand.

Once more Bethany hesitated.

Hayley lifted her hands and showed her fists, thumbs up.

Bethany smiled. She took Rick's hand and led herself lead away. Over the shoulder she threw a last look back at Hayley.

Hayley sighed quietly. She pulled the cloak firmly around her and crouched under the wagon. There she lay down and closed her eyes… but she couldn't go to sleep for a long time.

"Therefore I pronounce you husband and wife!" Priest Alfonso shut the book he had been reading from. "You may kiss the bride now."

Arthur turned to Bethany at his side and smiled lightly at her. He bent forward and pressed his mouth on her lips, tasting the soft lips before he went on.

The Fighters whistled mockingly and they clapped their hands.

Arthur solved his lips from Bethany's and noticed that she had closed her eyes. As she now opened her eyes again, he whispered quietly: "I hope you will be satisfied with me."

Bethany smiled. "Every time and every day." she answered in the same quiet voice.

Arthur pressed her at his body before they left the place in front of the altar and took all the best wishes from the other Fighters.

Harry tapped Arthur on the shoulder and smiled. "There is not much we can give you as a present and we hadn't much time to prepare something, as you know. But we have a small tent, which you can use for the rest of the night. Hopefully it will be all right for you both. It's in the corner over there." He pointed to a corner between the last wagon and the horses.

Arthur and Bethany exchanged a look. "Thanks a lot!" Arthur smiled. "It will be fine for now."

"Then have a good night!" Harry grinned again before he turned to the other side of the camp.

The rest of the Fighters, including Rick and Priest Alfonso, followed him slowly.

Arthur took Bethany's hand and led her over to the tent. "It's small but it's ours. At least for tonight." he smiled at his wife.

Bethany entered the tent and lay down at once, as there wasn't enough space to stand up. Arthur came just behind her and he lay down beside her. Harry had even thought about pillows and blankets so the couple was lying quite comfortable in the small tent.

"There is something I still have to tell you." Arthur said quietly during he pulled a blanket over Bethany's and his own body.

"You don't need to. I know what you want to say. It's about Hayley, isn't it?" Bethany murmured.

"You are right. I love Hayley – you have a right to know that. And I don't give her up only because we are married now." Arthur's voice sounded strong.

Bethany sighed. "I know – I love her too. You don't need to give her up; in fact I would be happy if we are still good friends with her. She will need us."

"I'm glad you think so. It will make everything easier – for us and for her." Arthur bent over Bethany and kissed her softly. As he pushed his hands under her clothes, Bethany sighed comfortable and gave herself completely into Arthur's hands...

25

"Here we are!" Hayley stopped her camel and pointed over to the last hills in front of them. "That should be where Azara, Susie and Lilly are at home."

"It could be." Arthur frowned.

Hayley threw an amused look over at him. She knew he had a lot on his mind at the moment and he wasn't really paying attention to her. "Let's try to find the village." She only answered and rode on again.

They still needed two days till they found the village, hidden away between the hills. The wagons kept them back sometimes but nobody wanted to divide the group. Especially not, as the last three women they had freed were travelling on the wagons. And they had to get them back to the village.

Hayley rode slowly till the first wagon, driven by Jeff, overtook her. Azara drove the second wagon and Hayley kept up with her. "Azara - What do you think?"

Azara smiled. "I'm coming home. That's a good feeling."

Hayley smiled understanding under her scarf. "We will stop near the village. I don't want to get into trouble like the last time." She remembered that the town people had been very unfriendly to them and had looked after that they left the town as soon as possible, even though they had brought back some of the town's women.

Azara laughed. "My people are not like the town people. They are friendly, especially when you bring them back what they want to have."

"You mean you three?" Hayley asked astonished.

Azara nodded. "Our village is not rich and there aren't so many young women to make sure it will survive. There had been some disappearances before. So they will be really happy to see that we come back."

"I take your word for it." Hayley pushed her camel forwards till she was at the top of the group again and searched for the way to enter the valley between the hills. She found it and rode onto the small path.

The Fighters followed her, the wagons only with difficulty. But finally they reached the village.

Hayley hesitated for a moment before she rode straight into the village and through it till she came to an open space in the middle of the village. There she stopped and jumped from her camel.

Curious village people looked out of windows and stood in the doorframes, watching the arrival of the foreign people with interest. Out of building beside the open space came three till four men, stepping over where Hayley had stopped her camel.

Suddenly one of the men, a young man with long black hair, left the group and ran over to the second wagon. "Azara," He called out loudly.

Azara stopped the wagon, jumped down to the ground and fell into the man's arms. They embraced each other for a long time without saying anything.

Susie and Lilly climbed down from the wagon and were greeted from the village people as well.

"Who of you is the leader?" One of the older men had come nearer and turned now with his question to Hayley.

"That's me." Hayley made the sign of Freedom before she bowed to the man.

The man crossed his arms in front of his chest and bowed back. "May I ask which business brought you here?"

Hayley smiled. "My business here is almost over. We found three women who belong to your village. We only brought them back."

"Don't believe her, Father. We were kidnapped and she freed us and brought us back. Please welcome her and her group here! Please, Father!" Azara fell into the arms of the older man and hugged him heartily.

"She," The man asked back astonished during he pressed his daughter firm at his body.

Azara threw a look over her shoulder at Hayley.

Hayley shrugged her shoulders and pulled the scarf down. She shook her long red curls and smiled at the man in front of her.

"I'm Azara's father, Dom Erdogan, First of the Village. I have to thank you for bringing my daughter and her two friends back. Is there anything we can do for you?"

"Well," Hayley hesitated for a moment then she continued: "We would need some food and water if you can spare something. Also – you haven't a camel to sell by any chance?"

Dom Erdogan bowed. "You will get food and water as much as you can carry with you. Also you will get a camel from us, a very good one. Is there anything else you need; a home perhaps and a husband?"

"Thank you but no thank you." Hayley smiled at the First of the Village. "I have a home and a husband and that's enough. But if we can get water for our camels as well…"

Dom Erdogan nodded. "Water you will find in the well over there." He pointed over to the edge of the space where a well was build into the ground. "We'll organize enough buckets for you." He bowed again before he turned around and led his daughter and her friend away.

Hayley turned to Arthur who just jumped down from his camel. "Go and tell Bethany and Orinda not to show up here. They shall stay inside in the safety of the wagon. Then get two men who shall guard the wagon."

"What do you fear?" Arthur murmured astonished.

Hayley sighed. "Look around. Here aren't so many women – they are in need of more. If we stay longer here than we have to then you won't have any wife anymore. Orinda will disappear and… and you won't have any leader anymore. We have to be damn careful here!"

Arthur looked around without moving his head. "You're right." He bowed shortly before he went over to the wagon where Priest Alfonso sat still on it. Arthur climbed on the seat beside him and talked to the women in the wagon without moving his head into their way so that it looked like he was talking to the Priest. Finally he clapped the Priest on the shoulder and jumped down again. Then he turned to Brad and Gerry and ordered them to keep an eye on the wagon.

Satisfied Hayley turned to the well and had a closer look at it. Arthur followed her as well as Rick and Harry.

"I think it's all right." Hayley murmured quietly. She noticed that some men with buckets in their hands came nearer and she made way for them.

The men started to get the water out of the well and Harry and Rick carried it over to the camels and checked that every animal got its share.

Adrian and Ian in the meantime brought the two wagons, which were now ballast to the Fighters, to one side of the open space and knotted the reins of the horses to a fence.

Then Guy climbed into the wagon of the Priest and pushed the women into a corner. "Stay there that they don't see you!" He murmured and started to push all the things in the wagon over to them, building up a wall in front of them. Then he sat down in the entrance and took the buckets with water and the baskets with food and pushed them into the wagon till the wagon was full till the top. At last he jumped down to the ground again and closed the curtains again.

"Let me show you the camel I decided to give to you." Dom Erdogan came over to Hayley and pointed over to a fence.

Hayley nodded and turned her head. She searched first for Arthur's eyes then for Jeff's and asked the two men with a nod of her head to come with her.

Dom Erdogan smiled mockingly. "Are you afraid of me? Or why do they have to come with you?"

Hayley smiled lightly. "I'm not afraid of you. I'm a very good fighter. But the camel you have for us is for one of my guys so I have to ask him to come with me to check that it is right for him."

Dom Erdogan nodded only. He led the three Fighters through a gate, over a green patch, through another gate and one more. Finally they reached a meadow where some camels grassed on it.

"This one is for you!" Dom Erdogan pointed to a big, powerful camel at the middle of the meadow.

Hayley stepped carefully nearer to the camel and stroked it softly. Also Arthur and especially Jeff stroked the camel then Jeff wound a rope around its neck.

"And now it's time that you give up!" Dom Erdogan's voice came over to them.

"What do you mean?" Hayley turned around. So she came face to face with around ten men who had showed up in a circle around them. She laid her hand in an automatic gesture on the sword in her back.

"Come on, Girlie! We need some more women here and you look damn pretty. You will be a good wife to one of my men and you will bear him a lot of beautiful children. Finally that's the purpose of a woman, isn't it?" Dom Erdogan's voice was cold and matter-of-fact. "If you give up now then we let your friends go without harming them."

Hayley looked around at Arthur and Jeff.

Both men had pulled their swords out of their covers and examined the men around them.

Hayley pulled her sword and answered quietly but calmly: "You won't get me without a fight. My purpose is not to make your village richer, and when it would be only in one way." She pointed her sword at the men.

The men didn't hesitate for long. They attacked Hayley and the two men so hard and merciless that the camels ran terrified away.

Hayley pulled her second sword and held the men at two sides on distance. She killed two of the men before the men started to back away from her when she came nearer.

Arthur who was well trained as well hadn't any problems at all to keep the men away from him but Jeff who had only just started to receive the training got fast into trouble. Arthur turned and got him at his side that he was able to help him when he was in danger. Still Jeff got a sharp hit on his arm, which left his arm without any power at all.

The village men stopped the attack, as they noticed that they had chosen the wrong people to attack. They hadn't any chance against them.

Hayley noticed that the men hesitated and called very quietly over to Arthur and Jeff: "Take the camel and then let's see that we get out of here!"

Arthur nodded and moved a bit that the men around him gave way and opened the way over to the corner where the camels were standing together.

"Go and get it! I'll watch them!" Arthur whispered to Jeff.

Jeff nodded. Carefully he stepped over to the camels and with his healthy hand he grabbed after the rope, which was still hanging around the neck of the big camel. Softly he pulled it over and back to Arthur.

Arthur waited till Jeff and the camel had passed him then he followed them, still having his sword in his hand and his eyes fixed at the men.

Hayley left her place and stepped forward, as Jeff reached her. Together, slowly and carefully, they left the meadow and went back into the village. Hayley too had still her swords in her hands.

"What's wrong?" Harry asked astonished, as Hayley, Jeff and Arthur reached the open space of the village, still prepared for a fight. But everything seemed to be fine in the village.

Hayley put one of her swords away. "We had only a little bit of trouble. Can you please see to it that somebody looks after Jeff's arm? Rick! Look that everybody gets ready to go – and tie this camel behind the wagon for the time being." She ordered.

Harry and Rick bowed and Harry took care of Jeff. Rick took the camel and got the Fighters back on their feet again, during Rick wound the rope around a ring at the back of the wagon.

Five minutes later they all were ready to leave again.

"You're going already?" Azara came out of one house and stepped over to Hayley.

Hayley looked frowning at her. "Yes, we're leaving. But before we go – you have to promise me something!"

"I promise everything." Azara nodded.

Hayley examined her, thoughtfully and still frowning. In the ankles of her eyes she saw Dom Erdogan and the village men coming back through the gate. They carried the three dead men between them.

"Promise me that you will teach your children the difference between a lie and a white lie. You lied to me over the friendliness of your village; a lie not a white lie. Normally I would punish you for that but I really think you will be punished here enough for that." Hayley pulled the scarf back into its place, in front of her face and climbed up the camel. Then she gave the sign for leaving and pushed her camel forward.

In silence the Fighters followed her, in their midst the wagon with the Priest and the two women.

26

"How long are we already on the way?" Bethany asked, looking down at her clothes.

Hayley smiled. "Almost a year is gone by since I... freed you out of Prince Alban's harem." She answered calmly. "But don't ask me about the year, the month or the day. I have no bloody idea."

Bethany grinned. "If I can't keep track – how should you?"

Hayley leaned back in the wagon and examined her friend. "You would like to set up a home for you and Arthur wouldn't you? You want us to have a place we can go back to; a place, we can call home, don't you?"

Bethany looked down at her hands. "Well, wouldn't you like to have a place you can call home?"

"I once had a place called home. I lost it and there will never be another place." Hayley answered quietly.

Bethany laid the arm around her friend. "You will always have a home to go to. Arthur and I will always have a room for you." She said quietly and pressed her friend's shoulder.

Hayley smiled. "Thanks but that's not necessary. When I did my job, I go back to the temple and fulfil my part of the oath, I gave to Harder."

"And that means?" Bethany frowned.

"It only means that I will leave you all – after I found a home for you all." Hayley wasn't ready to confess to her friend what it really meant.

Bethany still frowned. "But why do you want to leave us? Don't you like it at all being with us all?"

"Oh God, Bethany," Hayley sighed deeply. "I like you all and I like being with you. But I have no choice; when I finished my job, I have to leave. I swore it and I always keep my oaths."

"Does Arthur know that?" Bethany asked quietly.

Hayley nodded. "He does." She pressed her lips firmly together.

"After that – we won't see you again, will we?"

Hayley shook her head. "No, we won't. But there is no reason now to think about that. I can't turn the clock back and change my oath. And I won't turn the fingers of the clock faster forward than it is necessary." She was silent for a moment then she continued: "How are you and Arthur getting on?"

Bethany smiled. "Oh, he is lovely and so sweet. He reads every wish from my eyes."

"It's good that you are happy." Hayley smiled.

"There is more." Bethany confessed.

Hayley looked astonished at her. "What is it?"

"Well," Bethany hesitated. "There was a reason why I asked you how much time has gone by already. I counted; and I had my period the last time more than six weeks ago. I think I'm pregnant." She finally finished.

Hayley was surprised, "Already? I'm glad for you – and so happy! Does Arthur know it?" She embraced her friend friendly.

Bethany shook her head. "I wanted to keep it for myself till I'm really sure. You won't tell him, will you?"

"I won't. That's your job, not mine. But still – I'm happy for you two!" Hayley smiled.

And Bethany smiled back at her.

"Hayley?" a voice came into the open wagon.

Hayley bent forward and threw a look out of the moving wagon. "What is it?" She called, as she noticed Harry riding beside the wagon.

"The scouts are back. They have news." Harry called over to her.

"I'm coming!" Hayley called back and turned to Bethany. "I've got to go. We talk later, okay?"

"Certainly we do. Go!" Bethany hugged her shortly.

Hayley winked at Bethany then she solved the reins from her camel from the wagon where she had bound it to and jumped from the wagon. Still in movement the camel came up to her and with another jump Hayley caught the top of the saddle and pulled up till she sat correct in the saddle. Then she picked up the reins, pulled the camel to the left and pushed it forward. She rode till she reached the top of the small caravan where Arthur, Rick, Harry and the scouts Damon and Richard rode. Hayley led her camel over to the scouts and pushed it between the two men. "What did you find out?" She asked curiously.

Richard grinned. "We found a small lake and a waterfall in the next hills. There is no village or something else around. We thought that maybe a perfect place for us to…" He suddenly stopped.

"You mean a place to rest?" Hayley asked matter-of-fact. "You all need a break, don't you?" She looked from one man to the next.

Arthur was the only one who dared to look into her eyes and he was the only one who dared to answer: "You are right, we need a break. Since weeks we don't do something else than riding and fighting. Some days break would be heaven for us."

Hayley frowned lightly. She looked intensive at the men and noted only now how tired they all looked. As she looked at Arthur, she noticed the black marks under his eyes he hadn't had before. 'And still you had time to produce something else as well.' She thought but she was clever enough not to say it aloud. And she guessed quite right that he must be under an enormous pressure, having to look after his wife and to satisfy her as well.

Hayley stared to the hills, which lay just in front of her, warm and inviting. And she confessed to herself that she was tired too. "Well," she sighed. "Then show us where this lake is. When it is all right, we stay for some days and relax a bit."

The Fighters examined her astonished because that was the last thing they had expected to hear from her.

"Do I speak Spanish? Or why don't you move?" Hayley turned to the Scouts.

Damon began to stutter. "I'm… I'm so… I'm sorry, Hay… Hayley. This… this way!" he said and rode faster on.

Hayley frowned, as the two scouts rode in front of her up into the hills. "What's wrong with them now?" She asked Arthur, as she came up to his side.

Arthur smiled. "You shocked them. In fact you shocked us all. A break is a good idea, in fact a very good idea. But you are driven from something we don't know and it surprised us that you will give us a break. You always seem to be fit and powerful and you don't seem to need a break." He stopped, suddenly afraid that he had said too much.

Hayley shook her head. "Never be afraid to tell me anything, promise?" She looked intensive at Arthur.

Arthur looked straightforward. After a while he put his eyes down before he looked over at Hayley. "In the last days you were more like a slave driver. What's going on with you?"

"I don't know. Perhaps I'm only a bit… I don't know, sorry. We all need a break for sure." Hayley answered slowly.

Arthur looked at her and smiled a bit. "That sounds already more like the Hayley I know."

And Hayley smiled at him.

The evening came up already, as Hayley and the Fighters of Freedom reached the lake in between the hills. The lake looked very inviting in the evening sun and the green around it gave it a touch of warmth.

Hayley jumped from her camel and stretched herself. "It doesn't look bad – but I still want to have some guards around tonight. Can you organize everything?" She turned to Rick.

Rick bowed and with the help of Harry he got the people moving. The Fighters set up a big tent they had bought in the last town and looked after the camels.

Priest Alfonso stopped his wagon beside the tent and looked after his horses. Then he started a fire at the edge to the lake and looked after food and something to drink.

Orinda and Bethany helped him.

In the meantime Hayley had stepped over to the lake and put her hand into the water. She felt the water, still warm running over her hand. "Well, tomorrow I need for sure a bath." She murmured.

Arthur, who knelt down beside her, grinned. "We all need a bath but I don't think that one of us has a bathing costume."

Hayley couldn't hide a smile. "We have then to bath separate; one time the women, one time the men – and one time the couples." She teased him.

Arthur smiled. "We'll see. But I don't think you will be able to get that through. On the other hand I don't think that anybody would dare to touch you if you don't invite them."

"And what is with Orinda?" Hayley asked sceptical.

Arthur shrugged his shoulders. "We have to keep an eye on her." But he corrected himself at once again. "No, that's not necessary."

"Why is it not necessary?" Hayley asked astonished.

"Don't you know?" Arthur was really surprised. "Damon likes her a lot. And Orinda can't keep her eyes of him as well."

"Ohm - Damon and Orinda - I would never have guessed that." Hayley confessed. "But perhaps I'm too wrapped up in myself."

Arthur sat down on the ground. "Like to talk about that?" he asked quietly.

Hayley leaned back and supported herself on her arms. "Jeff reminds me every day of what I lost. It hurts a lot; you have to know. And to see you and Bethany doesn't make it better." Hayley bit on her lips.

Arthur sighed. "Aren't we on the way to the Horsemen's village? You will see then your husband again."

"We are on the way. And I dread the day we reach it." Hayley sighed.

"Why? Why do you dread it? Won't you like to see your husband again?" Arthur was really astonished.

"It's not that. I'd love to see Fletcher again. But then I got what I wanted and… and at the moment I'm afraid of going back to the temple to fulfil my oath. I don't want to leave you all." Hayley finally confessed.

Arthur slipped on the space beside Hayley and embraced her heartily. "I know your whole life has been difficult for you. But think about what you reached and think about what you leave back when you go. It maybe only small comfort but perhaps it helps you. – You were always so strong, don't give up just before you reach your goal." Arthur whispered into her ear. "And you know if you are lonely and sad, you always can come to me and Beth. Please!"

Hayley embraced him and pressed her body at his. "Thanks." She only murmured.

"Is there a reason of getting jealous?" A female voice interrupted Arthur and Hayley's conversation.

Hayley solved herself from Arthur and smiled up at Bethany. "There is no reason at all. I only needed a bit of comfort and I thought you would allow me to get it from your husband."

Bethany sat down beside the two people and smiled lightly. "I have nothing against it." She hesitated and looked at Arthur who nodded at her. "If you need comfort – come and join us tonight. Please do! You will feel better tomorrow, I promise."

Hayley hesitated as well. "If I don't disturb you…" She started.

Arthur interrupted her at once. "We wouldn't invite you when we thought you would disturb us. Please come. We stay for the night in the wagon."

Hayley looked at the couple seriously. Suddenly she smiled. "I love to come. Thanks."

"Fine," Bethany got up and stretched out her hands. "Let's go then. Supper is ready."

Hayley and Arthur took her hands and got up. Together they went back to the camp.

"Well, I think I go to bed. I'm on duty tonight." Rick stretched himself and looked around. "What's with you?"

It was already late; the moon was up and stars could be seen.

Harry got up as well. "I'm coming too."

The other men followed them into the tent till only Arthur, Bethany and Hayley were left beside the Fighters who were on guard.

"Let's go!" Arthur got up and pulled Bethany up as well. He threw a look at Hayley but he said nothing. He left the place at the fire and Bethany followed him hesitatingly.

Hayley stared into the fire. She waited till she heard nothing anymore then she got up, extinguished the fire and went to the first guard. "Everything okay?" she asked and she got a nod from Brad. Then she went on to the second guard, Will, where everything was all right as well. The third, fourth and fifth guard answered the same and Hayley grew calmer.

With quiet steps she went over to the wagon and lifted a bit of the curtain. "Are you already asleep?" She asked quietly into the darkness.

"Don't be ridiculous! We were waiting for you! Come inside!" Arthur's voice came back.

Hayley solved the belts from her swords and laid them down inside the wagon, direct at the entrance. Then she climbed up and entered carefully the wagon.

"Lie down here!" Bethany knocked on the ground in the middle of the wagon and Hayley followed the noise. She let herself down in the middle and felt the warm bodies of Arthur and Bethany beside hers. She sighed comfortable.

"Still troubled in your mind?" Arthur asked quietly, bending over her.

"No, it is just the opposite." Hayley answered slowly. "It's good to be with you."

"Is it only to be with us – or more?" Arthur inquired, coming with his face nearer to hers so that Hayley could feel his breath on her skin and it made her crazy. "Do you really know what you do to me?" She asked, lifting her head a bit till she reached Arthur's lips. Then she breathed a kiss on his mouth.

Arthur reacted at once. He pressed his lips hard on Hayley's mouth and started to kiss her wildly.

Hayley got breathless under his kisses. Her hand searched over the ground till it reached Bethany and went then over her body.

Bethany slipped nearer and started to open the leather strings of Hayley's waistcoat. Then she went with her hand under Hayley's shirt and stroked her naked skin.

Hayley turned her head away from Arthur's and sighed. "You both turn me completely on, do you know that?" She asked only hypocritical.

But Arthur laughed. "That was the reason, wasn't it, for doing it?"

"Well, yes, I think so." Hayley grinned. She opened her cloak around the neck and then pulled the waistcoat over her head. She had noticed that Arthur and Bethany were already completely naked and she helped them to unbutton her shirt. Then Bethany embraced her, pulled the shirt down her arms and opened the bra.

Hayley breathed the smell of Bethany's hair and leaned against her. She threw the shirt and the bra away and embraced Bethany.

Softly and longingly they kissed each other.

Arthur felt about the bodies of the two women and stopped, as he reached the breasts. Gently he started to massage Hayley's left and Bethany's right breast. Then he bent forward and licked first Bethany's breast, then Hayley's.

Hayley lay down again. Her hands lay on Bethany's head and stroked her softly.

Arthur went up to Bethany's ear and whispered quietly: "You up, I do down. Is it all right?"

"Okay." Bethany answered quietly and lay down beside Hayley.

Again the two women kissed each other, searching with their tongues through the mouth of the other one.

Bethany caressed Hayley's breast and massaged it softly.

But Hayley grew fast much more excited, as Arthur spread out her legs and knelt down between them. He laid his hand on the soft spot and tickled her so that Hayley's legs started to shiver and move.

Hayley solved her lips from Bethany's and groaned softly.

Bethany smiled. She kissed Hayley's cheek and her ear before she wandered down to her breasts. She licked and kissed her nipples till they grew hard and massaged her breasts wildly.

At the same time Arthur bent forward and started to lick and kiss Hayley between her legs.

Hayley groaned up. Her hands were still on Bethany's head, cramping softly into the hair. She was unable to do anything; she enjoyed only the feeling Arthur and Bethany released in her.

Arthur stopped licking her, as he heard her groan loudly and pushed Bethany a bit to the side. Then he stretched himself, led his penis into Hayley and lay down on her, pressing his penis deeply into her.

Hayley groaned up. She laid her legs around Arthur and pressed him hard against herself.

Bethany stroked both of them softly during the act.

Finally Arthur groaned up as well and pressed hard against Hayley.

Hayley groaned and let go of her hold. She lay down flat on the ground again and sighed.

Arthur kissed her softly then he rolled to the side.

"I keep you warm." Bethany said quietly and lay down on Hayley.

Hayley laid her arms around Arthur and Bethany and stroked them softly. She lifted her head and whispered something into Bethany's ear what Arthur couldn't make out.

Bethany looked at her, only seeing Hayley's eyes gleaming in the darkness. "Do you think it will work?" She asked suspiciously.

Hayley smiled. "Let's try it then we know."

"Well, then." Bethany grinned.

Together they turned and took Arthur into their middle.

"I don't think I can so fast again." Arthur murmured but Hayley stopped him with her lips. She kissed him, searching with her tongue through his mouth.

Arthur laid his arms around Hayley and kissed her wildly back. His hand pressed her head down at his and the other went over her back then her side to the front. He reached her breasts and started to massage them.

Suddenly he solved his lips from Hayley's and groaned.

Bethany had taken his penis into her hands and kissed now the top of it, which made Arthur groan for excitement. She licked him intensive till she felt his penis hardened in her hands. Then she sat down on him, leading his penis straight into her.

Arthur gasped. His hand cramped around Hayley's breast and his other hand searched for Bethany.

Bethany bent a bit forward, during she moved back and forwards.

Arthur reached her body and felt along till he reached her breast. He pressed and massaged the breast till Bethany groaned up as well.

Hayley in the meantime solved his hand from her breast and led it down between her legs.

Arthur groaned. He searched with his finger till he reached her spot and tickled her there again and again.

Hayley bent forward and kissed Arthur on the mouth. But it didn't last long; Arthur touched her so much like Bethany moved on him that both of them groaned up together.

Bethany groaned up in the next moment and she lay down on Arthur.

Hayley snuggled up to both of them and closed her eyes.

"Don't fall asleep! I hadn't had you yet!" Bethany laughed quietly, as she noted that Hayley was drifting away.

Hayley opened her eyes again. "I'm not tired. But I don't think that anything can excite me now."

"Well, I said the same and still you both managed it to get me to the point again. Don't you think Bethany and I will be able to bring you once more to orgasm?" Arthur grinned.

"Try it! I love surprises." Hayley answered laughing. But she didn't laugh anymore, as Arthur bent over her and started to kiss her all over her face. She laid her arms around him and enjoyed feeling his mouth and tongue on her skin.

Bethany massaged Hayley's breasts softly, kissed the nipples till they grew hard then she moved on down till she reached Hayley's soft spot. She started to kiss and lick her and smiled, as Hayley started to move her legs in excitement.

As Arthur laid his hand on her breast, Hayley groaned up deeply. She felt over Arthur's body and laid her hands around his penis.

Arthur couldn't stop a gasp and as Bethany stretched her finger into Hayley, it was Hayley who gave a gasp and started to shiver all over her body for excitement.

Arthur pressed again his lips on Hayley's and stroked at the same time over her breasts.

Bethany licked again over Hayley's spot and pressed her finger deeper into Hayley.

Hayley's hand held Arthur's penis firmly and she breathed out with a long groan.

"Did we get you?" Arthur grinned at her.

Hayley smiled back. "Did I get you? At least it feels like it."

Arthur laughed again. "Well, yes, I could again."

Hayley pushed him over to Bethany who had stretched out beside Hayley. "She needs it."

Arthur didn't hesitate at all; he lay down on Bethany and pressed his penis deep down into her.

Bethany gasped and laid one arm around Arthur and one around Hayley. After both of them had caught their breaths again, all three of them snuggled up together and fell asleep.

Next morning Hayley crept out of the wagon very early. She was carefully and very quiet in order not to wake up Arthur and Bethany. She dressed fast but she left her swords back in the wagon. Then she went over to the lake and tested the water.

"Care for an early bath?"

Hayley turned around. "Morning, Harry! Did anything happen last night?"

Harry sat down beside her and looked over the water. "The night was quiet. It seems to be a very quiet area here. How long do we stay?"

Hayley shrugged her shoulders. "Let's see how long we can cope with the quietness around here, shall we?" She tested the water again and grinned then at Harry. "I think I go for a swim. I need it."

"Enjoy it!" Harry got up and walked away.

"And when do you want to take a bath? You really need one as well!" Hayley called teasingly behind him.

Harry turned. "What did you say?" He asked with a frown.

Hayley let her cloak fall to the ground and her waistcoat followed at once. "I said you really need a bath as well." She grinned mischievously.

Harry stepped slowly back. At the same moment he pulled the arms of his shirt up. "Will you say that again?" He said seriously, coming nearer and nearer.

Hayley looked around for a way out; during she went one step after the other back. "Well, I don't think that you..." She stopped at the edge of the lake.

Harry grinned. "Then I heard right. Now I think I really need a bath. But not alone!" And he threw himself on Hayley.

Hayley lost her hold and fell backwards into the lake.

Harry fell into the lake beside her and he came splashing up. "Well, you got what you wanted. I'm taking a bath."

Hayley grinned beside him. "But don't you think it would be better to get rid of the clothes? It's easier to swim then."

"Err. When I take my clothes off, I'm able to chase you three times over the lake and will still be able to overtake you and win the fourth time." Harry threw his cloak on the green and let his swords follow. Then he pulled his wet clothes down from his body.

Hayley followed his example. She spread her clothes out on the green before she slipped down into the water again, completely naked. "Four times through the lake, right?" She said and without waiting for an answer she swam over to the other end of the lake.

Harry had problems to follow her so fast.

They chased each other over the lake and back, much to the enjoyment of the other Fighters who had gathered around the lake in the meantime.

"What's going on here?" Arthur came nearer and threw a look over the lake.

Rick grinned. "Hayley has a go at Harry. She chases him over the lake. Well, we are waiting only for the time they want to come out."

"Why that?" Arthur still didn't understand.

"Well," Rick grinned wide, "when you see the wet clothes on the ground over there, then you know why they're chasing each other. And then you should know why we are waiting."

Arthur looked at the clothes on the ground and finally shook his head. "You're crazy." He murmured. "You do all these only because you want to see Hayley naked?"

Rick threw a look at him. "You can talk easily. You had her last night, hadn't you? And to all you have a wife as well."

"Oh God," Arthur groaned. "Do you all know that?" As he saw Rick nodding, he continued calmer: "Because she didn't come into the tent?" Again Rick nodded and Arthur stared down at the clothes on the ground. "Well, I can understand that you all are grieving for a woman but do you really think she would take you all in?"

Rick laughed. "No, I don't. For that she has you and your wife. But a glimpse on her – well, that would be nice."

Arthur grinned now as well. "Okay, then let's get her out." He said and sat down on the ground. He started to prepare a fire then he put a kettle with water on it. As it just started to boil, he called loudly: "Anybody caring for a hot tea?"

"I do - every time!" Hayley called from the lake where she just pushed Harry under water. Then she swam nearer to the edge of the lake.

"Come and get it!" Arthur called out.

Hayley hesitated, as she noted that all the Fighters were staring at her. Then she understood. "Well, and now you are waiting to see me coming out of here?" She shook her head.

"You can't expect us not to watch you. When do we ever get to see a woman? Well, a woman in her natural state?" Brad grinned.

Hayley looked at him. "Guess, next time we stop in a town and not at a lonely lake. Bethany, be a pal and give me a towel."

Bethany smiled, as she turned to get a towel for Hayley.

"What a pity!" Will sighed loudly, and the whole group broke out into hilarious laughter.

Harry sat down on the edge of the lake and shook his head. He took a towel out of the Priest's hands and dried himself. Then he wound it around his waist and grinned down at Hayley. "You see I get my revenge."

Hayley sighed. She dipped into the water and shook her head, as she came up out of the water. Bethany reached her a towel, and Hayley climbed out of the lake. She wound the towel around her body before she turned to the guys. "Satisfied?" She mocked.

Brad sat down at the fire and nodded. "For the moment!" he grinned.

Hayley rolled her eyes. She grabbed Bethany's arm and pulled her away from the fire and over to the wagon.

The men gathered around the fire and started to cook breakfast.

Hayley looked at Bethany and Orinda who had followed them in silence. "Could you do me a favour? I want to clean my stuff but I need something to dress in the meantime." Her look was beseechingly.

Bethany grinned. "Do you want to get the guys all hot and bothered again?"

Hayley only shrugged her shoulders.

In this moment Orinda joined into the conversation. "I think I just have the right thing for you. The guys will have something to see – but nothing to be seen."

"Get it out!" Hayley grinned.

Twenty minutes later the women joined the men around the fire.

Hayley pushed Rick into the back and said calmly: "Move your ass to the side and let a lady sit down."

"A… What?" Rick turned and got confused, as his look fell on Hayley.

Hayley sat down and took a mug of tea into her hands. Astonished she looked around at the Fighters who were staring at her without exception. "What's now wrong?" She sighed.

"Well," Arthur searched for words. "Err, you look… different."

Hayley looked down at herself. "Nice dress, isn't it?" She smiled.

"It is." Arthur swallowed.

Hayley wore a white dress, which stood her very well with her still brown skin. It gave her figure very well over but it didn't show anything. It gave only her right shoulder and arm free; on the left side her arm was covered till her wrist, covering her tattoo on the arm completely.

"Well, we are not used to see you… like that." Gerry smiled at her.

"Then get used to it. I have to wear that a little bit longer." Hayley grinned.

The Fighters recovered moment to moment and started to enjoy their breakfast again.

Hayley winked at Bethany and Orinda and both women grinned back at her.

27

It was afternoon, hot in the sun and warm in the lake.

Hayley had finished cleaning her clothes and had hung them up at the back of the tent. Now she was sitting with the other Fighters at the edge of the lake, the feet in the water and lying back on a blanket.

Half of the men were sleeping and even Hayley couldn't keep her eyes open the whole time.

"We get visitors." Damon came up to Hayley. "They are riding just up the path we came up as well."

"Do you think they are on the warpath?" Hayley opened one eye.

Damon shrugged his shoulders. "Till now they don't know that we are here."

"Okay." Hayley got up a bit. "Guys, can you do me a favour?"

"What is it, Hayley?" Arthur opened his eyes.

"Take over, please. I'm not in the mood for a fight or even to change my dress." Hayley leaned back again and closed her eyes.

Arthur looked over at her and shook his head. "Aye, Ma'am." He murmured and sat slowly up. Then he got completely up, pulled his boots over and warmed himself up. Then he turned to the place where the path came out to the green and waited.

The riders came slowly nearer; they stopped short, as they noticed the Fighters at the lake but then they rode on.

"What are you doing here?" The first man at the top of the group of riders asked quite unfriendly, as he came up to Arthur.

"I would call it a break." Arthur answered mockingly. "And what are you doing here?"

The man stared down at Arthur. He got a push from another man into his back and he made the sign of Freedom.

Arthur gave the sign straight back.

The man sighed. "You know that this area here is holy ground?"

Arthur frowned, "Holy ground - and for whom?"

"Harder, God of Freedom," The man jumped down from his horse. "This country doesn't in particular praise him but for us he's important. And you desecrated his ground." The man examined Arthur from top to bottom.

Arthur stared back without any problems. "If you believe it or not but we don't desecrate his ground. Harder is holy to us as well."

The man laughed mockingly. "That I can see." he let Arthur stand where he was and entered the camp. Interested he looked around.

Hayley turned a bit and examined the man from top to bottom from under her eyelashes. She turned and pushed Priest Alfonso who was lying beside her and was sleeping. "Wake up, Al! I think Arthur needs your help!"

"Why mine?" Priest Alfonso murmured.

"I don't know. Only a feeling," Hayley answered.

Priest Alfonso murmured something, pulled his feet out of the water and got slowly up. He checked his dress then he turned and went over to the man who was standing in the middle of the camp. "May I ask what you are looking for here, my son?" He asked interested.

The man turned – and stared surprised into the Priest's face. He shook his head. "Al, isn't it? What on earth are you doing here?"

Priest Alfonso smiled, "Hi Paul! I think you know exactly what I'm doing here. But how does it come that you're here?"

Paul shook his head. "So we don't come forward, Al. Do you know that's holy ground here?"

Priest Alfonso was clever. "Harder's ground, I know. And you should come down from your big horse, as you know exactly that I'm a priest of Harder. And the guys I'm riding with are sworn to Harder as well. So tell your guys to climb down and join us at the fire."

Paul grinned. "You are still so straight forward as I remember you. – Okay, we will join you." He got up – and stopped in the same moment. "Are these chickens belonging to your group as well?"

Priest Alfonso turned and looked over to the lake where Hayley had sat up and talked quietly to Bethany and Orinda. He noted as well the hungry look of Paul. "Keep your fingers away from these girls – if you don't want to end up dead. Only a friendly suggestion!" he added, as he saw Paul frowning.

Paul grinned. "Let this be my problem." He went back to his companions and organized shortly where they could leave their horses and asked them over to the fire.

Arthur sat down beside the Priest. "You know them?" He asked astonished.

Priest Alfonso nodded. "They are a bunch of... of robbers to say it exactly. We have to be careful with them – and we have to keep an eye on our women or we won't have them anymore."

Arthur frowned. "With other words – they take everything they can get without taking any considerations?" And as Priest Alfonso nodded once more, he added with a sigh: "Well, perhaps Rick is the right one to keep his eyes open if they do something."

"And you are the right one", Priest Alfonso continued, "to look after your wife before it's too late." He pointed down to the lake.

Hayley, Bethany and Orinda had got visitors.

The men had brought their horses on the grass to the left of the lake and on their way back they had noticed the women at the lake. So they had joined them for a light conversation, which turned quite fast into a nasty one.

"So, what do you think about a nice day and night with us – and not with these stiff guys?" One of the men asked finally.

Bethany snipped mockingly back: "I'm sorry to disappoint you but I'm married to one of these stiff guys and for nothing in the world I want to change that."

"What a pity!" The man said but his eyes spoke a different language.

"And you?" Another man turned to Orinda.

Orinda shook her head. "Count me out. I don't care for you but I care for these stiff guys!" She mocked.

Paul laid his hand on Hayley's shoulder. "And what is with you, Sweetheart? You are for sure not given away, are you?"

"Not at this moment. But if you want to have this evening still a left hand then it would be better to take it away from me." Hayley answered coldly.

Paul laughed. "This you say now. But wait till tonight!"

The men started to laugh.

Hayley bent forward and whispered into Bethany's ear: "See that you keep in safety with Arthur and the others that nothing will happen to you both. These guys won't take any considerations."

"And you?" Bethany asked exactly so quiet like Hayley back.

Hayley smiled. "I'm able to look after myself. – Look, here comes Arthur!"

Arthur stepped up to the circle and said calmly: "If the gents finished flirting, we have a meal ready for you. Bethany, Orinda, Hayley! We would need you over there." He stretched out his hand.

Bethany took his hand and got up. "Certainly!" and she pulled up Orinda as well.

Hayley followed their example but leaving the circle she made a sign to Arthur and started to walk around the lake.

Arthur brought the other two women back to the fire and then into the tent. "Listen, both of you! I don't want you to go out there again before we got rid of these guys. They may be dangerous."

"This we already noticed." Bethany nodded. "We stay here – but, please don't forget about us at all." She looked beseechingly at Arthur.

Arthur grinned. "How could I?" He bent forward and kissed Bethany on her lips. But as he finally turned to go, Bethany stopped him once more. "Please, Arthur! Keep an eye on Hayley as well, will you?"

"Sure, I will." Arthur smiled before he left the tent.

The men had gathered around the fire by now, only Hayley – and Paul were missing.

Hayley noted quite fast that she still wasn't alone on her walk around the lake.

Paul came up to her and laid his arm around her. "It's beautiful here, isn't it?" He asked smiling.

Hayley became stiff. "If you don't take your arm from my body – you will regret it for the rest of your life!" She warned him intensive.

Paul took her warning as a joke and laughed. "Come on, girlie! Enjoy the beautiful country instead of getting crummy!"

"I warn you for the last time!" Hayley only answered. She stopped and stared out of eyes, dark from anger, at the man at her side. "Why you dared to talk to us about Harder and his holy ground here, is a puzzle to me. You do everything what goes against Harder and what he stands for." She added.

Paul grinned. "Why do you think he's holy to us? Then at least we know what we can do without getting in conflict with him."

"You can take it like that." Hayley shrugged her shoulders and turned to go back.

Paul caught her arm and stopped her. "It's just so nice here, stay with me. We could have a little bit of fun."

Hayley examined him mockingly. "You still don't understand, do you? Let me try to explain it better to you." Her eyes sparked with cold anger. "I'll kill you if you don't let go of me. And if you think about to force me to anything I don't want to do – let me tell you that there are already other guys who had to pay for it – with their lives! Is it clear now?"

Paul still grinned. "I think you need a cup of tea to calm you down. Then we talk again."

Hayley rolled her eyes, pulled her arm out of Paul's grab and went back over to the fire. She sought for Priest Alfonso's vicinity and sat down beside him. Quietly she asked him about the guys he seemed to know and Priest Alfonso told her everything he knew.

Paul had sat down with his guys opposite Priest Alfonso and Hayley and they had started to talk together in quiet voices.

Hayley felt the looks of the guys on her again and again and finally she couldn't bear it anymore. She sighed. "Al, listen. I have a look at the girls and change my dress. It's getting dark and I want to be prepared. Please tell Arthur in an unobserved moment to bring me my swords. There are in the back of the wagon."

Priest Alfonso nodded. "Will do." he only answered.

Hayley got up and wriggled her way through the Fighters over to the tent. She slipped inside and breathed out in relief.

Bethany and Orinda only looked grinning at her.

Outside Paul stretched himself out. "It's a pity, she left. She would have been great fun, as soon as she would have calmed down. Perhaps I visit her tonight."

"Well," Arthur said seriously, "then it's better when I'll be with her."

Paul laughed. "Don't be afraid! I won't do anything bad to her."

Arthur shook his head. "It's not her, I'm concerned about. It's you!"

"What do you mean?" Paul frowned for a second.

Arthur examined him thoroughly. "I mean that if you try to get Hayley – especially if she doesn't want to – then she will kill you without hesitating. I'll be there to prevent that you get killed."

Paul laughed. "I don't think she will manage." He was amused.

Arthur shook his head. "You have no idea." He murmured but he left it with that.

Neither Paul nor one of his men noticed around half an hour later that Arthur got up and went over to the wagon. He checked the back of the wagon, and then the complete wagon without finding anything.

"Are you looking for these?" Rick stepped nearer. In his hands he held Hayley's swords.

Arthur frowned. "She left them in the wagon; I saw them this morning. How did you get them?"

Rick smiled. "I kept an eye on the guys, as you suggested. They had already a good snoop around our camp even though it looks like that nobody ever left his seat at the fire. But I wasn't helpless as well. I brought everything back and stored it in the tent. Hayley's swords are the last ones; I thought she might need them tonight."

Arthur nodded. "We all will need all our power and swords tonight. Please, keep further on an eye on these guys."

Rick nodded only. He handed over the swords and left on silent soles like he had come.

Arthur turned to the back of the tent in order not to let the guys see the swords and pushed them underneath the cover into the tent. Then he got up, walked around the tent and entered the tent freely and without any problems.

Hayley looked over at him. "How is it going on?" She asked, now dressed again in her dark clothes.

Arthur shrugged his shoulders. "This guy called Paul is determined to get you tonight. I've warned him but he won't listen. So we have to count with an attack this night."

Hayley nodded. She looked at Arthur, asking, and Arthur nodded. He stepped into the back of the tent and picked up the swords, which he then handed over to Hayley.

"Thanks." Hayley murmured. "Where were they?"

"Rick found them somewhere in the stuff of the guys. They're robbing us already the whole time they're here."

"I know." Hayley smiled hard. "Rick brought already some stuff back." She pointed over to a corner where a lot of sacks were stapled up. Hayley sat down on a blanket and waved Arthur over to her. "We have to make a plan."

Arthur sat down beside her and in the next half an hour they figured out a plan for the night…

28

"They're coming!" Harry whispered quietly.

"Psst!" Hayley made and wound the blanket firmly around her. She closed her eyes and simulated that she was asleep.

The men who entered the tent were very quiet. They were aware that the Fighters were all sleeping in the tent and so they did everything that they wouldn't wake up. Silently they stepped over to the corner where they saw in the dark light of a torch Hayley curled up under a blanket.

Paul bent over Hayley and he pressed a hand with a plaster on her mouth. In the next moment he searched for her hands.

Hayley had enough. She felt Paul's hands on her body and she closed her hand firmly around the handle of her sword. She lifted it and pointed it at Paul. With the other hand she ripped off the plaster. "And now?" she asked mockingly.

Paul stepped back. "Come on, girlie! You don't mean that. All we want is a little bit of fun – and you want it too!"

"Well yes", Hayley got slowly up. "But my fun looks a little bit different to yours." She said and she played with the sword in her hands, making it clear that she knew what to do with that.

Harry got up. "Leave it, Hayley. They are not worth to get into trouble for only cause of you wanting to kill them. Let's see that we get them out of our camp."

The men looked around. They had to notice that they were surrounded from the Fighters and that not one of them looked approachable, not even Harry who had spoken for them.

"I have no problems to kill them and I won't have any problems afterwards." Hayley knew she sounded hard and unforgivable but that was what men had made out of her. And she didn't want to let a guy destroy that.

Paul stepped backwards, as he noticed that Hayley was serious. Her hold of the sword told him as well that he had to be careful. "Okay, okay." He said. "We're leaving – you win. But be a bit more careful the next time or it won't be so easy for you." He warned Hayley then he turned around and left the tent, his companions at his heel.

Harry nodded and some of the Fighters followed the men out of the tent. At last he tapped Hayley on the shoulder. "Good for you for not having done it. Now we have a clean cut."

Hayley shook her head. "It's not over yet."

"What do you mean?" Harry frowned.

Hayley sat back on her blanket. "They may be leaving now but they'll come back. And believe me – then I won't take any considerations at all anymore."

Harry nodded. "Go to sleep before they come back that you will be fit." He suggested.

Hayley lay down and with her did some of the other Fighters. She knew that she could trust her Fighters that they would get rid of the intruders – and that they would keep watch… Hayley fell asleep.

Nothing happened in that night and in the morning the Fighters, including Hayley, Bethany and Orinda, gathered around a fire for an early breakfast. Still some of the Fighters were on watch.

Hayley sighed. She nipped at her tea before she started: "Okay, listen. You all know that these guys won't accept that we turned them out. They'll come back. The question is: Do you want to stay here and fight it out or do you want to leave?"

Arthur frowned: "Why do you ask such a question?"

Hayley stayed calm. "We are here in an area we don't know it belongs to. We are here because we wanted to have some days rest and quietness. That's the reason why I ask. If we stay here and wait for the attack – it could be that we have to run afterwards. There won't be anything like rest and quietness anymore, probably for a long time. On the other hand if we go now, we still can search for another ground to get some peace and rest."

The Fighters looked in silence at each other. Nobody dared to say something and everybody avoided her look.

Hayley concentrated for a moment only on her cup of tea. She finished her drink and got up. "Think about it and let me know what you decided."

She said, calmer as she really was and went down to the lake. Nobody stopped her.

"I hate it." Nick murmured.

"What do you hate?" Arthur wanted to know.

Nick shook his head. "I hate that she's leaving the decision for us again. Why can't she make it?"

Arthur smiled. "Don't you know that she already made the decision? She only wants to know if we have the same opinion. – If we all have a different opinion, perhaps we can change hers but otherwise…" Arthur left the rest open.

Nick was confused and with him some of the others. "But why can't she say clearly what she wants?"

Now Rick grinned. "That has something to do with democracy. At least she leaves us the choice to decide different."

Priest Alfonso suppressed a smile with effort. "Guys!" and as his look fell onto the ladies, he added: "Sorry, ladies! But we should come to a decision now – don't let Hayley wait."

Again the guys were silent.

Bethany looked around. "I don't really know what you all are thinking. If you ask me – yes, I enjoyed a quiet time but when this is over now then it's over. I'll wait here with Hayley, even if you don't." She got up and followed Hayley down to the lake before Arthur could stop her.

Arthur smiled. "Well, I can't say more, as my wife already did. Has anybody else something to say?"

Once more the Fighters looked at each other. Then Damon leaned back and grinned: "Well, we are fighters, aren't we? Let's stay and see what happens."

And the men nodded in agreement.

"That's that then." Arthur got up and followed the women down to the lake.

The men spread out and started to enjoy the day.

Orinda snuggled up at Damon and talked quietly to him, making him promise to be very careful.

Arthur sat down between Hayley and Bethany and embraced both of them at once. "You both are the most courageous women I ever saw. What shall we do today? It's such a nice day."

Hayley smiled. "So you all decided to stay?"

"We are fighters, aren't we?" Arthur spoke with Damon's words.

"True." Hayley grinned. Then she sighed. "I don't know what you want to do but I want to take a bath as long as it is possible. After that we should see that we are prepared – in all ways."

"Leave that to me." Arthur nodded. "Enjoy your bath." He got up and went back to the fire where he gathered around Rick, Harry and Priest Alfonso to talk the next points of defence through with them.

Hayley looked over at Bethany. "It was brave of you to make a stand. But I don't want you or Orinda anywhere near here, when these guys attack us."

"But where shall we go to? Here is nothing else." Bethany shrugged her shoulders.

Hayley smiled. "Come and take a bath with me!" She said and started to undress. Shortly after she threw herself into the water and swam over to the other end.

Bethany followed her slowly, having not so much power anymore, as Hayley still possessed. At the other end she was half tired already.

"Look here!" Hayley pointed at the rocks in front of her.

The rocks came at this side down till the edge of the lake and even down into it. At one point, only reachable over the water, was a crack in the rocks, just wide enough to let a slim woman slip through it.

"I checked the cave. There's enough space for you and Orinda to lie down and have a good night's sleep. You will need it – you have to care for our wounds in the morning." Hayley smiled.

Bethany sighed, "As you wish." But as Hayley turned to swim back, she stopped her: "Can you do me a favour?"

"What is it?" Hayley asked astonished.

"Listen, Hayley. You know I'm pregnant. I have only one wish – my child shall get to know its father. Can you keep an eye on him for me, please?"

Hayley grinned. "Do you really think your plan will work? Telling Arthur to look after me, and telling me to look after him? What do you want from us?" She asked more serious.

Bethany sighed, "Oh Hayley! All I want is to see you both again – alive! Is it too much to ask for? – I... I haven't any other family left then you both." She added carefully.

Hayley swam over to Bethany and embraced her till they both started to struggle against the water. Then Hayley let her go and promised: "I'll see to it that we both stay alive. I promise – and you know I never break a promise."

"Thanks, Hayley!" Bethany swam behind Hayley back over the lake.

Hayley had already dressed, as Bethany reached land again. She winked at her friend before she left the edge and went back to the fire where she joined Arthur, Rick, Harry and Priest Alfonso. Shortly she told them what she had agreed with Bethany then she listened to the plan the others had figured out in the meantime and with a smile on her lips she thought the plan was good.

The night was dark; the moon hadn't come up at all that night.

Otherwise it was quiet, not one leave fell from the trees and not one breath of wind could be felt.

Hayley stretched out in the tent on the ground. For the first time since they had bought the tent she had enough place for herself. That came only because she was alone in the tent. She was the piece of cheese in the mousetrap.

As Damon reported to her that he had seen the robbers coming back, she had made sure that they noticed that she was alone in the tent.

The plan was easy: Bethany and Orinda were hiding in the cave far away from the fighting ground. Five men were hiding in the wagon beside the tent; the others had looked for trees and bushes to hide in, around the camp and well out of the way the robbers would sneak into the camp but near enough to close them in afterwards. But all of the Fighters had made sure that the robbers saw that they were leaving the grounds around the lake...

Hayley relaxed her muscles. She knew she would need them pretty soon and she wanted them in best working order. She was lying motionless and waited for whatever would happen.

Somebody crept into the tent; Hayley could hear it without making any effort. She sighed like in a bad dream and curled herself up, the handle of her sword firmly in her hand.

"You never thought I would dare to come back, did you? But you belong to me, my girl!" Paul laid his hand around Hayley's neck.

Hayley opened her eyes. "Did you really believe I would let you come inside here without being prepared? I knew you would come back." She pointed the top of her sword at Paul's throat.

Paul was still amused. "You can kill me if you want to. But my men will take you without mercy. How do you like that?"

"Well," Hayley smiled. "If they survive, I will ask them later on." She got up, her hand still around her sword.

"You wanted it like that. But don't think you get me without defending myself." Paul pulled his sword and weighed it in his hand. Then he attacked Hayley without any hesitation.

Hayley defended herself as best as possible in the tent. She didn't notice that she cut the tent on top, as she made a wide swing to get near her attacker. Then she made a short attack and Paul let his defence fall to catch her sword. In the next moment Hayley let her sword fall, caught it at the bottom again and drove it from there up into Paul's chest.

Paul stood in astonishment still then he fell slowly to his back and didn't move anymore.

Hayley pulled her sword back and turned to the other men who stood at the entrance of the tent. "Who's next?" She asked calmly.

The men turned to the entrance and stepped in a hurry outside. Here they had to notice what their friends who had waited outside already knew: The Fighters had closed them in and direct by the entrance of the tent waited five of them, prepared to fight.

Hayley came out of the tent and joined her friends. Together they attacked the robbers and within seconds a hell of a fight was going on.

Arthur had a hard man to fight against. He couldn't get him at all and came into a hard self-defence, as the man hit at him again and again. Finally the man managed to pull his sword over Arthur's chest, cutting his leather waistcoat like paper. Arthur went into his knees.

Hayley noticed out of the corner of her eyes that Arthur went down into his knees and she jumped over to help him. She caught in the last moment the death hit, which was supposed to hit Arthur, and turned to the man. She knew when Arthur had problems with him; she wouldn't have it easier with him. Covering Arthur with her back, she hit out at the man, again and again, not watching her defence at all. Anger had been swelling up in her and she made it short. She got the man to the point that he didn't know anymore where to catch her hits and she hit him neatly over the throat with a violent hit.

The man broke down and Hayley turned to Arthur. "Are you all right?"

"I'm okay." Arthur murmured quietly then he fell to the ground and didn't move anymore.

In the next moment Hayley got a violent hit into the side, led from the back. She groaned up, turned during she went into her knees and hit out at her attacker. She cut his legs open and as he fell down, she slid open his throat. Then the power left her; the sword fell to the ground and Hayley broke down beside it.

The fight went on for some more minutes, yet then the Fighters started to collect the dead bodies on one pile at one side of the lake.

"Anybody hurt?" Priest Alfonso went from one to the next Fighter.

Most of the Fighters had scratches, as the robbers had fought quite violent and unfair but there was nothing more than a slid belly.

Harry had looked around. He was searching for Hayley and Arthur who he couldn't see running around. He saw some bodies lying around near the tent, and he swallowed, as he recognized the Fighter's uniform at two of them. He grabbed after Priest Alfonso's arm and pointed over to the tent. "I think they need help." He said only.

Priest Alfonso turned and went over to the tent. He knelt down and searched the first body for any wounds.

Hayley felt a couple of hands on her body and she groaned lightly. Half unconscious she felt how her body was moved around then she lost completely consciousness.

"That doesn't look good. It's a deep cut." Priest Alfonso murmured during he still examined the wound. "Get Bethany and Orinda over here; I need their help. Rick, Harry! Can you bring her into the tent?"

Without saying anything Rick and Harry lifted Hayley up and carried her into the tent during Brad swam over to the other side of the lake to get Bethany and Orinda back. Nick in the meantime set the dead bodies under fire.

Arthur blinked. "What happened?" He asked quietly.

Priest Alfonso pressed a cloth on his chest and smiled lightly. "You have a nasty cut, which put you out of order for a moment. But that will be fine in some days. Can you get up?"

Arthur nodded. "I think so." And with the help of the priest he got up and went into the tent where he sank thankfully down on a blanket. Then he looked around and saw with astonishment Hayley lying not far away from him on the ground. Rick was trying to stop her bleeding but he wasn't much successful.

Arthur frowned.

Bethany was in a worried state, as she entered the tent. She went straight over to Arthur but Arthur could calm her down a bit. As she turned then to Hayley, her worried look came back.

For the next hours Bethany, Orinda and Priest Alfonso looked after Hayley; they stopped the bleeding and they clamped the wound together as best as possible. Then there was nothing left than waiting.

29

As Hayley woke up the first time, it was dark. She only saw some shadows and she closed her eyes at once.

As she opened her eyes for the second time, the sun sent her rays through the tent opening and put everything into a gleaming light. Hayley blinked till she got used to it then she tried to sit up. But as a violent pain went through her body, she fell back with a light groan.

"You shouldn't try that again for the next days. You're still not healthy enough for that." Priest Alfonso said quietly and knelt down beside Hayley.

"What happened?" Hayley asked, trying to cope with the pain.

"As far as we know", Priest Alfonso explained, "You were attacked from the back. Your wound shows it clearly. You killed your attacker but that was it."

Hayley nodded, not having the slightest idea about what had happened. The last thing she could remember was seeing Arthur in a difficult position during the fight.

"Are you thirsty?" Priest Alfonso tore her back out of her dreams.

Hayley nodded.

Priest Alfonso poured some water into a cup and helped Hayley to lift her head and held then the cup to her mouth. Hayley drank carefully before she sank back again. Priest Alfonso put the cup down beside the water bottle.

"Is anybody else injured?" Hayley asked interested, meaning to come up to date again.

Priest Alfonso nodded. "But you are the one who got the most difficult injury. Arthur had a bad cut over his chest but it healed well. Damon had another cut; that's all right again. Otherwise there were only small cuts and bruises."

Hayley frowned. "And the wounds of the others healed already?" She asked.

Priest Alfonso nodded once more.

"How long am I lying here already?" Hayley asked, deeply frowning. "Tell me the truth!" She added, as she noticed that Priest Alfonso hesitated.

· Priest Alfonso sighed. "Since around two weeks. We were afraid that you wouldn't come through at all."

Hayley swallowed. "Do we have at least enough to eat?" She asked after a while.

"Well, we found a farm not far away. Some of the guys help out there – for that we get everything we need."

Hayley calmed down a bit. She closed her eyes and breathed deeply through.

As she opened her eyes again, she was alone in the tent. She looked through the opening of the tent and noticed the sun going down. Only then she registered that she must have slept again for some hours.

Hayley heard the men talking and laughing outside and she felt the immense wish to be with them. She decided shortly to try it again.

Carefully Hayley got up. She ignored the pain in her body and went slowly, step-by-step, over to the entrance of the tent. Then she looked interested outside.

Arthur leaned back and passed with his hand over the still painful chest. "At least, Hayley woke up. Perhaps she will be fine again in some day's time." He sighed.

Priest Alfonso looked up. "If she is careful – maybe." he murmured his answer.

"What do you mean?" Rick asked astonished.

"Well," Priest Alfonso shrugged his shoulders. "You know Hayley; she is always so... so unpredictable."

"And I think we don't know her enough." Harry joined into the conversation and pointed over to the entrance of the tent.

Arthur, Bethany and Rick turned around during the others only turned their heads.

"Hayley - What in Harder's name are you doing out of bed?" Priest Alfonso sounded very angry. He got up and went over to Hayley.

Hayley smiled at him. "I was lonely and wanted to see what you are doing." She said calmly.

Priest Alfonso took softly her arm and pushed her back into the tent. "You stay here till I allow you to get up. If you don't, I'll give you a good spanking after you recovered that you won't be able to sit anymore for days!"

"That's a real threat!" Hayley murmured, still smiling and sat obedient down. As she lay down again, she groaned shortly in pain.

"You see – if you would have stayed where you were, you wouldn't be in pain now." Priest Alfonso pressed Hayley down and pulled the blanket over her.

"Do you have any more of these useful suggestions?" Hayley sighed, as she lay in her provisional bed again.

"If you don't want to be lonely", Priest Alfonso continued a bit calmer. "Then we will bring the fire to you that you can be with us. And next time before you get up – call me! Understood?" He asked sharply now.

Hayley nodded. "Yes, father." She murmured.

With half closed eyes Hayley watched the Fighters moving the fire nearer to the tent and all the Fighters sat down, half in the tent, half outside.

Arthur sat down beside Hayley and looked down at her. "And how are you now?"

Hayley pulled a face. "I wish I would feel better, as I do at the moment."

Arthur smiled. "That will be better in some day's time."

"We'll see. And how are you?" Hayley looked intensive at Arthur.

Arthur shrugged his shoulders. "Sometimes it still hurts but it will be over soon." He smiled.

"I thought I would lose you, as I saw the man hurting you. I made the promise to have an eye on you and I never break a promise but… in this moment I thought I failed." Hayley said quietly, almost in whisper.

Arthur lowered his voice as well. "You saved my life; I have to thank you. This guy was much too good for me."

Hayley laid her hand on Arthur's. "No need to thank me. I like to think you would have done the same for me."

"I couldn't." Arthur's face was overcome with the knowledge of his failure.

Hayley smiled once more. "Your time hasn't come yet." She murmured, closing her eyes. She fell asleep with Arthur's hand in her own.

A week later Hayley was able to get up, and again a week later she made her first ride over the nearest country. She enjoyed it thoroughly to be fit again and she didn't think about her wound anymore.

"How was it?" Arthur got hold of the reins of Hayley's camel and helped her to climb down.

"Brilliant!" Hayley pulled the scarf from her face. She shook her long red curls till they fell freely around her head again. Then she patted her camel, opened the lock and pulled the saddle down. "We should see that we get moving." She said calmly, putting the saddle down beside the tent. Then she took the reins out of Arthur's hands and let her camel run. She knew it would come back if she only would whistle.

Arthur examined Hayley from top to bottom. "I'm sure you should take a step back again. You are still not all right and we should stay till we are all one hundred per cent once more."

Hayley sighed. "I only would wish you all wouldn't worry so much about me. I'm fine!"

Then she suddenly grinned. "One hundred per cent, you said? Well, we'll see!" And she went into the tent.

Arthur stopped frowning outside. "What do you mean?" He asked suspiciously.

Hayley came back out of the tent. She had left her cloak inside as well as the scarf but for that she had her sword in her hands. "Let's see how fit we are." She said grinning and examined Arthur mockingly.

Arthur shook his head. "You're terrible." He turned half away from Hayley then in the next second he pulled his sword out of its cover and turning back he hit out at Hayley.

Hayley only had waited for it. She caught the hit and attacked herself then so hard that Arthur jumped backwards.

"What are you both doing here?" Bethany came up from the lake with a load of washed clothes.

"Training," Arthur pressed through his teeth during he caught a hit and hit himself out again.

Hayley grinned, as she stepped slowly backwards to get out of Arthur's fire. She prepared herself and finally outrun Arthur and got him in front of her sword without letting him any possibility for defence. "Well and now?" She asked mockingly.

Arthur shook his head. "One to zero for you!" he said, stepped back, lifted his sword and attacked Hayley once more.

During Hayley defended herself, more and more of the Fighters came nearer to the place where Arthur and Hayley were fighting each other. They started to whistle and clapped into their hands every time when one of the two Fighters got a good blow against the other one.

Harry, who stepped nearer at Priest Alfonso's side, shook his head. "If somebody tells me now that these two are not fit – I start to laugh."

Priest Alfonso shrugged his shoulders. "We will see how Hayley's wound looks like after the fight."

"Don't be so pessimistic!" Harry smiled and clapped, as Hayley managed with one blow that Arthur lost his sword and fell onto his back. "They are both fit again how you can see. And they both didn't forget anything I taught them." He sounded satisfied.

Priest Alfonso examined his friend thoughtfully. "I'll check her tonight through and – perhaps you are right and we will be able to go on our journey again."

Harry only nodded.

Hayley and Arthur finished their training fights, as it stood eight to eight for each of them.

Hayley sat down on the ground and fanned herself some fresh air. "That was good." She said satisfied.

Arthur lay down beside her. "You still have your special touch – and you're in a good shape after this long time."

"You're pretty good as well." Hayley grinned back at him.

"And what does it mean for us?" Nick asked curiously, sitting down beside them.

Hayley looked at him, at Damon behind him and then at all the other men who came nearer up to them. Then she sighed. "You're getting impatient, aren't you?" Again she looked from one Fighter to the next. "Perhaps I have to apologize to you…"

"Don't." Will interrupted her at once. "We know enough about your condition as to know that you didn't simulated. But if you are fit again…"

"You want to go on?" Hayley sighed.

Will nodded and with him the other Fighters as well.

Priest Alfonso stepped up. "At first I have to check you through. And if you are all right then we can decide if we go on or not." He said firmly and stretched out his hand.

Hayley, like everybody else, didn't really dare to contradict the Priest and she took his hand and got up. She put her sword back into its cover and followed the Priest back to the tent and into it.

"Be patient!" Nick warned the other Fighters. "We will go on – and if not today then tomorrow."

Damon grinned. "Going under the poets as well?" He asked mockingly and ran away in the next moment, as Nick got up and started to chase him.

The men laughed.

Inside the tent Priest Alfonso bent over Hayley and examined the wound very carefully. Then he checked her through from top to bottom. Finally he got up again.

"Satisfied?" Hayley asked calmly.

"Well, yes. Without one thing," Priest Alfonso looked down at her again.

"And that would be?" Hayley asked curiously.

"You are worried about something?" Priest Alfonso asked carefully.

Hayley closed her eyes for a moment. "I can't keep anything for myself, can I?" She answered back, opening her eyes and looking straight at the Priest.

"Not much." Priest Alfonso smiled. "So tell me what is it?"

Hayley sighed. "We are near the country I lived in before. That means…" For a moment she didn't know how to say what she wanted to say.

"I know what you mean." Priest Alfonso nodded. "You are concerned because as soon as you finished your job, you have to go back."

"Well, no." Hayley said surprisingly. "I know I have to do my job and then to go back to the temple. That's nothing to worry about. But…"

"But – what is it?"

Hayley sat upright and stared at the Priest. "What will become out of you? What will you do – and the other Fighters? And Arthur?" she asked urgently.

Priest Alfonso frowned. "You are on a job and after that you have to face death, as far as I know. And all you worry about is us?"

"It's too late to worry about me, isn't it?" Hayley asked with a tone of sarcasm.

Priest Alfonso sat down. "Well," he said and scratched his cheek. "If you are so worried about us, perhaps you can find us a place where we can stay. And what's with Arthur? – I know he will be very sad when you leave but if you tell him to lead us, he will do so. What do you think?"

Hayley thought about it. "Sounds good." she smiled lightly. "Then let's see that we find a place for you all. Come on!" She stretched out her hand and together, like they had entered the tent, they left it again.

The Fighters had set up a fire in the meantime and in a pot over it cooked something, which smelt heavenly.

In silence Hayley and Priest Alfonso sat down between the others and listened to the conversation, which went around everything under the sun.

Hayley observed Bethany who stirred sometimes in the pot and asked herself how she had managed till now not to put on any weight.

"What are you thinking about?" Arthur interrupted her thoughts.

"Ohm," Hayley looked at him. "I just was thinking that it is slowly time to set up a home for you and Bethany. Don't you think so?"

"How do you come now on this idea?" Arthur asked astonished.

Hayley turned to Bethany. "Didn't you tell him?"

"I… I had no chance." Bethany stuttered. She blushed like a tomato and avoided Arthur's asking look.

Hayley smiled. "Then it's time that you do it. Perhaps he understands then my suggestion."

"Can anybody tell me what are you talking about?" Arthur frowned deeply.

Bethany turned to him. "You have to know… I mean… I have… I am…" She stuttered helpless.

Arthur only looked at her.

Bethany swallowed. Then she bent forward and whispered into Arthur's ear: "I'm pregnant."

Arthur couldn't really follow. "What?" He asked confused.

Again Bethany whispered him into the ear. "I'm pregnant, you fool!"

Arthur looked blank.

Bethany turned to Hayley and shrugged her shoulders. "Is it every time like that when you tell a guy that he becomes a father? Or is there anything else I can do?"

"It's every time the same." Hayley confirmed. "I think you did fine."

"Wait a second." Arthur came slowly back to his senses. "Do you want to say that you are pregnant?"

"Well, this I told you two times." Bethany smiled at him.

Arthur passed with his hand over his face; he stared at Bethany, then at Hayley and all the other grinning faces around him. Finally he looked at Bethany again and following an impulse, he pulled her into his arms. "You are pregnant? And I'm the father? That's great!" He embraced his wife softly.

Bethany leaned against him. "Do you love me now a bit?" She murmured quietly.

"Don't tell me that you got pregnant only to hear from me that I love you a bit?" Arthur asked astonished.

"Well, you know…" Bethany searched for the right words.

Arthur shook his head. "You are stupid, Darling. I love you, more than a bit and pregnant or not. Do you understand?"

"Do you really?" Bethany leaned her head on Arthur's shoulder.

"I do. I really love you." Arthur confirmed and kissed Bethany softly on her mouth.

"Hey! Can you both stop for a moment? That's a terrible nuisance." Rick called over the fire.

The Fighters laughed.

Even Arthur and Bethany had to laugh and they turned back to the fire, sitting hand by hand beside each other.

Hayley pitched Arthur into the side. "How do you think about a home now?"

Arthur smiled. "I can't say anything against it."

"Well," Hayley looked around, "then we should see that we go on as soon as possible that we find something suitable – for all of us."

Arthur nodded, "Tomorrow?"

Hayley agreed, "Tomorrow."

And on the next morning the Fighters of Freedom left the quiet area around the lake…

30

"Nice village, I have to say!" Arthur put his sword back into its cover and looked around.

"Nice?" Hayley shook her head, her sword still in her hand. "I can't say I like it so much here."

"Come on, Hayley! We have seen much worse places, haven't we?" Rick stepped over to Hayley and Arthur.

"Probably," Hayley agreed grinning. "But now we are here. How many unfriendly villages did we meet on our journey now?"

"I think it was the thirteenth. And one, which was, well, not friendly but at least welcoming." Rick grinned.

Hayley nodded. "We are a long time on the way again. – That remains me – where are we exactly?"

"Well, as far as I know we are a ten-days-journey from our original goal. Let's see. That should be the last village we should meet on our journey." Priest Alfonso checked with the map he carried with him.

"Okay. Rick! Check the wells and search for anything suitable to eat! Arthur, look after the wounded that they get help! Harry, get somebody to help and burn the dead! Al, let me have a look at the map!" Hayley gave shortly her orders then she stepped over to Priest Alfonso and took the map. She looked down on it; her finger tipping on the spot where they just were; her eyes tracing through the endless desert till she found the spot she knew the Horsemen had their village there. "Less than ten days." she murmured.

"Don't forget we are slower with the wagon and with the wounded." Priest Alfonso reminded her.

Hayley shook her head. "You take all the time you need. What I have to do there I only can do alone – so I will go alone!"

Priest Alfonso grabbed after her arm. "You forget another thing! We are a team! We go together or nobody goes!"

Hayley looked at him with a shy smile. "My dear friend!" she said quietly. "I don't intend to go without you. You only have to stay a little bit behind. You know its private business I have to do there and, if everything goes well, perhaps I can make them welcome you."

"They are Fighters as well." Priest Alfonso shook his head. "Why do you think they would welcome us?"

Hayley smiled. "They are my people as well, did you forget?"

Priest Alfonso looked at her intensive. He searched for words, found none then he shrugged his shoulders. "Whatever you say." he said in resignation.

Hayley nodded. "Tell the others to wait for my sign just a day journey from the village. If you don't see my sign within four days – leave. Arthur will lead you further on."

"As you wish," Priest Alfonso nodded.

Hayley went over to the place where she had left her camel. She didn't notice at all that Priest Alfonso wiped a tear out of his eyes. Hayley climbed up her camel, took the reins and led her camel out of the village.

Bethany looked up, as she heard the sound of camel's hooves and stopped putting a bandage around Brad's arm. "Hayley!" she called.

Hayley heard the call; she turned her camel around and looked over at the wagon where Bethany was standing. For a moment she only moved when her camel moved then she picked up the reins again and she tossed with her camel away.

"But…" Bethany started and she stopped, as a hand was lain down on her shoulder.

"Don't!" Arthur said quietly. "Don't try to stop her! You know she has something to do where we can't help her. Let her do it, and we will get her back."

"Do you really think so?" Bethany asked quietly.

But Arthur didn't give her any answer anymore.

Next morning the Fighters of Freedom started to follow Hayley…

31

"Hayley told you about what she said to me, as she was tied up to the wooden rack?" Mandy frowned.

"At the well," The Fighter nodded. "Why?"

"I thought she would keep it for herself, as she said it as a warning for me." Mandy confessed quietly.

The Fighter couldn't keep quiet anymore. "What does it matter? You didn't take the advice for real."

"Why do you say that?" Mandy was offended.

The Fighter looked intensive at her. "You seemed to be on good terms with Brian, am I right?"

"And what if I was? I knew Brian quite well and he seemed to be trustworthy." Mandy defended herself.

The Fighter looked into the fire. "I said that you should be careful who you trust. Especially when you think they are trustworthy." He said quietly.

Mandy opened her mouth but suddenly she closed it again and swallowed. With wide-open eyes she stared at the Fighter of Freedom.

The others seemed to have noticed nothing.

Fletcher didn't listen anymore. He stared into the fire. "I knew it." He murmured quietly.

"What did you know?" Tim asked curiously.

Fletcher looked up. "Brian. I found it quite unbelievable, as we came back on that Sunday night that he was the only one to survive all and not being seen at all. I never could prove something to him but my trust in him was away. Now I know why."

Tim shook his head. "I know that you didn't trust him anymore but I would like to know where you knew from that you couldn't."

Fletcher shrugged his shoulders. "I don't know." He said quietly.

The Fighter looked carefully at him. It did hurt him to see Fletcher so sadly but he knew there was nothing he could do at that moment.

Tim turned around to the Fighter and examined him without really seeing him. "And you went along to put right what somebody did wrong to somebody else?" He asked him curiously.

The Fighter had problems not to laugh loudly about the sentence Tim had just said. He gave his voice a firm sound and answered calmly: "No, I'm not."

Tim frowned. "You told us all why..."

"But you didn't listen." The Fighter interrupted him at once.

"What do you mean?" Fletcher joined in.

The Fighter shook his head. "You only hear what you want to hear, don't you? But I'm surprised that you (he pointed at Fletcher) didn't hear anything else out of it."

Fletcher leaned back. "I don't understand anything anymore." He said.

Mandy laughed. Slowly she got up, sat down beside the Fighter and asked the Fighter quietly so that nobody else could understand it: "Give it up; they won't understand. But I'm curious: Why didn't you come back earlier?"

The Fighter smiled, hidden under his scarf. "I would have come earlier if I could. It was the first possibility."

Mandy snuggled into her seat beside Hayley, the Fighter in the dark black clothes. "Tell me, aren't you curious at all what happened for example with your son? Or with Fletcher?" she whispered.

Hayley nodded. In the same voice she whispered back: "I am curious, especially as I can see what happened with Fletcher. But there are powers I can't ignore; they kept me away and they will keep me away again. – I know that you cared for my son. You could bring him back?"

Mandy nodded. "He is here – and is at the moment the only reason, which keeps Fletcher going. He has so much from you and he is... well, lovely."

Hayley smiled again.

"I really don't know." Fletcher joined in again. "If I wouldn't know it better, I would say that there are two possibilities: This guy tries to steal your wife, Tim – or it's only girlie talk. What do you think?" He turned to Tim.

Tim frowned. He glanced at his wife and then at the dark person beside him. But before he could answer, Hayley cleared her throat: "Nothing of it all. Why?"

Fletcher turned to her. "Want to fight me as well?" He asked mocking back.

Hayley shook her head. "You can do what you want but I will never fight you."

"Are you sure?" Fletcher was suddenly driven by the devil. He grabbed around Tim and under the Fighter's cloak the Fighter had wrapped around him again and pulled out one of the swords the dark man carried. For a moment he looked at it then he turned the sword in his hand and held the top of it at the Fighter's throat. "And now?" he mocked.

Hayley examined him carefully. "Kill me if you need to do it. But don't expect me to defend myself."

"Why don't you want to defend yourself?" Fletcher pressed the sword a little bit harder against Hayley's throat.

Hayley didn't move backwards. The sword picked hard into her throat but still she managed to answer calmly: "I'm not angry with you and you can't make me angry. You never could make me really angry."

Fletcher stopped short. "It's the first time I try." He said astonished.

Hayley shook her head carefully, having the top of her sword still at her throat. "You tried it a lot of times, Fletcher, which made me impatient – and that's a big difference to anger."

Fletcher put down the sword then he lifted it again. He laid it on top of the scarf and pushed it down. "Hayley!" he said stunned, not believing what he saw.

Hayley examined him carefully. "You needed a long time to find that out." She said quietly. She listened to the astonished gasps around the fire. "I made so many mistakes in my story that I already thought you would find out sooner." She pulled the scarf completely from her head and shook her long red curls. "But Mandy was the only one who noticed that."

Mandy smiled lightly.

Fletcher let the sword falling down and his knees started to shake. He sat down where he had been standing and stared like mad at Hayley.

Hayley picked up the sword and put it back under her cloak.

Fletcher found his voice again: "Why now? Why did you come back – now?"

Hayley sighed. "First I wanted to have my revenge, which should be clear to you by now. Secondly, I need a place to stay for my guys, where they can recover for a time. We are already too long on the way."

"Are these the only reasons?" Tim mocked.

"They aren't – and you know that. So don't ask such questions, I plead you. But these are the main reasons for me at the moment!" Hayley confirmed.

Fletcher looked at her. "Where are your friends?"

"They are a day journey from here. They only know that I had something to do here." Hayley answered shortly.

Fletcher passed with both hands through his hair. "Listen, Hayley! I'm... stunned to see you again. I missed you... but I don't understand what's going on here."

Hayley smiled. She got up and stretched out her hand to Fletcher. "If you would please excuse us!" she said calmly and waited.

Fletcher hesitated but then he took her hand and got up as well. Slowly he stepped nearer and pushed her softly backwards. "I think you still know where our house is?" He asked quietly.

Hayley closed her fingers around Fletcher's hand. "I know where it is. But you know now as well that I had a bad experience there and I really don't want to go back in there. Can't we go... to the stables?"

Fletcher shrugged his shoulders. "It's all right with me." He said and took over the lead. Slowly he led her over to the stables, let go of her hand and opened the door. Hayley stepped inside and Fletcher closed the door from inside. Then he suddenly grabbed after Hayley's arm and pulled her over to him.

For a moment they both stood next to each other only an inch from the other person. Then Hayley bent forward and kissed Fletcher softly on the mouth.

Fletcher felt the kiss and tasted it still after Hayley had backed away again. With a sigh on his lips he murmured: "I waited so long for that. And still..." He shook his head, as he looked at Hayley. And suddenly he stepped nearer and kissed her wildly.

Hayley threw her arms around Fletcher and enjoyed the kisses.

But after a while they both grew quieter and finally Fletcher solved his lips from hers. "I never believed that you could be dead, didn't matter what the others said. And I knew that one day you would come back. But I never expected... that!" He pointed to the outside.

Hayley leaned against Fletcher. "The only thought, which kept me going, was to see you again. But I have to pay a price for it. Fletcher, listen to me please! All I need is a place for my guys to stay. They are good guys; you won't have any problems with them. I need a place for them because I can't stay with them. I have to leave again and I would like to know them in good hands. Can you do this favour for me?"

Fletcher looked to the ground.

"I know it's quite a lot to ask for, as we only found each other again. But I haven't much more time." Hayley said urgently.

Fletcher looked up into her eyes. "If I say yes, you will leave again, right?"

Hayley lifted her hand and wiped a hair out of Fletcher's forehead. "I have to leave, if you say yes or no. That's the price I have to pay. But you would make it easier for me if you would care for my guys as long as they need it."

Fletcher shook his head again. "I really don't understand. Why do you have to pay a price for seeing me? And what is it for a price?"

Now Hayley shook her head. "Our complete equipment we have to pay for. I can't tell you what the price is." Hayley leaned again against Fletcher. "And I need another favour from you, a personal one."

"What would be?" Fletcher gently stroked over Hayley's hair.

"Love me." Hayley whispered and kissed Fletcher once more.

Fletcher pulled her completely into his arms and kissed her wildly. But then he pushed her to the end of the stable where an empty box was.

Hayley stopped him smiling for a moment. She pulled her cloak off and laid it down on the ground. Then she took off the belts, which held her swords and laid them down beside the cloak at the edge of the box. Finally she sat down on her cloak and looked up at Fletcher.

Fletcher smiled at her. He sat down beside her and started stroking her, passing over her hair, her cheeks. Then he pulled her over to him and kissed her, again and again. Slowly, very slowly they laid down under each other kisses and Fletcher turned Hayley on to her back. Gently he pushed his hand under her shirt with the waistcoat, and Hayley twitched together under his touch. But then Fletcher stopped. "Can you tell me how you come out of this... dress?" He asked embarrassed.

Hayley laughed. "Look here, like that." And she started to solve the leather strings at the side of her waistcoat. Fletcher helped her to slip out of it then there was only the shirt left. Again he bent over Hayley and kissed her softly. Button after button he opened Hayley's shirt and pushed it finally away. His hand wandered over the bra, pushed it away and laid his hand on her breast.

Hayley twitched together again. She went with her hands under Fletcher's shirt and pulled it up.

Fletcher stretched himself and pulled the shirt off. Then he grabbed after Hayley's shirt and Hayley sat up and pulled it off. At last she opened her bra and let it fall to the side as well.

Fletcher breathed deeply in. He pressed Hayley back on the ground, laying his hands down on her breasts. Gently he started to massage them.

Hayley relaxed. She enjoyed feeling Fletcher's hands once more on her and she felt her body moving under his touch.

Fletcher bent forward and kissed the nipples from Hayley. He went with the tongue around and around them, biting them till they finally grew hard.

Hayley groaned softly. She trembled hard and as Fletcher came up to her to kiss her again, she opened her mouth willingly and full of expectations.

Fletcher didn't disappoint her. Wildly he kissed her during his hands still massaged her breasts. And Hayley wished she could feel so much how she was trembling. But she felt enough to enjoy thoroughly what Fletcher was doing with her.

Fletcher solved one hand from Hayley's breast and went over her stomach to the belt around her hips, which held the trousers. He opened the belt slowly and then the trousers. At last he solved himself from her and laid both his hands on Hayley's trousers. Carefully he pulled it down, pushed the boots off and threw her clothes away. Then he opened his own trousers and slipped out of them. Finally he lay down beside Hayley again.

Hayley stroked gently over Fletcher's face. Fletcher bent over her again and kissed her once more wildly. His hands found their way back to her breasts and massaged them wildly but softly.

Hayley laid her arms around Fletcher and stroked him over the back.

Fletcher solved his mouth from Hayley's and went over her chin, her throat down to her breasts. Again he kissed her breasts and licked her nipples till they grew hard.

Hayley groaned. She really enjoyed Fletcher's hands and lips on her and she got excited more and more with every second.

Fletcher discovered her belly, went with his lips over it, licking her navel and tickling her sides. Then he went down till he reached her soft spot between her legs and pressed his face on it.

Hayley gasped excited. She went with her hands down and cramped them firmly into Fletcher's hair.

Inspired through Hayley's touch, Fletcher kissed her around the soft place then he pushed his tongue inside her and searched for the right spot. He tickled her with his tongue and grew more wildly, as he heard Hayley groan deeply and felt her twitching under his hands. As he had Hayley on the point that she groaned with every breath she let out, he got up a bit and led his penis into her. He lay down on her and pressed again and again.

Hayley groaned loudly now. She laid her legs around Fletcher and pressed him against herself.

Now Fletcher gasped as well. Driven from excitement he moved faster and faster and finally he held in.

Hayley groaned up at the same moment, and Fletcher lay down on her again. After both of them had caught their breaths again, Hayley sighed. "I really missed you." She murmured.

"Don't go away!" Fletcher looked at her again. "I plead you. I just got you back and I don't want to lose you again. There is no reason why you should leave. I need you – Warren needs you! Stay, please!"

Hayley turned her head to the side. "Stop it, Fletcher!" She said quietly. "You didn't listen to me. Otherwise you would know that I have responsibilities somewhere else as well. And I told you that I have a price to pay for this possibility. I can't stay, even if I liked to. Please, try to understand."

"But I don't." Fletcher supported himself on his arms, his hands lying on her breast. "I heard your story and I know that you swore yourself to the Temple of Freedom and I also know that you have somewhere living another son. But that's all not a reason for not staying here. You can still do your job – whatever it is – and when you bring your son over here, everything will be all right."

"I wish it would be so easy." Hayley sighed again. For a moment she lay quietly under Fletcher then she pushed him to the side and got up. Slowly she started to dress herself again.

Fletcher examined her thoroughly and thoughtfully. Finally he got up and stepped behind Hayley. He laid his arms around her and laid his head on her shoulder. "One day – will you explain it to me?"

Hayley breathed deeply in. "One day I will." She confirmed quietly, knowing she was lying and she hoped he wouldn't notice.

In silence they dressed again then Fletcher stepped out on the corridor and turned around. "Listen, inform your friends; they can stay here as long as they want to. I trust you that they are all right. But one request I have as well."

"Which is?" Hayley stepped up to him.

"Tell me where are you going to and where your other son is."

"Why do you want to know that?" Hayley was astonished.

Fletcher smiled. "I want to know where I lose you to. And – shouldn't somebody look after your son?"

"Okay, but why do you want to look after my son?" Hayley frowned.

Fletcher laid his arms around her. "Don't you really know? The only thing, which kept me going all this time, was Warren. He was all I had from you. And now I know that there is somewhere another son of yours. If I can't have you, at least I want to have something from you – your sons, to look after."

"You want to look after my sons - even when one of them is not yours?"

"But he is part of you – that's good enough for me."

Hayley leaned against Fletcher and stroked him over his hair. "Now I know again why I love you so much!" She said and kissed him softly on the mouth. "I have to go back to the Temple of Freedom. My son, I called him Alban after his father, lives with a good friend of mine in a small village in the mountains. Perhaps you know it – it's called Aragon."

Fletcher nodded. "I was never there but the village is known because so many men disappeared from this town."

Hayley agreed. "Yes, that's right. My friend is called Ahmed. He is one of the men who disappeared but could get back. Ask him, he will show you my son. – Wait!" Hayley searched through her pockets till she found something. "As a proof to Ahmed – show him this and you won't have any problems with him." She opened her hand.

On the palm of her hand lay a small beautiful ring with a diamond in the middle.

"Well…" Fletcher picked up the ring.

"Pay attention to it. It's the only proof to who you are." Hayley turned again, picked up her swords and laid them around her hips again. After she had closed the belts, she took her cloak, swiped some straw away and laid it around her shoulders. "We should join the others before they search for us." She turned back to Fletcher.

Fletcher put the ring away into one of his pockets and nodded. "How do you want to contact your friends to come over here? Can I help you with that?" He went along the corridor and opened the stable door.

Hayley slipped outside. "If you could organize to have a torch lighted over the gate, it would be enough."

"Okay." Fletcher stopped the next guard and asked him to light a torch over the gate.

The guard saluted and hurried away.

As Fletcher and Hayley finally came back to the market place where Hayley still had her stuff and where the fire had been lighted, almost everybody had been gone to bed. Only Tim and Mandy sat, snuggled up at each other, still beside the fire. Now they looked curiously at Hayley and Fletcher.

"We'll get some visitors tomorrow." Fletcher informed Tim shortly.

Tim nodded. "And where shall they stay?" He asked interested.

"I thought of the house at the end, the big white one. It's empty. It will be just right for them – if they clean it a bit." He added with a side look at Hayley.

"That won't be a problem." Hayley grinned. "They are used to things like that."

Tim got up. He stretched out his hand and pulled his wife up. "We should go to bed that we are fit tomorrow when our guests arrive." He hesitated a moment before he continued: "I noticed that you didn't go into your house. Mandy and I agreed that we let you have our home for tonight that you can stay together. We'll be fine in your house – if that's all right with you." He added hastily.

Fletcher threw a look over at Hayley. "That's nice of you, thanks. Err…"

Hayley picked up her bag and smiled at the three people around her. "I leave my other things here. I don't think one of you will take them away." It sounded more like a question than a conclusion.

Tim smiled. "It's safe here, you know that."

Hayley nodded. "Then let's go to bed. Good night." She grinned at Tim and Mandy.

The couple smiled back, said good night and disappeared into Fletcher's house.

Fletcher and Hayley smiled at each other before they turned and went over to the house, which belonged to Tim and Mandy.

32

It was already late in the morning, as Fletcher and Hayley got up. And they finally only got up because somebody knocked penetrating at the door.

"What's up?" Fletcher called.

"Sorry, Fletcher, but Tim sends me. Your guests are arriving." Walt's voice came through the door.

"Thanks, Walt. We're coming." Fletcher answered back.

Hayley had already started dressing and Fletcher jumped into his trousers as well. Five minutes later they were ready and left the house to go over to the gate.

Tim waited for them in patience. As they came to the top of the wall, which surrounded the small village, he pointed into the desert. "Half an hour and they will be here."

"And for that you let us throw out of bed in a hurry?" Hayley hummed.

Tim grinned over at her. "I thought you would like to be ready when your friends arrive."

"Yes, yes." Hayley murmured, turned around and sat down with the back to the wall.

Fletcher sat down beside her. "What do you think?" He asked curiously, searching her face for any sign of excitement or something else.

Hayley sighed. "I only thought that with every second they come nearer, the time comes where I have to leave you."

Fletcher sighed now as well. "Do I have the chance to convince you to stay?"

Hayley looked at him. "Please, Fletcher, don't! We talked about that more than enough. Please don't destroy the last minutes we have together."

"It's okay." Fletcher pressed softly her hand.

In silence they sat together till Tim cleared his throat. "But now they are here." He informed Fletcher and Hayley and gave a sign to the two guards who were standing at the gate. They opened the gate without any big effort.

Hayley stepped down and over to the open gate. As she saw the riders on their camels outside, she lifted her arm, laid her hand on her heart and opened her arm in a half bow with the palm of her hand pointing to the top. It was the sign of Freedom.

The first rider gave the sign exactly back then he jumped down from his camel. He led it at the reins through the gate and stopped near Hayley. "Are you all right?" He asked quietly.

Hayley nodded. "Certainly I am. And how are you?"

Arthur shrugged his shoulders. "Without the sand all over – we are okay. Err. Are we really welcome here?"

"You are. Come on, I'll show you where you can leave the camels before Fletcher will show you the house where you can stay." Hayley stepped the street down and Arthur followed her calmly.

Also the other riders entered through the gate and followed them the street down. At last a wagon, pulled by horses followed the riders.

The arrival of the Fighters of Freedom didn't stay unnoticed.

Everywhere windows opened and men, women and even children looked outside. The village people, who hadn't their house in the road the Fighters took, left his house and watched them curiously from the market place.

Hayley led the Fighters over to the stables and said quietly: "You can leave the camels on the grass here behind the stables. Take only the things with you, you need urgently."

"That's easy." Arthur hummed. He solved the belt around the camel and pulled the saddle down. Then he went over to the green, solved the reins and let his camel run on to the grass.

One Fighter after the other followed Arthur's example and the place in front of the stables emptied quite fast. Finally only the wagon was left and the horses danced nervous.

The man who jumped down from the wagon was Priest Alfonso, still dressed in a fine white robe. "Where can I leave the wagon?" He asked quietly.

Fletcher stepped up beside Hayley, "Just where it is now. The horses you can bring over to the green beside the one with the camels." He answered calmly.

Priest Alfonso nodded; solved the belts from the wagon and led the horses over to another green where he let them run.

Arthur in the meantime had stepped over to the wagon and opened the curtain. He helped first one woman out of the wagon then a second one. The two women looked curiously around, as…

"Orinda!" a cry could be heard and through the people of the village a woman pushed her way over to the wagon.

The dark haired woman at the wagon turned around and looked searching into the crowd. She saw the woman who tried to come over to her and hurried now over to her. "Olivia!" She cried now as well and the two women fell into each other's arms.

Fletcher looked surprised at Hayley.

Hayley smiled. "I brought Orinda over here because it was her wish to be with her sister. And that Olivia loves to have her here, I think you can see."

Fletcher nodded. "Some more of such surprises?" he asked.

"One more," Hayley confirmed. But she didn't say anything anymore; she turned to Arthur and Bethany. "Fletcher – that's Arthur and his wife Bethany. Arthur, Beth – that's Fletcher, my husband." She introduced shortly.

Fletcher looked thoughtfully at Arthur and Arthur stared without problems back.

"Well, so you are the lucky one." Arthur grinned and stretched out his hand.

"I don't know if I'm lucky. Especially not, as I can't see who's standing in front of me." Fletcher mocked, looking into Arthur's eyes, which were the only ones to be seen from his face and shook his hand.

"Sorry!" Arthur grinned. He pulled the scarf from his face and his head. He shook his blond hair and looked straight back at Fletcher.

But Fletcher had turned his eyes over at Bethany. "Welcome." He said calmly and nodded at her.

Bethany smiled only.

"Perhaps we should show you now where you can stay." Hayley joined into the conversation again.

Fletcher nodded. He stepped on and Hayley waved to the Fighters to follow them. She didn't notice that one of the Fighters stayed back.

This Fighter had turned to the green where the horses were and had lured a horse over to him, which he stroked now softly.

Two, three of the horsemen noted him standing at the gate and walked over to him.

"Don't you want to see where your friends are going to?" One of them asked mockingly.

"No. Why?" The Fighter asked calmly back.

"Don't you want to know where you can stay here?" The second man grew curiously.

"I know where." The Fighter answered shortly.

Astonished the three men exchanged a look.

"Where do you want to know that from?" One of them asked.

The Fighter threw a mocking look over at the man. "Phil, don't play the stupid one! It's finally not the first time that I'm here."

Phil stared at him. "Do we know each other?"

"We do." The Fighter nodded. He stroked once more over the soft fur of the horse then he sent it with a gentle tap on the side away. He turned and went over to the place where he had left his saddle.

The second of the men, Jack, stepped into his way. "And where do we know you from?"

The Fighter stopped. "That you from all the people on earth don't know it – that's bad, Jack. Didn't you miss me one bit?" He asked quietly back.

Jack examined him thoroughly from bottom to top. But only as he looked into his eyes, he noticed something familiar. He grew pale. "Jeff?"

The Fighter nodded. "How did you get on, Jack?" He asked curiously.

Jack hesitated. "Can't you take off this scarf? And – for goodness sake – how did you come to this bunch of Fighters?"

Jeff grinned. He pulled the scarf away and passed his hands through his brown hair.

The similarity between him and Jack was astonishing but only for somebody who didn't know the twins. Still even though they had gone for the last months different ways, they were still alike like an egg with another.

Jack swallowed. "I missed you." He confessed.

"I missed you too. Finally it's the first time we were separated. And it was difficult to hear you all, riding away and without a chance to let one of you know that I'm still alive!" Jeff sighed.

"What happened?" Phil joined in.

Jeff shrugged his shoulders. In short form he described what had happened to him.

Jack sighed. "And you will still ride on with the other Fighters?"

"What would be so bad about that?" Jeff asked astonished.

"Well, it's so that…" Jack started but Jeff interrupted him at once. "You mean, you still have no idea about what we do, have you?"

"Probably not," Jack frowned. "But…"

Again Jeff interrupted him: "Then I suggest that you at first learn what it means to be a Fighter of Freedom. Perhaps after that we can talk further on. – I have to join the others." He added calmly. He picked up his saddle and left the stable area and went through the streets to the big white house at the end of the village.

It was an hour later, as Rick threw a look out of one of the windows of the house and said grinning: "Jeff! Did you put a big picture of yourself outside?"

Jeff who stripped his saddle of his stuff looked up. "From what in the hell are you talking about?"

"Well," Rick's grin grew even wider, "if I wouldn't know that you are here, I would say you are standing in front of the house."

Jeff got up and stepped over to the window, "Where?"

"Opposite in the doorframe of the other house," Rick informed him, still grinning.

"You have sharp eyes." Jeff said during he stared frowning outside. Then he turned around again and sat down beside his saddle to sort his stuff.

Rick examined him frowning. "Don't you think you have something to explain?"

Jeff shrugged his shoulders. "This guy is my twin brother Jack." He said shortly.

"Well," Rick threw another look out of the window, "do you want to know what Hayley is just doing?" He grinned again.

"What?" Jeff sounded almost uninterested.

"She's bringing him in."

Now Jeff got up again and went over to the window. He saw Hayley standing in the street and talking to Jack. He noticed that Jack stepped out of the doorframe and went over to Hayley. They exchanged some more words then Hayley pushed Jack over to the entrance of the house.

Jeff sighed. "I wish sometimes she would leave things like that. I don't know if that's good." He sat down beside his stuff again.

The other three men in the room exchanged an amused look.

The door opened and Hayley looked inside: "May I disturb you?"

"Come in, Hayley! We already saw you down in the street." Rick smiled.

"I know." Hayley stepped inside. "Then you can put on your best manners now and explain to Jack what happened and why Jeff is here." She grinned back at Rick and pulled Jack inside. "Don't worry!" She whispered to him then she left the room again.

Rick solved himself from the window and stepped over to Jack. He examined him from top to bottom and from every side. "It's astonishing. You both are really like two eggs. No difference – when you don't look at the clothes."

"Well, yes, there was some confusion as we were in the same group." Jeff murmured. He looked up and winked at his brother.

Jack looked half mocking at Rick before he sat down beside Jeff and apologized quietly: "I'm sorry when I was not so friendly at first. I was stunned to see you again after all these months I thought you're dead. Can we start again?"

Jeff sighed. "I would have come to you after I unpacked. Finally I wasn't quite so nice to you as well. I still have Fletcher's words in my ears, which I can't forget. That was the reason for my... bad behaviour."

Jack grinned, "Like ever. We behave the same, we re-act the same and we do the same. It doesn't matter where we are."

"Then you hopefully know that it's nothing bad what we do here." Jeff whispered to Jack then he turned around and said more loudly: "That's my brother Jack. Jack, that's Rick. With him you have to be careful; he steals everything what's not bound to the owner."

Rick grinned only.

"That's Harry; he is master of the swords. And Priest Alfonso; he thinks he has to look after our souls. At least he's good at preaching." Jeff finished grinning.

Harry nodded only at Jack but Priest Alfonso was not so impressed with his introduction. He turned to Jeff and said warning: "You should be careful, my son. Otherwise I stop praying for you."

"Yes, father." Jeff answered smiling.

Soon the five men were in a deep conversation; and Jack heard a lot more about the Fighters ways...

33

Two floors underneath the room where Jeff and Jack celebrated their reunion, Hayley sat on the windowsill of a big room and dangled with the legs.

Fletcher leaned beside her on the wall and looked still interested at Arthur who unpacked his stuff from his saddle. Bethany sat beside him and helped him as much as she could.

"How long do you want to stay?" Fletcher asked interested.

Arthur shrugged his shoulders, "As long as you can cope with us. Not counting the days we'll be out." He hesitated for a moment before he continued: "I know that you have a problem with me being here but for Orinda's and Jeff's sake try it! I'm no danger for you."

Fletcher frowned. "I'm not so sure about that. Finally you had a quite good time with Hayley and I don't think it'll be ever over. You swore it to each other."

Hayley jumped down from the windowsill and placed herself in front of Fletcher. "Stop it, Fletcher! You have no idea what you're talking about."

"I do. You told me yourself." Fletcher grew aggressive.

"But you didn't listen. You heard only what you wanted to hear – but that's only half of the truth." She stopped short before she continued: "Arthur and I swore to each other to be friends forever. He helped me out of a lot of problems and I'm very thankful to him for that. And you should be as well because otherwise you would have been alone last night. Also Arthur and Bethany are coupled now; there is really nothing to be afraid of. Please, don't destroy what I built up in order to be able to love you once more. Be friends with Arthur – you won't regret it."

Fletcher sighed. "I don't understand you anymore." He hesitated and looked over Hayley's shoulder at Arthur and Bethany who had used the opportunity to kiss each other. "I will be friends with Arthur when it makes you happy. But can you promise me that there is really nothing anymore between you both?"

"I can." Hayley snuggled herself up at Fletcher. "Come on, give your heart a push and welcome my friends. You will see – you can trust him, all of them with your life."

Fletcher pressed Hayley firm at his body. "They are welcome – I told you so before. I…"

But Hayley had enough of that talk. She lifted her head and pressed her lips on Fletcher's mouth. She enjoyed feeling his lips and she noticed that Fletcher enjoyed it as well, as she felt his response. After a while she solved her lips again and looked at Fletcher.

And Fletcher nodded at her what meant more to her than as he would have said something.

Bethany got up. "Where can I get here some water?" She asked interested.

Hayley solved herself from Fletcher and turned to her. "Come with me. I'll show you."

Together the women left the house and in the room the two men stayed back.

Arthur got up. "To be completely truthfully to you, Fletcher – I love Hayley and I will never give up her friendship. I know I can't have her because she loves you but I will never stop to do everything for her and to protect her when it's possible. I thought it would be good if you know that."

"I felt the energy in the room when you both looked at each other." Fletcher frowned. "You don't need to tell me how you both are feeling for each other. I know it. And if you think she doesn't love you – you are wrong. She does love you, but the way is different to the way she loves me."

"Perhaps you are right." Arthur smiled. "Where can we make a fire that we can cook something? We hadn't had anything since last evening." He changed the subject.

"Do you have still enough or do you need something?" Fletcher asked matter-of-fact.

"I think for today we still have enough." Arthur grinned. "About tomorrow we have to talk again."

"Okay." Even Fletcher grinned now. "The best fire place is on the market place where the well is. If you get everything together you want to cook, I'll show you where and how."

Arthur and Fletcher organized shortly for everybody to search what they wanted to eat then they left the house and went back to the market place.

An astonishing picture was waiting there for them.

Hayley sat on the wall of the well, Bethany at her side. They both talked with two sisters with long black hair and Asian touch: Olivia and Orinda. They talked friendly together.

On the other side of the well stood some other women, Mandy with them, and they eyed the women on the other side suspiciously.

Also on one side of the market place had gathered together some of the horsemen and talked together in quiet voices.

Fletcher shook his head. "When this is going on like that then we will have here a village with at least three different parties." He murmured.

Arthur was more down to earth. "They get used to it as soon as they get used to us. Then there won't be any parties anymore." He answered calmly.

"Let's hope so." Fletcher pointed over to the place where there had been the fire last night and explained shortly: "The best place we have for a fire. You can have it for today – perhaps we will join you later on."

"Would be an honour for us," Arthur smiled. He went over to the place and started to build up a new fire.

Fletcher turned to his comrades and joined them at the corner.

In the meantime Hayley had noticed that Mandy and some of the other women were standing at the other side of the well and she turned over to them. "Mandy! Do I get it right that you and Olivia were the whole time together, as you were the only ones with babies at that time?"

Mandy understood at once. "Yes, that's right."

Hayley wanted to say something more but she stopped, touching her neck. She got up, grabbed after Bethany's arm and pulled her only with her around the well. She let her go at the side and sat down on the well again. She shrugged with her shoulders, as she noticed the astonished looks from the other women and said calmly: "I would have got a stiff neck if I would have stayed over there." She smiled. "Or do you really want to tell me that you are afraid of Bethany and Orinda?" She added, as she saw that Orinda only had come over as well because Olivia had pushed her forward.

"Well," Mandy started, "we are not afraid but you can't be surprised about the fact that we are suspicious. What do we know about them? Do we know that they are not here to take our husbands away? Or do even worse? Finally we see them for the first time – and..." She broke up.

Hayley looked at her confused, "And... what?"

Mandy swallowed. "I must confess I was happy to see you again but I must also say that we don't know you anymore. Two years is a long time and your entrance yesterday made it quite clear that you changed. You didn't even have a look at your son."

Hayley looked for a moment down at the ground then she looked straight at Mandy. "You are wrong when you think I hadn't a look at my son. I only thought it wouldn't be good to explain to him who I am when I have to leave him soon again. Otherwise I have more experience and am a bit more... hard in some way. But I have the same feelings like before and no intention to change something. And especially you, Mandy, know me better than anybody else."

Mandy frowned. "I'm not so sure." She threw a look over at Christine who held herself more in the background.

Hayley followed her look and started to laugh. "Now I understand. I think neither Fletcher nor I did let something go bad. But don't worry, you'll get him back." She nodded over at Christine.

"The old talk of leaving?" Bethany asked, half mockingly.

Hayley turned to her and looked at her with a frown. "Be careful what you say."

"Stop," Orinda stepped between the two women. "It's not the right time for that."

"And with that we come to you." Mandy joined in again. "As we want to get to know you – what are your intentions?"

"I know my sister since a long time." Olivia stepped forward. "She would never take another woman the husband away, especially not, when there are a lot of men around who haven't a girlfriend. This guarantee I can give you."

Hayley joined in again. "And Bethany is already married. So you know now more about the two than they know about you. What about an introduction of yourselves?"

Mandy hesitated. After a moment she stretched out her hand. "I'm Mandy and I'm married to Tim who is here the second commander."

Bethany shook hands with her and smiled lightly. Then Orinda greeted her as well.

Now one woman after the other introduced herself but it was Christine who pulled the attention to her – even though it wasn't her intention. "I'm Christine, Jack's sister. And, well, I tried to comfort Fletcher in the last months. But not with much success."

It was Bethany who noticed it first; perhaps because she had the same problem, which she only had told everybody some weeks ago but Hayley first. "It seems to me that Fletcher was much more successful. In which month are you?"

Christine blushed. "Fourth month." she said quietly then she looked over at Hayley. "I'm sorry!" She stuttered then she turned around and left the group in a hurry.

Hayley stared behind her and sighed only.

Fletcher who was standing together with his friends saw Christine running away from the group of the women and he sighed as well.

Tim looked at him. "Did you tell Hayley about Christine?"

Fletcher shook his head. "There wasn't any time for that."

"Idiot," Tim hummed. "What do you think Hayley will do to you when she hears it?"

Again Fletcher looked over to the group. "She knows it." He sighed again before he turned and went over to Arthur who had set a fire up in the meantime. "Everything all right?" he asked calmly.

"Here is everything okay." Arthur grinned up at him. "But I think now you have a problem." He pointed to the women in his back. "If you need help..,"

Fletcher sighed. "No, thank you." He answered shortly. Slowly he stepped around the well over to the women. "Everything all right here?" He asked calmly.

"It is." Mandy smiled at him. "But I think now I have something to do. Please, excuse me." She turned and left.

Some of the other women followed her and Olivia pulled Orinda away. Bethany stepped on as well. "I have to see that Arthur doesn't do anything wrong or burns his hand." She explained and went around the well over to the fireplace.

Hayley finally stayed as only woman back. She looked at Fletcher. "Why didn't you tell me that you had someone else in your bed as well?"

"I wanted to. But you pushed me over the edge to be completely truthfully. I'm sorry – I shouldn't make you any problems when I'm the one who is not honest with you."

Hayley sighed. "You should go to Christine. She's pregnant and she needs you now. Go to her!"

Fletcher hesitated, "Any chance that you forgive me one day?"

"One day." Hayley nodded at him, and Fletcher went hesitatingly away.

Hayley made a fast decision. She got up and stepped around the well. "Arthur." She said quietly, and Arthur and Bethany looked up.

But Hayley shook her head. "Please, Bethany. Leave us alone for a moment, will you?"

With a sigh Bethany got up. "I have to get the food. I won't be long." She said and disappeared.

Hayley sat down beside Arthur. "Can you do me a favour?"

"Certainly," Arthur looked asking at her.

Hayley stared into the fire. "It's time to say goodbye now. I have to go and now it's just the right time. Would you please tell Fletcher that I love him and that I hope he will be happy with Christine?"

"That's it?" Arthur leaned back. "Then you are not coming back this time?"

"I won't. And you know why." Hayley looked over at him. "I'll leave over the green that nobody will notice it too soon. Would you please look after Fletcher?"

"I will." Arthur promised. "Any word to Rick or one of the others?" he asked matter-of-fact but Hayley could see that he was sad.

"I wish you all only the best and I hope you have it good here. More I can't do anymore." Hayley got up. "Please, don't show anything. If somebody wants to stop me – you know what happens then. Don't let them know before it's too late. Understood?"

"Certainly," Arthur sighed.

"Bye." Hayley whispered quietly before she turned to her saddle and said loudly: "I'll take care of my saddle now. Leave something to eat for me, will you?"

"I will." Arthur smiled at her, as she picked up her saddle and walked over to the stables.

The horsemen didn't stop her, as they had heard what she had said to Arthur; actually they walked over to Arthur and joined him at the fire in the hope to find something more out about the Fighters of Freedom.

Hayley managed – unobserved – to saddle her camel and ten minutes after she had said goodbye to Arthur she was on her way back to the Temple of Freedom.

34

"Well, how is it, working together with Hayley?" Tim asked curiously, as he sat down beside Arthur.

Arthur grinned. "You know it. You worked together with her as well, didn't you?"

"I did." Tim confirmed. "But that's already a time ago."

"I don't think it changed so much." Arthur's grin grew wider. "She's quite bossy but she knows what she wants and she normally gets what she wants."

"True." Tim grinned now as well.

Bethany came back and with her came the rest of the Fighters with Jack in their middle.

"I think we have enough to eat for you as well – today." Rick greeted Tim and the other horsemen with a nod of his head. He sat down and opened the bag he carried.

Tim examined the bag in Rick's hand. "How did you come to this bag? It belongs to me." He asked astonished.

Rick blushed lightly. "Well, it was standing so alone around. So I thought I can take it with me." He grinned again.

"It stood alone around - in the middle of our cool house?" Tim was sceptical.

Arthur rolled his eyes. "Rick! What did you do?"

"Well," Rick started to defend himself; "we noticed that we hadn't enough food anymore. So I thought it would be the best to... to organize something."

Arthur turned to Tim and shook his head. "I'm sorry but Rick takes everything with him what's not secured to something. He was a thief, he is a thief and probably he ever will be a thief."

"Thank you." Rick said dryly.

Tim shook his head. "I see that we have to keep an eye on him."

Rick pulled a face.

Fletcher came over to the fire and sat down beside Tim. At his side was Christine. "If stolen or not, let's see what you have there." He turned to Rick.

Rick looked into the bag and pulled one piece of meat after the other out of it. It was a big bag...

Fletcher looked over at Arthur who snuggled up at Bethany. "Where is by the way Hayley?" He asked curiously.

"She's fixing her saddle." Arthur answered and he didn't feel well with this lie.

Fletcher nodded and the conversation around the fire went on.

Only Priest Alfonso looked surprised at Arthur. "Why did you lie to us, Arthur? What's going on?"

The eyes of the men and women around the fire got fixed on Arthur's face.

Arthur blushed. Still he tried to hide the fact that he had lied. "What do you mean?"

"Come on, Arthur. You were never good at lying. And now you are red like a tomato. What are you trying to hide?"

Fletcher foresaw something. "Where is Hayley?" He asked again.

Arthur sighed. He leaned back and looked at Fletcher. "Hayley is gone." He said only.

Fletcher grew pale. "What does it mean?"

"It means," Arthur tried to explain, "that she's gone back to pay the price she has to pay. She for sure told you about that?"

"She did." Fletcher nodded. "But she never said what this is for a price."

Arthur looked over at Rick who had sat back and stared into the fire.

"You both are her friends. You have to know what it is for a price she has to pay." Fletcher didn't let go of the subject.

Rick lifted his look and exchanged a look with Arthur. Then he cleared his throat. "She swore to give her life for the opportunity of revenge and a last look at you." He nodded over at Fletcher. "She's gone to die how she swore it."

"And you both are sitting here and do nothing? How can you?" Fletcher jumped up,

Arthur followed his example and stepped into his way. "There's nothing we can do and there's nothing you can do. Everybody has to pay the price sooner or later. There is no help – she chose the price herself."

"Why? Why did she do that?" Fletcher suddenly seemed to be despaired.

Arthur shrugged his shoulders. "She was at the end. Probably she thought she has nothing to lose anymore. Get used to the fact that she won't come back anymore – and Christine needs you."

"She doesn't need me; she needs somebody who can look after her and this I can't." Fletcher looked around. "It's Hayley who needs help."

"Hayley is out of your reach now. Come on and sit down again." Arthur managed it to get Fletcher down on his place again. He also sat down and looked over at Rick.

Rick started to cut the meat in pieces but it looked more like trying to get his anger and feelings under control again.

The conversation turned still around Hayley but Fletcher didn't listen. He thought sharply over his problem then he stood quietly up and stepped slowly backwards. As he noticed that nobody was looking at him, he turned and ran over to the stables. Five minutes later he was on his horse and on the way out over the green.

"Christine! Where's Fletcher?" Tim looked around.

Christine shrugged her shoulders. "I don't know. He's already some minutes away."

Arthur got up. "Where is normally his horse?"

"On the green," Tim looked at him. "What do you think?"

"I think he's gone behind Hayley." Arthur started to go over to the stables. "Can you tell me if his horse is still here or not?" He turned once more to Tim.

Tim got up as well. "Let's see."

The two men went over to the green behind the stables. Tim climbed on the fence around the green and straightened his eyes. After a moment he turned around and shook his head at Arthur.

"I thought so." Arthur turned and called over the place: "Rick! I need your and my saddle! Hurry up!"

"What do you want to do?" Tim asked curiously.

Arthur shrugged his shoulders. "I will try to find Fletcher. As I don't think he will turn back, it's the best I show him the way. Otherwise he would get lost."

Tim looked intensive at him. "I don't know what I shall think about you. But if you help Fletcher – we may become good friends. Fletcher is very important here and very important to us."

Rick came over with the two saddles.

Arthur took one and whistled after his camel. For a change it really came running over to him. Arthur saddled the camel and climbed on it. He took the reins of Rick's camel and turned to Tim: "If you care for some days for the guys – I care for Fletcher. Promise!" he didn't wait for an answer; he let his camel run over the green – the same way Hayley and Fletcher had taken.

Tim and Rick stared thoughtfully behind him.

Arthur's camel was very fast and after half an hour Arthur found Fletcher how he was just searching for traces Hayley might have left.

"Fletcher," Arthur called out breathlessly.

Fletcher turned around. "Go back! I don't return, as long as I haven't found Hayley!"

Arthur shook his head. "That's why I am here. I know that you won't turn around so I decided to help you. I know where to find Hayley."

"Where is she? Can you show me?" Fletcher asked curiously.

Arthur nodded. "But you have to do me a favour. Your horse is not fast enough and you won't be able to keep up on it for days. Send it back – and take the camel I brought with me."

"I've never been on a camel." Fletcher hesitated.

Arthur jumped down from his camel and took the reins of Fletcher's horse into his hands. He secured them on the saddle with enough length then he gave the horse a clapping on the back.

Willingly the horse galloped the way back home.

Arthur turned to Fletcher and folded his hands together. "Try it! It's easier than you may believe now. I help you to get on." He said.

Fletcher stepped over to him and put his foot into Arthur's folded hands. Then he grabbed after the saddle and with Arthur's powerful help he came – somehow – into the saddle.

Arthur climbed again on his own camel and turned it a bit. "This way!" he only said.

In silence the two men rode on.

Fletcher had problems in the beginning to get used to the wide steps of the camel. Also it was higher than on a horse – it was altogether something completely different. But Fletcher had no problems after a while to keep up and he got used to the feeling.

Arthur broke the journey up in the evening for a break but he suggested going on in the night. He let his camel run and fell asleep in the saddle.

Fletcher envied him for that. He needed a long time to find out how that worked and even after he found out, he only fell asleep for some minutes in a row. So he used every break they made for his sleep.

But Arthur didn't let them stop for a long time. He knew Hayley and he knew she wouldn't stop a lot before she reached her goal. She never did. She didn't even now, where she had to face death. That was one of the reasons why they didn't get even the tail of Hayley's camel to see.

On the twelfth day of their journey, Arthur and Fletcher reached the hills and – taking a short cut – they reached one day later the walls around the Temple of Freedom.

Arthur hammered against the gate.

The door opened a bit.

"Well, today is the day the Fighters come back in single line." A monk looked out of the crack at the gate and opened finally the gate completely. "Come inside."

Arthur led his camel through the gate and Fletcher followed him slowly.

The monk eyed him suspiciously but he didn't say anything.

Arthur stopped.

Fletcher closed up to him and looked at him. "What is it?"

Arthur pointed over to a bit of green, "Hayley's camel. It's still breathing heavily so she can't be here since a long time. You have a chance."

"Where will she be?" Fletcher jumped off the camel.

"See the big white house over there? She will be somewhere in there. More I don't know myself." Arthur answered calmly. "From now on you have to go on alone. Good luck!"

Fletcher turned. "You know more than you are willing to say – but one day I will get you!" He said with a light smile then he turned back and ran over to the big white house.

Without hesitation Fletcher entered the house and looked around. He saw the doors and he opened one after the other. Most of the doors led into other rooms but one door seemed to be going down into the dungeons.

· After Fletcher had seen every room he stepped over again to the door, which led downstairs. He stepped into the corridor and went the staircase down, first slowly then faster and faster. Finally he came into another corridor and ran it along till he came to a big wooden door. He stopped.

35

"You came back for which reason?" The first priest looked at Hayley.

"I swore to come back after I got what I wanted. And I never break an oath." Hayley answered clearly.

"And you are ready to fulfil your oath?" The second priest stepped in.

"I am." Her voice was clear but still Hayley was trembling. She wasn't afraid of the death, she was afraid of the kind of her death.

"Lie down on the altar." The third priest ordered shortly.

Hayley got up from her place in front of the altar and stepped up to it. She sat down on the edge of the altar and slipped till she lay completely on it.

The fourth priest went around the altar and put iron clamps around her ankles and her wrists. Then he stepped to the end where Hayley's head were and stroked her hair to the side. Then he put two iron sticks on to the sides of her head and pressed them so firm against her head that Hayley thought he tried to press them through her head. But then he stopped and connected them firm to the altar.

The fifth priest, Priest Hassan, bent over her. "You know you won't wake up anymore?"

"Yes, I know." Hayley swallowed.

"Do you have any last words?" Priest Hassan laid his hand on Hayley's eyes.

"Hayley - no!" a voice shouted through the temple, and the priests shook together.

Priest Hassan gave an order with his hand and the four other priests went over to snatch Fletcher who had entered the hidden temple.

But Fletcher was much more fixer than the priests. He dodged twice away from their hands and finally outrun them.

Hayley opened her mouth. "I love the man who just spoke. Would you please tell him?"

She couldn't see it but on Priest Hassan's face shone up a smile. With one hand he pulled a small bottle out of his pocket and opened it in front of Hayley's nose.

Hayley felt the sharp smell in her nose and she fought against it. But the smell was penetrating and she felt her body reacting against it. Her breath grew deeper and it grew black in front of her eyes.

"No!" Fletcher called again, as he noticed the bottle in the hand of the priest who bent over Hayley. He ran forward but one of the priests stretched out his leg and Fletcher fell over it – with full power in front of the altar.

Priest Hassan looked down at Fletcher and shook his head. "Young man, get up! How did you come into our temple?"

Fletcher got up. Without looking at the priest he stepped to the altar and felt over Hayley's throat till he found her pulse. But somehow he was stunned still to be able to feel her pulse. "You didn't kill her?" He asked astonished.

"I didn't – I'm not a murderer." Priest Hassan smiled. "She gave me the right answer to the right time. And you did the rest for it."

"What do you mean?" Fletcher looked around, as the other priests closed him in. Suddenly he felt unwell in this company.

"Well," Priest Hassan turned to him, "you wanted to come to her rescue. You interrupted our holy celebration. For that you have to pay a price. – Don't worry! It won't be so difficult for you, as you did the right thing." He gave an order with his hands and the priests grabbed after Fletcher and forced him down on his knees.

Fletcher tried to defend himself but against four priests he had no chance.

"Hayley has still her price to pay. Err. I think we leave it with the tattoo, which belongs to her position." Priest Hassan continued.

"Which would be?" Fletcher asked, breathing out deeply and trying to ignore the pain the priests gave him.

Priest Hassan looked at him. "She's the Keeper of the Light – she told me so, as she heard your voice."

"What did she say?"

"She said she loves you. And you showed already how much you love her. She has the fire in her; the light guarded her already the whole time. From now on you will be her guard – see that the light she has in her never extinguishes." He pointed over to a chair and said calmly: "Tie him on to the chair."

The priests pulled Fletcher up and pushed him over to the chair. There they forced him to sit down and clapped iron clamps around his ankles and wrists and turned them so close till Fletcher couldn't move anymore.

Priest Hassan threw a look at Hayley then he stepped over to Fletcher. He took another chair and sat down just in front of Fletcher. He grabbed after his throat and turned his head, first to the right then to the left. "Here!" He said and pointed to the point between Fletcher's cheek and his ear, just where the jaw started.

One of the priests nodded and turned to the fire. He chose one of the sticks at the side and held it into the fire.

Another priest stepped behind Fletcher and took his head to turn it to the right. Firm he held Fletcher in this position.

The priest came back from the fireplace and reached Priest Hassan a gleaming stick. Priest Hassan nodded. "A scarab is the sign of the light. Pay attention that you will never lose the light, otherwise you will die." He warned Fletcher then he lifted the stick and pressed it against Fletcher's skin at the spot he had pointed out before.

Fletcher groaned lightly for pain.

Priest Hassan pulled the stick away and checked the mark. "All right." he nodded and the priest let go of Fletcher's head, "Now to the wrist. Left side will be the best."

The priest to Fletcher's left side opened the iron clamp and grabbed after Fletcher's arm. He pulled the sleeve up and both priests checked his wrist.

"Prepare him!" Priest Hassan ordered and left his place.

Fletcher felt a slightly pain running through his wrist, as Priest Hassan finally started to tattoo him. He waited impatiently till the priest had finished with his work then he cleared his throat. "And what do the sign mean?" He asked interested.

"They are scarab flowers. They'll give you the power to guard the light." Priest Hassan answered shortly.

"And what do you want to tattoo on Hayley? And especially – where do you want to do it?"

Priest Hassan smiled. "It's normal for a keeper to have its name printed on the face. We don't make an exception for her. – Will it be a problem for you?"

Fletcher swallowed but then he shook his head. "She will be for me what she ever was – a beautiful young girl with a will made out of iron. A tattoo won't change anything."

"I hope so for your sake." Priest Hassan got up. "Help him to get out of here that he can recover. Be quiet!" He lifted his hand, as he saw that Fletcher wanted to protest. "Hayley will follow you later. Go now!"

The priest undid the iron clamps and supported Fletcher on the way out. They brought him the staircase up, through the lobby till they reached the entrance. Then they opened the door and led Fletcher out into the evening sun. They closed and locked the door before Fletcher could turn around.

Fletcher sat down on the steps in front of the house and supported his head with his right hand. The left was hanging like lifeless beside him.

"Fletcher - What happened?" Arthur sat down beside him.

Fletcher looked up and examined Arthur for a long time. "I know you know more about all these, more as you want to say. But it's time now that you start."

"But…"

"No but." Fletcher interrupted him at once. He glared at him. "What do you know?"

Arthur sighed. "Come on, you can't sit here the whole time. We have a house here at the side. I'll tell you then everything." He added and stopped Fletcher's protest at the first breath.

Fletcher got up. He swayed lightly, as he didn't know anymore what had happened to him. He still felt how Arthur grabbed after him then it grew dark in front of his eyes.

36

As Fletcher woke up again, the new day just started. Confused he looked around. A light snore to his right let him turn around.

Arthur was lying on a bed beside Fletcher's and dreamed. Like ever when he was laying on his back, he snored lightly.

Fletcher shook his head – and regretted it at once. The small burned mark gave him some pain what reminded him at once on the day before. He looked down at his left wrist and frowned. The tattoo was clearly to be seen. He moved his hand a bit and was happy to feel it again.

Arthur turned around. "Go to sleep again! It's too early!" He murmured.

"I slept already too much." Fletcher said angrily. "Get up and tell me what you know about all these."

Arthur turned around again. "If you really want to know." he answered and wiped the sleep out of his eyes. Then he started to tell Fletcher the first part of the legend how he had once told it to Hayley.

Fletcher nodded. "That explains some things. But that's not all, is it?"

"It isn't." Arthur confirmed. He hesitated for a moment then he continued: "The legend says that the woman would become a Keeper of the Light, guarded by her original husband. They wouldn't be so often together, as she would still ride with her friends, and he with his, but enough to live a good life together." He looked over at Fletcher. "I didn't understand this part at once – that's the reason why I told you not to follow her. But it was suddenly quite clear after you had left. So I followed you – it is the price I have to pay – to bring you both together again and to see that it stays like that. It's a part of the legend as well – a bit I didn't understand." Arthur sighed.

Fletcher frowned. "You know about everybody from us, don't you? It's probably only in riddles that you don't know at once what it means, isn't it?"

"More or less," Arthur nodded.

"But where do you know all that from?" Fletcher was curious.

Arthur shrugged his shoulders. "It was laid into my cot. I don't know why but I carry this burden with me around since I can remember back." He pulled some sheets of paper out of his pocket from the waistcoat and reached it over to Fletcher.

Fletcher took the papers and threw a look at them. He whistled. "Everything written down – our all future. I don't want to read it, thank you." He reached them back.

Arthur grinned. "Then don't ask me any questions anymore." He put the papers back where he had got them out.

Fletcher observed him thoughtfully. "At least I know now who I can ask when something goes wrong." He laughed.

The sun was already high on the sky, as the two men went outside. It was visible for everybody around them that the two completely different men had become friends.

37

Hayley blinked.

She closed her eyes before she tried it again. She winked once more.

After the world got firm, she looked astonished around. Then she sighed loudly.

"That was a big loud sigh!" A voice laughed at her side.

Hayley turned her head around. "I never thought I would wake up again." She hummed.

"And leaving me all alone? You can't be serious." Another voice joined into the conversation.

Hayley turned her head to the other side. She blinked once more before she got up a bit. "What on earth are you both doing here?" She frowned – and fell on her back again, as a sharp pain ran over her face. Her hands went up to her face.

Fletcher caught her hands just in time. "Don't. You have some tattoos on your face and they shouldn't get scratched." He explained.

"What for tattoos?" Hayley was now completely confused. She turned to Fletcher. "I heard you down in the temple, calling for me."

"I did, yes." Fletcher confessed. "I couldn't stand the thought of them killing you. And if you for sure noticed in the meantime – I was successful."

Hayley sighed. "Can you explain to me what happened exactly?"

Fletcher smiled. Shortly he explained what had happened since she had left the village, how he had come into this walls and what had happened to him. Then he laughed: "What they did to you, I can see clearly. And I'm happy they let you off so lightly. Still I think it may be a big burden for you."

"Because I'm now signed for my life and nobody will ever look at me again?" Hayley had tears in her eyes.

"That's all right with me." Fletcher smiled and caught a tear carefully with his finger. "I mean then finally I have you for me alone." And he bent forward and kissed Hayley softly on the lips.

Arthur cleared his throat. "Sorry but you don't get rid of me so easily."

Hayley laughed lightly: "Hi Arthur! I have to thank you for bringing Fletcher to me."

"Don't mention it!" Arthur laughed. "But now – let's have a look at your tattoos. It should be soon all right." He bent over her face. "It looks good. If you don't move your face so much, you'll be fine."

"What is it for a tattoo?" Hayley asked curiously.

"They are Old-Arabic signs. It says so much like: Keeper of the Light." Fletcher answered calmly.

"And that means?" Hayley wanted to know.

Fletcher and Arthur exchanged a look. Then Fletcher cleared his throat. "We can only guess ourselves. But as it all is about us – I would guess it has something to do with the love we feel for each other. I carry the signs of the Guard of the Keeper of the Light. I have to give everything to guard you and the light between us."

"I don't think that will be a difficult job." Hayley smiled at him.

Fletcher got up and turned to the window.

Hayley looked asking at Arthur but Arthur shrugged his shoulders. Hayley got carefully up and stepped over to Fletcher. "What is it, which makes you feel bad?" She asked quietly.

Fletcher sighed. "During all this – I forgot completely about Christine. You know the girl who tried to replace you and got pregnant."

Hayley laid her arms around his shoulders. "We go home as soon as possible. Then you can look after her like you looked after me." She hesitated for a moment before she continued: "I envy her for the time she could spend with you. But I intend to make up for it. But that doesn't mean you have to forget about her completely. Finally she carries your child. – But nothing like that should ever come between us and destroy our love and us. Don't you think so?" She added.

Fletcher turned around. Softly he pulled Hayley into his arms and sighed again. "Then you are not angry with me anymore?"

"I'm not angry with you – I never was. We both were separated for two years and we both went on our own ways in every way. If we now want to try to live together then it wouldn't be good if we were angry at each other for what we did, as we were alone. Don't think about the past – let's get on with our lives!"

Fletcher bent forward and kissed Hayley softly on the mouth. "I never let you go again. I promise."

"I promise you never to leave you again in my heart. But you have to let me go on my way, which is similar to yours but not the same." Hayley snuggled up at Fletcher.

"Everything you say." Fletcher smiled.

Carefully they kissed each other again.

A knocking at the door interrupted the two lovers again.

"Come in!" Fletcher called and let go of his hold of Hayley.

Hayley sat down on the bed again.

Arthur looked through the crack of the door. "I didn't want to disturb you but the meal is ready." He smiled.

"I didn't notice that you had left." Fletcher grinned. "But thank you for that. We're coming."

Arthur nodded and disappeared.

Hayley stretched out on the bed. "Go for your meal. I'll stay; I'm tired and will sleep a bit longer." She murmured.

Fletcher stepped over to her and pulled a blanket over her. "I'll bring you something to eat later on." He said quietly but Hayley was already asleep again.

Four days later, Hayley was so fit that she was able to ride. She, Fletcher and Arthur saddled their camels one nice morning and said goodbye to the priests, monks and the normal people at the Temple of Freedom. Then they climbed on their camels and rode away.

None of them noted a young girl staring sadly behind them…

"Is that the right way?" Arthur rode up to Hayley's side and examined their surroundings.

Hayley smiled. "We are not straight going home. I have at first something else to do."

"And that would be?" Fletcher rode up at her other side.

Hayley looked at him. "I want to pick up my son if you allow." It was a question and that was clear to Fletcher.

"Certainly," Fletcher smiled at her supporting. "I'm curious myself how he is."

Hayley smiled only.

"How was the village called?" Arthur asked interested.

"Aragon." Hayley answered lightly. "There it is." She pointed over to a row of mountains in front of them.

Slowly they came nearer to the mountains, which grew bigger with every step they came over to them. At last they reached the foot of the mountains and Hayley led her camel on a small path up the hill.

Fletcher and Arthur followed her slowly.

Around noon they reached a small village on top of the first hill in the mountain row. They rode straight on to the well in the middle of the village and jumped from their camels.

Hayley and Arthur were both masked with their scarves but Fletcher everybody could see without problems.

"And where will we find him?" Fletcher asked curiously. "It doesn't seem that anybody is at home."

"It only seems like that." Hayley looked around. "I would more guess that they are afraid of us and hiding away." She hesitated before she confessed: "I've never been here before. I don't know where I can find my son."

"But how on earth did he come then to this place?" Fletcher asked astonished.

Hayley smiled under her scarf. "A friend took him over here. He promised to look after him till I come to pick him up again."

"What for a friend? Is he one of the men of this village who had the luck to find their way back?" Fletcher wanted to know it exactly.

"Right," Hayley turned to one end of the village where some old men showed up.

The old men walked slowly over to them.

Hayley stepped out of the group toward the men and made the sign of freedom.

One of the old man looked at her. "What do you want here? Here you can't get anything worthwhile for you."

"First we would need some water for us and our camels. I'm sure you can organize that for us?" Hayley answered clearly.

"The well hides the best water here in the mountains. You are free to take what you need."

"Thank you." Hayley answered with a small bowing towards him.

But the old man hadn't finished with her yet. "What else do you want?"

Hayley looked seriously at him. "I'm looking for a man called Ahmed."

"There are a lot of men around with this name. Why are you looking for him?"

Hayley hesitated. "I want to ask him something." She answered only.

"Sorry, we can't help you." The old man turned around.

Hayley looked over at Fletcher and Arthur and shrugged her shoulders. She pulled the scarf down and shook her long red hair. Then she turned to go back to her camel.

"Hayley?" a voice overturned the steps of the old men and echoed over to her.

Hayley turned once more around. She stepped back into the middle of the street and looked over to where the old men stood like frozen.

A man, middle-aged, let the men standing where they were and stepped up the street.

"Ahmed!" Hayley sighed relieved.

The man came up to her and embraced her lightly, "By God, Hayley! I thought I would never see you again. How on earth could you escape the revenge of Prince Alban's men once more? And how on earth do you look like?"

"A lot of questions for one moment," Hayley laughed. "How are you, old friend?"

"I'm home – I'm fine." Ahmed smiled. "Don't you want to come and see my wife? You can have dinner with us – you and your friends."

"That's an offer we can't say no to." Hayley nodded. "But tell me first: How is my son?"

"I knew you wanted to know. But come and see for yourself." Ahmed pointed the street down where he had come from. "Leave your camels here. Nobody will steal them."

"All right," Hayley waved over to Fletcher and Arthur to follow them. She stepped at Ahmed's side the street down till they reached a small house at the right.

"Izara - Come and greet my friends!" Ahmed called and opened the door of the house.

A thin woman with beautiful black hair came over to the door. She frowned, as she noticed Hayley.

"Izara, that's Hayley. You have to thank her because without her help I would never have been able to come back to you." Ahmed introduced Hayley shortly.

Hayley smiled shyly at the woman. "He likes to exaggerate. I didn't do much but Ahmed was a big help to me." She nodded over at Ahmed.

Izara smiled. "He told me before that you would say that when you finally come." She asked her with a hand movement to sit down. Then she looked over to the door where Fletcher and Arthur waited. "And who are your friends?"

Ahmed turned as well to the door. He examined the man in black till the man pulled his scarf down.

"Arthur!" Ahmed was astonished. "What are you doing here?"

Arthur smiled at Ahmed. "I swore to look after Hayley – and this I do." He bowed lightly over at Izara.

Ahmed turned to Fletcher. "I don't think that I know you." He confessed.

Fletcher shook his head. "We don't know each other. But I heard a lot about you and the help you gave to Hayley. I want to thank you for that." He as well bowed lightly over at Izara.

Hayley made a sign and Fletcher nodded. He pulled something out of his pocket and reached it over to Ahmed.

Ahmed took the small thing and stared at the ring in his hand. Then he looked up. "You must be Fletcher, Hayley's husband." He said, closing his hand around the ring.

For a second it was quiet, only Fletcher nodded at Ahmed.

Ahmed turned and opened the door to another room. "Bennie!" he called, "Farrah! Come and greet our guests!"

Through the door a girl of six years came inside; she had a small boy of just over a year at her hand.

The girl was a picture of her mother; thin with long black hair and black eyes. The boy in contrary was also thin with black hair but his eyes were from an astonishing green.

Hayley swallowed. She knelt down on the floor and looked over at the boy, stretching her hand out toward him.

The most astonishing thing was what happened then.

The boy solved his hand from the girl's and stepped with uncertain steps over to Hayley. He stretched out his hands and he smiled wide. As he came up to Hayley, he slung his arms around Hayley's neck.

Hayley embraced him softly and picked him up. She sat down on a chair, her son on her lab and caressed him without saying anything.

Fletcher stepped up to his wife and laid his hand on her shoulder. Then he stroked softly over the head of the boy.

Finally Hayley lifted her head. "You looked after him very well. I don't know how I shall thank you." She looked over at Ahmed.

"First of all, we should eat something. Then we can talk about everything else. Or do you have to leave at once again?" Ahmed asked back.

Hayley exchanged a look with Fletcher and Arthur. "We'll stay for one night. Then we have to leave." She decided.

Ahmed nodded, and Izara started to set up the table.

After a simple but very good meal, Hayley leaned back in her chair. "You wanted to ask me something?" She looked at Ahmed.

Ahmed swallowed. "I need a big favour of you. From time to time we get threads from other villages or another prince. We need someone who helps us when we need it."

Hayley nodded. "You'll get our help every time you need it. But how do you want to let us know?" She asked frowning. "We can't stay here forever."

"I don't ask you to stay here. I'll send my friend the owl with a message when we need your help. Will this be all right?"

Hayley smiled. "If the owl knows where to go to." she was uncertain about the fact to have to trust an owl.

Ahmed laughed. "I trained the owl in the last months. If we give her something from you, she will remember you and find you when needed." Ahmed got up, left the room and came shortly after back with a white owl on his shoulder. With one hand he picked up the owl and placed it on Hayley's shoulder.

Hayley sat perfectly still.

The owl moved on her shoulder and sniffed at her throat.

Carefully Hayley lifted her hand and started to stroke the owl softly. The owl seemed to relax and leaned against Hayley's face.

"She likes you. That's good." Ahmed nodded. "She will be able to find you when it's necessary."

"All right," Hayley gave her agreement.

After Ahmed had brought the owl back and Izara and Hayley had brought the children to bed, Ahmed showed them the whole village and introduced them to everybody in it. They looked after the camels and built up a night quarter for them.

The next morning, after a good breakfast, they said goodbye and left the village.

Hayley had in the saddle in front of her Bennie, how she had taken over the nickname of her son. Carefully with her cloak she protected him against the sun but Bennie seemed to enjoy the ride.

Five days later, late, very late in the evening they reached the gate of their hometown.

Fletcher gave the sign to open the gate, and at last they could enter the village.

Tired they jumped in front of the stables from the camels and stretched themselves.

Hayley held in her arms her sleeping son.

Tim came over to them, woken up from one of the guards. "If we would have known that you all come back tonight, I would have occupied your house, Fletcher, to leave my house for you. But so you have to take the house, which is left." He smiled apologizing at Hayley. "At least it's good to see you back, Hayley. We thought we lost you."

Hayley smiled. "If you really thought, you can get rid of me so easily – I'm sorry to disappoint you. It's good to be here again." She embraced Tim shortly.

"Only for your information: Christine is well – Rick is looking after her. Otherwise your friends are wicked but quite okay. The rest we should go through tomorrow."

Fletcher nodded. "Let's go to bed. I'm quite tired after this journey." He confessed.

Hayley snuggled up at him. "Let's go." She murmured tired as well.

Fletcher took her hand and led her over to their house. They found a small bed for Bennie before they fell into their own beds and were asleep a minute later.

Tim led Arthur through the streets to the big white house. "Your friends made in the meantime something out of the house. As far as I know your room is opposite the entrance, sharing with Bethany." He opened the door and pointed to a door on the other side.

"Thanks." Arthur murmured and stepped quietly over to the door. He opened it, slipped inside, walked over to the bed and fell down beside Bethany. He was asleep before even his head touched the pillow.

38

Next morning Hayley woke up from the cries of her son. She jumped out of bed and ran over to the room they had brought Bennie into in the night.

The boy cried loudly and Hayley sat down beside and took him into her arms.

Fletcher looked inside. "What do you think about a swim? Best way to get clean again."

"Yes, a swim would be great?" Hayley nodded. "But who is looking after Bennie?"

"Mandy is here, looking after Warren. She will look after Bennie as well." Fletcher smiled. "Come on." He stroked softly over Bennie's head, as Hayley stepped up to him.

Together they left the room and went downstairs.

Mandy was in the kitchen, looking after Warren that he ate his breakfast.

"Good morning, Mandy! How are you?" Hayley smiled at her friend.

Mandy turned around to her. "Tim told me that you came back. I'm glad to see…" She breathed deeply in before she continued: "You again. But what happened to you?" She came over to Hayley and touched her face.

"Long story," Hayley sighed. "Can you do me a favour?" She set Bennie up on the table and wiped him some hairs out of his face. "Can you look after Bennie as long as we are out for a swim?" She looked down at Warren who also looked interested at her. As well as Bennie he had beautiful green eyes.

"Certainly I can. The water is nice and warm today – enjoy it!" Mandy smiled and took Bennie up on her arm.

Fletcher picked up two big towels, took Hayley's hand and they left the house. Without meeting anybody they came to the two lakes with the waterfall.

Against everybody else's choice Hayley and Fletcher chose the upper lake for their swim and they left their clothes lying on the ground at the edge of the lake.

After three times crossing the lake, Hayley stopped near the waterfall. "It's good to be here again. I missed this – and I missed you!" She said quietly and put her arms around Fletcher's naked body.

"Do you know that you look more beautiful than ever?" Fletcher's voice was hoarse. He pressed his body firm against Hayley's. Then he bent forward and kissed her softly on the mouth.

Hayley replied the kiss warmly. She felt Fletcher moving and pulled him under the waterfall and then behind it.

Fletcher pressed with his body Hayley against the stone behind the waterfall and pressed his mouth again hard on hers.

Hayley soon got breathlessly through the hard and wild kiss and she had to breathe hard in, especially as she felt Fletcher's hands everywhere on her body.

Fletcher solved his lips from hers and went over to her earlobe. He touched it with his tongue and bit into it during he pressed Hayley's legs apart and found his way firmly into her.

Hayley groaned up, holding herself with the hands at Fletcher's shoulders.

Again and again Fletcher pressed his body against hers and his mouth touching the skin of her face during his hand lay on her breast and pressed her nipple.

Hayley groaned once more, and Fletcher groaned up at the same moment. His movements grew less and he leaned again against Hayley.

Hayley sighed. "You know exactly when I need what." She kissed him softly on the cheek.

Fletcher laughed. "You invited me. How could I say No?" He solved himself completely and stepped under the waterfall. He rubbed one time down on him completely then he threw himself again into the lake.

Hayley followed his example and together they swam over the lake back to the place where they had left their towels and clothes.

After they had dried themselves and dressed again, they walked slowly down the path and back into the village.

Mandy who was with the two children out on the market place discovered them first. She pointed them out to Bennie who at once started to walk over to his mother. Mandy whispered into Warren's ear: "Listen, Warren! The woman with your father – that's your mother! Go and greet her! Go!"

Warren got a soft push into his back and he stepped hesitatingly forward. Then it seemed suddenly that he remembered something, as his steps grew faster and finally he overtook his half-brother and ran over to Hayley. "Mum!" He called with joy and threw himself on Hayley.

Hayley caught him in her arms and swung him around. Then she set him down again, still her arm around him and caught Bennie in her other arm. Firmly she pressed her two sons at her body.

Fletcher bent down and picked Warren up. Hayley got up with Bennie on her arms. They joined the other men and women at the market place.

"Hi Hayley, hi Fletcher," The men and women greeted them friendly then they stopped. They stared stunned at Hayley, and it didn't matter if they were Horsemen or Fighters of Freedom. The women all stared at her.

Hayley sighed. "Perhaps I should tell you what happened to me before you start to speculate and to talk behind my back." She said more or less calmly.

"Good idea." Tim nodded. "We just wanted to build up a fire for lunch. Best time to explain then everything, as we will be all there."

Hayley just wanted to agree, as another voice joined in. "I don't know what you have. It's quite clear, don't you think so?"

Tim turned around. "What's quite clear, Rick?"

Rick pointed at Hayley's face. "Keeper of the Light." he spelled correctly out. Then he turned back to Tim. "Didn't you learn any kind of Arabic?" He asked mockingly.

Tim frowned at him then he looked back at Hayley. "Explain it later." He said and organized shortly everything for the fire.

In the meantime Arthur stepped slowly nearer. "There is something else you have to explain as well." He said calmly to Hayley.

Hayley looked asking at him.

Arthur smiled and stepped to the side. He pointed to a woman in the back.

Hayley followed where Arthur's finger pointed to and discovered a young woman in the back with beautiful black hair. She stopped for a moment and examined the woman from top to bottom. Then she suddenly smiled. "Look, Bennie, whose here!" she said to her small son and stepped over to the woman. She stretched her hand out towards the young woman and said calmly: "What on earth are you doing here?"

The woman smiled at Hayley. "I thought you might need my help again. I... I... I didn't want to stay anymore at the Temple." She confessed and pressed Hayley's hand lightly.

Hayley pulled her nearer and embraced her softly. "I'm glad you are here, Nell." She called her by her nickname. She never had really liked the name Arachnarella. "We both are glad, aren't we, Bennie?" She tickled the young boy till he started to laugh.

Arachnarella smiled at the boy. "You've grown." She noted.

Bennie stretched out his arms, and Arachnarella took him softly into her arms and cuddled him.

Mandy sighed, as she saw that picture. "Do I lose a job?" She turned to Hayley.

Hayley smiled at her. "No, you don't." She examined first Mandy then Arachnarella. "Nell here helped me in the temple during my pregnancy, and she looked after Bennie in the first months. She... I still think she has something from you, Mandy." She added.

Mandy looked over at Arachnarella. She only shrugged uncertain her shoulders.

Arachnarella pressed Bennie softly to her breast.

Hayley still smiled. "Well, I'm happy to have both of you here." She took Mandy's hand, laid her arm around Arachnarella and pulled both women with her to the well where others had started to set up the fire.

Half an hour later everybody sat around the fire and had something to eat on her or his plate. They ate till they had enough then Tim turned again to Hayley: "Let's hear your story."

Hayley shrugged her shoulders and told her story as far as she could. Fletcher helped her over the bits she didn't remember or couldn't remember because she had been unconscious.

Only Arthur was completely silent.

Finally Hayley finished off with the last bits then she leaned back against Fletcher.

"How is it going on now?" Rick looked at her.

Hayley and Fletcher looked at each other.

"We're going on. We do the same we always did – with the difference that we don't let anybody know that the Fighters have their quarters here as well." Fletcher said.

"Have they?" Tim asked uncomfortable.

"Do you have something against it?" Fletcher asked astonished back.

"No, not really," Tim shrugged his shoulders.

Arthur turned to Hayley. "And what are we doing?"

Hayley smiled. "We do the same like before as well. With the difference that we have now a home we can return to."

"Have we?" Rick asked suspiciously with a side look at Tim.

"Have you something against this place?" Hayley asked astonished.

Rick laid his arm around Christine and pressed her to his body. "Absolutely not." he answered smiling.

Fletcher and Hayley exchanged a look. "After we cleared everything, we can go on!" Fletcher said calmly, and Hayley nodded. "We should." She said and kissed Fletcher softly on the mouth…

The End